First Journal of the Ancient Ones

ELDER GODS

OF ANTIQUITY

M. Don Schorn

PO Box 754
Huntsville, AR 72740
www.ozarkmt.com
800-935-0045 479-738-2348

For permission, or serialization, condensation, adaptions, or for catalog of other publications, write to: Ozark Mountain Publishing, Inc., PO Box 754, Huntsville, AR 72740, Attn: Permissions Department.

Library of Congress Cataloging-in-Publication Data
Schorn, M. Don - 1947 -
"Elder Gods of Antiquity" by M. Don Schorn
The first book of a series based on the elder gods theory of a revised account of human history.
1. Ancient History 2. Archeology 3. Lost Civilizations
4. Extraterrestrials
I. Schorn, M. Don 1947 -   II. Title

Library of Congress Catalog Number: 2007939981
ISBN: 978-1-886940-99-4
Cover Art and Layout by www.enki3d.com
Book Design: Julia Degan
Book Set in: Times New Roman

Published by

OZARK
MOUNTAIN
PUBLISHING

PO Box 754
Huntsville, AR 72740

www.ozarkmt.com
Printed in the United States of America

Other books by M. Don Schorn:

Second Journal of the Ancient Ones

Legacy of the Elder Gods

Third Journal of the Ancient Ones

Gardens of the Elder Gods

A Spiritual Belief, A Way of Life, And Much More

Reincarnation...
Stepping Stones of Life

A Novel of Modern Exploration, Discovery, & Ancient
Revelations...Set in the Near Future

Emerging Dawn

The author extends his gratitude to the numerous researchers and other authors whose diligent work helped inspire this book. Special thanks to Robert Bauval, Art Bell, Jacques Bergier, Charles Berlitz, William Bramley, Herbie Brennan, Robert Charroux, Maurice Chatelain, David Hatcher Childress, W. Raymond Drake, Frank Edwards, Charles Fort, Graham Hancock, Thor Heyerdahl, Richard C. Hoagland, Peter Kolosimo, George Noory, Eric Norman, Robert Schoch, Zecharia Sitchin, Warren Smith, Merlin Stone, Andrew Tomas, Brinsley le Poer Trench, Craig & Eric Umland, Jacques Vallee, Erich von Däniken, and Don Wilson; naming merely a few.

Table of Contents

PART ONE

FALLACY, FACT, and THEORY

Chapter 1

Flawed Beliefs

Remember when the Earth was flat? The belief in a flat Earth at the center of our universe, around which all other celestial bodies revolved, was once an accepted scientific fact. This false concept first emerged during the second century AD and continued into the 17th century when it was ultimately replaced with the heliocentric theory of planetary motion conceived earlier by Copernicus in 1543. This widely accepted and mostly unchallenged fallacy did not alter the true reality of a vastly larger and much older universe wherein our spherical planet is but a small and relatively recent newcomer occupying merely a small speck within a much larger grand design.

This classic example is presented to illustrate how some scientific theories can be inaccurate yet endure as accepted beliefs. Advocates advancing such concepts then seemingly force all new discoveries to fit within their ascribed belief system, thus mandating conformity with an accepted scientific paradigm. Consider the possibility that certain modern theories may be equally as wrong as the prior belief in a 'flat Earth.' Present theory explaining Earth's primordial past and the evolution of planetary life might be one of those securely held but flawed beliefs.

Such skepticism is not intended to cast doubt over our modern scientific community, or question the raw data and underlying facts they have uncovered. Rather, it merely questions their final interpretations and subsequent packaging of deductions into rigid doctrines. Differing conclusions can be drawn from evaluation of identical raw data. As information is woven into a hypothesis, deductions can vary greatly among researchers, resulting in differing conclusions without subverting any underlying fact. Substantial contradictory evidence exists to refute our present orthodox beliefs pertaining to Earth's development and humanity's origin as a species.

History is only able to describe events that have left some form of evidence. With limited certainty, we can go back to *circa* 7500 BC for the reconstruction of human culture and events, with about 2,500 of those years being quite sketchy. Prior cave paintings, stone carvings, and rock drawings can extend prehistory back to *circa* 35,000 BC, but with even less certainty. Geological indications and artifacts left by previous cultures are the only means to reconstruct events prior to that time frame.

But Earth seems to reveal her secrets begrudgingly. When relics are exposed, they do not come with instructions that assure the finder will make the correct observation or conclusion pertaining to those discoveries. Often the most likely explanation might quickly be discarded simply because it seems so implausible, especially if it conflicts with the prevailing scientific belief. Yet the same facts are often capable of producing numerous conclusions. Once venturing beyond the written record that has been fully verified with artifact evidence, only speculation exists, regardless of the credentials possessed by its discoverer. Only when written records exist can artifacts and archaeological suppositions be confirmed, allowing verification of fossil evidence with their recorded description.

Archeology does not always agree with findings of anthropology or geology, or even with some extant texts from olden cultures. Numerous exhumed ancient treasures, apparently of high technological achievement, simply do not reflect actions of a primitive people. Early humans simply could not have built certain archaic structures with only the basic abilities ascribed to them by modern anthropologists. Yet scholars continue to explain these contradictions with simplistic explanations, forcing conformity with orthodox beliefs while ignoring known facts.

Occasionally, human perception or interpretation of past events alters, distorts, or falsifies Earth's exposed history. That allows our factual past to be reshaped and presented in a manner conveying the historian's agenda, tailoring events to conform within the narrow view of its presenter. When factual but contrary information exists, it is often misinterpreted and discarded as extraneous, or simply ignored. Yet contrary data continue to surface in increasing quantities.

Even long extant data can add to such anomalous evidence, as it undergoes reevaluation through the filter of more enlightened understanding as a result of new technological advances. Such revelations have forced broad revisions of prior conclusions, requiring new theories. We can continue to accept flawed conventional views, or become skeptical and examine other explanations for the many mysteries associated with humanity's origins.

The true record of civilization might have even been deliberately suppressed or falsified by continued adherence to prevailing secular and religious histories. Some New Age researchers have accused academia of deliberately covering up significant archaeological finds that conflict with orthodox beliefs. David Hatcher Childress, an archaeologist and prolific author of the *Lost Cities* book series, reported on several cases where the Smithsonian Institution apparently not only lost important artifacts, but actually suppressed their own discoveries of Egyptian relics uncovered during their Grand Canyon excavations in northern Arizona.[1]

In December 1992, Mr. Childress detailed documentation of this Smithsonian cover up during an extensive interview on a Seattle radio program.[2] Similar conclusions were also expressed by French scientist, Jacques Bergier, who reported that: "The vaults of the Smithsonian Institution in the United States, for example, are full of crates of incomprehensible objects that no one is studying. The same situation exists in other museums...."[3]

Ancient historians were only able to describe events in the language and knowledge of their day. Current translators of ancient texts are able to decipher technical aspects only within limits of their own scientific understanding. Modern developments have only now risen to a level from which we can more correctly interpret and comprehend certain messages from antiquity, which were left not to confuse us, but rather to assist us. One can not state with any certainty what the true intent or meaning of any ancient idea might have been, when conveyed by people of a different culture, language, nationality, or time period. Modern translations and interpretations of those ancient messages have rendered them susceptible to errors and misunderstandings.

Thoughts and ideas are often difficult to convert from one language to another, even during contemporary times, let alone over the expanse of thousands of years. The original intent may become distorted, however minor, regardless of the method employed to communicate such thought. We know how contorted modern newspaper accounts can become when describing events during contemporary times. Yet those distortions do not negate the factual occurrence of the reported event, even if narration errors exist. Modern reinterpretations of ancient texts have allowed the formulation of new conclusions, especially when coupled with technical reevaluation of related artifacts. Those new explanations often eliminate the many contradictions associated with prevailing theories, thereby allowing all the known evidence to finally fit.

While this text is not intended as proof for a new paradigm, it does expose the flaws and missing pieces associated with our prevailing orthodoxy. The basic facts and evidence necessary to construct an alternate conclusion, one pointing in a different direction from present beliefs, will be supplied within this text. The reader will then be adequately equipped to evaluate explanations pertaining to Earth's early development and the origins of humankind.

This author's conclusions will also be revealed, supplying a unique and credible theory that not only answers most if not all lingering questions, but also accounts for all the anomalous relics and enigmatic aspects associated with numerous ancient cultures. However, no attempt will be made to compel acceptance of that explanation over another. Most likely, some major revelation yet awaits discovery, one that will encompass all known facts including contradictory evidence, thereby linking them in agreement with the extant archaeological record of our world.

Several theories attempt to explain Earth's early development and emergence of intelligent life. Orthodox beliefs offer an essentially linear development of both geological and biological components of Earth, confining events into neat compartments, eras, cultures, or strata layers. Such natural evolution claims progress was achieved by building on previous accomplishments from earlier levels of evolution, achieving just a little higher plateau of obtainment each time. It is expedient to accept the prevailing belief that humankind naturally evolved from an ape ancestor into a stone age caveman, developing later into today's more refined creature, all in a simple step by step process of natural progression. This belief concludes that humankind, solely through our own creativeness, invented and formulated our way into modern civilized societies.

But evolution of our species has not been a simple building-block process. Archaeological examinations indicate distinct regressions, while revealing earlier and more advanced cultures at those same locations. Professor Howard Carter, the noted Egyptologist who discovered the Tutankhamun tomb and its treasures, noted that flint artifacts found in the higher

Nile Valley region near Luxor were older than the crude stone implements dating from the site's later eras.[4]

Certain other cultural aspects, especially architectural complexity and artistic levels of jewelry, were higher in the earliest periods of Egypt than those found in later ones, according to author Andrew Tomas.[5] Many modern Egyptologists continue to underestimate achievements by the earliest dynasties, where levels of science, mathematics, medicine, and astronomy were much higher than admitted. A similar observation is equally true for those earliest civilizations in the Indus Valley, as well as numerous other cultures scattered throughout antiquity.

Often, the most ancient structures represent better craftsmanship, skill, and accuracy. But we are told that the further back in time, humankind's status becomes more primitive, barbarous, and savage. Yet evidence contrary to that belief exists. The earliest branch of *Homo sapiens* was more advanced than the later Neanderthal subspecies, a curious occurrence often explained as 'recessive genes.' Rather, these two subspecies were perhaps incorrectly grouped within the same genus, a decision rendered merely to accommodate the modern prevailing theory.

Evidence of a similar non-linear path exists for learning and knowledge. The ancient Sumerians, Egyptians, Hindus, and Greeks were more scientifically advanced than the much later cultures that lived during the 'Dark Ages.' The Arabian rediscovery of a forgotten high level of ancient science may have initiated the later Renaissance Period, an era that merely restored a prior level of advanced knowledge that had been lost or hidden during the centuries after Ptolemy until Copernicus. Yet substantial evidence indicates that the earliest human ancestors apparently converted from 'savage-to-civilized' almost overnight, utilizing impressive technology throughout that rapid transition.

Another widely accepted alternative to academia's *natural evolution* is the theory of Divine Intervention, put forth by numerous religious convictions around the world. Such beliefs state that the Creator of all things intervened with Earth's natural progress and developed humankind as an extraneous addition to the original Master Plan. Thus, humans are deemed a special creation, enjoying a lofty position over other living creatures, but below the level of the Creator.

Perhaps both concepts are correct within a broader context. Regardless of its origin, certain minimal evidence indicates that an advanced civilization apparently existed during remote antiquity, long before the emergence of humankind. Much later, elements of that high culture were also evident within primitive groups of later humans. However, insufficient quantities of evidence exist to adequately explain either its origin, or its apparently abrupt disappearance.

Legends, myths, and oral traditions claim those advanced elements were 'gifts' provided by heavenly 'gods,' the original bearers of civilization and teachers of ancient humanity on Earth. A universal belief exists around the world in the arrival of ancient gods during remote times when life was chaotic, bringing civilization and knowledge to the people of Earth. Such beliefs were common in Egypt, India, Mexico, Greece, China, Peru, and throughout the Near East.

Those accounts can be grouped into two periods or ages. The first was inhabited only by gods, with or without their helpers, during a time when humanity did not yet exist; while a Second Age of gods, along with their assistants, later presided over the early emergence of humankind. Most of our ancient oral traditions state that those gods had civilized and ruled our early world, but not created it. Such gods possessed human attributes, since they were the true progenitors of humankind. Those gods created human servants to perform shepherding or herding functions and workers to construct irrigation for fields and orchards, as well as laborers for farming and ranching duties. Those gods were deemed to be the first mathematicians, astronomers, architects, inventors, and land surveyors of Earth. Later, their influence or contact seemed to suddenly vanish, leaving little hard evidence of their interaction with our world.

Yet some form of ancient influence and intervention apparently shaped early humanity. The evolutionary process alone can not account for humankind as a species. No missing link has ever been found directly connecting man to any known animal ancestor. That missing link has actually never been missing at all. Such a link has always been openly exposed, documented, and readily apparent throughout the earliest myths and religious beliefs. That link was God, the One who created man...in His own image. But which God is being identified? Was that God the Creator of All, from the beginning of time? Or was that god merely a visitor to our planet, a mortal being with immense technological abilities and vast knowledge, who was viewed by his earthly creations as a god? Or is there yet another completely different theory that could also explain most or all of the mysteries surrounding our planet?

Chapter 2

Alternate Conclusions

The cultural core of many ancient civilizations was based upon creation myths that documented activities now recognized as genetic engineering performed by highly evolved beings, producing workers that fulfilled purposes deemed necessary by those 'Divine Masters.' Such accounts are labeled 'mythological' due to supernatural elements they contained, and thus were thought to be fictitious when read without modern technological comprehension. Those ancient texts are only now being reevaluated through the perspective of our latest scientific understanding. However, these new interpretations do not consist of hidden messages or secret meanings, but rather expose highly advanced ancient knowledge.

But archaic records can be interpreted in numerous ways, with some seeming to contradict other accounts. When contradictions and errors are found within olden sacred scriptures, those discrepancies do not negate the whole work, or cloud it with doubt. But most ancient texts are not deemed to be 'sacred' or 'holy,' and thus are not afforded that same 'respect.' They are often dismissed as mythological tales that are allegorical, ones through which 'hidden truths' might be revealed. Truth must never be hidden and should always stand on its own merit. Uniformity in evaluating the veracity of any written record should be applied to all ancient texts.

Most historic records likely contain some mistakes, with oral traditions often considered to be the least accurate. But singing ballads and epic poems usually preceded their written accounts. Those were memorized verbatim, usually in song or rhyme, with emphasis on each and every word. Such accounts became as much a part of family heredity as any biological link handed down from generation to generation.

The epic storytellers and orators such as Homer existed long before our first 'recorded' historians such as Herodotus. Their accuracy should not be questioned any more than similar written accounts. After those narratives were recorded, their later reinterpretations and translations into different languages by ensuing cultures, as well as their recopying by subsequent revisionists, would have resulted in distortions of the original author's intent and perhaps the actual event being described. Hence, oral literature is not as suspect or as easily dismissed as one might surmise, just as written literature is not as stable and accurate. Both probably contain factual data and some errors.

Although ancient myths and legends have been embellished and expanded over the ages, these tales often possess core elements based on factual events. This makes them more than fictionalized history, moral fables, or the misinterpretation of natural phenomena. Many mythological narratives describing historic events were likely based on antiquated facts passed down through oral tradition. They became even more distorted when finally recorded by 'authors' who were unable to fully comprehend what had previously been described. These ancient narratives support the reality of a lost advanced race or culture during remote antiquity, or perhaps even several races and multiple influences that are not recognized within our modern paradigm. This includes intervention by advanced visitors from the heavens who bestowed civilization and gifts upon humankind.

But high technological levels during archaic periods conflict with the orthodox belief in humanity's savage and primitive past. Yet ancient megalithic structures, archaic medical knowledge rivaling modern comprehension, detailed descriptions of flying machines, enigmatic relics, and the depiction of animals that became extinct long before the emergence of humans are all factual realities. However, that ancient technology differed from our modern levels, and was even more advanced in certain ways. Cultural differences in construction practices are also evident, with longevity and durability emphasized over comfort, as simplicity took precedence over ornate grandeur. Many ancient cultures apparently had some type of association with this unknown but common source.

Mythologist Joseph Campbell believed that a common mythology existed throughout the ancient world, with different interpretations by each diverse culture. He also noted that a general sameness could be detected regionally, which was further connected by universal symbolism. That resulted in a shared belief in a Golden Age, when order was created and peaceful times prevailed. Additional shared or common incidents can be found in epic stories such as the Great Flood legends. The earliest flood story is found in Sumer, with Ziusudra as its hero. Next was the Akkadian version, where its hero Utnapishtim is known from the *Gilgamesh Epic*. A Babylonian narrative followed, with its hero, Xisuthrus, immortalized in the Berosus account.

Accounts by numerous other cultures came later, each with their named hero, all before the Biblical Genesis story of Noah. Regardless of origin, every version revealed essentially the same tale. These olden narratives and Biblical accounts apparently represent historic events, even though they became exaggerated, confused, or distorted through human imagination and memory as they were handed down over time.

Many of these ancient texts and oral traditions seem to indicate some type of intervention by otherworldly beings. Other authors have advanced theories that these records, along with strange archaic artifacts, prove that advanced beings of extraterrestrial origin visited Earth during its formative past. Those visitors were perceived by ancient humans as 'gods,' with this theory combining both evolutionary and religious components into a single belief. It is perplexing that humanity readily embraces a believe that they evolved solely from apes, but are offended to consider possible genetic links with advanced humanoid visitors from another world.

The concept of astronauts visiting Earth during its remote past has been explored and discussed by contemporary authors such as Messrs. Bergier, Charroux, Drake, Kolosimo, Sendy, Sitchin, Tomas, and von Däniken to name merely a few. However, the concept of ancient astronauts is not new. In 1859, London publisher John Taylor believed that Noah had built the Giza pyramids with direction and assistance from advanced otherworldly beings. Authors Alan and Sally Landsburg reported that the Astronomer Royal of Scotland, Professor Charles Piazzi Smyth, had released data that seemed to support Mr. Taylor's hypothesis.[1] It is not that ancient records fail to reveal and support such visitations to Earth by beings of extraterrestrial origin, but rather their *message* was later distorted due to incorrect interpretations and perhaps deliberate omissions and changes.

The possibility of intelligent beings inhabiting alien worlds is not implausible. The basic molecules of living matter have been detected drifting in space within our solar system.[2] Life, in some manner or form, is evidently not that rare, with many researchers now believing that life may actually be commonplace beyond Earth. Biologists know that life is more robust than once thought, with some microbes known to thrive on chemical energy alone.[3] According to planetary scientist Bruce M. Jakosky at the University of Colorado, new discoveries suggest that life is simple, straightforward, and easy under the right conditions.[4] Within our own solar system, there are at least four places where life could have evolved outside of Earth. Those candidates include the planets Venus and Mars, along with the moons Europa and Ganymede, two of the natural satellites of Jupiter. All four worlds show evidence of volcanic activity, as well as other internal geological processes that have deformed and shaped their surfaces to some degree.

Europa is believed to possess a frozen crust of thin ice covering an ocean of liquid water. The heat necessary to maintain its melted state of water is thought to be from radioactive decay within its metallic core, or possibly from volcanic activity below its surface. Additional but less likely candidates would include Io and Callisto, two other moons of Jupiter. Both Callisto and Ganymede, Jupiter's two outer moons, exhibit lower densities midway between rock and ice, as well as a possible internal heat source that could permit underground water.

Although Venus is now a torrid planet due to its greenhouse effect, it is thought to have once been cooler, possessing more pleasant temperatures capable of supporting some form of life. The presently cold and barren planet Mars is believed to have once been more earthlike, with vast oceans of water, an oxygenated atmosphere, and warm winds. A mid-1999 study published in the journal *Science* revealed the discovery of magnetic striations on its surface, indicating Mars once had an earthlike geological separation of its crust, including continental drift.[5] Only Earth and Mars are known to exhibit this unique phenomenon. Many millions of years ago, Mars evidently possessed a more habitable environment than the less hospitable and convulsive Earth of that era. Those conditions could have allowed basic or primitive microbes to form on Mars before its similar occurrence on Earth, with resultant evolution toward higher lifeforms potentially occurring first on Mars.

In our understanding of planetary formation, as well as the mechanism for subsequent development of life where it might be possible, it is theorized that planets within our solar system formed at roughly the same time, within one-half billion years of each other. But noticeable differences exist between the outer frozen gas giants of planet Jupiter and beyond, and the innermost terrestrial planets of Mercury through Mars. The inner planets are metallic and stony, while the gas giants are mainly composed of hydrogen and helium, with lesser quantities of methane, ammonia, and water. The asteroid belt separates these two planetary groupings. Most cosmologists conclude that the outer or most remote planets from their central star (their sun) would have coalesced, condensed, and cooled-off first. This would be followed by the next innermost planetary group within their solar system, and so on.

The normal probability for life development would thus be greatest on outermost planets, since they are comprised of lighter elements, a condition closer to the general composition of the universe as a whole. It would further stand to reason that life would start or evolve on an outer planet that first cooled to a moderate 'livable' temperature and would thus be capable of spawning life, followed by inner planets that cooled later. The concept of 'seeding' life from one planet to another via expelled materials traveling through space is a likely one. Such shared-source life would usually result from outer planets transferring to inner planets, since debris 'falls' inward towards the center of its solar system, due to gravitational attraction from its sun.

Such an early inhabited outer planet would eventual become overcrowded, with ever-depleted natural resources, while its climate continued to cool. Eventually, such a planet would not be able to support its originating lifeform, or perhaps only sustain a small portion of its population. Those planetary conditions would prompt its inhabitants to migrate to a more hospitable inner planet that would have then cooled sufficiently to support its species, or perhaps an adaptation of its original biological lifeform. Those adaptations to conditions on a new planet might be achieved using genetic engineering or mutation, perhaps requiring repeated manipulations to obtain the desired result.

Such intervention by otherworldly sources would certainly influence developments and subsequent evolution on contacted worlds. The seeding of emerging planets could have been undertaken through means of remote landers, temporary visitations, direct colonization and terraforming attempts, or during the mining of planetary resources on those contacted worlds. Such intervention may have even been accidental rather than deliberate, with seeding of inner planets such as Earth possibly resulting from random asteroid or meteorite impacts.

Perhaps many early plant and animal species of Earth originated ancestrally from other worlds, through similar acts of accidental migration, rather than from an independent mechanism of natural evolution. Or perhaps ancient Earth might have simply been a planet of exile, where unwanted animal species, such as dinosaurs or the criminal elements of another society, were sent to live out their lives. Earth might have even served a multitude of purposes for numerous otherworldly species or races, over eons of time.

The legacy of humankind may lie in its past. Science supposedly reconstructed man's early evolution into acceptable and progressive stages from primitive to modern, but this no longer appears true. Once humanity believes all the answers to Earth's development and the origins of its planetary life have been discovered, a startling new find is unearthed that conflicts with our present theories, upsetting the balance between fact and speculation. Humankind should never assume that all facts have been discovered and adequately explained.

Numerous ancient texts seem to contain a level of scientific knowledge far in excess of what would be expected from a primitive culture. The Wonders of the Ancient World simply could not have resulted from technological levels assigned to early man. Anomalous relics routinely surface to plague scholars who often discard or label them as fakes or frauds. But these artifacts and ruins exist, defying conventional beliefs. Examination of certain archaic structures and ancient equipment indicates early utilization of advanced devices and application of scientific principals that were millennia before their accepted invention or discovery. Yet the creation of those innovations is often attributed to the genius of much later times.

In more modern times, humanity evidently rediscovered certain devices without realizing that such innovations were apparently known and used during the remote past. Perhaps ancient texts even inspired the development and construction of certain later inventions. Alexander Graham Bell may have hinted at such archaic influence when he stated: "The old devices have been reinvented, the old experiments have been tried once more...."[6]

Evidence of a rudimentary lifestyle is not apparent during certain remote ages when a high degree of art and accomplishment was clearly demonstrated. Such high cultures can be observed in ancient Europe, South America, India, and throughout the Near East. Evidence left by those advanced cultures does not suggest primitive societies. Yet modern anthropology suggests that the further back human ancestors are traced, increasingly savage, barbarous, or primitive behavior can be found. A closer correlation should be expected between people and their culture, reflecting a more consistent and linear development between the two, if scholars were factually correct. Too often that is not the case, based on the discovered evidence.

Such anomalies represent an inexplicable divergence from the 'main highway' of historic evolution described by orthodox science. If one were to think of this highway as Earth's own path towards natural evolution, mutation, development, and eventual progress, these anomalous artifacts represent unexplained merging 'on-ramps from nowhere' that can only be attributed to some unknown outside influence. Such enigmatic interventions seemingly would have produced a profound impact on our planet's development, infusing numerous inexplicable and advanced new elements into the mix.

But merely recognizing such inconsistencies does not reveal Earth's true history. Some explanation must exist that can account for all known facts, as well as the anomalous relics. Lost civilizations or extraterrestrial intervention are two of the more plausible explanations for the profound achievements exhibited during humanity's remote antiquity. Yet most scientists and historians are reluctant to accept such possibilities as a realistic explanation for the anomalous artifacts and contradictory evidence uncovered. That would require a complete reassessment and wholesale restructuring of the prevailing paradigm that defines Earth's history and scientific development. But these numerous mysteries and enigmatic finds seemingly defy most other explanations.

Chapter 3

Continuation of False Theory

The confinement of scientific specialization to smaller areas within a narrow scope shields new discoveries from the larger picture. Although producing a wealth of new discoveries, each specialization focuses on ever smaller confined research domains that do not necessarily connect with other findings within a broader perspective. As a result, general knowledge can suffer as these research fields fail to link each new discovery within overlapping areas of other affiliated technologies. Thus, bits and pieces of 'breakthrough' knowledge are merely showcased, but not interconnected with other contemporary finds.

New information must be interwoven to obtain its greatest benefit. Compared with past generations, our modern scholars undoubtedly possess the best education within their field of specialization, but may be unable to grasp or contemplate the broader implications of their work. The art of 'connecting the dots' is becoming lost. They appear to guard their own conventional orthodoxy, refuting any outside challenge to their strictly ordered theories, personally discrediting any questioner, rather than the questioner's new concepts.

A major obstacle to the advancement of human knowledge is blind acceptance of current belief without periodic challenge or review. Evolution of prevailing theories should be the goal of all new scientific discoveries. The theory of a flat Earth at the center of the universe was previously exhibited as a long held belief before 300 AD that continued well into the 1600s. While the knowledge of individual planets and our sun was essentially accurate, the correct arrangement and interaction between those celestial bodies was entirely wrong.

Modern cosmological understanding reemerged with the 1543 AD publication of the belief by Copernicus, which described Earth revolving around its sun. That correct concept was met with great resistance, and was not generally accepted until many years later. His followers were persecuted by the Church, burning one supporter, Giordano Bruno, at the stake in 1600, as reported by astronomer Patrick Moore.[1] Then in 1633, the Inquisition also forced Galileo to denounce the Copernican theory, forcing his endorsement of a centralized, motionless Earth claimed by the Bible. Yet the Greek historian, Musaeus, knew that our planet was spherical back in 1400 BC. Pythagoras later learned from the Egyptians in the 6th century BC that the Earth rotated on its own axis and revolved around the sun. If the false theories and beliefs held by 17th century religion and science had continued, such obstacles would certainly have prohibited humankind from ever advancing to the space age. Conversely, if humanity had continued and expanded upon the knowledge of the ancient Greeks, Hindus, and Egyptians, we might have reached the moon much sooner than the 20th century.

If ancient cultures were as primitive as traditional science claims, they could not have produced the achievements known from their artifacts. Academia perpetuates such obsolete beliefs by dismissing hard evidence that contradicts their accepted theories and chronologies. Author C. W. Ceram cites the continuance of such 'closed-thought' by revealing one assignment expected from doctoral candidates in archeology. They are typically required to explain which 'recognized' construction plan and method, or combination of methods, were used to build the Great Pyramid.[2] Only those students who reiterate the 'accepted' construction theory can expect to pass. Such adhesion to flawed beliefs is not education. The building of the three Giza Pyramids is perhaps one of the classic misinterpretations of history, perpetuating flawed theory with unsubstantiated conjecture.

The Giza Pyramids are unique and distinct from all other pyramids in Egypt, and are arguably the most researched and measured structures on Earth. Yet they continue to be represented in a false manner. Early Egyptians, or people of any other early culture, could not have built the Great Pyramid with their primitive obsidian tools (no metal was used according to Egyptologists) by utilizing only a land-based construction method. The scholarly belief that the Giza Pyramids were built with brute force, rising layer by layer, is both incorrect and dubious.

Of the seven 'Wonders of the Ancient World,' the Great Pyramid is the only surviving remnant. It was built to last, from bedrock limestone and granite. It stood as the largest man-made structure until the completion of the Hoover Dam in the 1930s. Dr. Gunther Rosenberg has extensively studied the Great Pyramid from every aspect, including computer analysis and X-ray. He concluded that no present day construction company could build it, even with modern basic tools.[3] Sir W. M. Flinders Petrie made the first accurate survey of the Great Pyramid between 1880 and 1881. He stated that the mean gap of the northern casing stones was only 0.020 of an inch, with some gaps displaying accuracy to within a mere 0.002 of an inch. The stones had been cut with a mean variation from a true edge within 0.010 of an inch over a length of 75 inches, an incredibly accurate trueness in any material, especially stone.[4] Such accuracy would indicate the use of precision machinery, rather than free-hand tools utilized by manual workers.

The Great Pyramid is level to within less than an inch of error over its base area of nearly fourteen acres, and is the world's most accurately oriented and aligned structure to true North. Yet it was constructed around a central outcropping of limestone that would have caused considerable problems in leveling its base and 'squaring' the structure; since direct diagonal measurements would have been impossible between opposite corners. Although complicating its layout and construction, that outcropping also contributed greatly to the stability of the structure.[5]

Such precision would have seemingly required laser levels and positioning satellites. The sheer complexity and magnitude of such construction would be beyond the technology and sophistication of any known ancient culture, requiring aerial and computer assistance. It was constructed using about 2.5 million blocks, which were quarried, cut, lifted, transported, placed, and precisely fitted to form mortarless joints, by some yet unknown process and means.

All this work was reportedly done without metal tools, only implements made from diorite (a hard, greenish colored stone) and volcanic obsidian, according to most Egyptologists and historians. Oddly enough, the steel chisels of the later invading Arabs bounced-off the limestone and granite surfaces in 820 AD, when Caliph Abdullah al-Mamun ordered his troops to break into the Great Pyramid. Only a repeated cycle of heating and cooling eventually cracked the stones, allowing entry. Most accounts indicate that the troops found nothing inside, although they were believed to be the first to enter the Pyramid since it was sealed during remote antiquity.

From the copper chisels and long copper saws (some over nine feet in length), it is known that metal tools were used on later pyramids. Sir Flinders Petrie uncovered such artifacts at the pyramid builder's village west of Giza. That construction village can only be associated with the subsequent group of pyramids built during later times. Yet, even using such superior implements, those later pyramids were quite inferior to their prior counterparts, the earliest 'great ones' on the nearby Giza plateau.

According to I.E.S. Edwards in his book, *The Pyramids of Egypt*, altogether only 80 pyramids were built in Egypt.[6] Yet the construction of the three Giza Pyramids is estimated to have accounted for about half of all the quarried stone during the entire pyramid-building period. All ancient pyramids varied greatly in style and construction, with some described as nearly unrecognizable ruins. Numerous archaeologists, including David Hatcher Childress, claim that no mummy or buried body has ever been found interned within a pyramid of Egypt.[7] Most pharaohs were buried in rock crypts cut into the cliffs of the Valley of the Kings, located along the bank of the Nile near Luxor. It becomes increasingly clear that the pyramids must have been erected for some other purpose.

The Great Pyramid was no exception. According to author Robert K. Moffett, it was not a tomb, or ever intended as one, based on the conclusions voiced by John Taylor, the 'Father of Pyramidology.'[8] The polished pink granite stone chest or coffer found in the King's Chamber was placed there during construction, since it was too large to fit through the entrance passage. Mr. Taylor further determined that the Egyptians could not have built the Great Pyramid. He observed that its construction incorporated mathematical knowledge that was unavailable to the area's inhabitants until much later times.[9]

One speculation as to the possible purpose of the Pyramid emerges from the fact that an equable temperature controlled environment (warm in cold weather, cooler during high heat) is created by such a stone edifice. Such a 'temperate room' could act as a repository for the most sensitive instruments, delicate equipment, weight/measure standards, charts/maps, or other unidentified scientific artifacts. Another speculative purpose emerges from its original brightly polished white limestone casing stones, which would have enhanced the pyramid's visibility, especially from the air, by reflecting sun or moon light. With its sides precisely oriented to the four cardinal points, and its location bisecting the Nile Delta, the Great Pyramid forms a perfect geodesic landmark for navigation from the air. The Great Pyramid's location and orientation would have provided an excellent place to establish a prime meridian, similar to the present Greenwich meridian. Such an archaic meridian would have divided the inhabited ancient world, as well as the Pacific Ocean, into equal parts.

While the Pyramid's original purpose still remains a mystery, its construction should not. No ancient Egyptian record describes the construction of the Giza Pyramids, or refers to any of their builders; unlike the accounts of the later, smaller, and more inferior pyramids that were indeed efforts of men, accomplished through brute force. The Greek historian, Herodotus, is the earliest written source of information on the Giza constructions, per his Egyptian visit of *c*.450 BC. Herodotus was told of the secret hinged door located on its north face, and the underground chamber of the Great Pyramid. He also wrote about the labor involved in another building project to move and transport one granite block weighing 300 tons from a quarry in Syene to the Delta via the Nile River. That single block was reported to have required 2,000 men and three years worth of labor for cutting and transport to its building site.[10] Based on such records, Dr. Gunther Rosenberg, the previously mentioned pyramidologist, estimated a period of construction lasting between 70 to over 600 years to complete the Great Pyramid.[11] Such a feat would have consumed all of the available labor force, bankrupting the Egyptian national economy of any era, without even accounting for the food requirements of the workers and their support citizens.

The Great Pyramid, which is universally portrayed as the Pyramid of Khufu (the Greek Cheops), was not built during the Fourth Dynasty around *c*.2600 BC, but much earlier. It should be noted that the Giza Pyramids are the only true equilateral pyramids, with square bases and equilateral triangular sides inclined at 51 degrees, 51 minutes; and are further distinguished by the area of their sides equaling the square of their height. All the other later copies, which are known to have been attempts made by ancient humans to duplicate the earlier edifices, were quite unsuccessful at duplicating this unique feat of construction. Those subsequent inferior structures had to settle for slopes of less than 45 degrees to simplify and facilitate their completion. Those later constructions exhibited no correlation with the earlier grand architectural feats, and continued to deteriorate in quality, design, and workmanship over ensuing years.

One of the unique features of the Great Pyramid is its complete lack of hieroglyphics. In ancient Egypt, anything that did not move (and probably a number of articles that did) was covered with hieroglyphics: walls and ceilings of temples, memorial plaques, stelae, obelisks, statues, burial chambers and crypts, walking canes and staffs, coffins, urns and vases, boxes, furniture, and virtually everything else. The Great Pyramid has only been attributed to Khufu because of supposed quarry identification marks found in one of the stress-relief vaults above the King's Chamber by the English explorer, Colonel R. H. Vyse in 1837.

The author of The Earth Chronicles book series, Zecharia Sitchin, a most dedicated and competent scholarly researcher, presented evidence suggesting this quarry mark was a forgery by Colonel Vyse. In his second book, *The Stairway to Heaven*, Mr. Sitchin cites the painted characters used in the Khufu identification as being from the wrong dynasty, with mixed and incomplete script that even contained some unknown symbols.[12] In Mr. Sitchin's third book, *The Wars of Gods and Men*, he supplied confirmation for his forgery suspicions by obtaining family records from the great-grandson of Humphries Brewer. Mr. Brewer was employed by Colonel Vyse during his excavations conducted in 1837, and reportedly had personally observed Colonel Vyse forging the now questionable inscription. Mr. Brewer's objections to such a deceitful act resulted in his expulsion from the work site, compelling him to leave Egypt.[13]

Records prior to Khufu's time mention the Sphinx and the Great Pyramid, a remarkable feat for structures that were not yet built, according to our historians. An engraved limestone slab known as the *Inventory Stele* was discovered by the French archaeologist, Auguste Mariette, in the 19th century. This artifact is now housed in the Cairo Museum. It states that the Sphinx and the Great Pyramid were constructed long before the reign of Khufu, and were dedicated to the goddess Isis.[14] While this stele has been dated to a time after the reign of Khufu, it is accepted as being a copy made to replace a much earlier one, which had fallen into disrepair over the ages. Such replication of earlier records to replace aging ones was a common practice in ancient Egypt.

Chapter 4

Implausible Explanations

Perhaps the popular explanation of the methods of construction utilized for the Giza Pyramids (as well as numerous other ancient megalithic structures) represents one of the most obvious inconsistencies in our modern beliefs. Such monuments are claimed to have been erected using elementary or basic physics principals, such as levers, wedges, and rollers, along with application of brute force. Speculation over the plausible methods employed to raise such huge stone blocks included the use of earthen ramps, built as inclined planes. But such speculation appears to be historically contradicted. Diodorus, the first century BC geographer, stated in Volume I of his *Library of History*: "...not a trace remains either of any mound (ramp used in construction) or of the dressing of the stones...they do not have the appearance of being the slow handiwork of men but look like a sudden creation, as though they had been made by some god...."[1]

Without our huge modern mechanized earth moving equipment, the construction of compacted earthen mounds rising at a credible inclination to move large stones would encompass as great an engineering feat as the actual pyramid construction itself. The same would hold true for wooden scaffolding as the possible method of stone conveyance. Author Erich von Däniken reported that Professor Georges Goyon, an archaeologist specializing in ancient technology, eliminated the possible use of wood scaffolding in the building of the Great Pyramid, citing the scarcity of wood in the region.[2] Further, the tensile strength of wooden levers, sleds, and rollers is simply inadequate to have withstood such construction demands. The same would apply to the woven or braided ropes used to secure, pull, and raise the massive stone blocks. To fulfill the strength requirements sufficient to handle the larger stone monoliths, the diameters of wooden levers and fiber ropes would become so large and cumbersome it would make them useless to handle manually.

Both the rope and wooden implements would abrade quickly during their use with the much harder stones and bedrock surfaces, thus deteriorating rapidly. Before 3000 BC, ropes were made from flax. Only later was rope constructed using stronger fibers for such heavier work. It is unlikely that any early fiber rope weavers would have had the skills or necessary resources to produce suitable ropes capable of sustaining such heavy loads and rough usage. Realistically, materials compatible with such construction use would require high tensile strength steel alloy cables or chains, or strapping made from synthetic composite fibers.

One example tending to disprove the use of basic implements is revealed from the rare red granite stones used in the King's Chamber, a type of stone that could only have been quarried from a site over 600 miles away. With each of those blocks weighing over 70 tons, log rollers would have disintegrated rapidly, as would the ropes used to secure the blocks. Further, such rapid abrasion to wood and woven implements would require tree and plant resources that did not exist within the entire Egyptian desert area. The palm trees, which were an important source of dates for food, would not be candidates for cutting into rollers. The mighty cedars of Lebanon were the main source of wood for the entire Near East region, including Egypt. The cutting, logging, and transport of a sufficient number of cedar trees from Lebanon to Egypt would pose its own dilemma, again raising even further unanswered questions.

The use of brute force as motive power to move and place stone blocks requires an implausible number of workers within or around a confined area. Modern contractors will attest to the fact that there is a limiting number of workers able to congregate around a given space in which to maneuver and manhandle massive loads. The addition of 'extra' manpower quickly becomes counterproductive and dangerous, with workers merely getting in each other's way, or running out of room. The ability to precisely coordinate the push/pull efforts of manual laborers at the same instant is further questioned. There is simply a limit to the cumulative effort derived from simple brute force, without utilization of mechanization.

Many of us have watched modern construction re-creations of a minuscule portion of an isolated corner of a pyramid, using smaller than half-sized blocks that are raised only a limited height above the ground. Such demonstrations are undertaken to 'verify' prevailing construction theories, using mostly primitive equipment and methods ascribed by the historians, although steel levers and modern strapping is always employed in these recreations. Viewers are also supplied all the excuses why it looks so difficult and why the precision and accuracy is missing, along with other justifications for their inferior modern construction results. We are constantly told of how much easier and faster the construction process would become with more practice.

On the contrary, the work would only become progressively more difficult with increasing height, on a constantly diminishing work space, allowing ever fewer workers with limited access, as each successive course of stones was laid. But the stone blocks physically demonstrate the best proof that simple brute force was not employed. The corners are not rounded, which would be the result if slid and pried into place. The edges are not chipped, but crisp and sharp, indicating no brute force was used in their transport or placement. Rather, they appear to have been gently placed in position from above, as if weightless until reaching their intended location.

While the builders, the date of origin, and the intended purpose of the three unique Giza pyramids remains a mystery, Egyptologists discount any extraterrestrial component being associated with their construction. They strongly claim that Egyptians built those structures through their own cleverness and dedication. They point to the balls of diorite stone used by the ancient masons, along with the cemetery where those workers were eventually buried, as proof that man, and man alone, built those ancient monuments. They simply argue that we know man built certain later pyramids, so all pyramids built prior to those known constructions must also have been built by man, an 'all or nothing' belief. But it is obvious that multiple methods and types of construction were employed, along with differing levels of craftsmanship, as evidenced in the various structures, all clearly pointing to different groups and skill levels being employed.

Many other structures pose equally baffling archaeological dilemmas. Often the oldest edifices of a culture are the most complex in design, reflecting the best quality, even without evidence of a prior learning period. The later Egyptian pyramids are greatly inferior to the ones at Giza and are of much simpler design, as if the archaic master builders were no longer around, or their techniques and skills had been lost to the younger builders. Perhaps a more reasonable answer is that some unknown outside influence built the oldest structures, and man built the later ones by attempting to copy those prior ancient edifices.

The concept of extraterrestrial visitors creating certain archaic structures on Earth does not devalue or diminish the many great achievements accomplished by humankind over the ages, through our own ingenuity, inventiveness, and resolve. Perhaps any 'extraneous influence' merely instructed humanity during archaic construction periods, supplying technology that later became lost or hidden. Some ancient texts suggest that the purpose of an older, wiser 'benefactor species' was limited to only imparting knowledge; instructing encountered younger races in new skills and techniques, not conducting such work themselves. Only the most massive structures that were built during times when their construction would have been beyond the abilities of its indigenous people are thought to be the products of otherworldly visitors. Such structures were either necessary for the visiting benefactors to carry out their mission, or were intended for the direct benefit of the infant earthly cultures, perhaps as a protective fortification to assure the longevity of those indigenous 'students' undergoing instruction.

The stepped pyramid believed to have been built by Imhotep at Saqqara during the Third Dynasty reign of Pharaoh Zoser, about 2660 BC, is probably the first pyramid structure in Egypt that was made by man, but it was not the first pyramid on Earth. An acknowledged older one, the Cholula Pyramid, is found in the 'New World', located high on the Anahuac Plateau in the state of Pueblo near Mexico City, Mexico. That structure began its modern excavation from under a mantle of lava as a result of an ancient eruption from the Xitle Volcano that buried three of its sides. The result of an ancient eruption from the Xitle volcano. But the last known Xitle eruption occurred sometime between 6000 and 5000 BC.

Even with certainty of its age before the 5000 BC date, the pyramid is believed to be much older. A National Geographical Society excavation, led by the United States archaeologist Dr. Byron S. Cummings, studied stratigraphic layers of the site and declared the pyramid to be the oldest on the American continent.[3] It was further determined that this pyramid was abandoned and fell into ruins by 6500 BC.[4] Clearly, this structure grossly predates the archaeological dating for the pyramid building period in Egypt or elsewhere on Earth. Mexican legends attribute the building of the Cholula Pyramid to a group of deformed giants during remotely ancient times.

A reasonable and informed populace should no longer simply accept such false premises. The indigenous natives that formed early primitive cultures could not have constructed the ancient megalithic structures without assistance. Either those communities were much more highly mechanized and technically adept than described by our historians, or some extraneous intervention or assistance was involved. One source of such intervention is recorded in the texts of numerous ancient cultures as the gods from the heavens, the extraterrestrial visitors to our planet during its impressionable past. There is nothing improbable with the concept of ancient astronauts and their civilizing deeds contributing to the formation and shaping of Earth history. It is as believable, if not more so, than orthodox theories, or the various competing religious beliefs that attempt to explain the origins of humankind and our earliest cultures.

The likelihood that flaws exist within our current belief is based partially on anomalous artifacts and numerous unanswered questions. The present paradigm contains obvious omissions and missing pieces, as it pertains to the development of Earth and the ultimate emergence of humankind as its dominant species. To demonstrate that the present orthodox belief system contains errors and contradictions, it will be necessary to present basic facts as a primer, in order to establish the actual sequence of occurrences.

Such a study will commence with known cosmological knowledge, focusing on the Big Bang event. This will provide the necessary basis from which to introduce a unique and credible explanation of perhaps our true past, in the form of the *Elder Gods* theory, which can account for the anomalous evidence and exceptions that plague our present scientific hypothesis. This theory emerges from extrapolation of known data, as well as the reinterpretation of ancient texts, mainly from Sanskrit and Egyptian records. Additional fundamental data will also be provided regularly throughout this writing to establish the knowledge necessary to adequately place such ancient developments within the context of factual reality, as accompanying portions of the *Elder Gods* theory are revealed.

Chapter 5

Origins of the Universe

The factors underlying the creation of our universe have become more apparent with each new cosmological discovery. An eight-year study to estimate the age of the universe was conducted by an international team of 27 astronomers. Their findings, verified with data from an Australian physicist, were released in May of 1999. The results established that the universe was formed as long as 13.5 billion years ago as a product of the Big Bang genesis.[1] Yet a puzzling observation that focused on portions of our universe suggested an older formation, in the range of 14 to 15 billion years, creating a debate about an even earlier origin of the universe.

Perhaps our current formation that resulted from the Big Bang event 'captured' portions of an even earlier configuration that preceded our present one. Further, it has been determined that our universe is expanding faster now than at the dawn of the Big Bang, due to a strange phenomenon known as gravitational repulsion, a kind of anti-gravity effect. Such a more rapidly expanding condition is thought to indicate that the universe is likely to continue expanding into infinity without end, rather than collapsing back upon itself.[2]

Within a microsecond of the initiation of the genesis event, as a concurrent result of the immense heat and energy release of the explosion, an extremely dense subatomic primordial cosmic sea emerged. At that very same instant, the universe began to expand in all directions and cool, never to experience or attain such an immense temperature extreme again. The resulting primordial inflation and condensation continues into our present time. That unique and intense heat and pressure that occurred during this creation inferno produced the first ever conversion of energy into mass. This resulted in the formation of subatomic particles known as leptons and quarks, the first creation of physical form.[3] These particles carried a predetermined code from which order would ensue and the universe would be built.

The instantaneous energy and particle release from that genesis event is further believed to have created a bubble, a web, or a veil that encapsulated this furious expansion. This bubble became the ever-expanding, flexible fabric of 'space-time' that enshrouds our physical universe. This Big Bang energy release propelled the fundamental particles of primordial mass in all directions, inflating the envelope of space-time and displacing the void of nothingness that initially encompassed its single-point of origin. This space-time fabric is influenced or deformed by mass of any size, due to the effects of gravitational force that warps or distorts this envelope, forming a racetrack-like depression. Hence, the actual size and geometry of our universe is determined by its physical mass content. Further, the very basis for all physical reality, which emanated as a result of the Big Bang event, exists either as particles or waves.

That genesis inferno also ushered in other new commodities known as cosmic strings, along with the formation of energy forces and a massive release of photons. Photons are the particles of light that exhibit the unique characteristic of possessing a 'zero mass.' They belong to the family of carrier or exchange particles known as *gauge bosons*. Gauge bosons are the 'carrier' particles that convey *forces* between other particles. Such energy forces are believed to exist and apply uniformly everywhere in the universe. They include both the gravitational (the weakest of all four forces, but the one that works over the greatest or longest range) and the electromagnetic forces (that acts over an unlimited distance). Additionally, the lesser-known *strong* and *weak* nuclear forces (that work only within a microscopic range of distance within the nucleus of the atom) also exist; perhaps as well as a fifth unknown force yet to be discovered or understood.[4]

Natural laws acting on our physical world are both impersonal and dispassionate, possessing no special reverence or dispensation for any form of physical life. Thus, natural forces appear to act uniformly everywhere within the universe, without any consideration of consequences, while conforming to a master plan that provides order and predictability.

The initial formation of physical structure within this early emerging universe required interaction between all those commodities. Such formation commenced with the elementary particles that comprise all mass, which cannot be further divided or destroyed, only exchanged or converted. Hence, everything physical is comprised of quarks and leptons, nothing more and nothing less. The simple and solitary leptons, which consist of six structureless particles (plus their associated antiparticles), include the electrons and neutrinos. However, quarks act in a more complex fashion, and comprise six different types or 'flavors' (plus their six oppositely charged antiparticles), some of which act in combination to form protons and neutrons.[5]

Initially the different types of quarks combined together in groups of two or three to form *hadrons*, creating more than 100 distinct combinations. Hadrons are defined by the number and type of quarks they contain and are separated into two general classes known as mesons and baryons. The atomic components of protons and neutrons are types of baryons. [6] The earliest subatomic particles of charged protons and neutral neutrons eventually arranged to form a nucleus, the atomic structure held together by the *strong* force. Repeated pairings of these discrete particles continued over time, forming countless nuclei. Those fundamental subatomic components, in the form of continuously constructed nuclei, crashed together with free electrons (formed from leptons) in a chain

37

reaction of continuous collisions. Eventually, those primordial components came together via energy forces, as the unified structure of the atom.

The earlier cosmic strings are believed to have provided the initial gravitational forces and nucleating sites around which the various types of quarks and leptons combined to form such subatomic components, eventually resulting in the unification of the first atoms. Such cosmic strings are believed to be infinitesimally thin structures, extremely dense, perhaps even hollow tubes, which exhibit massive gravitational forces along with certain other wondrous properties.[7]

The base building block of all matter is the atom, which is comprised of three parts: protons, neutrons, and electrons. As previously described, protons and neutrons bond together forming a core or nucleus. An oppositely charged electron is randomly attracted to that pairing and orbits around such a nucleus. The electrons, orbiting at tremendous speeds around its nucleus, create a *shell* (or shells) comprising various layers around each atom. This unified structure is all held together by electromagnetic forces of attraction. Atoms differ from one another by the number of electrons and protons comprising each elemental atomic structure or shell.

According to the recognized governing body, the International Union of Pure and Applied Chemistry (IUPAC), as of 2003 there were 111 base elements on the Periodic Table, 92 of which are naturally occurring. Five additional substances that have been 'produced' or 'separated' from other compounds are undergoing evaluation for authentication and inclusion, and could increase that number to 116 'acknowledged' elements. However, some candidates such as Element 115 have only been produced from particle acceleration experiments, while certain other rare and exotic atoms are the resultant product from the quick decay of heavier elements, thus prohibiting their extensive study. The complexity of the universe occurs when these basic elements or 'building blocks' interact with each other.

Our perception of the true state of solid objects is misleading. Material objects are more nebulous than they appear. Solid objects are an illusion, being comprised of a very porous structure. Author William Bramley uses the example of a hydrogen atom, when enlarged to the size of a marble, would have its one electron orbiting about a quarter of a mile away from its center, creating an obvious vast gap of empty space. Hence, all atoms consist of immense empty spaces, with the density of the 'heaviest' matter still quite porous. The illusion of 'solidness' results from the very rapid speed and motion of the electrons orbiting the core of their atomic structures, which form a 'shell of solidness.'[8]

Over the eons of time, fundamental particles had joined in various combinations to create the first atoms. From these atoms, molecules formed to comprise the fundamental light gasses of hydrogen and helium. These basic simple gasses, along with early primordial dust, the debris from repeated collisions of elementary particles, clumped together around cosmic strings as gaseous 'super clouds' or nebulae to form the first stellar nursery. The cosmic strings provided the gravitational attraction to bring those molecules of dust and gases together.

The continued molecular interaction of such pristine interstellar material within those nurseries ultimately caused the light primordial gases to became dense enough to congeal and eventually transform or mutate, forming the earliest stars approximately 13 billion years ago. All stars are born in batches within their stellar nurseries or nebulae, which consist of compressed gas clouds. As a young star emerges from its nursery, it is surrounded by wisps of the residual glowing stellar material from which it was formed, releasing that surplus into 'free' space.

The conversion of energy into matter as a result of the Big Bang event created two types of matter: ordinary (or bright) matter and dark matter. Ordinary matter formed the observable structures of stars and planets, while the unfamiliar and unique commodity of dark matter filled the voids between the visible cosmic bodies. Dark matter is known only through its gravitational effects, since it does not interact by producing, absorbing, or reflecting light or any other type of radiation.[9] Cosmologists speculate that a portion of this dark matter may exist as WIMPs (Weakly Interacting Massive Particles) or a commodity known as a MACHO (Massive Compact Halo Object). An even more unusual commodity is dark energy, perhaps a massless counterpart to, or a component of dark matter. It is estimated that the universe is comprised of 4% bright matter, 23% dark matter, and 73% dark energy. The cosmic strings may also form or provide the boundary separating bright matter from dark matter. While cosmic strings are believed to have formed during the Big Bang event, the two types of physical matter definitely formed later.

Once stars were formed, the fusion process emerged, which provided their ability to shine or emit photons. Suns shine by 'burning' (actually converting) hydrogen into helium, loosing mass in the process through such conversion of its internal elements as a 'fuel,' eventually consuming itself to the point of supernova and exploding violently. Those resultant eruptions, which spew volatile jets of gas and dust, eventually mutate into heavier elements such as the metals. Such heavier elements further reform into new stars, along with molten-mass by-products that slowly cool into planets and other celestial bodies.[10]

Those bodies can obtain a steady-state condition with their surrounding neighbors to create solar systems. Some of those solar systems eventually collide or join with numerous other systems to create galaxies. Those galaxies continue to come in contact with one another to form mega-galaxies, such as the Virgo Super Cluster that includes our own Milky Way galaxy. New star systems were also created or fueled by planets and suns that lived their lives, expired, and were recycled into new cosmic bodies or converted to pure energy, ever altering and adding to our very active and expanding universe. It is believed that there are at least 50 billion galaxies, with estimates as high as one trillion galaxies, each containing about 100 to 300 billion stars. Our own Milky Way galaxy forms a spiral about 100,000 light-years across and is estimated to contain well over 150 billion stars, with some estimates approaching 400 billion.

Those same elementary particles comprise the nature of all things throughout the physical universe. Hence, all matter and life is made from the same things, quarks and leptons, the essential ingredients of stardust. Since everything in the universe is comprised of these quarks and leptons, perhaps things are not so different between the remote extremes of the universe as one might first imagine. For the same reason, perhaps physical life may not be all that different elsewhere in the universe where somewhat similar conditions might exist. The grand scheme of the Big Bang genesis shouts of preplanning that resulted in ordered construction from nothing.

Such design intent, which apparently existed prior to its initial energy release, brought eventual order to the universe after its instantaneous chaos. Its single central origin and universal consequence tends to indicate its inception as the work of a divine Godhead, with creation being an inevitable result through fundamental interactions that had to occur as a result. Such an act, from thought concept to elemental particles, to subatomic, to molecular, to microscopic, to microbes, to cells, to macromolecular structures, to tissue, to organs, to life, to thought...was apparently the grand cycle from conception to reality, which completed this circle of creation.

Animated Life

The initial seed responsible for the flora and fauna within a solar system may also be universal in its origin. Perhaps the original spore that first spawned life elsewhere in the universe is the very same for every celestial body. Such an original

41

spore would be allowed to evolve and develop independently on each world, mutating, adapting, and conforming to the unique environment encountered on each planet. That would result in a final and unique species or variety associated with each world. Those lifeforms could then further evolve according to the changing individual terrestrial conditions of each planet. Sentient beings may have developed in a similar way, from one single source of life. That would allow each world to develop and evolve its own unique indigenous species, even though the original source of such life was identical elsewhere within its neighboring region, although very different outcomes might ultimately be produced.

On a secondary level of formation, the commonalty of a universal spore as the original seed of life everywhere may be a concept similar to that of the quarks and leptons, the original building blocks for all matter within the universe. That would allow a vast and varied array of life forms to mutate from a common fundamental source, solely dependent on the environment in which each spore might find itself. Such universal spores may have created humans from apes, in a manner similar in which alien beings might have evolved from amphibians or reptiles. Both could be humanoid in their appearance, neither one actually resembling an ape or a lizard.

Prior to the formation of 'younger' later planets such as Earth, more than ample time ensued for simple life to form and evolve into sentient status on much earlier worlds. An untold countless number of intelligent and creative beings could have come into existence throughout the far reaches of the early universe. Those ancient races may now be extinct, or progressed to levels beyond our comprehension, perhaps even evolving beyond the need for corporeal-form existence. It is quite conceivable that sentient life would have occurred elsewhere in the universe prior to its formation on Earth. It is now a known fact that other solar systems exist, as evidenced by three huge planets orbiting the star Upsilon Andromeda, some 44 light years from Earth. Other planets are known to exist in orbits around other stars, but those planets are believed to be only single bodies, not a collection of planets that would qualify as a solar system.

As of the fall of 2001, a total of 76 planets have been detected outside our solar system.[11] It is no longer science fiction to believe that intelligent life elsewhere in the cosmos likely preceded our species on Earth, and may still exist somewhere within the universe. In November 1961, a secret meeting of noted scientists including Drs. Carl Sagan and Frank D. Drake, the director of Project Ozma, gathered at Green Bank, West Virginia. Their scientific group assembled to evaluate and estimate the number of cosmic worlds capable of harboring intelligent life that would be capable of communication with Earth. Known as the *Green Bank Formula*, it was estimated that there are between 40 to 50 million worlds that are either trying to signal us or are listening for messages from Earth. According to calculations by Otto Struve, the 1959 Director of the National Radio Astronomy Observatory at Green Bank, five solar systems that possess intelligent life are expected to exist just within our own Milky Way Galaxy.[12] Clearly, even respected scientists no longer believe we are alone in the universe.

Chapter 6

Elder Gods Theory

Be suspicious of anyone claiming to know with certainty the answers to all the mysteries pertaining to the Creative Godhead, the formation of the universe, the essence of life, or the origins of humankind on Earth. Harbor some skepticism toward the prevailing orthodox beliefs, when based only on the few known facts. Apparently the only universal certainties are found in mathematics. Other scientific branches simply do not display their truths in such mathematical absolutes, despite their apparent predictability or perceived procedural repeatability.

As new discoveries are made, it becomes more apparent that multiple unknown forces, however minor, demonstrate their influences and effects in ways still beyond our present human understanding. The following speculative interpretation of what may be Earth's true history is based on extrapolations from a combination of known historic facts, extant artifacts, existing circumstantial anomalous evidence, and geological indications; as well as from modern reinterpretations of ancient records, oral histories, and cultural traditions.

The correlation of all those individual elements produces a detectable pattern. From that pattern, deductions emerge from which comprehensive conclusions can be drawn, allowing the formation of a revised theory explaining humanity's past. There could still be other theories or explanations that also connect all the factual elements with the known contrary evidence, while additionally providing answers for all the outstanding perplexing mysteries. With the following event chronology provided, along with the exposed fundamental facts pertaining to the evolution of the universe contained in the preceding chapters, the reader is urged to formulate their own theory. Various different conclusions are capable of being drawn from the same facts. Therefore, this writing must remain a work in progress, as further knowledge and data are obtained, which may influence or alter the present conclusions.

Considering our modern cosmological knowledge, it is now likely that prior sentient life would have formed eons ago somewhere in that ocean of stars that resulted from the primordial furnace known as the Big Bang genesis. Emergence of that initial lifeform may have even occurred before our Earth condensed as a planet, or our sun became a twinkle in the night sky of a far distant world. Later, numerous other lifeforms likely also emerged in neighboring galaxies, somewhere within the vastness of that infant starry sea, perhaps in numerous locations throughout the universe. Eventually, those sentient *First Beings* would have likely achieved an intellectual aptitude, evolving into productive and creative sapient societies, growing in both knowledge and achievement. Their civilizations may have even flourished, perhaps through their proficient utilization of advanced technology.

Ultimately, those *First Beings* would have reached a degree of development and power that could threaten their progress, and perhaps even the existence of their region of space, possibly even the entire universe. Such threats might have involved pollution of their solar systems, deployment of doomsday weapons, extinction of lower species, or any number of other acts that would reflect the self-centered exploits of a species ignoring the consequences of their actions.

Such selfish, unconstrained actions might have intruded into unimaginable venues, without observing the physical and natural laws, perhaps completely unaware of such laws and their repercussions, with catastrophic results. Possibly their technical achievements grew faster than their moral composition, creating a permissive and decadent environment incapable of recognizing their own deterioration. Or perhaps the nature of corruption that threatened their corner of the galaxy might have simply involved acts beyond our present understanding, causing incomprehensible consequences, or some unimaginable imbalance within the universe.

Whatever act of perversion or manipulation of advanced powers, some devastating action or event caused a disruption within the continuity of universal order, resulting in chaos. Perhaps the effects of such acts even spread to nearby planets within their own solar system. Many worlds may have been destroyed, along with the vast extinction of numerous life forms. Other regions of the universe experienced similar disruptions by their earliest species. Similar ensuing chaos spread throughout the cosmos. Somewhere, one species of *First Beings* eventually altered such a cycle of destructive behavior and moral decay, perhaps altering the course of history, and maybe preventing total universal annihilation.

Once an enlightened level of understanding emerged from the chaos, that species of *First Beings* then focused their energies, skills, and expertise on more altruistic pursuits. Their culture and accomplishments flourished, achieving peace and tranquillity through order. New levels of technology were reached, ones concentrated on more beneficial pursuits, with less intrusive consequences. Space exploration eventually expanded beyond their own solar system, revealing numerous less developed life forms apparently on an evolutionary path not unlike their own chaotic ancient past. They observed that the encountered primitive creatures exhibited similar patterns of flawed actions and moral deficiencies that were identical to those of the *First Beings*, prior to their own enlightenment. Other worlds revealed the same levels of decay and disorder. It became evident that such imbalance and chaos was common among all emerging life forms.

Such a universal pattern revealed that any developing culture, one capable of achieving ever higher levels of technology and science, would eventually utilize their knowledge and inventions for self-centered and immature purposes, always resulting in universal disruption and chaos. Eventually, such primitive, emerging species would obtain the ability to self-destruct, a potential that also jeopardized innocent nearby worlds. Basically, all infant races would eventually reach a level of attainment, one that they were unable to fully control or understand, which resulted in disruptions within the universe. Destruction of their own species and their planet followed, ultimately threatening perhaps complete universal annihilation.

In their travels, the enlightened *First Beings* ultimately encountered another different *First Being* species from a remote part of an adjacent galaxy. Over time, several other dissimilar species of *First Being* survivors were encountered from even further reaches of the universe. By comparing experiences, those unrelated *First Beings* concluded that all primitive lifeforms progress through virtually identical evolutionary stages, culminating in the same self-created problems originally found within their own worlds, eventually threatening themselves and others. Such an inherent instinct for self-destruction was deemed to have been a universal affliction that could eventually affect one or all *First Being* species. The minimal consequences involved warfare, environmental and biological pollution, species extermination, depletion of natural resources, and delayed or even subverted development of new advancements. The ultimate consequence could mean universal demise and annihilation of everything physical.

It was further concluded that only an extremely small fraction of emerging lifeforms would succeed in overcoming such a basic and inherent pattern, prohibiting their own evolution to higher cultural and enlightenment levels. Even then, some of those species would eventually revert back to their prior destructive ways, ultimately resulting in extinction. The extremely few surviving species followed a strict but simple code of conduct, permitting eventual evolution to higher enlightenment levels reflecting altruistic motives, rather than the self-centered emotions possessed by those other doomed chaotic societies. Such a code of conduct envisioned all possible outcomes their actions could have on the cosmos, realizing all acts have permanent consequences on everything within our universe.

The few surviving *First Being* species ultimately joined together in an effort to create universal harmony. They constructed a simple code of conduct that was based on their own experiences, as well as the rules utilized by the more successful cultures they had encountered. They pledged their conformity to such a code, and realized the necessity for its compliance by all emerging primitive cultures, in order to ensure the successful continuation and evolution of the universe. This code was not viewed as merely a set of laws that were to be enforced by 'catching' lawbreakers. Such secular laws were considered secondary to this code, which was a way-of-life, with certain responsibilities and rights. It was a universal paradigm, intended to control the actions and developmental direction of all emerging races, while teaching those species morality and core values. This universal code, the *Cosmic Order*, was adopted by all the surviving *First Beings*, uniting them within this common goal.

The *Cosmic Order* dictated that any ensuing technology developed by an infant race would be restricted by their comprehensive ability to envision the total and ultimate effects of its implementation. No conduct was allowed that focused solely on the self-interests of any one species. This code professed that the rights of a species ended when they infringed upon the rights of other lifeforms or the well being of the universe. Any nonconforming technology required containment within that planet's atmosphere, so only its inhabitants might be harmed if miscalculations occurred, without affecting other worlds. Intervention would be deemed necessary to contain such actions and inventions that could spread chaos. All *First Beings* pledged their life's purpose and efforts to instill within all the primitive races throughout the cosmos their requirement for compliance and harmony with all other species, under the united mantle of the *Cosmic Order*.

The *Cosmic Order* was to be the primary and fundamental rule or commandment, coming before and taking precedence over the laws of each and every member planet. In return, the *First Beings* would impart knowledge to the infant races, in appropriate degrees, bringing civilization to their worlds. The *Cosmic Order* became the foundation of universal harmony, a prime directive intended to permanently alter the prior repetitive cycle of destruction in the physical realm. This linked the *First Beings* through some interconnectivity with a Godhead or Universal Consciousness, the Creator and Source of Power behind the Big Bang from which all physical reality ensued.

This hypothesis, the *Elder Gods* theory, could be considered by some as mere speculation. But nearly every ancient record provides some evidence supporting such a concept. Professor Cornelius Loew observed that archaic cultures believed that a sacred world order existed, with which humanity must conform; a *Cosmic Order* that permeated every level of reality.[1] This same conviction was closely associated with the tradition of Divine Kingship that was prevalent during ancient times.[2] The early Egyptians believed in a higher spiritual power of the cosmos, from which order and creative power flowed throughout the universe.[3] The Mayans believed in an orderliness in the heavens to which the gods, and thus humanity, must conform.[4] The Mayans further observed that the hierarchy of the divine beings changed periodically, as if in unison with some regular celestial movement.

This *Cosmic Order* was also known as the *Great Order* or *Universal Reality*. It was a common belief with the Greeks, Hindus of Ancient India, Egyptians, Chinese, and the Native

Indians. It was known by numerous names within each separate culture. Such Order was called R*ta* in Sanskrit texts. According to the tenth book, hymn 154, verse 4 of the *Rig Veda* (10.154.4), the Great Fathers who had reached high levels of spiritual attainment were: "Those who first nursed Order, who had Order and made Order grow great...." It was called *Logos* by the earliest Greeks, the divine reason or thought that ordered the universe. *Logos* occurred as a revolution out of chaos, and represented reason and logic.[5] It was the creation of material reality from the cosmic plane of manifestation, transforming energy into mass. Later, over time, the concept of *Logos* became the Law known as the *Cosmic Order*.

The *Cosmic Order* was a metaphysical divine force that produced the regularities and balance in nature, including the physical and natural laws that governed the pattern or direction of all matter in the universe. Harmony resulted from this *Order*, which was the connecting force between the Godhead and the physical world. According to the *Gospel of John* in the New Testament, Jesus is identified with the *Logos*. The English translation of the Greek *Logos* is "Word." In John 1:1-3: "In the beginning was the Word (Logos), and the Word was with God, and the Word was God...." This Word was the ultimate Law, the natural rules to which all actions must conform.

The Urantia Book also reveals the existence of a central administration over the universe, a kind of celestial government for the cosmos, acting as a coordination agency over the inhabited regions of space.[6] This cosmic authority, the administrative Joint Council, serves as coordinators over the Grand Universe, where the cosmos is supposedly divided into seven specific regions, the seven Superuniverses, containing numerous inhabited planets.[7] A 'local-universe-overseer' presides over regional cosmic sectors that manage about 1,000 inhabited worlds, with each inhabited world having its own planetary leader.[8] Such a purpose or plan, known as the Mortal Ascension Plan, attempts to ensure that infant races are properly guided throughout their development by more enlightened beings. *The Urantia Book* professes a belief that planets and their animal population do not occur by freak chance, but from deliberate acts of seeding by higher attained beings who are following some master plan.

Once such seeding produced a lifeform capable of self-determination, along with their ability to comprehend and learn knowledge, the 'overseer beings' reveal themselves and help guide the emerging species. That is accomplished by the authorities stationing a small group of enlightened beings on the 'primitive' planet to guide, instruct, and civilize the inhabitants for eventual interaction with other worlds.

The *Cosmic Order* evolved from the spiritual enlightenment obtained by the surviving *First Beings*, which prompted a commitment and dedication to their mission of guiding the fledgling, infant races to the same harmony of coexistence. Such intervention was an effort to eliminate possible destructive actions before they could occur. It further intended to spare the infant races the suffering and losses the *First Beings* had wrought upon themselves and the universe, prior to gaining the necessary wisdom to overcome their own destructive actions and path. It must be stressed that such a mission was not undertaken merely as a benevolent act. Nor were such actions based on any spiritual conviction promising an afterlife reward, or with any 'secretive' malevolent intent.

The *First Beings* were evidently dispassionate, unmoved by emotions, but acutely focused on their goal. Their contact with emerging solar systems was not an attempt to exploit, ravage, enslave, or implement any similar motives. Rather, their mission to create order, thus insuring a universal balance, was ultimately in their own self-interest. Their intervention with infant races was intended to instill core values of morality, orderliness, and laws; not because such actions are noble, but because it is in everyone's best interest for universal self-preservation. Spread of the *Cosmic Order* through such contact undoubtedly also provided raw materials necessary for the *First Beings* to continue their mission, providing them with some form of compensation. Their discovery of certain uninhabited planets that were deemed capable of supporting life may have also been used as new homeworlds for infant races that had suffered some natural devastation of their own planet.

The *First Beings* utilized education as their greatest tool. By soliciting compliance with the *Cosmic Order*, all participating members could also reap its benefits. Such emerging infant races would receive civilization and invaluable knowledge, all while the guiding influence and diligent intervention of the *First Beings* assured the continuation of universal harmony. Such compliance also eliminated the necessity of having to annihilate an emerging species that could be identified as a potential threat. Knowing that many primitive species would eventually reach technical levels capable of destroying themselves, as well as their surrounding neighbors and perhaps the entire universe, preemptive measures were sometimes employed.

As the highest evolved beings in the universe, the *First Beings* understood the principal of 'the sacrifice of a few for the good of the whole.' The elimination of a rogue world that could be projected to someday disrupt the well being of neighboring solar systems and galaxies would be deemed expendable, in the best interest of the universe. Such action would not be beyond the capability of a vastly advanced race.

By bringing education and civilization to an emerging world, the *First Beings* could also control its rate of progress by imposing certain restrictions. Such managed development of the infant races was accomplished by educating the populace, and controlling what was learned, resulting in the regulated growth and measured progress desired. Any advancement depended upon the achieved maturity and morality of each culture's values system. Such constrained evolutionary progress, which was neither malevolent nor benevolent, was to prevent chaos that could threaten universal order.

One can only imagine the exponential difference in the technology of the *First Beings* over that of later worlds, with a headstart of thousands, millions, or even billions of years. An earlier species would undoubtedly attain higher levels of technology than a later one, if essential developments were approximately progressive in their occurrence. That is, the higher one attains, the more resources become available to obtain even more advancements. Attainment levels would become exponential, until reaching some finite plateau.

A logical conclusion professes such discoveries and inventions will occur when each species reaches a given level, regardless if that species is seeking such knowledge or innovation. New developments will occur when the recipient is ready, perhaps even by accident, but the resultant attainment would always be self-evident. No divine bond or connection is known to intertwine technical advances with a species' spiritual development. A species may obtain great technical levels without achieving high spirituality. Conversely, a highly enlightened being may have little or no need or use for technology. The *First Beings* apparently had attained both.

The surviving *First Beings* eventually became known as the *Ancient Ones*. They traveled the stellar regions from one solar system to another, and even to different galaxies, spreading harmony to the emerging worlds they encountered, through the introduction and adherence with the *Cosmic Order*. The term 'Ancient Ones' does not refer to the age of such beings, but rather to the primordial origins of their species. They were a united group of evolved beings; comprised of descendants from the *First Being* survivors who had overcome their inherent propensity for self-destruction, while also eventually achieving elevated levels of enlightenment. According to the *Rig Veda*, they were the *elder gods* who possessed the greatest magic and powers.[9]

A speculative conclusion, based on extrapolation of ancient texts, suggests seven original home worlds that produced seven distinct species of *First Beings*, who later joined collectively to form the initial coalition of the *Cosmic Order*. Evidence derived from Stanza VII of the *Book of Dzyan* refers to the 'First Lord' as the Shining Seven, the Builders, "...they who watch over thee and [the Earth]."[10] Other references in Stanza V of that text also refer to those same Seven Sons, describing the Primordial Seven, who were the seven primordial self-born gods.

The term *Primordial Seven* definitely refers to the seven *First Beings* species, those earliest intelligent lifeforms that survived to the next level of enlightenment by overcoming their inherent instinct for self-annihilation. They survived without the assistance or aid from any outside influence, because they were 'self-born' as the first species, existing before such help was available. The Jewish esoteric *Cabala* (aka *Kabbalah*) makes reference to "the seven other revealed inhabited worlds,"[11] further collaborating this speculative assumption. *The Urantia Book* speaks of the seven Sacred Worlds of the Father, the satellites of Paradise.[12] Those same seven worlds may also be the sole sources from which all life in the universe originated, either through accidental seeding or deliberately by direct relocation of lifeforms from planet to planet.

Archaic texts clearly differentiate between the Godhead and the Ancient Ones. The Sanskrit commentaries on the *Book of Dzyan* state that the Godhead was the Creator, the Initiator who sat in the Circle of Darkness peering at the threshold of Light, conceiving and initiating the Big Bang from which the universe was created.[13] The seven self-born primordial 'gods' (species) resulted from the original Big Bang event of the Creator. All else thereafter was the result of the Primordial Seven, the Ancient Ones, the Builders.[14] The Ancient Ones were the 'builders' of the worlds within that universe, 'creating' the cultures, civilizations, inventions, and collected knowledge.

Therefore, the Ancient Ones are the 'highest' beings in the physical world, and represent species of different forms and shapes that are indigenous to other worlds.

According to the *Book of Dzyan*, these Seven Sons were the "first seven breaths of the dragon of wisdom."[15] *The Urantia Book* distinguishes the Creator, the First Great Source,[16] from the seven Master Spirits (presumably the Ancient Ones) who are the 'highest life forms under the Creator.'[17] The later Zoroastrians knew them as the Seven Amshaspends, although their true identity eventually underwent alteration, distorting their original composition and 'designation.'

The *Book of Dzyan* further claims that three main groups of Ancient Ones exist, with each group divided into seven sub-groups. The first group rebuilt the universe after the massive self-destruction by the early primitive races, becoming Master Builders. The second group civilized newly emerging infant races, while the third group seeded desolate worlds. They also became known as the Watchers over their architectural accomplishments, but that term also applied to their 'Helpers,' who often became the rulers, regents, and leaders over many of those individual worlds. Those Helpers, or related members of their species, were the ones known as the Hindu Pitris, the Judeo-Christian Angels, and the ancient ancestors of the Anunnaki or 'gods' of ancient Earth cultures.

All species in the universe may be based on or from those original 'Seven Sources,' the seven worlds that were the sacred planets of antiquity. Those 'surviving' primordial beings included amphibious races, humanoids of both large and small stature, reptilian species, and insect-like creatures. A few of those species may have reached a quasi-physical state of existence, able to inhabit both the ethereal and physical worlds. Descriptions of such strange beings are numerous in ancient accounts. Such different species help explain the often contradictory appearance of 'alien creatures' described in various ancient texts around the world. The mere notion that humanoid beings could have evolved from insects or reptiles is no more farfetched than humans having evolved from primates. A sentient and sapient reptilian being would therefore be as closely related to a lizard as any human would be linked with an ape.

Locations of the seven homeworlds of the Ancient Ones are unclear, but certain repetitive mention and common focus on specific celestial bodies may provide a clue. An unusual amount of attention was paid to the Sirius, Orion, and Bootis star systems during archaic times. Specific tales from antiquity actually state that the visitors from the sky had their home in the Pleiades. Ancient Peruvians were thought to have been descendants of the gods from the Pleiades, which Peruvian legends considered to be the 'Celestial Gates.' Mayan oral tradition even claimed that 400 of their youths returned to the Pleiades.[18] Other texts specifically state that Arcturus was their home of origin. Islamic texts of the *Annunciation* reference Archangel Gabriel as being associated with the star Arcturus, the largest and brightest star in the constellation Boötes, with a connection to the star Epsilon Bootis.

The previously mentioned Project Ozma was an early scientific program established to search the heavens for extraterrestrial intelligent signals using the Green Bank radio telescope located in West Virginia.[19] The project was initiated in April of 1959, but did not commence its first search until April of 1960.[20] The first focus was directed at Epsilon Eridani and Tau Ceti, star systems located about 11 light years from Earth.[21] Such a search seems to support the belief of Joseph Shklovsky, a Russian astronomer. He reasoned that Epsilon Indi, Tau Ceti, and Epsilon Eridani are likely candidates that could support intelligent beings, based on his hypothesis of a ten light year distance between civilizations, a premise also supported by an American scientist, Professor Robert N. Bracewell.[22]

According to Dr. Frank Drake, the program director, strong intelligently coded signals were heard on the first day from the

Epsilon Eridani system. The transmissions were a series of high-speed pulses so uniformly spaced that they were deemed to have originated from an intelligent source. After about five minutes, the signal ceased, but additional similar pulses were recorded intermittently over the next five months.[23] The signals were judged to probably be of Earth origin, perhaps aircraft interference, and after only roughly 150 hours of searching, the program was abruptly terminated in July of 1960.[24]

Ancient Sanskrit records further indicate that the alien species overseeing each emerging world would change from time to time, being replaced by a different member or species from the *Cosmic Order*. That would help to explain the differing accounts of diverse Ancient Ones being variously described as humanoid, amphibious, or insect-like creatures. Such personnel rotations might reflect a periodic changing of the Ancient Ones overseeing each world, when a different species assumed the duties and responsibilities associated with that specific infant planet.

Perhaps those periodic changes were connected with a celestial phenomenon, such as the cyclic advancement through the twelve Zodiac Ages, which have also been linked to the *Cosmic Order* as referenced in the *Rig Veda* 1.164.11: "The twelve-spoked wheel of Order rolls around and around the sky and never ages." The exploration, education, and civilizing efforts of the Ancient Ones are apparently a perpetual, ever expanding venture, one deemed necessary for the *Cosmic Order* to prevail throughout the universe.

The pursuit of such a mission was evidently with the intention of achieving enlightenment and higher evolution toward godlike obtainment for all species. Any other hypothetical motives, or speculations regarding their homeworld locations and precise appearances, is of secondary importance when compared to their actual influence and intervention within our solar system, which will be explored in subsequent chapters. But first, factual background data must once again be presented, supplying the essential details necessary to further develop the *Elder Gods* theory.

Chapter 7

Solar System Development

After the universe aged for nearly nine billion years, our own sun commenced incubation in a gaseous nebula located in the region of the universe that would become known as the Milky Way galaxy. Our sun's core was prematurely expelled from this nursery accompanied by trails of stellar material, which is the normal birth occurrence for stars in the outskirts or 'arms' of a spiral galaxy. Birthing is different in elliptical galaxies, globular clusters, or at locations further within the central core of spiral galaxies where little or no stellar material is normally left to surround its formed stars. The nebula surrounding our sun was a swirling disk of material comprised of various gasses and plentiful water molecules. After its birth, our yet to be fully-formed sun continued to attract the active trailing stellar material, gathering in all it could absorb, and eventually spewed-out any unused excess, leaving those unabsorbed scattered remains from this process to cool and condense into individual planets.

Scientists, including the renowned astrophysicist Sir Fred Hoyle, estimate such 'excess' material required merely one to three percent of our sun's mass to produce all the celestial bodies within our solar system. Such 'waste products' as planets, satellites, asteroids, and comets from our sun's formation were theorized to have involved a process involving very hot gasses that were influenced by electrical currents and magnetic fields, a concept referred to as magneto-hydrodynamics. Such a process may have also been influenced by the rotational inertial motion imparted to the sun's nebular cloud as it initially exited its nursery. The planets eventually achieved a steady-state balance with each other, forming our solar system. As mentioned earlier, there are distinct differences between the inner planets and the outer gas giants, with these two groupings separated by the asteroid belt.

The four inner terrestrial planets and their satellites are those with solid surfaces that are cratered to some degree, with interiors made of rock and iron. Those crater impact scars are the result of celestial objects hitting their surface, with the Asteroid belt believed to be a main source. The Asteroid belt first became known from the 1801 discovery of Ceres, its largest asteroid, which features a 700 to 800 mile diameter. Continuing study disclosed more than 40,000 rocky chunks orbiting between Mars and Jupiter. Very few of the asteroids are over 150 miles in diameter, with many of the smaller chunks measuring less than a mile across. Most asteroids 'fell' toward the sun, but the unusual asteroids known as the Trojans lie beyond the asteroid belt, sharing the same orbit as Jupiter. They are comprised of two groups, with one set orbiting in a mean position about 60 degrees ahead of Jupiter, while the second aggregate trails in a mean position about 60 degrees behind the planet. Both groups are loose aggregates, spread out over many millions of miles.

The asteroids are fragments that were torn violently from some larger body, as evidenced by their jagged shape and the highly unusual motion of certain larger chunks that rotate on their long axis, an unnatural action. Their charred and pitted surfaces generally exhibit areas of fused crust, with the fragments grouped into three broad categories. One grouping consists mostly of silicates, believed to represent the more rocky or stony crustal-surface composition of the original destroyed parent. Another collection known as the siderites consist mostly of an iron-nickel composition, presumably indicating its origin from the inner core of the original parent body. The third grouping, the siderolites, comprise varying proportions of both iron and stone, likely from more internal or subterranean regions of the original body, but short of its central core. Some stray chunks that broke from their orbit and later impacted our planet display a composition strikingly similar to Earth.

Analysis of the most pristine specimens reveal no 'foreign' substances or elements that are not also found on Earth, and are further known to contain organic molecules of the same type that some experts suggest might have been the original raw materials for the formation of life on Earth. It is known that the original Asteroid Belt planet had abundant water to support life. A meteorite chunk from the asteroid belt that landed in Texas contained liquid water, indicating that resource did exist on that destroyed planet.[1] The age of similar specimens have been dated at 5.0 billion years old, making its extraterrestrial parent as much as 300 million years older than Earth. Such a formation earlier than that of Earth equates to roughly a six percent 'headstart' before any similar development on Earth, and may have allowed sentient life in our solar system to have originated there first, rather than on our world.

The prevailing theory states that a planet had long ago been torn apart by some unknown process. Perhaps the cosmological process or formation conditions that determine planetary types, producing either a gas giant or a rocky crustal one, somehow produced a defective terrestrial planet at the very border between these two different classifications. Such a unique condition may have created fissures or faults that weakened the structural integrity of such a 'boundary world.'

Regardless of its congenital conditions, such an inconceivably massive force that would be required to obliterate a whole planet would also vaporize the vast majority of its mass during its original cataclysm.[2] A catastrophe of that nature would have resulted in roughly half of the remaining fragments continuing to orbit along the path of its shattered planet, with the other remaining half of the non-vaporized fragments thrown free from orbit, with most hurtling inward toward the sun due to its gravitational attraction. Initially, that original bombardment of asteroids would be expected to have produced the largest meteorite shower ever experienced within our solar system.

Some of those chunks would have impacted all the inner solar bodies, starting with Mars. Such fallout would have continued to collide with the moon, Earth, Venus, and Mercury, with any non-colliding fragments eventually reaching the sun where they were incinerated. The smaller chunks invading those planets would have burned up in the denser atmosphere of the major worlds, while larger pieces would have impacted their surfaces. Due to the magnitude of such a phenomenally powerful destructive force, a few asteroid chunks would likely be expelled 'backward' away from the sun and be captured by the gravitational field of its closest outer neighbor, Jupiter. The unique Trojan Asteroids seem to confirm such a scenario. Over time, additional rocky masses would dislodge from the debris field orbit and occasionally collide with the inner celestial bodies, further cratering their surfaces.

Author Brinsley le Poer Trench wrote that an ancient legend told of just such a planet that "destroyed itself"[3] and created the asteroid belt we now know. That legend referred to this planet using the name 'Lucifer,'[4] although references in other archaic accounts called it Aravoth, Tiamat, Theos, Olam, Phaeton, or Maldek; with Maldek being the most accepted and frequently used name identifying that destroyed world. The 9th century Archbishop of Lyons, Agobard (779-840), stated that the ancient gods came from Magonia (aka Matagonie), perhaps yet another name for the Asteroid Belt planet.

Further substantiation of such a destroyed world can be found in a celestial formula known as Bode's Law, a postulation compiled by the 18th century German astronomers Johann Titius and Johann Bode.[5] Their hypothesis is an empirical observational conclusion that places the formation of planets within given distances from the sun, based on a mathematical formula. This theory requires a medium-to-large planet to be located between Mars and Jupiter, precisely where the present Asteroid belt exists. Within our solar system, that asteroid field is unique only to that one location, suggesting a planet could have once existed in that orbit. The debris is insufficient to account for a whole planet, agreeing with the preceding theory of vaporization, expulsion, and impact, as well as orbital cluster.

Mars

The neighboring planet Mars was once very similar to our present Earth conditions, with certain earlier periods more hospitable than those existing during identical times on Earth. Scientist and astronomer Percival Lowell, founder of the famed Lowell Observatory, concluded that Earth and Mars were the most suitable planets capable of similar and compatible lifeforms. It is our nearest planetary neighbor, achieving its closest orbital position with Earth roughly every 15 to 17 years, at a distance of about 35 million miles. Mars has a diameter about half that of Earth, with gravitational attraction only about 38 percent of Earth's, with a weak magnetic field. Mars' smaller size would have allowed its condensation and solidification before larger planetary bodies. Its more distant location from the sun at the outer reaches of the terrestrial planet boundary would also allow quicker cooling, further enhancing its comparably early solidification.

Its landscape consists of mountains, valleys, volcanoes, and a few craters. There are polar ice caps, floating white clouds, seasonal changes, raging dust storms, and even a 24 hour day (24 hours, 37 minutes). It is believed that Mars once had the equivalent amount of flowing water as Earth, based on its proportionate size. Mars is also believed to have once possessed a dense atmosphere containing considerable oxygen and water vapor within the last several million years. That atmosphere has since slowly dissipated, with the remaining atmosphere appearing to come from a persistent release of gas from the Martian rocks, and perhaps even rare volcanic activity.

The present atmosphere is composed of 95% carbon dioxide, 3% nitrogen, and 2% other gasses, including water vapor. No ozone exists, so high levels of ultraviolet radiation would presently prohibit plant and animal survival on its surface. Its weakly attractive magnetic field, due to a minimal or non-existent liquid core, would also allow other dangerous cosmic rays and particles to bombard the surface of Mars.

Mars experiences the same variables of axis tilt, orbital eccentricity, and precessional wobble believed to contribute to Ice Ages, although to even greater extremes than on Earth. It is believed that Mars is presently experiencing its own form of Ice Age. During the interglacial warming periods, water is believed to flow freely on Mars. Such flowing water conditions were believed to have existed as recently as 8000 BC. Subterranean aquifers are also believed to be numerous, with some pools mere inches below the surface. Water is still present as permafrost over vast areas of the planet and in ice caps at its northern pole.

Prior volcanic activity is evident, and supports the existence of a past hot molten core. It is known that molten lava flowed over vast areas, covering more than several hundred miles in the northern lowlands millions of years ago. Other observations support the existence of some internally generated heat sources, perhaps hot springs, radioactive decay, or even volcanic activity. Although Mars is presently inhospitable and desolate, it took a very long time to reach that state. Such a slow decline of its once very livable environment would have allowed any inhabitants ample time to alter their world or colonize other planets.

If such inhabitants once existed, they could have prepared for that slow degradation by building underground dwellings, where atmospheric pressure would be higher, with greatly reduced temperature extremes. Nine respected astronomers discovered a huge unnatural bulge at the Martian equator, after meticulous observations in 1962.[6] A noted astrophysicist, Dr. E. J. Öpik, concluded that the empirical data even supported the theory that such a bulge may be hollow,[7] perhaps a type of protective roof, built by the inhabitants as their survival shelter against the inevitable loss of atmosphere. Such a subterranean domain would provide a sheltered environment with a somewhat warmer temperature and an elevated atmospheric pressure.

Earth's Moon

Mars' nearest neighbor, as well Earth's closest celestial body, is our own moon. As stated, all the planets in our solar system are believed to have formed or condensed at roughly the same time, but evolved at different rates due to their variance in mass and distance from the sun. Our planet formed about 4.7 billion years ago, while its moon is dated at 4.5 billion years old, with a quick solidification, although a great lava flow occurred between 3.9 and 3.1 billion years ago. The moon has a small metallic core, cooler than Earth's at about 1,500 degrees Centigrade. There is no magnetic field on the moon now, but one existed in the remote past, perhaps three billion years ago. It supposedly has no atmosphere, and one is not believed to have ever existed, although controversial evidence suggests a possible atmosphere. Moon rocks reveal no trace of organic material either past or present.

Several billion years ago the moon was closer to the Earth than now, but the probable cause for the resultant increased separation is in dispute. The major moonquakes and volcanic activity that formed the mountains, valleys, and 'sea' landscape occurred eons ago. There has been no appreciable surface change over the past 50 million years, except for the sporadic celestial impact craters and the occasional planting of the United States flag.

Such conclusions depict our moon as a dead world, without any geologic activity. Yet in 1843, German astronomer Johann Schröter (aka Schröeter) recorded changes in the Linne crater, a well-known and defined lunar feature that he described as a deep crater between five and six miles in diameter.[8] Mr. Schröter recorded his observations of the crater's discernible changes over a period of time exceeding 35 years. However, the respected German astronomer Johann Mädler described this crater in 1866 as being only about 1.4 to 1.5 miles in diameter, but having an extreme depth.[9] More recent photographs from Apollo 15 revealed that Linne is now only a tiny bright pit, about 1.5 miles across, which displays very little depth. Some have credited such changes to possible mining activity in that area.

The craters on the moon are believed to be the result of meteorite impacts or the remnants left from extremely ancient volcanic activity. Both processes would display certain pattern randomness, with volcanism being somewhat more clustered. It has further been determined that the long gully of the Rheita Valley is not a true valley, but rather a crater chain along its entire length. Astronomer Dr. Patrick Moore contends that many of the valleys of the moon are really crater-chains similar to that of the Rheita Valley. It has also been suggested that such craters exhibit a detectable arrangement resembling modern aerial bombing patterns. If they are eventually determined to represent such bombing patterns, they occurred in the remote past, making it difficult to ascribe them to either warfare or the use of the moon as a 'practice range' target.

Chapter 8

Development of Life

On such terrestrial worlds, it is believed that the formation of life, where possible, would have followed roughly the same procedure. To understand that process, life development on Earth will be reviewed. In prior chapters it was revealed that the stellar companions of our sun all formed at roughly the same time, within about 500 million years of each other, eventually achieving a steady-state equilibrium with one another, forming our solar system. Hence, planet Earth formed about 4.7 billion years ago, and solidified into our world about 800 million years later. Fossil studies reveal that life developed quickly after that, probably within the first 200 million years,[1] or about 3.7 billion years ago.

Beside the heat associated with the forging of Earth, great internal heating was also generated by ongoing interior radioactive decay. Such decay yielded only proportionately slow cooling, permitting abundant volcanic activity that released gasses previously dissolved within the expelled liquid rock. Those eruptions spewed carbon monoxide, sulfur dioxide, methane, hydrogen chloride, nitrogen, and vast amounts of water vapor all around our planet. Utilizing gravitational and other forces, Earth ultimately retained a combination of toxic gasses to finally form its acidic and poisonous early atmosphere.

With further planetary cooling, atmospheric water vapor condensed as rainfall, creating vast oceans augmented with additional water from comets entering the atmosphere. The presence of liquid water allowed life to form in the oceans, with the water acting as a filter or 'shield' to protect any developing life from the harmful cosmic radiation. The water would have also created a stable temperature, acting as a thermal moderator.

Molecular mutations eventually occurred within that ocean, following a path of natural selection, creating a primordial 'soup' or solution of ammonia, hydrogen, methane, and water. This chemical mixture interacted or fermented until an energy source initiated the creation of a rich organic broth. Some type of energy would have been a necessary ingredient to promote such evolution. Neither inorganic nor organic matter can mutate or evolve into more complex forms without the absorption or conversion of some form of energy. That energy may have come from a natural spark or discharge of lightning, ultraviolet solar radiation, volcanic eruptions, or hot vents on the ocean floor. The introduction of such energy breaks molecular bonds, allowing them to interact, rearrange, and reunite to form more complex bundles of atoms as a different or new molecule. A portion of the energy responsible for breaking the initial bonds of a molecule can also be absorbed by the new molecule itself, thus strengthening its newly formed chemically bonded structure while making it even more stable than its prior original arrangement.

That primordial energized soup eventually produced even more complex molecules that included amino acids. Amino acids are relatively simple organic compounds of specific combinations of atoms that bond together by electromagnetic forces or chemical bonds.[2] Although numerous amino acids can be formed, only 20 are basic or fundamental for life.

Utilizing only the reactive combinations of the 20 basic acids, known as alpha amino acids, the resultant concoction can be structured by the cell to form the building blocks of simple biological proteins. This occurs when one amino acid group links with another, forming subunits; producing long chains that form a specific molecule called a polypeptide. A single polypeptide molecule can form a protein, or combine

70

with other molecular chains to form thousands of different proteins, each having a vital and specialized role or purpose in each cell. Such proteins compose the most important ingredient of a cell's cytoplasm.

Cytoplasm (aka protoplasm) is the living-substance portion of a cell where the synthesis of proteins takes place. The 'worker' proteins of a cell are the enzymes, the molecules that serve as a promoter or catalyst for all the chemical reactions involved in every cellular function. A single cell is comprised of its nucleus (or nuclei) that is surrounded in cytoplasm, all encased in an outer membrane. One may visualize a single cell in terms of an egg, although incorrectly, with the yolk representing the nucleus, the egg white as cytoplasm, and the shell as its membrane.

Cells obey codes that determine how organisms develop, part by part. A chemical unit called a gene, which is passed on by the parents, provides this pattern or code. These genes, in tightly packed bundles, are contained on very long segments or chains of DNA [deoxyribonucleic acid] molecules. DNA is a complex chemical molecule shaped like a helix or spiral staircase. Its entwined railings are made of sugar and phosphate, with those 'rungs' or 'treads' composed of nitrogen compounds called nucleotides or 'bases.' There are four such bases, or amino acids, namely: adenine, thymine, cytosine, and guanine, which are abbreviated by their initials A, T, C, and G. They arrange in pairs, with A always linking with T, and C always linking with G. Their precise order of 'pairing arrangement' provides the instructions or codes that are then relayed to each cell, determining its final development.

The human genome or 'genetic map' possesses about 80,000 genes, arranged in about 3.1 billion base pairs.[3] Genes are stored in parts of the cell called chromosomes, localized in the nucleus, where their information is passed into that cell's cytoplasm by its RNA [ribonucleic acid], a short-lived 'messenger' that disappears shortly after conveying its information. All human DNA is contained within its 23 pairs,

71

or 46 total chromosomes, with half coming from each parent.

Astrophysicist Eric Chaisson revealed that viruses are the smallest and simplest entities that can transition or bridge the gap between cells that are alive and molecules that are non-living or unanimated.[4] Viruses, which are smaller than the typical cell and may consist of only a few hundred atoms, appear to possess both the attributes of nonliving molecules as well as living cells. According to Professor Chaisson, the first true cells on Earth were *heterotrophs*, which resulted as a product from the earliest amino acids produced from the fermentation of basic or simple elements.[5] That primordial production of early cellular life occurred perhaps as early as 3.7 to 3.5 billion years ago, when the first primitive organic material developed from inorganic matter, as a chemical reaction that allowed life to evolve from non-life. The resulting heterotrophs were prokaryotic organisms that converted or processed simple organic materials from various carbon compounds for food.

All living organisms belong to one of two major groups, the *prokaryotic* or *eukaryotic*. All bacteria and algae are members of the prokaryotes, which lack a distinct nucleus and any surrounding membrane. The eukaryotic classification consists of all other living organisms that have an organized nucleus and a distinct nuclear membrane, with each eukaryotic cell also possessing chromosomes.

Earth's first life, a type of rudimentary bacteria, consisted of a simple cell belonging to the primitive kingdom *Monera* of the prokaryotic group. Over time, the surrounding simple elements that had provided food for those heterotrophs began to vanish, brought about by the irreversible changes in the environment of early Earth. Eventually, nearly all organic material in the ocean was ultimately devoured, forcing those primitive cells to mutate into a more advanced form of life. That produced the first *cyanobacteria*, the prokaryotic cells resembling a rudimentary algae or vegetation that subsisted on carbon dioxide. Those 'protoplant' cells, which are called *autotrophs*, were the forerunners of all future plants.

Early autotrophs consisted of a type of fuzzy bacterial moss and primitive algae, some resembling blue-green algae, which produced oxygen. Between 3.0 and 2.8 billion years ago, that first simple vegetation blanketed the ocean floor, clumping together in a type of symbiotic relationship with calcium carbonate 'spongelike' deposits, forming structures or reeflike mounds known as *stromatolites*.[6] Those organic mounds existed on a diet of very simple elements, producing a by-product of oxygen. That abundant oxygen then enriched the surrounding waters, with some of it escaping into the atmosphere of early Earth, which then contained ammonia, methane, sulfur dioxide, hydrogen chloride, nitrogen, and water vapor. Oxygen released from the ocean eventually built-up within Earth's early thin atmosphere, forming minimal ozone that further served as a limited protective shield to the sun's ultraviolet radiation.

Between 2.5 and 2.1 billion years ago, the early single cell Chlorophyta or green algae then formed, often clumping together in colonies. Such simple vegetation represented the earliest plantlike organisms capable of true photosynthesis, converting light energy into chemical energy by deriving its sustenance from a process that combined carbon monoxide and carbon dioxide with water, while giving off a by-product of oxygen. That early vegetation flourished, producing ever-increasing levels of oxygen, resulting in an oxidizing atmosphere that further enriched its protective ozone layer. Yet, as recently as two billion years ago, all those Earth changes still had produced only unicellular life.

Environments extraneous to the ocean waters occasionally formed from rock shield outcroppings. Rock shields are localized areas or regions of magma uplift that occur throughout geological time. This process may have started as early as 3.9 billion years ago, eventually forming isolated 'island' areas of exposed rock outcroppings within the primitive ocean, perhaps as early as 3.0 billion years ago.

Archaebacteria, the transitional single cell organisms that reflect a lifeform basically between the prokaryotic and eukaryotic groups, then formed around the hydrovents on the ocean floor. Still other *Archaea* kingdom organisms include microbes called *Methanococcus jannaschii*, which live on the ocean floor and survive in near-boiling water, while thriving on carbon dioxide.[7]

For some unknown reason, after more than two billion years of single cell life, perhaps including some life existing on rock outcroppings that would have derived oxygen directly from Earth's new 'altered' atmosphere, a new type of cellular organism formed. They were the distinctive eukaryotic cells that first appeared around 1.5 billion years ago. Those advanced cells formed the early protozoa and ameba organisms of the *Protista* kingdom, the earliest proto-animal ancestors. They also created the first true plants, the multicellular green organisms belonging to the *Plantae* kingdom.

Perhaps as early as 800 million years ago, continued Earth changes further led to even more complex organisms, which some classify as Earth's earliest form of animal life. That new invertebrate creature possessed a soft-body, and might best be described as being 'wormlike.' It is believed that the earliest jellyfish ancestors then quickly followed the emergence of that creature.

While primitive elemental life thrived, Earth's environment underwent drastic changes, ushering in its first Glacial Ice Age about 600 million years ago. Ice Ages occur about every 150 million years, lasting about five million years in duration. Each duration typically consists of a 100,000 year repetitive cycle, during which ensuing climatic temperatures alternate between warm and cold phases. A glaciation or cold period usually lasts about 90,000 years, with its shorter interglacial or warm period separating those frigid phases, one that normally lasts only about 10,000 years in duration.

The shelled trilobites, the first creatures with mineralized skeletons, then emerged around 570 million years ago, not long after the start of the Cambrian Period. That event was followed by the appearance of segmented worms, primitive crustaceans, brachiopods, snails, and sea spiders around 550 million years ago. Those invertebrates eventually gave rise to the early vertebrates between 530 and 500 million years ago, with the emergence of early primitive fish.

Eventually, after numerous tectonic plate movements and ensuing volcanic eruptions on the ocean floor, a great land mass formed, which is identified now as *Panagaea*. That allowed the first creatures, the ancient ancestors of the horseshoe crab, to temporarily venture onto land to lay their eggs along the muddy shores around 450 million years ago. Earth's oldest known mass extinction event then occurred sometime around 430 million years ago, as the 'boundary event' between the Ordovician-Silurian Periods. Earth's second Ice Age immediately followed, perhaps as a result of whatever caused that mass extinction.

Shortly after the start of the Silurian Period, the earliest vascular plant species, those capable of existing on dry land, emerged around 425 million years ago. Over time, a primitive centipede and scorpion emerged, becoming permanent dwellers on dry land around 395 million years ago. By 370 million years ago, a certain lobe-finned fish species, the crossopterygians (commonly known as tetrapods) had developed the ability to breathe air. They were the ancient ancestors of the first amphibians, creating additional creatures that were able to thrive beyond the sea. They cohabited with newly emerging insects and ferns, adding further variety to early life on dry land.

Then the second known mass extinction transpired about 365 million years ago. But life quickly bounced back, with some lizardlike amphibians giving rise to the reptiles around 320 million years ago, roughly the same time certain insects, which are thought to be the ancestors of the dragonfly, mutated into species with wings, allowing first flight. This evolutionary process was once again hindered around 300 million years ago with the emergence of the third and longest Ice Age, the Permocarboniferous. Sometime between 262 and 225 million years ago, the great land mass of Panagaea then split into the northern supercontinent of Laurisia and a southern supercontinent of Gondwanaland. The granite portions of the tiny Seychelle Islands in the Indian Ocean are the last remaining vestiges of primordial Gondwanaland. During that same period, the first species of dinosaurs appeared as early as 250 million years ago, followed by the third and most severe mass extinction between 240 and 230 million years ago. That occurrence, known as the Permian-Triassic boundary event, exterminated an estimated 95% to 96% of all species, and effectively ended the Paleozoic Era.

Surprisingly, various additional animal species quickly emerged, including new dinosaurs and early mammals. A fourth mass extinction then occurred shortly after the end of the Triassic Period, sometime between 215 and 195 million years ago, which is hypothesized to have been the result of a celestial impact. Birds then formed around 185 million years ago, which some theorize to be a mutated evolutionary branch from reptiles. Various dinosaur species continued to thrive, even during natural ordeals such as the fourth Ice Age that started about 150 million years ago, with new species formed continually. With the start of the Cretaceous Period about 136 million years ago, the first primates and flowering plants quickly emerged.

Supposedly, the dinosaur's reign ended about 65 million years ago, which occurred over an extended period of thousands of years after an asteroid hit within the Yucatan region, creating a massive worldwide conflagration. That collision sent debris into the atmosphere, blocking all sunlight. It is believed that earthquakes, volcanic eruptions, and tidal waves ensued, drastically altering the topography of the planet. Numerous meteorites would have also showered Earth causing vast forest fires, with smoke and dust saturating the atmosphere for more than a year. Such blockage of sunlight would have resulted in conditions similar to an Ice Age. It is estimated that such an event would have killed off about 75% of all plant and animal life, with the largest species being most affected. Later, about 35 million years ago, two celestial impacts, one hitting Chesapeake Bay and a second impacting Siberia, caused yet another mass extinction.

As Earth purged the devastating effects from those natural disasters, life slowly came back, erasing most traces of those conflagrations. The eventual new rulers of our planet became the mammals, with primates within that classification taking the leadership role. Monkeys emerged about 30 million years ago, preceding apes in this lineage. One of Earth's first proto-apes, the *Pliopithecus*, appeared about 23 million years ago. A creature known as Proconsul, which first appeared about 22 million years ago, then followed the ancient ancestor of the gibbon. Proconsul is considered a generalized mammalian species, neither ape nor man, comprising a wide variety of statures from pygmy chimp-size to gorilla-size. The first true primates, the *Adapis parisiensis*, developed approximately 20 million years ago. The lemurs are modern descendants of those most ancient primates. Primates appear to have taken three separate paths in their evolution:

1. The Old World monkeys, which consist of the African and Asian monkeys.
2. The New World monkeys, which include the marmosets, spider, and howling monkeys.
3. The hominids, which include the various apes and man, represented by our present day species of gibbons, orangutans, chimpanzees, gorillas, and modern humans.

It is believed that all hominid lineages originated in Africa and/or Asia. One of the earliest candidates for inclusion into the hominid lineage was *Oreopithecus*, which first appeared about 16 million years ago. It was a pithecoid creature, more apelike than man. Then about 15 million years ago, an early primate left the treetops to become the first ground-dweller called *Equatorius*. This genus was not believed to be an ancestor of either later apes or humans, but rather a dead-end species. The generally accepted first true hominid, *Ramapithecus*, appeared about 14 million years ago, and stands as the ancient ancestor of our own ancient ancestors.

Ramapithecus was considered an anthropoid creature, more manlike than ape. While *Oreopithecus* outlived *Ramapithecus* by more than four million years, both proved to be dead-end branches in the hominid family. With the extinction of *Oreopithecus* about eight million years ago, all manlike apes vanished, leaving only true apes. Apes then split sometime between 6.4 and 4.4 million years ago during the late Pliocene Age, resulting in both the continuation of apes and a new apeman species. The Homininae subfamily represents the new and separate human line that split from the true apes. The emergence of apeman was a major division in the hominid line due to its ability to walk erect, which was made possible by its unique skeletal and muscular design. That lineage of apeman is called *Australopithecus*, with their remains found in the Near East as well as in East and South Africa.

Certain fragmentary remains that date to roughly five million years ago have been tentatively identified as possibly being an early Australopithecine, but insufficient anatomical details and additional fossils exist to accurately classify those remains. Thus, the confirmed and commonly acknowledged *Australopithecus* lineage had at least five initial branches of evolution, consisting of the following distinct species:

1. *Australopithecus ramidus* (aka *Ardipithecus ramidus*) was found in Kenya, Africa, dating to approximately 4.4 million years ago.
2. *Australopithecus anamensis* first appeared in Kenya about 4.2 million years ago.
3. *Australopithecus afarensis*, the famous 'Lucy' specimen, was also found in Kenya, with their branch dating between 3.7 and 3.2 million years ago.
4. *Australopithecus africanus*, a branch that lived in both East and South Africa, started their existence about 2.8

million years ago.

5. *Australopithecus garhi* lived in Ethiopia, Africa, and dated to about 2.5 million years ago. The artifacts left by these apemen suggest or indicate that they were meat eaters, with some even fashioning and using crude stone tools. Somewhat later, two additional branches of the *Australopithecus* family emerged. They are classified as:

6. *Australopithecus paranthropus boisei*, who first appeared about 2.4 million years ago and roamed throughout East Africa.

7. *Australopithecus paranthropus robustus*, a branch indigenous to South Africa, which initially emerged about 2.2 million years ago. The remains of these two later Australopithecine species suggest or indicate that they were vegetarians. While these subsequent Australopithecine branches were later arrivals, they are considered more primitive than their earlier branches.

Australopithecines were a gentle and peaceful species that lived in small groups. They were of short stature, with females standing about 3'6" and males approaching almost four feet in height, while weighing about 90 pounds. Their brain size averaged about 508cc, ranging from 400 to 600cc. The meat-eating branches may have been primarily scavengers rather than true hunters. Much is known of this species from numerous fossil specimens, although their fossil evidence became very sparse during the time span between three and two million years ago, the period when rudimentary stone tools first appeared. A stone tool factory utilized by the later Australopithecine branches was recently found in the Rift Valley of Kenya, Africa, which has been dated at 2.3 million years old. The tools consisted of sharp flakes of stone, chipped from a single rock, which were believed to have then been used to cut and scrape plants and meat.

Shortly after the emergence of our fifth and last (or perhaps current) glacial Ice Age of 2.2 million years ago, another apeman branch emerged, one that still remained a member of the *Australopithecus* family, but of a different and distinct subspecies. This apeman was called *Homo habilis*, meaning 'handy man,' due to its use of simple stone tools. This branch emerged in Africa about 2.1 million years ago. While this subspecies is classified under the 'Homo' designation, meaning 'true human,' it is an inappropriate classification since this subspecies was prehuman and represented merely a transitional branch of *Australopithecus*. We now know that the *Paranthropus* branch of Australopithecines had utilized crude stone tools prior to *Homo habilis*,[8] so this was not a new event worthy of a separate genus classification.

The earliest form of near-man, or our oldest traceable human lineage, is the genus *Homo erectus* at 1.7 million years old, which ushered in the earliest men that walked in a fully upright gate and stance. Many scientists now differentiate between two separate species of *Homo erectus*.[9] The first was the earlier *Homo ergaster* that emerged in Africa, then later migrated into Asia where they evolved into *Homo erectus*. All were warlike, practiced cannibalism, and formed small hunter-gatherer groups. The earliest specimens possessed an average brain size of 775cc, ranging from 750 to 900cc, but the later examples had evolved to possess a brain size approaching 1300cc near their extinction in *c*.375,000 BC. They also introduced more complex tools and utilized fire. The use of cooking with fire greatly aids digestion, and reduces the incidence of contaminants. Again, fossil remains of *Homo erectus* are plentiful, thus providing a very clear picture of this family branch. Some paleoanthropologists combine all subspecies of *Homo erectus* into a single genus, the *Pithecanthropus*. By either name, this genus included:

1. *Pithecanthropus*, represented by the Java man specimens of Asia who first appeared about 675,000 BC. They were of short stature, and did not utilize tools.
2. Heidelberg man, the European branch of the family

that first emerged some time around 500,000 BC.

3. *Sinanthropus*, also known as Far Eastern *Pithecanthropus*, which first appeared around 450,000 BC, and is represented by the Peking man specimens found mainly within the Choukoutien caves of China. This species used both fire and tools.

Humankind

True man did not emerge until the genus *Homo sapiens*, perhaps as far back as 400,000 years ago, although it is difficult to precisely identify their start, due to extremely scant fossil evidence left by its earliest branch. Their coexistence with *Homo erectus* was very brief, with the earlier species becoming extinct around 375,000 BC, shortly after the first appearance of *Homo sapiens*. No specific classification name has been assigned to this earliest subspecies of *Homo sapiens* that preceded Neanderthal man, due to the discovery of only an extremely few specimens. No clear picture of this branch can be developed, due to a similar lack of artifact evidence. For identification purposes, this text will refer to that subspecies as the 'proto-Sapiens,' in order to designate its few known variants. It is possible that their 250,000 years of existence may have concluded as a dead-end branch, or the subsequent Neanderthals may have exterminated them.

It is known that those earliest humans, the proto-Sapiens, emerged with surprising abilities. Foremost was their advanced hunting skills, which were possessed right from the start. The fossilized wooden spruce spears that were discovered by the German archaeologist, Hartmut Thieme, in 1995 near Schoeningen, Germany, substantiate that conclusion.[10] Such skillfully made spears dated to 400,000 BC, much before the generally accepted age during which anthropologists normally claim that organized hunting first started. Other evidence further indicated that the proto-Sapiens employed systematic hunting techniques to kill big game, mainly horses, which would have required advanced planning and organization.

Similar wooden spears were likewise used to hunt straight-tusked elephants, as demonstrated by additional fossils also found in Germany. Other bits of wooden artifacts, which have also been identified as spears, were found in Torralba, Spain, indicating a wider and earlier use of wood implements than first believed, rather than the exclusive use of stone implements ascribed for that time period. Evidence of wood sawn by mechanical means was found in the strata of ancient forest beds near Cromer, England, also dating to c.400,000 BC.[11]

Perhaps the people that made those spears were related to Vertesszöllös man, one of the earliest suspected proto-Sapiens specimens. Vertesszöllös (also Verteszölös) man was named after a limestone quarry site about 30 miles from Budapest, Hungary, near the village of Vertesszöllös where it was discovered. Anthropologist John E. Pfeiffer suggested a date between 500,000 and 400,000 BC for such remains, based mainly on their unique artifacts and cultural indications.[12]

Vertesszöllös man is also the earliest identified human ancestor to have hunted large game such as bear, deer, and bison. Traces of their unique culture were also found at Clacton, England, although no skeletal remains were detected. Other very loosely associated specimens from that time, or perhaps even older, might include Lantian man of China and 'Poor George' man found in the Olduvai Gorge of Africa.[13]

The first 'officially' named subspecies within the *Homo sapiens* genus, Neanderthal man, emerged during the start of the third interglacial period of our last Ice Age phase, known as the Würm glaciation, perhaps as early as *circa* 150,000 BC. The Neanderthals were also a sparsely populated species at their outset, with very little increase in population numbers until around 115,000 BC when they became quite numerous. This species was followed by Modern man, which had two phases of development. Classifications for the genus *Homo sapiens* presently include the following main subspecies:

1. 'Proto-Sapiens,' the branch often incorrectly labeled as 'early Neanderthals,' are known by their early fossils found in Kenya, Africa, but are better known from the later Swanscombe man of Europe. They existed from *c.*400,000 to *c.*150,000 BC.

2. Neanderthals, who extended all across Europe, the Mediterranean, Africa, and Southeast Asia, dated from *c.*150,000 BC to 30,000 BC (although controversial specimens found in Croatia are dated to *c.*26,000 BC). This subspecies represents a wide variety of fossils that include:

-Solo man, the Asian representative found in Java, is known to have practiced cannibalism, and was one of the earliest, if not the earliest specimen of Neanderthal man.

-Ehringsdorf man, another of the very early representatives, dating to 120,000 BC. They were very primitive when compared to 'proto-Sapiens,' regressing toward more apelike traits.

-Tabun man, also known as Shanidar man, was the Near Eastern representative found in Palestine, who emerged around 44,000 BC.

-Skhul man, another Near Eastern and Mediterranean representative that consisted of a number of extremely varied specimens, from very primitive to quite modern.

-Rhodesian man, the African representative and one of the last of its subspecies, dating to around 35,000 BC.

3. Cro-Magnons, the early version of Modern man, were mainly concentrated in Europe. They existed from *c.*43,000 BC to *c.*10,500 BC, although inconclusive indications are found suggesting an earlier appearance as far back as 90,000 to 110,000 BC.

4. *Sapiens*, or truly Modern man, emerged around 11,600 BC and continues to represent our present species. Other groupings have been found, suggestive of the expected levels of normal evolutionary mutation and cross-breeding within a genus, but not sufficiently different to warrant their own

subspecies classification. Most of these minor branches, like Mount Carmel man and the Boskops, either dead-ended or blended with one of the main subspecies of this genus through interbreeding.

Chapter 9

Examination of the Species

Attention is focused on the unnamed but earliest representative of *Homo sapiens*, identified in this text as the proto-Sapiens. They existed at least as far back as 400,000 BC, surviving until the appearance of Neanderthal man in 150,000 BC, when they were evidently driven out of Europe and disappeared. So few fossils exist that little can be concluded for this branch. The enigmatic proto-Sapiens are incorrectly but commonly included in the Neanderthal subspecies as 'early Neanderthals.' But these two branches were distinctly separate and quite different species.

Believed to be one of the oldest specimens of the proto-Sapiens is a lower jaw found in Kanam, Kenya, dated between 400,000 and 375,000 BC. Nearby, fragments of four additional skulls believed to be from this same subspecies were found in Kanjera, Kenya, which date to *c*.350,000 BC.[1] These early African specimens appear to be virtually modern in most aspects, except for a thicker bone structure and slightly larger pre-molar teeth, but without the protruding bone over the eyebrow, which is characteristic of the much later Neanderthal man.

Their earliest known European representative was perhaps the previously mentioned Vertesszöllös man discovered in Hungary, with that branch or its ancestors also dating to around 400,000 BC. Other fossils of this subspecies include a portion of a skull, including its occipital bone, which was discovered in 1935 near London, at a Thames Valley gravel pit in Kent, England. That specimen, known as Swanscombe

man, dates to $c.250,000$ BC.[2] Over a twenty year period, both
the left and right parietal bones from this same skull were
found in excavations at that original site. In his comprehensive
book *The Emergence of Man*, anthropologist John E. Pfeiffer
categorized Swanscombe man as: "a distinct advance over his
fossil predecessors...an apparent evolutionary leap, the sudden
appearance of a man who was nearly fully modern."[3]

Over the ensuing years, no other bones or partial
fragments were ever found at the Thames Valley excavation,
but similar human skeletal remains were discovered at Galley
Hill, England, a village near London, which dated to about the
same time period. Another find at Ipswich, also near London,
was thought to be as old.[4] Still other specimens were
discovered near Stuttgart in Steinheim, Germany, which dated
between 240,000 and 190,000 BC;[5] although that specimen did
exhibit a slight eyebrow protrusion. According to Professor
Pfeiffer, artifacts associated with this species were also found
at the English sites of Birmingham, Hoxne, and High Lodge
near Cambridge, as well as in the Somme Valley region near
Amiens, France. Although displaying less similarities, other
vestiges of this branch may be connected with finds at the
Escale and Vallonet caves in France; at Terra Amata, also in
France; and with finds at valley sites near the villages of
Torralba and Ambrona in Spain.

The most recent fossil, a jawbone dated to 200,000 BC,
was found in southern France by Canadian paleontologist,
Serge Lebel, in July 2000.[6] Other remains dating to $c.175,000$
BC include Montmaurin man, known from a lower jawbone.
Still other skull fragments from both a male and female of this
subspecies, dating back to 150,000 BC, were found in a cave
shelter at Fontechévade, France.[7] Those skulls are the
youngest known remains of the early proto-Sapiens, and are
believed to mark the end of this branch. Both skulls exhibited
the hint of more primitive features, ones slightly resembling
those of Neanderthal, and may have even been the products of
mixed breeding with the emerging Neanderthals, which first

appeared around that same time. However, the specific subspecies classification of Fontechévade man remains in great dispute, mainly between French archaeologists and their United States counterparts.

More recently discovered fossil data even suggest that a representative thought to be from the Cro-Magnon subspecies may have first appeared as long ago as 90,000 to 110,000 BC. Such conclusions are based on extant remains that could also be either a 'late appearing' proto-Sapiens, or from an early but rare dead-end branch of the Cro-Magnons. Such anomalous fossils tend to indicate that limited genetic specimens can occasionally appear from time to time, for some yet unknown reason.

However, such finds could also represent anomalous fossil remains from otherworldly humanlike beings, ones that may have visited Earth during remote times. Either explanation is credible, due to the age of these finds and their expansive time-gap between other established or accepted species and these unusual fossils. Further, the absence of any continuing evolutionary development or cultural relics during such times, prior to the known emergence of Cro-Magnon man around 43,000 BC, tends to indicate such a species had a very brief existence on Earth.

The proto-Sapiens more closely resembled Cro-Magnon rather than Neanderthal man, with their slight difference from later Modern man mainly in their increased skull thickness. Yet they appeared suddenly on Earth in the midst of an established species, *Pithecanthropus*, but clearly did not evolve from them. They had emerged with a relatively small population, which was apparently maintained throughout their existence, followed by an equally sudden disappearance a quarter of a million years later when a much less refined subspecies, Neanderthal man, first appeared. Their existence as a species seems to makes little sense. But actually it is Neanderthal man that seems out of place in the overall scenario, with their lack of similarity or definitive connection with other subspecies of *Homo sapiens*, which is usually credited to regressive genes. But perhaps a more revealing explanation exists.

Neanderthals differed in both physical appearance and structure from both earlier and later *Homo sapiens* subspecies. Neanderthal man was big boned, furless but hairy, and stood about 5' 6" tall. They exhibited slightly bent knees, a forward thrust of the head, a massive chinless jaw, and proportionately shorter arms than Modern man. Arthritic problems were common among middle aged Neanderthals. They had a larger brain size by about 35cc than that of Modern man, averaging 1425cc with a range from 1200 to 1620cc, yet are believed to have been limited mentally when compared to Modern man whose brain averages 1390cc with a range from 1200 to 1500cc. Still, the Neanderthals were wide ranging, with large populations in Europe, the Mediterranean, Asia, and Africa.

Neanderthal man was first discovered in 1856 when their remains were found in the Neander Valley near Dusseldorf, Germany. The Neanderthals displayed numerous variations, with sharp differences within their species, and are much more representative of the genus *Pithecanthropus* than *Homo sapiens*. The true nature and origin of Neanderthal man remains unclear and highly suspect, casting doubt over their link with Modern man. Author and researcher Gregg S. Braden referenced a little publicized mid-1990s scientific study that revealed an insufficient genetic link existed between Modern man and Neanderthal man to establish true ancestry between the two subspecies. Similar findings also emerged from several subsequent studies, including a major analysis undertaken at the Max Plank Institute.

Mitochondrial DNA extracted from a Neanderthal arm bone was also researched at both the University of Munich in Germany and at Pennsylvania State University. The DNA material was compared to modern *Homo sapiens sapiens*, with results reported in the July 11, 1997 issue of the journal *Cell*. The DNA base pair sequence differed substantially from modern humans, suggesting that Neanderthals were at best distant relations to Modern man, perhaps from a divergent evolutionary branch between 550,000 and 690,000 years ago. According to Svante Paabo at the Max Planck Institute, their DNA testing indicated that Neanderthals apparently shared a common ancestor with Modern man (*Homo sapiens*) sometime around 150,000 BC, but was not a related species. From those tests, it was further determined that Neanderthals were a dead end branch of a separate lineage that traced back to an origin around 500,000 BC.

Additionally, the *New York Times* reported results of DNA tests that were released in 1998, which strongly suggested that Neanderthals were a separate species that had no common ancestor with *Homo sapiens sapiens*.[8] Neanderthals are generally considered too primitive to be ancestors of modern humans, and thus could not be a contributing factor in our direct line of descent.

There can be little remaining doubt that Neanderthal man is not a direct ancestor of Modern man. Any minimal enduring connection likely occurred merely as the result of infrequent crossbreeding with earlier proto-Sapiens or later Cro-Magnon man. Since limited studies have been done comparing only mitochondrial DNA, the genetic material contributed from the mother, the results do not rule out possible interbreeding between Neanderthal males and Cro-Magnon females. Such an offspring would not reflect any Neanderthal genetic material contained in its mitochondrial DNA, only that of its Cro-Magnon mother.

The belief that mating, at least on a limited basis, occurred between the younger Cro-Magnon subspecies and Neanderthal man is reinforced from Neanderthal bones found in the Vindija cave site in Croatia. According to anthropologist Fred Smith of Northern Illinois University, those fossils were radiocarbon dated to a time between 27,000 and 26,000 BC.[9] Still, it would appear that Neanderthal man has more in common with the *Homo erectus* genus, such as the crude *Pithecanthropus* Java man, than with that of Modern man.

Evidence indicates the Neanderthals practiced cannibalism, with a preference for the brains of their victims. However, some anthropologists claim Neanderthals believed in an afterlife, since food and weapons were found buried with a few of their dead, along with flowers in one specific case. In a cave near the village of Shanidar in the Zagros Mountains of northern Iraq, a 1970s Smithsonian Institution expedition unearthed a grave containing flowers. The age of the adult male corpse was determined to be about 40 years old at the time of death, a very long life for a Stone Age man. Further, the man had lost his right arm as a child, yet was still able to achieve a mature age, a most remarkable survival achievement for a crippled individual during primitive times. Based on the pollen evidence, that burial dated between 60,000 and 55,000 BC.

Since most anthropologists classify all ancestral humans that existed between 400,000 and 43,000 BC as 'Neanderthals,' no distinction is made between the advanced proto-Sapiens and the actual Neanderthals who first appeared around 150,000 BC. Hence, the few ritual burials alluding to an afterlife belief may reflect proto-Sapiens practices, not Neanderthal ones.

With attention focused on the burial flowers, it is likely that the skeletal remains were those of a later, although scarce descendant of the proto-Sapiens, rather than from a Neanderthal man. The flowers in question were found to be mostly herbs used for medicinal purposes during later times, knowledge that was completely unknown to Neanderthals, but would have been a common practice utilized by the more advanced proto-Sapiens.

The oldest extant intentional burial grave is recognized as the one found in a limestone cave near the village of Chou-K'ou-Tien, north of Beijing China, which has been dated to 400,000 BC, a date long before the emergence of the first Neanderthals around 150,000 BC. That burial was seemingly prepared by the proto-Sapiens, virtually at the onset of their emergence as a species.

It is still possible that certain later Neanderthals might have simply copied or mimicked the burial practices of their contemporary brethren, the Cro-Magnons, while not understanding the true intent of such a procedure. Even with a plausible explanation for such Neanderthal burials, it is likely that a few would have met accidental death from falls, floods, or some other similar natural demise, resulting in a burial with both their food and weapons. None of those instances would necessarily indicate a rationalized belief in an afterlife existence, or a purposeful burial.

There was not a simple transition or even a rapid evolutionary phase from Neanderthals to Cro-Magnons. Cro-Magnon man simply appeared suddenly on Earth, within the midst of the Neanderthals. Science simply does not know how such an event occurred, mentioning the process of evolution without any further explanation, essentially ignoring this paradox. Human intelligence also seemed to occur almost overnight, noticeably around 40,000 BC, about the same time as the Cro-Magnons first appeared.

The Cro-Magnons all started out as a powerful, big boned, white race with a high brow, reaching up to 6' 4" in height. Cro-Magnons wore sewn and embroidered clothing of skins, with paintings also showing modern trousers, jackets, and hats, all of a fashionable design. Cro-Magnons quickly inhabited the entire world soon after their first appearance, seemingly with little or no resistance from Neanderthal man. There may have been some cross-breeding between the two races, perhaps producing the presumed mixed-race Mount Carmel man and the even earlier Skhul man who varied widely in their appearance, both found in the Near East around ancient Canaan.

In November of 1998, Joao Zilhao, the director of the Portuguese Archaeological Institute, found the hybrid skeleton of a child in the Lapedo Valley near Leiria, Portugal, about 90 miles north of Lisbon.[10] That specimen is believed to be the result of breeding between a Neanderthal and a Cro-Magnon, suggesting that limited interbreeding did occur between those two species.

It is known that Cro-Magnons diverged into a few specific branches that existed contemporaneously. One example was Combe man, a smaller more delicate-boned specimen with a Mediterranean-appearance that was frail by comparison to the original Cro-Magnon man. Another example was Brunn man who was different from both the original Cro-Magnon and Combe branch, seemingly fitting between the two in appearance and size. There is very little difference between Cro-Magnon and our present subspecies, *Homo sapiens sapiens*, which first appeared about 11,600 BC. Traits of that latest subspecies are distinguished by the physicality of a nearly vertical forehead, thin-boned skull, slender neck, and a squarish mouth structure that is better suited for forming difficult sounds.[11] While Cro-Magnons banded together in small groups to assist in hunting and defense, true civilization seemed to suddenly appear with the refinement of fully Modern man, *Homo sapiens sapiens*.

The concept of race in humankind is attributed to the process of evolution, with the origins of the races suspected to be one of mutation, selection, and drift. Mutation refers to the appearance of new traits through accidental new genes. Dr. Franz Weidenreich postulated a pattern of indigenous evolution of the races from early man, such as: Peking man into Mongoloids, Rhodesian man into Africans, and Solo man into Australian Aboriginals. But it is now accepted that the 'Wadjak' skulls found in Java are believed to be the forerunner of the Negroid aborigines of Australia. The all-white Cro-Magnon subspecies, which completely displaced Neanderthal man, tends to disprove this supposition at first glance, unless recessive genes went haywire or some other as yet unknown influence was at play. Science simply does not have an acceptable explanation for the emergence of numerous races, or humankind's advancement, followed by regression and return again to a pattern of progress within the *Homo sapiens* genus.

The process of civilizing humankind occurred after billions of years of planetary evolution, a complex process ruled by natural selection. But the effect of natural selection, the survival of the fittest, diminishes with the level of medical and scientific advancements possessed by a society. Basically, higher levels of technology allow the weaker, the diseased, and the physically impaired to live much longer, allowing their genetic seed greater opportunity to spawn 'inferior' offspring resulting in a 'diminishing' of the future gene pool. Rather than evolution, mutation is probably the better term to describe such changes. That usually involves quicker and starker changes, ones thought to have been initiated by a reaction to some suddenly occurring massive Earth change or major natural catastrophe. Yet such an explanation would not account for the drastic change of disposition from the nurturing and gentle Australopithecine species found in Earth's remote past, to that of the aggressive and often hostile later *Pithecanthropus* genus.

The evolution of the cognitive abilities of humankind is even more baffling. Neither the environment nor the life style of primitive humans sufficiently taxed their mental aptitude to a degree that would require their evolution toward a larger brain capacity. Survival could have simply relied on inborn instincts, as is the case with many other lower animal forms. There was no reason for humans to mutate into a more complex 'thinking' animal with higher intelligence, yet man clearly became a contemplative and rational creature. That occurrence further developed over a surprisingly short time and within a newly emerged species, even though past species that had existed for much longer periods never developed such an ability. Again, science simply has no plausible answer for such developments.

Closer examination of this question only reveals more mysteries. After the demise of the dinosaurs, apes did not become the next dominant species. Apes did not yet exist, nor would they exist for many millions of years. No clear ruler over the planet seemed to appear between 65 million and 35 million years ago. The anthropoid ape did not yet exist even at the end of that era, although *Parapithecus*, a small distant cousin existed, but resembled a squirrel more than an ape. An ancient tree dwelling lemur of the prosimian family also existed around 35 million years ago, but was not a dominant figure. The earliest monkeys did not emerge until about 30 million years ago. Of all those distant ancestors of humankind, none possessed the highest intellect or cunning dominance over other creatures of their time.

Rather, scientists have determined that dolphins possessed the highest brainpower of any species on Earth 30 million years ago. Why this most advanced brain functioning lifeform did not evolve into the dominant intelligent creature on our planet is also perplexing. Rather unpredictably, the primates developed into such an intellectual leadership position. It is known that human intelligence is not linked merely to brain size, but is also determined by the number of convolutions and neurons present in the brain, as well as with increased genetic or chemical activity within the brain.

Modern man has a brain size of 1390cc, while his Cro-Magnon predecessor had a slightly larger brain at 1400cc. An extinct African Negroid, Boskop man, had an even larger brain size approaching 1800cc. The Boskop race appeared suddenly, without any known intermediate development stages, and also disappeared just as abruptly. Perhaps, as religious beliefs attest, humanity's ancestors occasionally benefited from some form of divine genetic intervention or manipulation during various early Earth periods.

While Neanderthal man was a primitive subspecies, his subsequent and contemporary contender for Earth dominance, the Cro-Magnons, were vastly more advanced and cultured. While Neanderthals often camped at cave openings, the Cro-Magnons penetrated deep into those caves, using them for sanctuary. They also lived in underground shelters, tents, and summer wickiups made from brush and twigs, with Paleolithic oval hut houses becoming the norm by 15,000 BC. Caves actually appear to have been used more as a social gathering place for religious purposes, community centers, and schools.

The first appearance of the universal Mother Goddess cult can be traced to those ceremonial caverns that date to the late Pleistocene. The earliest known-recorded chronicles of humankind can be traced to the art displayed in those caves that concentrated on religious or god motifs and hunting themes. The level and degree of artistic achievement by the Cro-Magnons, revealed by their highly detailed cave and rock paintings along with the intricate bone, antler, horn, and stone carvings, rival even modern achievements. Such artistic displays began during the early Upper Paleolithic period of c.35,000 BC. The Cro-Magnons are known to have also kept detailed and meticulous records of lunar observations and cycles.

Traditional history describes such 'cave men' as savage and primitive, but that was clearly not the case. Their skilled and prodigious display of talent indicates a large amount of leisure time available for such pursuits, and perhaps even the delegation of duties among selected work groups within a highly structured society. Such artistic and ascetic creations must have also involved some sort of art school training in technique, perspective, and proportion. But no known prior civilization existed to teach such proficiency, certainly not the Neanderthals. The source of such training remains yet another mystery surrounding the origins of humanity.

Chapter 10

First Contact

At some point, the Ancient Ones and their Helpers would have personally visited our solar system during an unknown archaic primordial time. They would have explored and mapped our entire solar region, including Earth, but may have focused on one or more of the outer planets. At the time of their earliest extended-stay visits, it is unclear whether primitive life on Earth had formed, was forming, or may have been produced by an act of seeding from one of the prior deep space capsules sent by the Ancient Ones' ancestors during past eons.

At that same unknown primordial time, intelligent humanlike life had evidently started to emerge on at least one of the outer planets, prior to its formation on Earth. Numerous archaic records tend to support the belief that humans did not yet exist on Earth during those earliest visitations. Mythological accounts clearly state that the gods ruled over the Earth during times before man, while oral traditions also indicate that the seeding or creation of humankind occurred later. Verification of such events is documented throughout numerous ancient manuscripts.

Regardless of its origin or method, intelligent humanlike life evidently first developed and evolved on an outer planet, satellite, or an asteroid within our solar system, not on Earth. Such early humanlike beings grew with the intervention, guidance, and assistance of the Ancient Ones and their Helpers. Such 'Helpers,' or their ancestors, had been selected from other 'infant races' previously encountered and nurtured by the Ancient Ones.

After an 'infant race' was civilized, educated, and brought into the Cosmic Order by the Ancient Ones, certain of their 'graduates' were also selected to become Helpers. Such a group of assistants evidently included feline creatures, amphibious races, yellow or blue-skin beings, and various giant or titan hominoids, species that were described within the narratives of numerous ancient texts.

Such Helpers were themselves at various different stages of individual development within their own evolution, with diverse levels of attained enlightenment. The Helpers acted as intermediaries between the Ancient Ones and other contacted infant races. Each individual Helper species was further selected based on their appearance for each specific mission, depending on which species most closely resembled the beings that would be encountered on a specific developing world. Such Helpers became the prime contact, educators, and often times the eventual leaders of the numerous encountered infant races on those emerging worlds.

It was a normal practice to employ such like-species intermediaries, since the appearance of an alien being would certainly be a terrifying experience for any primitive lifeform. The fear response from a race of primitive beings confronted by creatures of alien appearance would be quite traumatic and negative, outweighing any positive influence. The primitive response would be to flee in panic or attack out of fear, the classic 'flight or fight' response. The deployment of similar appearing intermediaries to make first contact with indigenous emerging races minimized such hostility, distrust, and misconception.

Such involvement as an interface with newly encountered infant races was an honor, which the chosen Helpers freely gave, perhaps as 'repayment' for the Ancient Ones' earlier guidance and evolutionary aid. Perhaps it was also the price 'paid' as admission into the Cosmic Order. The extraction and utilization of natural resources from each visited planet was yet another form of repayment, similar to missionaries spreading the word of God to the 'heathens,' while taking indigenous materials of livestock, crops, precious metals, and even sex from the natives.

The outer planet homeworld where the earliest humanlike beings emerged within our solar system became the central focus of civilizing efforts by the Ancient Ones. Lacking absolute certainty, that planetary homeworld was either Mars or Maldek, the Asteroid Belt planet prior to its destruction. The efforts to civilize and educate its infant race were very successful, creating an exemplary relationship with the Ancient Ones. Technical knowledge was always imparted in measured portions, based on the moral development of each civilization.

Such a restriction was a central mandate of the Cosmic Order, implemented to allow the emerging culture to slowly absorb such progress, technology, and growth without overwhelming the spiritual development and comprehensive ability of its people. A rapid introduction of advanced technology was found to exceed the limited aptitude of most fledgling societies, affecting their ability to recognize and understand all the consequences associated with such advances. The Ancient Ones had detected the necessity for a balance between progress and moral development, from their earlier missions with numerous encountered infant civilizations.

The highly technical devices and lifestyle spawned by the introduction and implementation of such technology could be so seductive and corruptive as to undermine the moral fiber and spiritual consciousness of many infant civilizations, eventually leading to their own demise. Recognizing that potential possibility, the Ancient Ones carefully metered and controlled the rate of progress and growth for all subsequent emerging species. The humanlike beings on the outer planet in our solar system prospered under the controlled guidance of the Ancient Ones, accepting the restricted introduction and use of such advanced devices and knowledge.

Their homeworld eventually evolved into a model culture, one committed to the Cosmic Order and the harmony of the universe. In time, the humanlike beings evolved sufficiently to also become Helpers that assisted the Ancient Ones. They were recruited to prepare nearby planets and moons for survey, seeding, colonization, natural resource extraction, and other similar activities. In time, with assistance from the Ancient Ones, they built small but flourishing colonies on Earth and its moon, and perhaps on several of the moons of Jupiter. But their main off-world settlement was built on their nearest celestial neighbor, referring to whichever planet was not the homeworld of the humanlike beings. Hence, if Mars was the original homeworld, then its main colony was located on Maldek before its destruction; or conversely, with such a settlement constructed on Mars if Maldek was the homeworld.

Limited evidence of such colonies can be found in the anomalous structures and enigmatic features that have been documented from astronomical studies and space probes. Such evidence is found on our moon, suggesting some type of base or colony may have once existed. Respected astronomers have been identifying artificial monuments on the moon for more than several centuries. In 1822, the highly regarded German astronomer Baron von Paula Gruithuisen observed what he described as the ruins of a lunar city, near the center of the moon, on the border of the Sinus Medii (The Central Bay).[1] He described the structure as: "A collection of gigantic ramparts...extending about 23 miles...on either side of a principal rampart down the center...."[2] Other astronomers described the structure as 'low ridges' extending approximately parallel for some distance. Two years later in 1824, Baron Gruithuisen announced his discovery of "colossal buildings" just north of Schröter crater.[3] That claim was followed with similar confirmation of numerous additional and apparently artificial structures that were revealed by other astronomers.

One of those structures, known as the Mädler Square after the German astronomer Johann Mädler, is suspected to be of artificial construction, dating to ancient times. Dr. Mädler and his partner, Wilhelm Beer, studied the moon for more than ten years and mapped its surface. Their results were compiled in an 1838 book, *Der Mond*. The Mädler Square edifice lies at the edge of the Mare Frigoris (The Sea of Cold), near the eastern edge of the crater Fontenelle. It has enormously high walls in the shape of a square enclosure.[4] A later description by the British astronomer Edmund Neison (aka Edmund Nevill) in his 1876 book, *The Moon*, further describes this formation as: "...a perfect square, enclosed by long, straight walls about 65 miles in length and one mile in breadth, from 250 to 300 feet in height."[5] While more recent study concludes that the shelter is incomplete and not quite straight and square, it remains a source of debate. An abandoned structure in ruin from eons ago would seemingly exhibit similar deterioration.

From 1950 to 1987, Howard Hill, a British astronomer, identified fascinating lunar formations, including mammoth walls located at the eastern extensions of the Hypatia Rille, along with pyramidal formations within the crater of Moretus.[6] The Alpine Valley is suspected to also be a possible artificially engineered structure. Its 80 mile long formation is considered to be the finest of its type anywhere on the moon. Other anomalies include what appears to be 'domes' formed in discernible clusters, not in random patterns of natural distribution. Such domes are large, gently sloped structures, which are mostly located in or near craters.[7] They have also been described as possible extinct volcanoes, but their true nature remains unknown.

One photograph of the Sea of Tranquility, taken by NASA's 1964 Ranger 7 probe, displayed several artificially-appearing structures inside one of its craters, flanked by concentric shafts that appear to be subterranean entrances.[8] Another photograph in that series displayed what some identify as a flying saucer. Author and amateur astronomer George Leonard described this large object as having: "a dull metallic finish...smoothly rounded, symmetrical, and has what appears to be a turret-shaped protuberance...."[9]

In the western edge of the Sea of Tranquility, six cone or pyramid-shaped spires, apparently arranged in a purposeful geometric pattern, were photographed by Orbiter 2, a 1966 NASA space probe.[10] Those photographs were extensively studied by William Blair, an archaeologist and anthropologist with the Boeing Institute of Biotechnology. Very distinct shadows became apparent, with the largest one likened to the distinctive shadow projected by the Washington Monument. Triangulation allowed measurements to be taken of the highest obelisk, revealing a height of nearly 700 feet.[11] Just to the west of that spire, a very distinct rectangular depression is found, clearly displaying right angle corners.

Author Peter Kolosimo reported that photographs of strange structures, in the shape of a cross, were taken by astronomer R. E. Curtis and published in the Harvard University Review.[12] They were deemed to be too purposefully arranged to be merely natural formations. Another oddity was discovered first hand by the Apollo 17 team of Dr. Schmitt and Commander Eugene Cernan while driving the Lunar Rover back from the South Massif Mountain. A small crater named "Shorty" by the Apollo crew was observed to contain orange colored glasslike beads.[13] Analysis of those beads dated the material at 3.8 billion years old.[14] No where else on the moon has such a comparable material yet been found or observed.

The highly respected astronomer, F. H. Thornton, briefly observed a brilliant flash of orange-yellow light on the moon's surface along the eastern rim of Plato on April 15, 1948. He described that flash as being similar to an artillery shell exploding in the air from about ten miles away.[15] The light was definitely not from a falling meteor or a volcanic explosion, and no explanation for that phenomenon was ever given.

According to a late 1970s report from *The New York Daily News*, NASA had refused an investigative group's request to release 125 photographs taken by their moon probes and missions.[16]   Prior scientific consultants to NASA have admitted that NASA has not released all information they gathered about the moon, keeping some data absolutely secret.[17]

Mars Base

A Martian base or its ruins may have been photographed by NASA's 1971 Mariner 9 probe in transmission frame 4209-75. That frame recorded a strange arrangement, located along the equator at longitude 186.4, displaying clearly defined areas of rectangles interconnected with a circular nucleus by a series of straight channels.[18]   This formation resembles a series of blocks, arranged in a radial pattern around a central hub, similar to separate wings or rooms leading from a circular hall. It is also the arrangement used by numerous modern airport terminals.   Such artificial-appearing forms or groupings are often speculated as being linked by subterranean shafts or tunnels, which connect them with various points between different complexes.   Such an underground community could provide livable accommodations on a dying planet.

Such a subterranean world may have even transcended both time and space, with the lingering ancient recollection or belief on our own planet of a 'hollow' Earth region.   The Greeks, Japanese, and the Buddhists of Central Asia shared such a belief in ancient times.   That belief continued to persist into modern times with the creation of the Hollow Earth Society, formed by Cyrus Read in 1870.   Until specific probe data or physical examinations by a landing party are made, no final determination can be made of a possible Martian subterranean complex.

Since Mars is adjacent to the asteroid belt, on its 'sun-side,' it should have the greatest incident of crater impacts from 'falling' meteorites freed from the belt.   The thin atmosphere would also offer little resistance to such rocky invaders, with minimal frictional heat burning away its mass, allowing larger and more numerous chunks to reach the surface. But the actual frequency is much lower than would be expected, especially in the Northern Hemisphere where very few craters are found. Erosion does not appear to be at work in leveling or removing the evidence of the expected numerous impacts.

Such lack of crater impact evidence on the northern half of Mars may indicate artificial excavation of the planet's surface during past ages, made necessary for construction or farming purposes. Or it may reflect some form of artificial protection, such as a shield or dome, which may have been erected in the ancient past to protect against asteroid and meteorite impacts. Or perhaps the creation of the asteroid belt reflected an intense period of activity, but only one of short duration. Mars simply may have had celestial luck working for it. It could have been on the far side of the sun, opposite its neighboring planet at the time of its catastrophic destruction, the one that resulted in the formation of the asteroid belt. Such an orbital position would have minimized the effects of the ensuing 'rain of rock.' But the most plausible explanation may be found in the belief that the Northern Hemisphere was once predominantly an ocean when the asteroid belt was first created as a result of Maldek's destruction.

The planetary three-dimensional mapping of Mars by NASA's Global Surveyor, which reached Mars in 1997, revealed that the Northern Hemisphere was an average of three miles lower than the more mountainous land of the Southern Hemisphere. Such extreme lowland topography could indicate the floor of an ocean that once existed. Its waters would have slowed any asteroids hitting that aquatic region, thereby negating or minimizing any resultant impact craters. The southern half of Mars reveals more volcanic activity, with massive mountains as high as fifteen miles, along with canyons vastly larger than the Grand Canyon, running for thousands of miles. The huge depressions in the Southern Hemisphere, such as the Hellas Basin (aka the Hellas Crater), which measures six miles deep by 1,500 miles across, may have formed from devastating asteroid collisions or volcanic activity. It also may have once been an ocean or sea during Mars' distant past.

NASA's 1976 Viking I mission photographed a giant stone face on Mars that was apparently designed to be viewed from above.[19] This monument measures 1.6 miles long by 1.2 miles wide, rising almost one-half mile in height. Other photographs reportedly also clearly show this formation, making it unlikely that the object is a 'trick of light' or an optical illusion. It has been calculated that the head would have been aligned with the sunrise of the Martian summer solstice around 500,000 BC.[20] Disputes arise over two additional similar 'face sculptures' that are reported to have also been photographed on Mars, according to author William Bramley.[21] Richard C. Hoagland, the popular lecturer, researcher, and author, is one of the leading experts on this face, along with numerous other structures located in the Cydonia region of Mars. Mr. Hoagland has been investigating such anomalous structures since the early 1980s.

Objects resembling three-sided pyramids, two enormous in size along with two smaller ones, were found located in the Elysium Basin. Dr. Vladimir Avinksy, a prior-Soviet geological researcher, concluded that those objects consisted of three true pyramids and a possible fourth. The largest ones are reported to be about 9,800 feet across the base and about 3,275 feet high, while the smaller one is estimated to be 3,000 feet across at its base.[22] All appeared to be severely eroded and of ancient origin. Other pyramid shaped objects were photographed on Mars during the 1976 Viking mission. Approximately ten miles from the stone face, a rectangular pyramid is found. That structure is reported to be about one mile wide by 1.6 miles long, with one side pointing due Martian north. A few miles southwest of the face, a series of organized and aligned objects are found. They form a nearly perfect pentagon of mountains shaped like pyramids, along with an adjacent triangular structure near two upright walls. It is doubtful that such structures are all natural formations.

Much mystery surrounds Phobos 2, the 1989 Soviet Mars probe. According to Boris Bolitsky, a then-Soviet science correspondent, several unusual images were transmitted back to Earth just prior to its demise. The final pictures were described as "quite remarkable features."[23] The last picture was about half-transmitted when everything suddenly stopped. This last image has never been officially released. According to David Hatcher Childress, a Russian astronaut with the rank of colonel, Dr. Marina Popovich, passed a copy of this photo to UFO investigators in 1991. It reportedly showed a huge cigar-shaped mothership, about 12.5 miles long by nearly one mile in diameter, near the Martian moon Phobos.[24]

Three days before the destruction of Phobos 2, another photo showed a shadow projected onto the surface of Mars. It was determined to have come from an enormous object in space just beyond the orbit of the moon Phobos. Perhaps it was the same object seen in the final photo transmission from Phobos 2, and might have been the cause of the probe's ultimate destruction. Also prior to its sudden demise, Phobos 2 revealed a network of straight rows of parallel lines at the equator of Mars. This geometric pattern covered a vast area of over 200 square miles, and appeared to be purposeful, not natural in origin.

Other anomalies of Mars are found in the surface markings that run for countless miles in both intersecting and parallel layouts. Such tracks have been compared to similar ones found on the Nazca plain in Peru. Pictures from the 1965 Mariner 4 probe showed straight-line canals that followed true 'great-circle' courses, which represent the shortest distance between points on the surface of a sphere. That would tend to support an artificial construction origin, prompting speculation that they represent actual canals used to convey melted water from the polar ice caps.

Author Zecharia Sitchin reported on an area displaying a unique surface 'waffle pattern,' believed to be caused by hardened lava being broken into geometric shapes by certain subterranean movements, even though similar patterns are not found elsewhere. Those patterns resemble a type of farming practice used in South America, on land served by underground aquifers in rainless regions. Such a method involves construction of an 'island terrace' that is then surrounded by irrigation channels.[25]

At the Cofrates depression, an area presumed to once be an ancient sea, a series of structures are found that resemble ruins of docks, streets, and rectangular buildings that one would expect to find around a port city. As recently as the summer of 1998, wind storms formed huge sand dunes on the surface of Mars. As a result of known dust storms spreading massive amounts of sand around the planet, it is likely that the majority of ruins that might reflect the prior existence of an ancient civilization would have been buried beneath the Martian surface long ago.

Like the moon, unexplained flashes of light, perhaps from explosions or eruptions, have been observed on the surface of Mars. Tsuneo Saheki, an Osaka Planetarium astronomer, wrote of three separate occurrences when: "...a pinpoint of light that scintillated like a star"[26] was observed. The first was in 1937 and lasted for five minutes, which was the same duration for the second sighting in 1951, which was followed by a cloud that hovered over the origin of the flash, much like the mushroom cloud over an atomic explosion. The last anomalous light flash occurred in 1954, but lasted only five seconds.[27]

No acceptable explanation has ever been given for such intense transient light phenomenon. Astronomers have repeatedly observe mysterious clouds and color changes in the planet's surface during its closest orbital approach to Earth, which occurs roughly every 26 months. Author Eric Norman reported that Dr. Felix Y. Zigel, a noted Russian UFO authority, noted the frequency of UFO sightings increased during those periods when Mars was closest to Earth.[28]

Phobos, one of two moons of Mars, displays unusual orbital traits. It is the only satellite in our solar system to revolve faster than its parent planet, completing one rotation approximately every eight hours, compared to Mars' 24 hour rotation. Phobos has a nearly circular orbit that averages about 5,829 miles from the planet, situated almost in the plane of the Martian equator. Its orbit is decaying in a peculiar manner, with its inertial movement being eroded by some unknown drag. It is believed that a further orbital deterioration, one allowing the moon to descend 1,000 miles closer to the planet, would result in tidal stresses that would destroy Phobos.

Probes have recorded gravimetric readings much less than its irregular size should exhibit, helping to explain this decay. Such a condition has also led some scientists, including the prior-Soviet astronomer Professor Shklovsky, to speculate that Phobos is an artificial, hollow satellite, based on its lack of expected density. Further measurements and study have diminished that conjecture, but not eliminated it completely.

The size of Phobos, its longest 'diameter' believed to be between 11 and 17 miles long, is too small and fragile to have sustained the impact of its largest crater, which is four miles across, without breaking-up. Apparently, such a huge crater must have occurred while Phobos was still a part of a much larger celestial body, most likely a portion of the Asteroid Belt planet before its destruction. Phobos' lack of the classic red color of Mars further suggests it was not originally a Martian outformation as a natural satellite, and therefore was probably a captured chunk from another extraterrestrial formation.

Our own planet displays similar anomalous relics found in strata layers dating to times known to be millions of years before the emergence of humankind's earliest ancestors, suggesting extraneous or unconventional sources were involved in their placement on Earth. An extensive review of such artifacts will be presented later in this writing in Chapters 13 and 19.

Such early colonies were established for a multitude of purposes, but were limited ultimately by each planet's own indigenous lifeforms, which had rights and preference over all other considerations, according to the mandates of the Cosmic Order. The Ancient Ones had evidently conducted extensive research on all those colony sites. That was undertaken to determine the future potential and suitability of the indigenous lifeforms on each world, since such life would have priority ahead of all other offworld life. Such studies included global mapping and geological surveys, which determined a planet's stability and its mineral resources. Evidence of such an evaluation and survey of Earth is suggested by extant ancient maps that depict the Antarctic continent free of ice, a condition last known to have occurred sometime before three million BC. Such documents will be reviewed in Chapter 14.

During the distant past, extraterrestrial animals were likely also introduced at colonies that included Earth, to determine their compatibility with each planet. Some likely survived, cross-breeding with indigenous animals, while others died-out or mutated into new species. It is probable that Earth species were also taken back to the outer planet homeworld, as well as some of their other colonies. Genetic engineering may have even been employed to further augment such multi-world compatibility of animal and plant species.

Very sketchy archaeological evidence, along with vague archaic textual references, point to several colonizations of Earth prior to the emergence of ancestral humankind. One of those high civilizations was evidently located at a vastly ancient Antarctic location, during a time when the region was tropical. Additional settlements may have included a smaller site at the North Pole; a Gobi Desert Celestial City that existed when the area was an island plateau surrounded by an inland sea; and various archipelago paradises that are now buried beneath the silt, deep below the ocean surface. Such sites may be the 'lost civilizations' of earthly legend, but ones with a distinct otherworldly connection.

The identity of the inhabitants that populated those most archaic colonies remains unclear. They may have been occupied by a completely undiscovered early lineage of humankind that ended in a dead-end branch of evolution, creating an expansive gap in time before the next emergence of an indigenous hominid species. Or, a more likely scenario finds otherworldly beings occupying our planet, either as temporary lodging while their own homeworld purged the devastating effects of a planetary cataclysm, or as an unsuccessful attempt at a permanent colonization by 'alien' life on Earth. Such early Earth visitations and colonizing attempts may have been efforts by the Ancient Ones and their Helpers, or perhaps autonomous missions were undertaken independently by the outer planet humanlike beings. Such now-inhospitable sites, which were established by some long lost civilization or otherworldly visitor, have precluded their discovery and assessment by Earth's later inhabitants.

Natural catastrophes and severe climatic changes would have occurred periodically on each of the colonized worlds, including Earth, occasionally requiring desertion of those colonies, resulting in long periods of abandonment without otherworldly contact. The earthly period between 3.0 and 2.5 million BC reflects such a period of planetary disruption. Fossil remains have been found of very early *Homo sapiens* dating to that period, a time millions of years before humankind and our ancestors supposedly even existed.

Such finds may represent the remains of humanlike outer planet independent explorers, or humanlike Helpers of the Ancient Ones that may have been stranded on Earth during such natural catastrophes. Those fossils will be further discussed in Chapter 19. Space probes or routine orbital observations may have tracked the living standards at each site during such ensuing periods of colony abandonment, in an effort to determine when favorable conditions returned for rehabitation and additional exploration.

Chapter 11

Destruction of Maldek

Even though the Ancient Ones maintained close observance and influence over the humanlike beings and their outer planet homeworld, direct intervention was not normally allowed under the Cosmic Order. Emerging worlds were allowed great freedom and latitude to pursue their own direction and destiny, as long as they complied with the precepts of the Cosmic Order. As infant races matured, and their conduct and direction were deemed acceptable, their independence was expanded further. Such autonomy was certainly bestowed upon the outer planet humanlike beings, a privilege that might have even contributed to their eventual downfall. That same level of independence likely was also a factor contributing to the minimal amount of information now known about these humanlike beings and their homeworld. Archaic texts of Earth are mostly devoid of any useful information pertaining to the fate of the Asteroid Belt planet. Only a few fragments and vague legends exist from which to reconstruct any feasible speculations of what may have actually occurred to that homeworld and its indigenous species.

As planets age, certain attrition occurs. Volcanism and inner core temperatures diminish, adversely affecting both climatic and atmospheric fitness. Evidently, the planetary conditions on the humanlike beings' homeworld had started to deteriorate, perhaps creating a chronic but slow loss of atmosphere, resulting from a gradual internal cooling of both its solid inner iron core and its surrounding molten outer core. Its weakened magnetic field and decreased axial spin may have further reduced the planet's ability to hold its ever-thinning atmosphere, exacerbating such deteriorating planetary conditions.

Although this humanlike species had achieved impressive levels of spiritual and scientific development, they may have still lacked adequate abilities to solve their own planetary dilemma. It is unknown if the Ancient Ones had reviewed or approved their correctional plan, although the humanlike species evidently had full confidence in their own intended solution.

Although purely speculative, perhaps such a plan involved focusing certain energy pulses, possibly gamma rays or microwaves that were propagated through waveguides placed deep within planetary fissures and ocean floor vents, or conceivably integrated within laser beams as carrier waves, positioned at strategic locations around the globe. Such radiation would have been directed to converge at the central core of the planet, with the intent to increase the temperature within the outer liquid portion of its internal core, thereby intensifying the heat within its rocky mantle, effectively reactivating volcanic activity. The resultant volcanism would have renewed the production and release of critical gases, which could then replenish the planet's atmosphere.

Perhaps such a procedure was carried out concurrently with a secondary process intended to slightly increase the rotational speed of the globe. Such a procedure would have been intended to augment the planetary inertial forces resulting from any slight enhancement of the rotational differential between its outer molten core and its solid inner core, thereby imparting a stronger magnetic field to the planet. The resultant strengthened magnetic field would then provide a greater force of attraction with which to retain the newly enriched and denser atmosphere. Even an infinitesimally small increase would have been sufficient to improve the planet's gravitational attraction for better atmospheric retention. One can only envision such a scenario that utilized some form of unimaginably elaborate technological procedure known only within the realm of science fiction, which still remains beyond our present comprehension and abilities.

Another secondary intent associated with such an experimental procedure might have involved the implementation of a novel process that present Earth science has envisioned. That process is an attempt to harvest the massive electrical energy created by the spin-rate differential between the inner and outer portions of a planet's central iron core. Such spinning core sectors act as a massive generator of electrical energy. By somehow harnessing the ensuing electrical potential produced, a natural energy source could be created for their planet as a supplemental benefit associated with their planned 'corrective process.'

While unsure if the homeworld of the humanlike beings was Mars or Maldek, the Asteroid Belt planet, it is certain that Maldek was the recipient of their intricate restorative procedure. Such a corrective measure was performed on the Asteroid Belt planet either during process refinement as a 'trial run,' or as implementation of the final plan. For whatever reason, the plan failed, resulting in the explosive and cataclysmic destruction of Maldek.

It is known that the total destruction of a celestial body would require an incredibly massive energy release to achieve such a feat. Astrophysicists generally believe that a planet can not be exploded into bits and pieces, even by an atomic blast detonated at or somewhat below its outer surface.[1] While such a strategically placed global nuclear conflagration could extinguish all life on that world, that planet would still remain intact. It is believed that the destructive power necessary to shatter a world would require a massive explosive force centered within that planet's innermost core.[2] Complete destruction may even require contributing factors such as unusual gravitational or tidal influences, perhaps a conjunctive alignment with a nearby huge planet like Jupiter, or possibly an undetected fissure or fault within the rocky mantle of the planet itself.

As a secondary result from such a fracturing disaster, massive chunks of the shattered planet would have been propelled toward neighboring celestial bodies, causing impact craters and climatic changes on the worlds hit by those rocky missiles. Such an immense cataclysm would have drastically affected most of our solar system.

Although extant ancient records are inadequate to allow conclusive determination of which world was the origin of the humanlike beings, the few clues that do exist appear to indicate that it was Maldek. Such a speculative conclusion is based on the knowledge that the survivors who escaped the catastrophic destruction of the Asteroid Belt planet were few in numbers. Mars is only slightly less likely to have been the homeworld, since a greater number of survivors would be expected, based on its status as merely a neighboring planet to that disaster. Evidence of such a high civilization, including major city ruins and infrastructure decay, should therefore be greater than the few pyramids, walls, and 'sculpted-face' artifacts found on the Martian surface. Also, the credible evidence indicating subterranean shelters on Mars further suggests a 'refugee status' for the few survivors that would have been relocated to other nearby worlds, after a complete destruction of their home planet.

Regardless of their true origin, the humanlike beings were acutely affected by the Maldek cataclysm. Their homeworld was either destroyed (the Asteroid Belt planet), or its atmosphere (that of Mars) was partially 'blown away' as a result of the huge ensuing explosion. The bulk of the inhabitants, and most everything else of that civilization, were eradicated, along with many other extensive consequences within our solar system.

This scenario goes beyond mere speculation, and includes extrapolation of ancient records and examination of physical evidence. The cataclysmic destruction of the Asteroid Belt planet would have affected most of our solar system, especially its closest neighbors. The moon, Mars, and Earth would have undergone severe bombardment at roughly the same time over a relatively short period. This would have been an extremely violent episode for those surviving planets.

Author Frank Edwards observed that many craters on the moon are perfectly formed, indicating they have not been subsequently impacted again. Such a condition indicates a sudden, confined, and violent duration of bombardment,[3] during a relatively recent epoch, one occurring less than a million years ago, instead of billions of years ago. The massive explosion of a planet would certainly also send a few large asteroids hurling toward the sun, a few of which would have seemingly struck Earth. One would expect the largest of all meteorite or asteroid impacts on Earth to have occurred during that same event, our solar system's most cataclysmic episode.

While it is known that a planet or planetoid orbiting between Jupiter and Mars was destroyed in the ancient past, it should also be possible to determine the approximate date of that specific catastrophic event. All inner planets and its nearest outer neighbor, Jupiter, would have felt its effects, leaving some form of geological evidence. As previously stated, the explosion of a rocky planet would vaporize a major portion, with about half of the remaining debris remaining in orbit, forming an asteroid belt. The other debris-half remnants would then create the largest meteorite shower ever experienced within our solar system. Evidence exists on Earth of two such massive meteorite showers. The first one occurred about 35 million years ago, and was the second largest shower ever, depositing an estimated 110 billion tons of debris on Earth.[4] Two massive impacts are connected with that event, one hitting Chesapeake Bay, with a second strike impacting Siberia, causing a widespread mass extinction.

While science can not precisely determine the cause of that phenomenon, conceivable explanations have been offered. One theory claims those meteorites were a result of our solar system passing through the densest portion of the Milky Way Galaxy, accounting for such massive meteorite evidence. Our normal 'orbital' path through such dense portions of our galaxy occurs about every 35 to 37 million years, so Earth may be nearing a repeat episode. Another alternate theory for that massive shower is credited to the gravitational field of the Earth tearing away a portion of the outer crust of the moon, for some still unknown reason. Regardless of its cause, with a high degree of certainty this second largest meteorite shower was not a result of Maldek's destruction.

Fallout from that 35 million BC shower was greatly surpassed by Earth's largest meteorite bombardment ever, an event that occurred around 700,000 BC, according to a *New York Times* article.[5] Other geological estimates have dated that event between 700,000 and 650,000 BC, associating it with a magnetic pole reversal. That occurrence included the highest incident of rare tektite meteorites, which fell to Earth in select areas. Tektites are small, dark, irregular shaped, glasslike remains of meteorites ranging from less than an inch in length to almost as large as a small egg. Eighty percent of their composition consists of silica, and are most unique because they have gone through two molten stages, the first being of fantastic intensity.[6]

These rare specimens should not be confused with regular meteor showers, which are entirely different. Meteors, commonly referred to as 'shooting stars' or 'falling stars,' are actually tiny grains of debris, some remnants smaller than a mustard seed, left behind by a comet. Such debris trails or swarms are found throughout the orbital path of the parent comet. When Earth's orbit intersects the orbital debris field of a comet, a regular meteor shower occurs. Since the Earth's movement through the orbital path of each comet is predictable, that results in regular meteor showers such as the Lyrids that arrive about April 20th, the Perseids around August 10th, the Leonids of mid-November, and the Geminids of December 10th through the 13th.[7]

The unusual tektite specimens are found in a selective S-shaped distribution on Earth, with the largest concentration found in the southern part of Australia. They are also found in the East Indies, southeastern Asia, along the western coast of Africa, in the Indian Ocean, in Eastern Europe (especially in Czechoslovakia), and in scattered parts of the United States, mostly in Texas and Georgia.[8] The locations prove that the initial heating was not of terrestrial volcanic activity, since no volcanoes exist where they are found. Additionally, volcanism has been scientifically excluded as the cause for the dual-heated condition. They may represent the fragmented rock survivors that were close to the energy force that caused the breakup of the original celestial body once residing in the asteroid belt orbit. Such survivors were close enough to become molten but not vaporized by the ensuing phenomenal destructive force, and were subsequently blown free from the parent body.

Such resolidified remnants were then reheated to a second molten state as they later entered Earth's atmosphere. Bits of the parent body much further from the unknown destructive energy force would not have undergone similar vitrification, and would have experienced only a single molten state from frictional heating upon entering Earth's atmosphere. The scarcity of tektites reflects their association with some extremely rare extraterrestrial event. The destruction of the planet originally occupying the asteroid belt orbit would therefore be a good candidate for such a rare cosmic occurrence.

This 700,000 BC date was further confirmed with the largest-ever asteroid to hit the Earth at a location near the South Pole, which evidently occurred around that time period. Charles Berlitz revealed that John Weihaupt, a scientist at Purdue University in West Lafayette, Indiana, claimed to have proof of that largest asteroid to have ever impacted Earth.[9] Although still undiscovered, its massive crater is believed to be near the South Pole. John Weihaupt further claims to possess

117

evidence of such a crater under the thick ice cover of northern Antarctica, estimated to be 150 miles wide by one-half mile deep and weighing an estimated 13 billion tons.[10] A meteorite or asteroid of that size would have produced a massive crater four times larger than any other one known on Earth, one measuring between 2.5 and 3.75 miles across. Its crash velocity was estimated at 44,000 miles per hour, with its impact dated between 700,000 and 600,000 BC.[11]

The time frame for the destruction of the Asteroid Belt planet can be further defined. With the combination of a massive asteroid impact, the largest meteorite shower, and the rare tektite shower, such events would have caused a rapid and massive reduction in the amount of water vapor in the upper atmosphere of Earth, resulting from prodigious rainfall and a reduction of greenhouse gasses. The resultant colder temperatures would either start an ice age glaciation, or continue and deepen one if it was already in process. The only period of time that fulfills such a scenario is *c.*700,000 BC.

That time period falls during the climax of the Günz glaciation of our last Ice Age, when its effects were extended by perhaps as much as 10,000 years, prolonging its end to around 690,000 BC. As previously stated, the distinct phases that occur during Ice Ages follow a somewhat predictable and repetitive cycle of roughly 90,000 years or less, during which the climate alternates between two or more long-duration cold phases, separated by shorter interglacial warm periods lasting around 10,000 years. Our most recent glaciation, the Würm, had four such distinct cold/ice maximas. Overall, our last or still present Pleistocene Ice Age started about 2.2 million years ago, and has gone through four such major phases or glaciations, including the Günz (800,000-690,000 BC), the Mindel (450,000-400,000 BC), the Riss (220,000-150,000 BC), and the Würm (68,000-10,500 BC). Their periodic glaciations covered all areas of Canada, Belgium, Holland, Germany, and Scandinavia, along with a part of the United States and a portion of Eastern Europe. Although the glaciations were not worldwide, they had widespread global effects.

The vastly extended interval of ice cover during the Günz Ice Age lasted approximately 110,000 years, which represents the longest duration of known glaciation encountered during any of the four glacial periods within our most recent (or perhaps still present) Ice Age. Combining all these unusual incidents that are validated with geological corroboration, they provide solid evidence consistent with the aftermath that would be expected from the destruction of an outer celestial neighbor within our solar system.

This catastrophic event adversely altered the intended progress planned and anticipated for our solar system as a whole, affecting Earth in a most unusual way. Those influences went beyond the massive meteorite bombardment and subsequent climatic and environmental changes that ensued. It also altered the sphere of external influence affecting Earth and its indigenous species, intervening with our planet's ultimate development.

Chapter 12

Unauthorized Intervention

Only an extremely minimal portion of the original humanlike population would have survived the devastating effects of Maldek's destruction, with ensuing life drastically changed for those survivors. The few humanlike beings that did survive were on various motherships assisting the Ancient Ones with routine duties. Others were manning the offworld colonies on the moon and the 'far side' of Mars, away from the explosion's blast effect. Despite that, an unknown number were likely killed in isolated areas on Mars, from the percussion of the massive neighboring explosion and the partial stripping of the Martin atmosphere that was ripped-away by the shock wave. An additional few would have been on space stations before their eventual destruction, likely surviving by utilizing escape pods that were later retrieved by the Ancient Ones.

The dispassionate Ancient Ones immediately intervened, and undertook the task to minimize the effects of that catastrophe where possible. The Ancient Ones' efforts would have centered on creating a more permanent living environment for the few humanlike survivors. The Ancient Ones quickly relocated many survivors to the base on Earth's moon, since meteorite fallout remained greatest on Mars. Emergency excavations were then undertaken to build underground shelters on both Mars and the moon of Earth. Eventually, protective shields or domed structures were erected around the equatorial region of Mars, to help contain and maintain the remaining 'partially stripped' atmosphere, at least in isolated areas, as well as to provide protection against the continuing bombardment of stray meteorite impacts coming from the errant exploded debris.

Later, the colony settlements on our own moon were also upgraded with similar shelters, to provide for additional long-term occupancy. Over time, Mars became the main refugee base for the descendants of the humanlike survivors, although the Ancient Ones had established multiple worlds for subsequent generations to assure that at least one colony prospered, thereby preserving the species from extinction. Short term relocation was also undertaken on Earth, but involved only brief stays, due to the limited allowable exposure to Earth's more 'hostile' environment.

Earth seemingly offered less hospitable living conditions compared to the humanlike beings' homeworld, where somewhat lower atmospheric pressure, oxygen content, and gravity existed. Earth was also deep into the severe and extensive glaciation of the Günz Ice Age, which only worsened after the effects of Maldek's destruction were felt. Consequently, regardless of their original homeworld planet, Mars became the apparent primary homeworld of the humanlike beings after 700,000 BC. Much later, genetic alterations were undertaken by the Ancient Ones to 'modify' the physiology of the resultant offspring of the rescued humanlike survivors, in order to improve their adaptation with the higher solar radiation levels, gravitational forces, temperatures, and atmospheric pressures associated with Earth.

Those genetic modifications were introduced into both the indigenous Earth species as well as the humanlike beings. On Earth, only an isolated group of *Pithecanthropus* apemen received such 'commonly shared' engineered recombinant DNA material. A much wider distribution was introduced into the Martian populace of the humanlike beings that survived the Maldek disaster.

The 'altered' *Pithecanthropus* parents and their offspring were continuously segregated on protected island locations or other isolated sites, so as not to interfere with a parallel evolutionary track of 'natural' mutation on Earth. That assured the continuation of at least one branch of indigenous earthly life, fulfilling mandates of the Cosmic Order. Perhaps the emergence of the proto-Sapiens sometime around 400,000 BC (with certain earlier indications as old as perhaps 500,000 BC) represented the initial 'release' of that altered species. On Mars, the descendants of the survivors from the Maldek disaster did not enjoy that same 'dual' option. Their 'required' mutation was more urgent, based on continued deterioration of the Martian climatic conditions, with its life-sustaining environment projected to continue for only a limited amount of time. The Ancient Ones' goal for the successful genetic mutation of the humanlike beings, one permitting dual-world habitation with Earth, was regarded as essential for their species' ultimate survival.

DNA modifications made to the humanlike survivors were intended to provide prolonged exposure on Earth, with eventual full and permanent adaptation. One early mutation was the deliberate increase in bone density and thickness of the skull, meant to compensate for the higher atmospheric pressure and gravity associated with Earth. Such a heavier bone structure was also evident in the proto-Sapien skulls on Earth. By 400,000 BC, the DNA alterations introduced to the indigenous Earth species had resulted in an evolutionary humanlike being, basically an amalgamation between primitive man and the original outer planet humanlike being.

Perhaps the Ancient Ones carved a stone monument on the Martian surface to commemorate the original humanlike species, the source from which both the altered humanlike survivors of the Maldek destruction and the new human species on Earth emerged. The controversial Face of Mars may stand as mute testimony to the original indigenous lifeform within our solar system, the humanlike beings of Maldek or Mars. Although it is presently impossible to establish the construction date of such a monument, speculations dating the sculpture's orientation with various

Martian occurrences have been made. Respected researcher and author Zecharia Sitchin stated that the face displays an alignment with the Martian solstice sunrise around 500,000 BC.[1]

The surviving outer planet humanlike beings can not simply be called 'human,' because they were a distinctly different genus. The term 'pre-human,' referring to the species that came before humans, connotes a being less developed than human, when in actuality that earlier ancestor was decidedly more advanced. Their differences in physiology from present humans was the reason why they could not merely be transported by the Ancient Ones to Earth for permanent relocation immediately after the destruction of Maldek. But the biggest obstacle may have been the precepts of the Cosmic Order itself, which gave the indigenous sapient species of each planet preference over all other lifeforms.

The Ancient Ones simply could not undertake the wholesale immigration of an off-world species to another developing planet. That would be a blatant violation of the Cosmic Order. Such an intrusive act of alien intervention on an emerging world was viewed as a disruption of the regulated and slow development of the evolutionary progress on such planets. The key aspects of 'controlled' and 'gradual' should be noted. To the Ancient Ones, a million years or so could be viewed as a 'quick' time frame.

The widespread introduction of advanced technology upon a primitive world would also not be acceptable, violating the Cosmic Order. But the outer planet humanlike beings did not have a million years to wait. Such a dilemma may mark the earliest dissension between our 'distant' ancestors (in more ways than one) and the Ancient Ones, as well as their Cosmic Order rules.

With the small number of humanlike survivors relegated to underground bases on Mars and the moon, their lives, culture, and future became totally disrupted. Their greatest inventors, scientists, and educators had been lost, their cities, wealth, and possessions essentially destroyed. They had to basically start over, although they knew what inventions and obtainments awaited them. Being aware of the direction in which to proceed, such insight should have been a positive influence. Rather, it became a detriment, as the populace grew impatient, knowing that the Ancient Ones could do much more to 'replace' their lost civilization. The Ancient Ones would not have considered the duplication of past accomplishments as 'replacement,' but viewed such restoration as too rapid a rate of progress for merely the descendants of a prior high civilization. Those recipients would not have achieved the same moral maturity possessed by their ancestors, a level necessary to fully appreciate such technological concepts and their consequences.

In a manner similar to a spoiled child having his lost or broken toys replaced as a result of his own neglect, the humanlike beings would also not grow and learn from merely having their lost culture and civilization replaced. Such survivors were merely the descendants of those originators who originally built their once-great culture. Those ancient ancestors had 'earned' their accomplishments, through their methodical and regulated growth, progressing and maturing as an enlightened species during that process. The simple replacement of lost prior achievements would teach nothing to the then current recipients, nor instill any moral maturity or core values.

The Ancient Ones were also concerned that the humanlike beings would expect future 'bail-outs' if they were to make reckless mistakes, or proceed with their progress too rapidly. The Ancient Ones may have had prior experience with numerous 'natural' disasters that essentially devastated the advanced cultures of certain species on other worlds, with those beings coming back stronger and better than before. The humanlike beings on their home base of Mars did not share that same philosophy, resulting in bitterness and resentment toward the Ancient Ones. That reaction acutely altered their outlook and moral values. Over time, the bases on the moon and Mars drifted apart, differing in both philosophy and development. The ongoing slow loss of atmosphere on Mars further exacerbated that schism with the lunar base, as well as with the Ancient Ones. Such impending peril made any tangible progress an imposing task, as long as the Martian populace was fighting for their very survival.

The Ancient Ones began to focus their attention on the humanlike beings based on the moon of Earth, mainly due to their more compliant attitude. Ensuing replacement humanlike Helpers were selected from that group to civilize and educate the earliest genetically modified indigenous Earth species, the proto-Sapiens. Initially the Helpers monitored the compatibility of the proto-Sapiens at sites in Africa, which was a tropical paradise at that time, rich in wildlife and natural resources, with settlements established near modern day Kenya. Other settlements were also dispersed around the Mediterranean, mainly in European lands. Their compatibility with Earth was not very successful, even after more than 250,000 years of dedicated effort.

Meanwhile, the humanlike beings' fight for survival on the bases of Mars and the moon continued to overshadow any real cultural progress, which prohibited them from ever obtaining the prior grand levels of their ancestors. Those at the Martian base became increasingly bitter toward the Ancient Ones, believing they should intervene to an ever-greater extent to alleviate their plight. They also harbored resentment toward the indigenous beings of Earth, 'creatures' they perceived as rivals for possession of that world. The history of the outer planet humanlike beings after 700,000 BC became one of survival and dissension, rather than one of progress.

Their future as a species would later become ultimately intertwined with Earth, one predicated on their eventual achievement of long term compatibility with our planet, resulting in indigenous earthlings being used as pawns. Their continuing story is included in the subsequent chapters on Earth history, where they eventually became known as the gods depicted in many ancient mythologies. Those accounts include the Anunnaki described in various ancient texts of Mesopotamia, Egypt, and India; and later as the Nefilim, Elohim, and angels in both the Old and New Testaments of the Bible. Their later division into two opposing groups would cause great turmoil for humans, which likely slowed or even negated the rate of progress the Ancient Ones originally intended for our world.

Chapter 13

Indications of Early Earth Contact

Focus now turns back to Earth, where it appears impossible to determine the first or very earliest contact the Ancient Ones made with our planet. Such contact may have occurred in extremely remote Earth epochs long before humankind, perhaps during times when dinosaurs dominated the planet. Such speculation is derived from certain indirect and wholly inexplicable indications, such as the much later archaic rock drawings that depicted numerous recognizable species of long extinct dinosaurs.

The first dinosaur bone was found in 1838, and consisted of only a single fossil. Additional bones were discovered over the ensuing years, although the first complete skeletal reconstruction occurred much later. Prior to that time, man would have had no idea of how the many different dinosaurs would have looked. However, enigmatic depictions vastly predating humankind's first knowledge of such 'terrible lizards' were drawn during ancient times, accurately showing various species of dinosaurs that supposedly became extinct 65 million years ago. In prehistoric times, such knowledge could only be known if it had been imparted by some advanced culture that either viewed such creatures, or unearthed their remains and reconstructed their appearances.

Ceramic artifacts, known as the Acámbaro Collection of Mexico, depict humans interacting with extinct dinosaurs. Those ceramic representations are dated to *c*.3600 BC, as determined by the thermoluminescence dating method.[1] The Hava Supai Canyon of Arizona contains ancient rock carvings depicting a giant human fighting a dinosaur.[2] Another ancient petroglyph, found by the 1924 Dohenny Expedition in the Grand Canyon, depicts a man about to be attacked by a Tyrannosaurus-like dinosaur.[3] A Rhodesian cave painting depicting a Brontosaurus was drawn by primitive bushmen sometime between 30,000 and 15,000 BC.[4] Author Andrew Tomas stated that a representation of a stegosaurus was found near the Big Sandy River in Oregon.[5] Other cave drawings found in Central America also depict unmistakable renderings of dinosaurs.[6]

In an area northwest of Tucson, Arizona, a Roman broadsword that dated between 560 and 800 AD was discovered by archaeologists from the University of Tucson in 1925.[7] It is believed to be from a Jewish outpost that broke from Roman rule and later established a settlement in the region,[8] a shocking revelation and discovery on its own merit. But this sword also featured an intricate carving of a Brontosaurus.[9] Although such depictions all dated to times long before the first dinosaur bone was even found, it is clear that some beings or ancient cultures knew of such creatures, and evidently had an accurate understanding of their appearance.

Dr. Daniel Ruzo, a Peruvian explorer, discovered an unusual ancient hidden art gallery in 1952 by following fragmented and unrelated passages from ancient legends and texts. The site of this gallery is on the Marcahuasi Plateau about 50 miles northeast of Lima, Peru, high in the Andes at 12,500 feet. The site contains drawings of extinct prehistoric creatures dating to remote ages. It also has strange megalithic sculptures, a few recognizable only on the summer solstice when human faces are revealed by the unique refractive solar alignment. Other figures are only visible at noon and vanished as the sun moved.[10] This stone 'art museum' is dated by some to an indeterminate time before 8000 BC. Jacques Bergier and Andrew Tomas both reported that the site dates to times before 10,000 BC,[11] while Dr. Ruzo speculated that the sculptures could be much older. Constructed during any age, this great granite amphitheater was obviously sculpted by beings knowledgeable in optics, refraction, perspective, and the anatomy of extinct animals.

A report by H. L. Armstrong in a 1960 issue of the journal *Nature* revealed that fossilized human footprints were found around the Paluxy River bed near Glen Rose, Texas,[12] where dinosaur prints were also found within that same strata layer. However, certain 'giant human' prints found within that same strata have been proven fraudulent. A 1983 report in the *Moscow News* revealed the discovery of a fossilized human footprint adjacent to the print of a three-toed dinosaur, in the Turkmen Republic of southwestern Asia.[13] Such reports of humanoid footprints found in the same strata layer as fossilized dinosaur prints are common, but may have other explanations than the coexistence of the two species, although that possibility should not be excluded when visitations by otherworldly humanlike beings are considered.

Between 26 and 12 million BC, the period that encompassed the Miocene Epoch, the fourth epoch of the Tertiary Period that started about 65 million years ago, the Ancient Ones apparently continued to send probes throughout our galaxy. They searched for signs of celestial worlds that were displaying development, or ones already in process of evolving life and planetary resources. The Ancient Ones likely sent such probes during various times throughout Earth's development, without necessitating physical contact. Perhaps evidence of such probes can be detected from certain anomalous artifacts or unexplained objects recovered from remote antiquity.

A polished metal block was found in a coal seam of a mine[14] located high in the Austrian Alps in 1877[15] by Dr. Gurlt,[16] an Austrian physicist.[17] The object was determined to be of an iron-nickel alloy, not of meteoric iron or iron pyrite, since metallurgical analysis detected no trace of sulphur.[18] The cube, or more correctly the squared prism, measured approximately 2.75 inch by 2.75 inch by 2.0 inch, with a mass of 785 grams.[19] The steel block displayed a finely machined deep groove around its periphery, with its two square-faces perfectly rounded,[20] producing what were described as convex surfaces.[21] The coal vein in which the block was found dated to the Miocene stratum of the Tertiary coal period,[22] which is between 12 and 26 million years old. The object was finally reported to the public in 1885 in the journal *Nature*,[23] and put on display in the Salzburg Museum for a number of years until it was 'misplaced,' and disappeared around 1910.[24]

Perhaps the publicity made people more observant, since a very similar object was found in the foundry owned by Isidor Braun, which was located in Vocklabruck, Austria. In 1885 Mr. Braun's son passed by a load of coal awaiting use in the furnace when he noticed a lump of coal that had partially encased a small steel block. Retrieving the article, its size was determined to be about 2.63 inches by 2.63 inches by 1.85 inches, but its weight was not disclosed.[25] The block also displayed a small but deep incision, with two edges rounded on opposite faces, with both features appearing to have been machined.[26] That find was announced in the November 1886 issue of the London *Times*, and put on display in the Linz Museum from where it also became 'lost' during the early 20th century.[27] Reportedly a cast was made of the original block,[28] but its later status is also unknown.

Apparently both articles were of artificial origin, produced by some intelligent being. However, steel mills, tool shops, and skilled machinists did not exist millions of years ago, at least not on planet Earth. Additionally, it should be noted that the mass of the first steel block would have been well over 1,500 grams if it were solid. Its 785 gram weight would suggest a hollow or chambered interior core, perhaps housing even more complex items. The original intent of such an advanced machined-assembly simply remains a mystery.

In June of 1851 near Dorchester, Massachusetts, a bell-shaped cone resembling a chalice was found to have been embedded in solid granite after blasting operations had split the stone.[29] The cone was of obvious artificial construction, made from some unknown metal thought to be perhaps a silver and zinc alloy,[30] which measured 6.5 inches at its base, tapering to 2.5 inches at the top of its 4.5 inch height.[31] It displayed engravings of intricate designs that were described as having a floral appearance,[32] but could have also been some type of script. Presumably the cone was older than the millions of years old granite that had formed around it. Such a discovery was reported in the June 1852 issue of *Scientific American*.[33] That object toured numerous museums until it too eventually disappeared.[34]

According to a June 22, 1844 issue of the *Times* of London, a length of fine gold thread, artificially produced by some manufacturing process, was found embedded eight feet deep in solid stone by workers cutting rock in a quarry near Rutherford Mills, England, in an area close to the Tweed River.[35] The stone had been removed from the Miocene stratum that formed 12 to 26 million years ago.[36]

Similar finds have also been found in coal seams dating to the Tertiary Period. A modern day British Naval Intelligence officer, Ivan Sanderson, reported his knowledge of a manufactured gold chain found embedded in a Pennsylvania coal deposit, thus dating it at millions of years old.[37] Another find of a nearly ten inch long low-alloy gold chain was found in 1891 by Mrs. S. W. Culp in the United States.[38] The chain, completely embedded within a coal lump, only became visible upon breaking open the chunk, suggesting the chain was made before the coal deposit formation.

An iron screw, or rather its oxidized remnant outline, was also found embedded in solid granite after being exposed by miners who had split the stone.[39] Again, such an artificial screw had to predate the formation of the granite rock, which could be as old as 60 million years. That fastener-entombing rock was discovered near Treasure City, Nevada, in November of 1869.[40] Another old fastener, this time a seven inch long iron nail, was found encrusted in a rock taken from a Peruvian mine by the Spanish Conquistadors during the sixteenth century.[41] Since the explorers did not identify the type of rock, its ultimate age remains unknown. However, the very youngest volcanic rock in that Peruvian area would have dated that relic to tens of thousands of years old, long before the discovery and use of iron on Earth.

In 1844, Sir David Brewster, a Scottish physicist, reported the discovery of an iron nail embedded in a block of sandstone from the Kingoodie Quarry of northern Britain.[42] An 1851 London *Times* article revealed that the quartz was found by Mr. Hiram Dewitt while visiting in California. When accidentally dropped, the quartz split, exposing an iron nail.[43] The brothers and archaeological co-authors, Eric and Craig Umland, reported that eleven steel nails have been found in limestone from the Cretaceous Period, dating as old as 70 million years.[44] Numerous other fastener items have reportedly been found in similar ways, with an unknown number of such discoveries simply going unreported over the years.

In 1912, Frank J. Kenwood, a worker in a power plant in Thomas, Oklahoma, exposed a fully embedded iron cup after splitting a large lump of coal. The coal was determined to have come from the Wilburton Mine in Oklahoma.[45] Another similar anomalous artifact was reportedly later found within that same mine in 1928, but lacked adequate confirmation. Also in 1928, but in a different coal mine in Heavener, Oklahoma, a concrete block wall was found fully encapsulated within a coal seam, at a depth of almost two miles. The blocks were described as smooth-surfaced, twelve inch cubes, with their internal cores filled with gravel. The blocks were later determined to have formed a 300 to 450 feet long wall.[46]

Several lines of a script similar to hieroglyphics were found in 1868 by James Parsons, carved in bold relief on a slate wall in an Ohio coal mine.[47] Further west in 1912, a clay figurine was found in Nampa, Idaho, which had been removed from a strata that dated to approximately two million years ago. Still further west, a five inch square pavement tile, reportedly made of artificial materials, was found by Mr. Thomas Kenny in 1936, buried within a Colorado strata that dated to the Miocene.[48] This would indicate that the tile was millions of years old, yet of synthetic composition.

Focusing on the embedded artifacts, one compelling enigmatic question concerns their apparent ability, regardless of their actual origin, to withstand the extreme temperatures of molten magma that engulfed such items during their initial encapsulation, without melting or vaporizing the article. Yet their composition and shape were retained, even over the many millions of years of slow cool down that is associated with the formation of igneous rock granite.

Such articles may reflect an imparting of some unique property, perhaps an impervious barrier or coating yet beyond our comprehension that allowed them to withstand the vaporizing temperatures encountered, either from frictional heating upon entering our atmosphere or their encapsulation within molten magma. Based on our current scientific understanding, most other explanations for such a phenomenon would entail explanations derived from science fiction, perhaps suggesting teleportation, with reassembly mistakenly directed within a solid object. But such an act, even if possible, would have split the granite with the internal displacement of molecules from the invasive item, while also crushing the intrusive object.

Another speculative explanation could be the alteration of molecular bonds at the atomic level of both objects, while merging and then rebonding each of their distinct molecular structures. Technology to explain such anomalies is far beyond our capability or comprehension, but may be a simple procedure for a vastly superior species. The mere fact that such articles had retained their original shape and composition would tend to indicate that some type of unknown science was employed in their embedding process, perhaps utilizing some low temperature method, one that yet remains beyond the abilities of modern man.

The machined metal cubes found in Europe may have been components of a detachable sensor pack that landed in strategic locations, or perhaps they were basic individualized targeting devices.   Their hollow or chambered interior structure tends to support the possibility that other instrumentation may have once been housed within the blocks. With their intended purpose of gathering and analyzing mineral deposits or soil samples having long since passed, their internal components would have eventually oxidized or become deeply carbonized over time.   The cone-shaped chalice, embedded deep in a Massachusetts granite stone, may have actually been a portion of an outer casing or shell, perhaps even a heat shield for a space probe. The metal screw remnants also discovered in the United States may simply be fastening devices used in the assembly of such probes. The anomalous gold thread found embedded in European granite may have been part of the wiring used for various electronic packages and power packs utilized to energize the internal components within each probe.   The out-of-place manufactured gold chains might be grounding straps or power cords for such monitoring or sensing devices.

Presumably during this 26 to 12 million years ago period, other worlds were encountered that possessed more advanced lifeforms, with the Ancient Ones deciding to concentrate on those planets.   Earth was probably categorized as a more primitive planet, scheduled for later intervention. Undoubtedly additional probes were sent, perhaps even some 'manned' missions, allowing periodic checks of Earth's development. This period also represents the time when primates and hominids first appeared on Earth, perhaps as part of 'seeding' experiments.

The following Earth period between 12 and 5 million BC encompassed the start and vast majority of the Pliocene Epoch of the Tertiary Period, reflecting a time when rudimentary apeman hominids became extinct, leaving only apes. Such a discovery could indicate another early but failed seeding attempt, or even 'manned' visitations, perhaps with the demise and burial of one of their landing party.

Author Martin Ebon described a remarkable discovery made in an Italian coal mine at a depth of several hundred feet by Dr. Johannes Heurezeler from Basle University in Switzerland, where a complete skeleton of a humanoid was found along with plant and animal remnants.[49] Those fossil remnants and bones were deemed to be of the same age, dating to ten million years ago. The plant and animal species were identified, but were of varieties thought to have only first appeared during much later times. A similar discovery was reported in the December 1862 issue of *The Geologist*. That specimen was also humanoid, found at a depth of about 90 feet within an Illinois coal seam, dating the remains to before or during the Tertiary Period.[50] Anthropologists date the earliest humanoids, such as the Australopithecines, as existing between five and six million years ago. A specimen approximately twice as old clearly contradicts that traditional and accepted belief.

This era displays indications of numerous settlements being periodically established on Earth for various purposes, perhaps including penal colonies or temporary sanctuaries for otherworldly infant races while their home planet purged the devastating effects of their own planetary cataclysm. The numerous previously documented anomalous nails found in stones and quartz dating from both these ancient periods poses an interesting dilemma. Abundant evidence exists that the Ancient Ones apparently preferred to construct permanent structures that lasted over extended periods, building them from massive megalithic stone blocks. Hence, the use of nails tends to indicate merely a temporary stay that suggests wooden structures were utilized as short-term shelters.

Other anomalous artifacts found within the strata of this archaic period included a five inch cut-tile of artificial

137

composition found in Colorado, perhaps a heat-shield tile from a remote probe or sensor. Similar tiles have been found in much later strata, and will be presented in Part Two of this writing. Other anomalous artifacts will also be revealed, perhaps representing articles that may have simply been lost or misplaced by the short-term visitors or explorers while temporarily on our planet.

Chapter 14

Continuing Early Earth Visitations

Disclosure of the *Elder Gods* theory continues with a review of the major developments undertaken or implemented on Earth by the Ancient Ones and their outer planet humanlike Helpers, presented in distinct chronological periods for greater clarity. This review commences with the time period following the previous chapter, and includes some of the mysterious anomalous artifacts found on our planet, which contradict the prevailing belief theories intended to explain our planet's early history. However, such enigmatic relics actually reinforce and verify the *Elder Gods* theory and the Ancient Ones' primordial contact with Earth over many millions of years.

5 to 2.5 Million BC:

This ensuing Earth period represents the later end of the Pliocene Epoch of the Tertiary Period, and reflects an increased level of active contact and intervention with our planet. The first apeman appeared during this period of Earth's history, and may mark the earliest successful seeding of our planet with primitive hominids. Perhaps such creatures were 'low or mid-level' life forms, which were acquired from an earlier developing celestial world within our solar system.

Many ancient legends tell of a time when only the 'elder gods,' the Ancient Ones, were on Earth, long before humankind's existence. Other accounts reveal that humanlike Helpers or Watchers later also assisted them. Such extensive early visits may have introduced the outer planet humanlike

139

beings to Earth, the same beings that would later contribute DNA material for infusion into the genetic mutations that would eventually become our true ancestors.

It is generally accepted that only Australopithecine apemen existed during this time frame, so *Homo sapiens* definitely did not exist during this period and would have been chronologically out-of-place. But enigmatic evidence exists, suggesting either a lost and unknown branch of ancient ancestors, or perhaps humanlike explorers who visited Earth during its remote past. Such humanlike presence is substantiated with anomalous imprints found around the planet.

In Cow Canyon, about 25 miles east of Lovelock, Nevada, a fossilized distinct footprint of a *Homo sapiens* human was found.[1] This print was discovered in a coal vein dating to the Tertiary Period more than two million years ago. In 1979, paleoanthropologist Mary Leakey discovered an early human (hominid) footprint in northern Tanzania, fossilized in volcanic ash, dating to 3.6 million years old.[2]

In 1959, while on a joint Chinese-Soviet expedition in the Gobi Dessert, Dr. Chow Ming Chen found a ribbed-sole or grid-pattern shoe sole imprint fossilized in sandstone.[3] The impression was so distinct that the shoe was determined to be a size 9,[4] with the print dating to between two and three million years old. Another shoe print was discovered in a coal seam deposit in the Fisher Canyon of Pershing County, Nevada. The fossilized impression was so defined that traces of the thread used to stitch the shoe sole were clearly visible.[5] Again, that artifact also dated to millions of years ago, long before the cobbler's trade. William J. Meister also found a fossilized shoe print inside a broken slab of shale near Antelope Spring, Utah, in 1968.[6] The distinct print was determined to be a shoe for the right foot.[7] Yet that print was embedded along with trilobite fossils preserved within the same stone, indicating their potential contemporaneous existence.

140

Dating of such fossils is inexact, often relying on relative dating, which is done by the stratigraphic method where it is assumed that the stratum becomes older with each lower level of excavation. Fossils dated by this method rely on the general stability of earthen layers or strata in which they are found. This process can be contradictory when pursuing the concept of linear evolutionary development. Earth layers can become distorted, mixed, and intertwined by natural events such as earthquakes, floods, hurricanes, and glaciers. Such catastrophic natural phenomena can fold an older layer and its fossil contents over later or newer strata. But the most intrusive of all conflagrations would not distort such layers by millions of years, ruling out that excuse for some of the oldest and most fascinating anomalies.

Such anomalies also include inexplicable organic evidence. A remarkable discovery was announced in 1974 by a joint American, French, and Ethiopian anthropological expedition near the Awash River in central Ethiopia. They recovered a complete upper jaw with all teeth, half of an upper jaw with some teeth, and a portion of a lower jaw with most teeth, all belonging to the *Homo sapiens* genus. Those fossils were determined to be about 3,500,000 years old, although no explanation for such fossils ensued.[8] An earlier 1972 discovery was made by renowned anthropologist Richard Leakey in the East Rudolph Basin at Lake Turkana near Kenya, South Africa, where he found a human skull and leg bone.[9] The skull, labeled as "Number 1470,"[10] is clearly that of a modern *Homo sapiens*, with a vertical forehead absent any heavy eyebrow ridge, and possessing a thin bone structure. But this skull is dated to 2,800,000 BC.[11] Perhaps no single find could do more to disprove the prevailing theory of humankind's origins than this specimen, yet it has received little publicity, with even fewer attempts to explain the existence of a human skull during such a remote period.

Those humanlike beings may have been part of a colonization attempt to determine their compatibility with

Earth. Or perhaps they were Helpers of the Ancient Ones that may have been stranded after becoming separated from their landing party, during some natural cataclysm on Earth. Geological evidence indicates that Earth underwent massive upheavals between 3.0 and 2.5 million BC. Massive volcanic activity and ensuing lava flows are known to have covered much of the western portion of the United States.[12] Similar eruptions around that same time formed many of the South Pacific islands, along with Easter Island. Such planetary disruptions were likely to have also contributed to the start of a new Ice Age, the Pleistocene, which commenced shortly after this global period of upheaval.

This period evidently encompassed the earliest known and extensive exploration of Earth, which included a major global survey and mapping effort conducted during this time frame. That effort is known from the ancient extant maps that reveal accurate details of a fully ice-free Antarctic continent, a condition that last occurred around 2.5 million BC. A subtropical climate is believed to have existed in the Antarctic then, with evidence of a major Antarctic settlement, along with indications of a smaller but similar settlement at the Arctic North Pole as well.

Among the many anomalous records and artifacts found throughout history, ancient maps depicting accurate land mass locations and their relative positions are some of the most dramatic. It now appears that civilizations of antiquity had a much greater knowledge and understanding of geography and space than many later generations, a fact confirmed from more recent 'discoveries' made between 1500 and 1900 AD. Such olden charts accurately show details that can only be obtained from an aerial perspective. But those maps emerged during times when aircraft did not exist, and therefore seem to defy explanation. Yet many medieval maps are surprisingly accurate delineations of land masses that are depicted in correct relative position, correlated with other landmarks and features.

One olden and enigmatic chart is the 1513 AD *Map of the World* drawn by Piri Reis. This map was found during modern times at the old Imperial Palace of Istanbul in 1929. Piri Reis was the Admiral of the Turkish fleet in both the Red Sea and the Persian Gulf. He was a successful and well-known cartographer of his time, charting the Aegean Sea and Mediterranean regions. He later became Commander in Chief of the Egyptian fleet, and was eventually wrongly beheaded by order of the sultan of Cairo in 1554, over misinterpretation of facts surrounding a naval battle with the Portuguese.

The map was drawn on gazelle hides in Gallipoli, Turkey, but only two fragmented portions of the original still exist today. Piri Reis compiled a book, the *Bahriye* (*Book of the Seas*), which was a brief autobiography and an atlas containing 210 accurate maps. In that book, he stated that his 1513 map was based on twenty different, much older, source maps and eight fragmented Arabian charts; some dating from the days of Alexander the Great. Piri Reis referred to himself as 'a poor copyist,' merely reproducing archaic charts originally made during ancient times. It is believed that at least one map used by Christopher Columbus was based on an ancient map from Alexander's collection. Another map used by Columbus was drawn by Toscanelli del Pozzo in 1475 AD, which showed numerous islands in the Atlantic Ocean, including one identified as Antilia, from which the Antilles are believed to have been named.

Some of the remarkably accurate features drawn by Piri Reis depict the eastern coastlines of both North and South America, including the entire profile of Brazil. The layout of the South American interior is also detailed, including the Andean Mountain range and the unexplored waterways of the Amazon, Orinoco, Parana, and the Uruguay Rivers. It also showed the islands lying below the southernmost tip of South America, including the Falklands and Shetlands. This map also featured the contours of Antarctica without its two mile thick ice cover, virtually fitting the continental contour known during modern times.

As with other olden maps, the Piri Reis chart reflects a knowledge and ability to correctly determine positions of latitude and longitude, as evidenced from the correct alignment of the continents. Yet such modern survey skills were not mastered until the 1700s. The Piri Reis chart also employed sophisticated map projection techniques that required the use of high-level mathematics. Charles Hapgood, a New Hampshire college professor who specialized in the history of science, conducted a modern study of ancient maps. His findings were published in his 1966 book, *Maps of the Ancient Sea Kings*. Professor Hapgood laboriously determined the original projection point utilized in the creation of the Piri Reis map, identifying that location as Aswan in Upper Egypt.[13]

This enigmatic chart also contained some glaring inaccuracies. Although the map depicts the southern continents in a distorted and elongated manner, sinking away and downward as if viewed from space, the representation does not fully fit with modern day space photographs. Also, the South American continent is drawn about 900 miles shorter than its true length, and appears to join the South Pole, with the size and placement of certain interior features also distorted. If the primary source for such later maps originated during remotely archaic times, human copy errors and distortions would be expected to occur over the ensuing millennia.

Perhaps an even more astonishing map was the so-called 'Glareanus Map.' This map, in its rough form, was contained in a 1482 book, the *Ptolemaeus Cosmographia*. It was updated and completed in 1510 by Glareanus, a Swiss scholar also known as Heinrich Loris. This work was based on chart and map information from the time of Claudius Ptolemaeus, the second century astronomer of Alexandria. This map depicts Greenland, Iceland, and both North and South America. It accurately shows both east and west coasts of the Americas, and correctly depicts the actual shape of South America, including its southernmost portion as a 'tip,' which was correctly shown disconnected from Antarctica and the South Pole. There were also inaccuracies, which included an erroneous size attributed to Africa.[14]

The Greek scholar, Eratosthenes, drew a map of the world in the shape of a sphere to within 1.3% of its true diameter around 250 BC. A map drawn by Pomponius Mela in 40 AD shows the continent of Australia (then called Antipodes). However, Captain James Cook did not formally 'discover' Australia until 1775. Most early European maps were believed to have been based on charts possessed by Ptolemy of Alexandria or those of Marinus of Tyre, *c.*120 AD, with such data reportedly based on even older works. The *Medicean Map* of 1351 and the *Pizingi Map* of 1367 both show Japan as a large island in the western Atlantic, with another island named "Brasil" midway between Japan and Europe.[15] The Athanasius Kircher map of the world, dated 1675, is alleged to depict ancient Earth just after the cataclysmic sinking of Atlantis.[16]

The Venice, Italy, Zeno brothers, Nicolo and Antonio, were mapmakers that specialized in Arctic and Icelandic maps. A Zeno brothers' map dated 1380 shows Greenland without its ice sheet of historic times. Twentieth century polar expeditions conclusively prove that this map was based not only on very ancient data, but that the mapping must have been done when Greenland had a temperate climate without an ice cover.[17]

A *circa* 1504 chart drawn by Nicolo Caneiro, a Genovese cartographer, depicted the coastal outlines and islands of the North Atlantic. The work was reportedly based on secret Portuguese data and knowledge. A 1507 AD map of the New World showing the lower portion of South America was drawn by Martin Waldseemuller and labeled "America." Other remarkable maps were drawn by Gerardus Mercator dated 1538, and Ptolemaeus Basilia dated 1540. The French geographer, Oronteus Finnaeus, drew another enigmatic map in 1531 that utilized an advanced map projection technique that would have required the use of spherical coordinates and angular trigonometry.[18]

Yet another French geographer, Philippe Buache, published a map of Antarctica in 1737 that showed the precise subglacial topography as it would appear without any glacial ice. As stated previously, Antarctica has been covered with ice for more than two and a half million years, although certain small areas enjoyed a brief ice-free period about 125,000 years ago. Charles Hapgood's research of this map determined that the source data used to construct Buache's chart would have dated to the end of the fifth millennium BC.[19]

None of the olden cartographers are believed to have known one another, or to have copied each other's work. All such maps were alleged to have been based upon much older source charts of unknown origin. Many of their maps accurately depict the coastline and contours of the Antarctic continent without its ice cap, a remarkable feat during the sixteenth century, realizing that the continent of Antarctica was not even 'discovered' until 1773. It was not until 1952 that its sub-glacial topography was first mapped from seismic surveys, revealing the actual coastline and contours of its landmass. Those surveys agreed with the ancient contours depicted in many of the enigmatic maps produced between the late 1300s and the early 1700s. It should be noted that glacial ice cover is a protective one, not an erosive one, allowing most land masses to retain their original outline, regardless of ice cover.

2.5 Million to 700,000 BC:

This time interval encompasses the start and earliest segment of the Pleistocene Epoch of the Quaternary Period. Due to the extensive Earth disruptions and climatic changes that were still occurring on our planet at the start of this period, exploration would have been quite difficult and dangerous. Hence, colonization efforts may have focused on other worlds during this time, a fact that is seemingly suggested by Chinese legends and oral histories of their creator god, P'an Ku, who 'traveled around the cosmos' in 2,229,000 BC.[20] Earth's fifth and latest glacial Ice Age then started around 2.2 million BC, further contributing to this temporary interruption in contact with Earth during such inhospitable times. Very little happened until 1.7 million BC, when Earth's indigenous and warlike *Homo erectus* first appeared. That genus was undoubtedly the natural product of our planet's evolutionary process, and would have likely caused concern for the Ancient Ones.

The early *Homo ergaster/Homo erectus* (aka *Pithecanthropus*) was likely not well received by the Ancient Ones due to its aggressive predisposition, so extensive contact was curtailed for additional assessment to determine future intervention with that new species. Perhaps those studies revealed an almost certain probability for a dead-end evolutionary path for that species, so continuing cautious contact eventually resumed.

Perhaps the next phase of contact and colonization then occurred around one million BC, as evidenced from the many artifacts of a semi-civilized culture that emerged in a western region of the United States. According to author Peter Kolosimo that ancient race lived in caves found in the Canyon of St. Mary, an area identified by Mr. Kolosimo as being in the Bronco Mountains.[21] That obscure site may be part of a range or spur of the Western Coastal Mountains or perhaps a part of the Rockies. Their Stone Age culture was notable for domesticating livestock and burying their dead in jute baskets. Surprisingly, they were not a red race culture but a Caucasoid one, or one very similar, based on analysis of bone fragments left by this ancient civilization.[22] That seeding attempt apparently ended abruptly around 800,000 BC with the start of the Günz ice cover, as the next phase of Ice Age glaciation. That severe cold period then lasted for more than 100,000 years, a period during which the greatest cataclysm within our solar system occurred.

700,000 to 690,000 BC:

Possibly the biggest event to ever occur in our solar system happened during this time. Although this event did not occur on Earth, the numerous resultant effects from the destruction of Maldek, the Asteroid Belt planet, had a lasting impact on all neighboring worlds, perhaps most of all on our planet. The immediate 'fallout' from such devastation was the most massive meteorite shower ever to impact Earth, resulting in the prolonged continuation of the Günz ice cover by about 10,000 years, extending it until *c.*690,000 BC. Such harsh climatic conditions kept any new Earth developments in check, with minimal off-world contact. That same absence also reflected the survival and relocation efforts that were being concentrated on the bases of Mars and Earth's moon. However, the greatest consequence for Earth from Maldek's destruction was yet to be realized, manifesting its true aftermath at a much later date.

690,000 to 450,000 BC:

This era of Earth history ushered in an interglacial period or warm phase of the Ice Age, resulting in relief from the bitter cold and extended ice cover. During this period, the devastating effects were purged from the massive meteorite and tektite showers, caused by the explosion of Maldek. The flora and fauna of Earth were slowly replenished and actually flourished during this ensuing period, helping to reestablish the dominance of the indigenous *Pithecanthropus* species.

450,000 to 400,000 BC:

This period encompassed the Mindel glaciation, the second ice cover of our last Ice Age, which started and continued during this era. Wild game and edible plants diminished as a result. This event greatly strained and eventually weakened the indigenous *Pithecanthropus* species, and may have even contributed to their cannibalistic tendencies. Such an abrupt reversal in that species' prosperous environment created an opportunity for renewed seeding attempts by the Ancient Ones. This time period also reflected an increased urgency to improve the deteriorating living conditions of the humanlike beings on the base of Mars, where the slow loss of atmosphere continued to threaten their long-term existence.

400,000 to 220,000 BC:

This was apparently a pivotal period in Earth's history. With the arrival of an interglacial warm phase following the Mindel ice cover, Earth's climate became ideal. Yet the 'highest' indigenous species, the *Pithecanthropus*, was becoming marginal, leaving Earth without its own viable, heir apparent offspring. By 375,000 BC, *Pithecanthropus* would become extinct, again leaving Earth open to accept 'new' lifeforms from beyond its borders, without compromising or usurping the rights of any indigenous planetary species; one of the Cosmic Order's prime mandates.

The spontaneous introduction of an unrelated and very advanced species then occurred around 400,000 BC with the proto-Sapiens, seemingly a most abrupt development. The proto-Sapiens were also remarkably unlike any other prior 'ancestor' seen on Earth, except for the enigmatic anomalous jaw bones and skulls, such as Dr. Leakey's "Number 1470" skull that was nearly three million years old. Further, the proto-Sapiens always possessed only a limited population number, much like a 'control lot,' and were perhaps used as a test to determine their ultimate compatibility with their new surroundings. They also possessed new and advanced implements, exemplified by the first manufactured wooden hunting spears, utilized in conjunction with modern, highly organized hunting strategies.

Such beings were evidently the Ancient Ones' first genetically engineered species that was specifically intended for permanent colonization of Earth. Those early humans would have been partially based on recombinant DNA from the outer planet humanlike beings, altered to comply with the environmental conditions found on our planet. Such alterations evidently included an increased bone thickness in the skull, perhaps to better withstand the higher atmospheric pressure and greater gravity associated with Earth. Other less apparent genetic alterations were likely also undertaken, through numerous continuing experiments over many centuries.

The 'base' DNA material used to produce the proto-Sapiens was obtained by the Ancient Ones from the humanlike beings, perhaps without voluntary permission or their full knowledge, conceivably even extracting developing embryos in a manner similar to the way modern UFO abduction subjects describe their own encounters. Such genetic engineering would likely have integrally involved the *Pithecanthropus*, perhaps utilizing them as 'gestation units' for the genetically modified DNA 'seeds' or embryos.

The timing for this introduction may not have been the most opportune. The resultant genetically engineered specimen might not have been the optimum candidate for Earth, having undergone their development initially as a cohabitable species, capable of dual existence on both the underground bases of Mars and the moon, as well as also on Earth. The demise of the *Pithecanthropus* had provided a somewhat quicker than anticipated indigenous species vacuum on Earth, opening a window of opportunity for the Ancient Ones to test their candidate as a permanent colonist, instead as merely a 'compromised' dual-inhabitant of several worlds. The warm interglacial period further accelerated this process, rushing the Ancient Ones to take quick advantage of the emerging temperate climate. Artifacts indicate that endeavor was not a great success, as evidenced by the low number of specimens, with limited expansion of settlements.

220,000 to 150,000 BC:

The less than stellar compatibility of the earliest proto-Sapiens with Earth was further tested during this time frame with the emergence of the third glaciation, the Riss, which started at the onset of this period. While not the longest duration ice cover, it had the most extensive coverage, affecting a larger area of land than any other since the inception of our last Ice Age. That may have ultimately caused the demise of this experimental candidate, which finally disappeared around 150,000 BC after limping through their quarter of a million year 'experiment.'

150,000 to 70,000 BC:

Major changes were occurring on Earth during this era. As the proto-Sapiens disappeared, an interglacial warm period finally arrived. With its more temperate climate, the next vestige of indigenous evolution from *Pithecanthropus* then occurred, producing the Neanderthals. That new subspecies was not much further advanced than the *Pithecanthropus*, and more closely resembled that older ancestor, displaying little similarity with the more modern proto-Sapiens. By all indications, Neanderthals were not part of the Ancient Ones' next experimental phase, but merely a normal evolution of Earth's own *Pithecanthropus* genus. Although Neanderthal man first emerged about 150,000 BC with an initially low population, they eventually flourished and became well established, with a substantial number of inhabitants by around 110,000 BC.

Neanderthals posed a problem for the Ancient Ones, since Earth no longer exhibited a species vacuum. Any imminent introduction of a new, genetically altered candidate was put on hold, thwarting their active program to relocate an altered species of the outer planet humanlike beings to Earth. Still, the Ancient Ones continued their planned genetic refinements on the outer planet humanlike survivors, for their improved dual-world compatibility. The Ancient Ones also continued similar work on their 'cousins,' a proposed species based on recombinant outer planet humanlike DNA infused with the prior genetically modified and recently extinct proto-Sapiens, the 'future' species intended to eventually colonize Earth. Over the ensuing years, the differences between the two species diminished, as certain successful modifications resulting from such genetic experimental work were introduced into the general population of both worlds.

Eventually the later descendants of the original humanlike species became capable of withstanding longer durations with Earth's environment, becoming valuable Helpers of the Ancient Ones during their ever-increasing visits to our planet. The only negative result from such increased Earth compatibility was their reduced tolerance with the ever deteriorating conditions on the Martian and moon bases.

The skeletal remains of a *Homo sapiens* infant, ceremoniously buried along with various individual adult bones that included a complete skull, may indicate evidence of such humanlike visitors on Earth during this period. According to author John Wallace Spencer, those remains, along with a reported 300,000 additional artifacts, were found by researchers Adrian Boshier and Peter Beaumont in a cave of the Bomva Ridge in an area of South Africa between Swaziland and Natal,[23] which was a known area of ancient mining. The modern human remains were dated older than 100,000 BC,[24] yet the earliest Modern man did not appear until *c*.43,000 BC with the Cro-Magnons. If such remains were not those of outer planet humanlike visitors, the remains may be from a final branch of the proto-Sapiens, or perhaps from certain very early prototypes resulting from the Ancient Ones' ongoing genetic work that eventually produced the later Cro-Magnons.

70,000 to 45,000 BC:

Neanderthal man continued to flourish and spread over Earth in increasing numbers during this time period, although no real species refinement or cultural development resulted. That species was essentially a roaming scavenger, traveling in small groups that occasionally succeeded in catching or killing wild game. But, they were the dominant indigenous species on Earth during this time frame. Around 68,000 BC, the Würm ice cover started, ushering in the fourth and last phase of glaciation associated with Earth's fifth and last Ice Age. The Würm ice cover was somewhat unique since it encompassed four distinct cold and ice maxima, separated by three interglacial warm periods. The first of those cold peaks occurred from 61,000 to 60,000 BC, followed by a warmer period extending from 60,000 to 54,000 BC. A second cold peak occurred briefly between 50,000 to 49,500 BC, but neither cold maxima appeared to drastically affect Neanderthal man.

Chapter 15

Emergence of Modern Man

The continuing chronology associated with the *Elder Gods* theory now converges on perhaps one of the most significant events within the origin and development of humanity as a species, the introduction of our earliest 'confirmed' ancestor.

45,000 to 15,500 BC:

This period commenced during an unremarkable time. No major cataclysms occurred, and the climate was neither undergoing a cold peak, or a warm phase. Still, an inexplicable event occurred without known origin or intent, greatly altering Earth's destiny. Around 43,000 BC, Cro-Magnon man suddenly appeared, seemingly overnight from some unknown inception. This subspecies initially cohabited among Neanderthal man, but did not evolve from them. The classification of Cro-Magnon conjures up an image of a primitive and savage cave man. Nothing could be farther from the truth. Cro-Magnons were modern in virtually all aspects. They lived in organized groups, possessed religious beliefs, underwent training, practiced skilled-trade work, and produced grand artwork.

By 41,000 BC, they operated and worked iron mines in Swaziland, Africa,[1] a remarkable skill for a stone age culture that did not use metals, at least according to orthodox belief. The environment on Earth at that time produced no reason for the *Homo sapiens* genus to mutate or evolve into Cro-Magnon man, especially in such a spontaneous and unexplained manner, yet such an amazing milestone occurred.

The emergence of Cro-Magnon man can best be explained as a result of genetic intervention by the Ancient Ones, perhaps an action that 'stretched' or even violated protocols of the Cosmic Order. The deteriorating conditions at the Martian base, the principal homeworld of the humanlike beings during that time, imparted urgency for such a genetic solution. The culmination of all past genetic work, on both the outer planet humanlike species and their recombinant DNA indigenous earthly 'cousins,' finally produced a success. The genetically engineered solution had proceeded at the usual deliberate and metered pace of the Ancient Ones, since the disappointing outcome of the earlier proto-Sapiens experiment. The seemingly abrupt appearance of Cro-Magnon on Earth was merely the methodical and long-awaited result.

Although this species was almost immediately tested with the introduction of the third cold maxima of the Würm glaciation that dominated the climate between 40,000 and 35,000 BC, the Cro-Magnons easily met the challenge successfully. To some degree, meteorites impacting Earth as a result of tidal forces occasional dislodging debris from the asteroid belt may have caused that cold spell. The Barringer Meteor Crater in Arizona, which occurred during this time frame, provides lasting evidence of those meteorite showers.

That catastrophic impact may have also precipitated the establishment of a permanent base on Earth for the Ancient Ones' Helpers, the assistants that were selected from the population of humanlike survivors on the moon base. They provided guidance for the Cro-Magnons, teaching them art, mining, and civilization. Such contact also introduced certain forms of early religious reverence, in which the Cro-Magnons venerated the Helpers as divine beings. The earthly guidance and assistance provided by the Ancient Ones' Helpers was apparently intended to benefit only the Cro-Magnons. That can be concluded from the demise of the last Neanderthals sometime between 30,000 and 26,000 BC, although remnants of the Neanderthal bloodline may have continued with a few offspring that resulted from interbreeding with certain Cro-Magnons. The outer planet humanlike beings on Mars equated such lack of concern for the Neanderthals as similar to the Ancient Ones' efforts to solve their environmental dilemma on Mars, even though that was not the case.

Many legends state that the Cro-Magnons had watchers or teachers who assisted them, but did not live with them. They were the 'Workers of Wonder,'[12] the Helpers who had a separate colony or home in a faraway land, usually on an island or a separate continent. Their homeland or sanctuary was known by various names, including Eden, E.din, Ta-Ur, or Atlantis. Such settlements were likely the bases of operation for the Ancient Ones and their loyal outer planet humanlike Helpers.

Those secluded bases provided sanctuaries from which genetic refinements conducted by the Ancient Ones could continue, while keeping those experimental specimens protected from the wild animals and savages of Earth, while remaining isolated so any failure would not be unleashed upon the planet. Those bases, such as the mysterious ancient fortresses found at many isolated sites, were the nucleus from which advanced cultures emerged, and may explain the numerous legends connecting civilization with Atlantis. The locations for those isolated bases of operation appeared to have changed periodically, perhaps relocating to new population centers to bring civilization to additional groups, as later migrations expanded.

It is believed that a few semi-permanent settlements or population centers existed prior to the Great Flood. The Cro-Magnons were known to have had encampments throughout Western Europe, often near cave complexes. Other geographic regions also display evidence of similar pre-flood civilizations. Chinese legends abound of a great ancient civilization in the Gobi Desert of East-Central Asia, the Land of Hsi Wang Mu (aka Hsia Hwang Mu),[3] a goddess of the ancient Chinese. That empire was reportedly centered along the border area of

Northern Tibet and the Gobi Desert, and was also referred to as the Land of the Immortals.[4]   This legendary land was mentioned by the great Chinese philosopher, Lao-tzu (aka Lao Tsu and Lao tse), in his book, the *Tao Te Ching* (aka *Tao Teh King*).[5]   Lao-tzu supposedly retired to this mystical land and was never heard from again.

That civilization was reportedly destroyed in a cataclysmic war, a trace of which perhaps still exists today. The surface of the Gobi Desert contains certain scattered areas of opaque glassy sand, indicating vitrification from intense heat.[6] Radiation traces have been found during geological tests, but are typically explained as the spontaneous combustion of naturally occurring radioactive elements. It is just as likely such traces are remnants from the legendary accounts of atomic warfare reported to have occurred many thousands of years ago, which left the area vegitationless and desolate even to this date.

The archaic South American race known as the Ancient Peruvians are thought to be responsible for another antediluvian civilization. Artifacts have been found from Tierra del Fuego to Peru that seem to group their remotely ancient cultures into three epochs. The first appeared for only a brief time around 34,000 BC, followed by a more long-term culture that flourished between 23,000 and 19,000 BC.[7] The final pre-flood culture formed by the enigmatic Ancient Peruvians, or a similar people, existed between 15,000 and 10,500 BC, the period that displayed the greatest number of artifacts. Those cultures were apparently associated with a now-sunken civilization that once existed on an island in Lake Titicaca that also established a mainland settlement at Tiahuanaco.[8] The world's oldest language is believed to be that of the Aymara Indians from the Tiahuanaco area. It has been utilized as a 'bridge language' through its transformation into computer algorithms that are then used to translate one language into another.[9]   Yet none of the ancient South American cultures were known to possess a written script, or to have kept written records.

The Ancient Peruvians created perhaps the oldest cultures in South America, and may have been the builders of Tiahuanaco, or assisted its builders, or merely occupied that complex sometime after its construction. They worked magnificent iron mines at Ancoriames, on the west shore of Lake Titicaca, even though no Iron Age ever existed there.[10] They were the ancestors of the proto-Quechua Indian tribes that originated in a small area of the southern highlands of Peru. The proto-Quechua are believed to have originally been a fair-skin race, with auburn hair and blue eyes.[11] Evidence indicates that they possessed large bodies with unusually large heads that exhibited regular facial features,[12] traits reminiscent of the equally mysterious race of ancient Egyptians known as the Shemsu-Hor.[13] The later and much younger Quechua culture was one of the most advanced in the Western World before European conquests. Their descendants became the main cultural element and racial component in the formation of the much later Inca Empire.

It is likely that the Ancient Peruvians also migrated into North America during very remote times. At Tule Springs in southern Nevada, evidence was found of man-made scraper tools and camp fires containing charred bones from extinct animals, indicating food cooking, all relative-dated to 26,000 BC.[14] On Santa Rosa Island, off the coast of Santa Barbara in southern California, numerous artifacts were found that radiocarbon date to various times from 28,000 to 13,000 BC.[15] Similar finds were also discovered in the exposed cliffs near San Diego, California, with artifacts dating to as early as the third interglacial period of the Pleistocene Ice Age around 25,000 BC.[16] Hence, New World migration seemingly could have originated from the south or the west, perhaps before 28,000 BC, rather than the orthodox belief in migration over a land bridge from Siberia sometime between 10,000 and 9500 BC.

A brief warm period then occurred around 25,500 BC,

which coincided with the highest peak of artistic achievement by Cro-Magnons during the Aurignacian period. An extended cold maxima, the fourth and last of the Würm ice cover, lingered from 21,500 to about 16,500 BC. Stratigraphic evidence also alludes to a large meteorite shower or possibly an asteroid strike, resulting in a pole shift around 21,500 BC,[17] perhaps initiating that 'cold peak.' Reglaciation then covered most of the Northern Hemisphere, evidently accounting for the regression in artistic levels during the Solutrean era. Such harsh conditions caused the Ancient Ones to shift their focus to more hospitable parts of Earth in the Southern Hemisphere. That resulted in the Ancient Ones concentrating their efforts on the Ancient Peruvians of the Andes Mountains, during their second cultural phase that occurred between 23,000 and 19,000 BC.

15,500 to *c.*10,500 BC:

This time frame represents the European Magdalenian period of Earth history. The compatibility of the genetically-tailored Cro-Magnons with Earth's environment continued to improve, which was also true for the outer planet humanlike survivors who benefited from the same genetic enhancements made to their earthly 'cousins.' By this time, the outer planet humanlike beings were also able to withstand much longer intervals on Earth, with their prolonged exposure requiring only occasional use of a respirator, depending on location and altitude. Use of such equipment is even depicted on numerous cliff and rock drawings. The Cro-Magnons were able to quickly adapt to most climates and environments of our planet, increasing their population numbers and spreading their culture accordingly. The European Cro-Magnons excelled in their artistic drawings, paintings, and sculptures during this Magdalenian period.

Other major settlements were located in Asia. Deep below the ruins of ancient Khara Khota in the Gobi Desert, near one of the areas of vitrified sand, Soviet Professor Kosloff (aka

Koslov) reportedly found a tomb that he dated to as old as 16,000 to 14,000 BC,[18] although others have dated the remains to 12,000 BC.[19] This burial chamber reportedly held a sarcophagus containing two men. Other details were not revealed, but such artifacts seem to indicate that some sort of culture or civilization existed in the Gobi prior to the universal flood. Artifacts of an ancient Stone Age culture have also been found throughout the desolate area high in the Altai Mountains along the western edge of Mongolia, and may represent a link with this mysterious culture. The headquarters of 'a race of dwarfs from space' that arrived during ancient times was reportedly traced to the Gobi Desert by researcher Charles Fort.[20] It is interesting to note that the Uigur language of the Gobi and Western Mongolia is totally unrelated to any other Earth language.[21]

That region's related Tibetan culture remains equally as mysterious, without knowing which is older. The area of the Tibetan high plateau surrounded by mountains ranging from the upper mouth of the Khuan-Khe River, down to the Kara-Korum hills lying within the central and eastern regions of Nan-Schayn and Altyne-taga, contains ancient settlements with some still remaining inaccessible for excavation.[22] The oasis of Tchertchen, located about 4,000 feet above the Tchertchen-D'arya River, is surrounded by ancient city ruins claimed to be the remnants from antediluvian cultures that were reportedly ruled by the 'great genii of the desert.'[23]

Advanced civilizations originating from Lake Titicaca and Tiahuanaco were apparently well established throughout the Andes Mountains by 15,000 BC, as were other semi-permanent early settlements that likely originated from that nucleus. As stated, prevailing belief suggests that the Ancient Peruvians extended from the Andean Plateau, through Mesoamerica, and into the United States all the way to the shores of the Great Lakes, the location of ancient copper mines.[24]

Hence, such migrating Ancient Peruvians may have also been the unknown builders of those earliest olden mounds found in the United States. Historians claim that such Mound Builders reflected the oldest culture found in North America. Those unidentified people built round and square-walled structures displaying perfect geometry, while other configurations formed conical or pyramid shapes, some covering vast areas. Typically, the mounds range from six to 70 feet in diameter, with most about eight feet high.[25] Such structures were not the result of a continuous building period, but occurred over interrupted intervals spanning long periods of time.[26]

Author Ignatius Donnelly believed that the much younger builders of the later mounds were associated with the archaic ancestors of the ancient Nahuatl natives.[27] But it is also generally believed that Native American Indians, particularly the tribe of Muskhogean descendants who eventually became known as the Natchez Indians, built those subsequent structures.[28] It is likely the younger mounds were constructed by Native Indians as an effort to copy or duplicate the much more ancient earthen mounds. Most of the younger 'copies' have been dated to a period after 800 AD. No Native Indian legend explains the earliest mounds, or takes credit for them. However, oral traditions of most Native American Indians clearly attributed the structures to a mysterious race of white gods, and the 'chosen white race people' that followed them.

Such structures were mainly concentrated throughout the Mississippi Valley, the Ohio Valley, and the Pacific Northwest. Some of the western mounds near the southern tip of Puget Sound, called Mima Mounds,[29] are scattered over hundreds of acres. The densest area houses about 10,000 mounds within a square mile. Those mounds were first mentioned by the 1841 United States Exploring Expedition, which was under the command of Charles Wilkes.[30] The mounds were found on the eroded plains of the Vashon Glacier that covered the area between 15,000 to 13,000 BC.[31]

Similar mounds are found in Russia, Mongolia, China and on the southwestern Pacific islands of New Caledonia and the

Isle of Pines.[32] Those island mounds were built from sand and gravel, averaging 300 feet in diameter, by eight to nine feet in height.[33] They differed from the American ones by the inclusion of cast pillars that protruded from those mounds. Those posts ranged from 40 to 75 inches in diameter, and stood from 40 to 100 inches tall. The cylinders were cast from a homogeneous, man-made, hard lime-mortar cement, which contained bits of shell, iron, and silica gravel fragments, all hardening within the mortar after being poured and cured. Various bits of shell aggregate have been radiocarbon dated from 10,950 to 5120 BC.[34]

While permanent settlements are associated with all the mounds, gaps of unoccupied periods are also evident. That tends to reflect different builders and cultures, possibly by later unrelated groups inhabiting previously built but later abandoned mound structures. Although considered to be burial mounds, no bones dating to the time of the original periods of construction were ever found. The few skeletal remains were known to have been buried by the later inhabitants that took over the edifices in more recent times.

The million year old western mountain culture reported in Chapter 14, best known for their jute basket burials, were speculated by some to have been the early ancestors of the Mound Builders.[35] Cultural similarities have been linked with Mound Builder settlements in Wisconsin, Illinois, and the Mississippi and Ohio River Valley regions.

Researcher Peter Kolosimo revealed accounts made by Serge Hutin, the French scholar and author, that described numerous other mysterious ruins scattered throughout California, Oregon, and Arizona, which evidently showed some association with the remnants found on the islands off the coast of Santa Barbara. Reportedly, those destroyed fortified structures were erected by a vanished race called the Chumash, whose culture possessed a highly scientific and technically advanced level of achievement.[36] Other reports state that a Native American Indian race much later adopted the Chumash name for their tribe.

Mr. Kolosimo further reported accounts describing curious ruins found within the desert southwest that had been explored by the adventurer William Walker. Those mysterious remains are scattered from the extreme southeastern corner of California where the Colorado and Gila Rivers converge, northward along the Colorado River basin.[37] The ruins reflect a high culture, and show traces of destruction from exceedingly powerful weapons, not from natural phenomena. The southernmost settlements were burned-out, leaving partially vitrified and fused stones that revealed distinct missile craters, ones reminiscent of mortar fire or aerial bombs. Similar areas of destruction continued along the Colorado River, approaching the Mojave Desert, where circular patches of sand are covered with an opaque, glasslike substance resembling the remnants of a nuclear explosion.[38]

The remains of a female were reportedly found off the coast of Santa Barbara, California, on the previously mentioned island of Santa Rosa. The fossils dated to between 11,000 and 10,000 BC, with studies revealing the woman was a member of the Caucasian race, or one that was very similar. Such discoveries affirm that a Caucasoid race predated other races in the United States, and seem to support the belief that the fair-skinned Ancient Peruvians migrated northward.

Evidence of a slightly older culture was discovered in the Big Horn Range of Wyoming on Medicine Mountain, where a 70 feet diameter circle of stones was found that displayed a 12 feet diameter center hub connected by 28 stone spokes.[39] That formation dated to c.12,000 BC, and was unlike any other found throughout the Great Plains area.[40] It was not one of the ancient Native American Indian 'Medicine Wheels' that served as celestial calendars, although it may have been a prototype from which they were copied. According to author Frank Edwards, later formations may have even had a Mayan influence.[41]

Additional settlements also existed throughout North Africa and the Near East along the Nile Delta. Geological analysis revealed that the Giza area was a fertile region with abundant rainfall between 15,000 and 10,500 BC, since the Sahara Desert did not yet exist during that period. Rather, that region was a green Savannah with lakes, forests, and abundant game animals, with a cooler and wetter climate than today. By 13,000 BC, Giza had permanent settlements focused around farming. That conclusion has been substantiated from excavated stone sickle blades and grinding-mill stones that dated to that time.[42] The region's large reduction of fish bone refuse further indicated a shift to plant food during that period.[43] That idyllic age of early-Egyptian culture continued without interruption until around 10,500 BC, when it was abruptly ended by the Great Flood. All such advanced early cultures had directly benefitted from the guidance and assistance provided by the Helpers of the Ancient Ones, who brought civilization to the Cro-Magnons. Perhaps the best known Helper of that era was the one named Osiris, who was made memorable through his numerous legendary Egyptian accounts.

During this time frame, further refinements were made on the genetically modified Cro-Magnons, leading to the latest version known as fully Modern man, emerging as the *Homo sapiens sapiens* about 11,600 BC. The most notable alteration or improvement over the Cro-Magnons was in the shape and structure of the mouth and jaw of this latest specimen.[44] Such changes allowed our species to form more difficult words and sounds, thus expanding our ability for more precise communication.[45] According to legends, *Homo sapiens sapiens* were developed at the isolated bases of the Ancient Ones, the sites generally known as the legendary Gardens of the Gods. The *Homo sapiens sapiens* reflected the Ancient Ones' success during that Golden Age of mankind, with harmony under the Cosmic Order becoming a reality for Earth.

Ancient records further support this approximate date for the creation of truly Modern man. Extrapolation of religious and astronomical cycles of the lunar calendar used by the Babylonians, as well as the solar calendar of the Egyptians, both converge to a common remote date determined to be 11,542 BC.[46] The Hindu calendar started with the year 11,652 BC, while the Mayans' last great cycle started around 11,653 BC, when extrapolated from the commencement of its current cycle in 3113 BC. Biblical chronology concerning the lineage of Adam reveals a time quite close to that same period. An approximate date of 12,150 BC is obtained by working back from Noah's age at the time of the Great Flood of c.10,500 BC, to the 'creation' of Adam, the first 'man.' Such ancient focus with the time period around c.11,600 BC seems to signify some common worldwide event of major importance, one that was recognized by numerous ancient cultures. That significant milestone was evidently the creation (or refinement) of truly Modern man.

A sparse population of such newly 'refined' modern humans prospered in their 'Garden of the Gods' paradise, separated from their earlier version of Cro-Magnon man, perhaps until their numbers increased and their ultimate compatibility was determined. They were sequestered at various sites including the 'closed' Egyptian cultures at Abydos, Giza, and Saqqara. Others were established at the now-lost Gobi Desert civilization; on the island fortresses of Malta and Gozo; at Tiahuanaco during the third cultural phase of the Ancient Peruvians; as well as on numerous sites known simply as Atlantis, a name that apparently applied to multiple island locations.

A final decision was made for a major integration of *Homo sapiens sapiens* around the world, until an impending global catastrophe was calculated to occur in the near future. Routine celestial monitoring conducted by the Ancient Ones had concluded that an unusual alignment of planets was imminent, and would create massive gravitational and tidal forces. That occurrence was determined to coincide with the approach of a massive comet or asteroid that would have a 'near-miss' trajectory without actually impacting Earth. The combination of those two events was determined to likely cause an impending and abrupt catastrophic devastation on Earth.

Such conditions were further exacerbated by the climatic situation that existed at that time on Earth. The less severe cold phase that had emerged between 16,000 and 15,000 BC during the later portion of the Würm glaciation had still caused wide spread reglaciation to occur over much of the Northern Hemisphere. That was followed by an extremely sudden and rapid interglacial warm period with aggressive thawing between 11,000 and 10,500 BC, perhaps caused by the unusual cosmic phenomenon. The result was a massive and devastating universal flood known from numerous ancient accounts as the Great Flood.

In preparation, knowing the magnitude of the impending event and its resulting potential conflagration, the Ancient Ones gathered a wide array of earthly genetic materials. That consisted of extracting DNA from a comprehensive and diverse selection of flora and fauna, including *Homo sapiens sapiens*. Just prior to the onset of the looming disaster, the Helpers also collected a number of select live specimens, which were taken onto the mothership of the Ancient Ones. Escaping Earth and the ominous flood, they returned to the base on Earth's moon. Apparently the Cro-Magnons, along with a number of other Earth species, were left unprotected from natures' impending wrath. Their ultimate fate was extinction, either during or shortly after the Great Flood of *c*.10,500 BC.

Chapter 16

Great Flood & Unexpected Results

The ensuing cataclysm would have had a major global impact as the result of such an unusual alignment of planets and the close approach of that large celestial body. Such conditions would have set up massive gravitational forces, causing a tilt or shift in Earth's axis and disrupting the magnetic field at its poles. The diurnal rotation of our planet would have been temporarily altered or changed, creating inertial and centrifugal forces allowing water to rotate out of the seas under its own momentum, with entire oceans believed to have emptied onto land. The unusually rapid melting of the ice cover, which had been underway during its current interglacial warm period, would have further exacerbated the deluge of water. The planet's atmospheric gasses would have also continued to move under inertial momentum, causing great hurricanes to sweep over oceans and continents. The resultant massive tidal waves would have easily carried numerous fish to land, and animals to the seas.

The gravitational forces associated with such a cataclysmic event may have even altered the Earth axis-tilt, further contributing to a magnetic pole shift. Such reversals of the North and South geomagnetic poles can be evidenced in rock formations, which results from a sudden disruption of the Earth's magnetic field that quickly reforms with an opposite polarity. A new polarity record is made each time iron-rich rocks are either liquefied or heated above their Curie point of 575 degrees Celsius, becoming non-magnetic. When later cooled below the Curie point, the rock acquires the magnetic state of its present environment, reflecting the polar field orientation existing at the time of its re-solidification. Many such pole shifts have occurred over time, with the last shift occurring sometime between 20,000 and 4000 BC, most likely around the *circa* 10,500 BC time period of the Great Flood.

Volcanic eruptions and earthquakes would have also occurred as tectonic plates convulsed, moving seas to land, and exposing dry ocean floors. Underwater research probes, which have revealed that much ocean floor sediment had been exposed to air and sunlight around 11,000 BC,[1] tend to confirm both the date and catastrophe. Since the Great Flood, it is believed that sea levels have risen about 300 feet as a result of the incessant torrential rains and huge sheets of land-based ice crashing into the oceans.[2] All the dust and gasses released from the ensuing volcanism, combined with smoke from the many accompanying massive forest fires, would have created a condition similar to 'nuclear winter,' blocking most sun light and its radiant heat. In time, evaporated water would have caused torrential rains that eventually changed to prodigious snowfalls. Mountains of snow would have then formed glaciers, ushering in a most sudden Ice Age, quick-freezing all life in its vicinity. Geological evidence confirms just such a scenario.

The Pleistocene Extinction of *c.*10,500 BC clearly reflects the result of the conflagration that ensued from the Great Flood, killing over 40 million animals.[3] Their bodies were crushed, torn apart, or drowned in water and mud; their mangled whole and partial carcasses mixed with trees, rocks, and other debris. Entire herd populations were exterminated *en masse* within minutes. Both indigenous and foreign animals were crammed together in caves, crevices, and numerous other inadequate sanctuaries. Such shelters only formed death pits for huge conglomerations of many different species of animals, all entwined with each other at their moment of demise. Marine creatures were transported to mountain heights in the Himalayas, Urals, Caucuses, and the Rockies. The brunt of such devastation appears to have occurred in Siberia and Alaska, especially throughout the Yukon Territory extending into Canada.

The extinction's suddenness can be evidenced from the preservation of whole bodies of animals, quick frozen within a thirty minute time frame as they stood eating, with the contents of their last meal still intact in their stomachs.[4] Permafrost conditions that prevail to this day are responsible for preserving those carcasses. Such quick destructive forces created huge Earth changes, evidenced by great worldwide climate alterations. It caused the extinction of mastodons, giant ground sloths, toxodons, woolly mammoths, saber-tooth tigers, and giant cave bears. Five million mammoths alone have been found along the coasts of Siberia and Alaska, although annihilation occurred everywhere. The greatest losses were in Canada, Alaska, Siberia, Europe, Florida, and throughout the Andes Mountains. While the bulk of the extinction occurred around 10,500 BC, such extermination appears to have started as early as 15,000 to 13,000 BC.

A most surprising contradiction followed the Great Flood and its mass extinction. Such massive destruction should have produced certain predictable results. Any survivors would first be faced with the immediate need for fresh drinking water and food. With the massive kill-off of wild game resulting from the Pleistocene Extinction, along with the complete destruction of all plant stocks, starvation would await any survivors. If life could overcome such immediate needs, it would then face devastating widespread epidemics of disease, resulting from the rotting dead and subsequent contaminated water. Typhus, cholera, or numerous other contagions would have proved fatal for most lingering life that was unfortunate enough to have survived the initial flood and the later starvation and thirst.

The Bible states that after the Great Flood, man's lifespan was reduced to 120 years, from its prior longevity of over 800 years. Such a shortened lifespan was further eroded during the Dark Ages, with longevity only now being reextended, due to modern medical treatments. Such a change in longevity might reflect genetic manipulation by the Ancient Ones, altering the human immune system to combat new strains of disease, which imparted improved resistance, but with the trade-off of some diminished longevity. The utilization of cloning to repopulate the planet may be another explanation. Recent scientific findings reveal startling surprises associated with the cloning process, which will be detailed later within this writing.

Instead of the expected disastrous effects to humankind, one of the greatest survival and revival aberrations occurred. Modern man, *Homo sapiens sapiens*, seemed to flourish as a result of the Great Flood, rather than being harmed by that event; coming back better, smarter, and stronger than before. Instead of starting over as if back in the most remote eons of time with primitive tools and nothing else, progress quickly ensued as civilization suddenly bounced back. Such a sudden and drastic cultural change can not be explained by conventional beliefs, but is easily recognized as intervention by the Ancient Ones in the *Elder Gods* theory.

Civilization is not an automatic result of being human, nor is it spontaneous. Unless taught, it does not seem to be apparent,[5] as exemplified by primitive tribes in New Guinea and the rain forests of the Amazon Jungle that still live in the uncivilized manner of prehistoric traditions. Explicit civilization also implies the teaching of behavioral traits, such as the discipline to live and interact peacefully with others within a group setting.[6] It further requires the modification of certain instinctive behaviors such as selfishness, inconsiderate acts, and the use of thievery as a survival tool. The ability to alter such behavioral traits allows individuals to live in a complex society, either within a tribe of a small region, or as a planetary species within a much larger community of the cosmic universe. Such behavioral changes occur only with intervention and active instruction. But orthodox beliefs can not identify the first benefactors, while the *Elder Gods* theory recognizes the Ancient Ones and their Helpers as those earliest teachers.

Civilizations do not simply burst on the scene and reach amazing heights without some preparation. They require a preliminary period in which to learn basic fundamentals, including mathematics, astronomy, physics principals, and building techniques. Perhaps the megalithic structures of remote antiquity best exemplify such a teaching enigma, where prior learning and development periods are not supported by any archaeological evidence. While archaeologists admit puzzlement with such a lack of prior trial and error corroboration, they avoid examination into the reasons for such an absence, fearing the answers may disrupt their conventional theories.

But quickly after the Great Flood, human and animal life, civilization, and noticeable progress seemed to occur overnight, a completely contradictory occurrence from what would be expected. The plow was invented and agriculture became the norm during the new PostGlacial Temperate Climate, which commenced around c.9000 BC. Domesticated herd animals were raised for food stock, and represented 95 percent of the meat those cultures were consuming by 8500 BC, as determined from bone and fossil evidence that dated to those times.[7] Hunting became a minor element in both the cultural and social structure of those communities. Both farming and livestock domestication requires a stationary or non-nomadic life style in order to tend flocks as well as plant, till, and harvest crops.[8]

Settlements quickly formed around the most fertile sites, creating the earliest known true cities and cultures. Not only was food no longer wild, but new grains such as corn and barley were introduced into those societies, a surprising occurrence considering the devastating flood effects. The very fact that human culture emerged is equally inexplicable. Culture is defined as the product or growth resulting from a group of people joined as a common society. The addition of culture to a species' society is what defines or establishes its unique civilization. Professor William Howells, noted historian and author of *Back of History*, stated that culture is what it takes to be human.[9] He further describes culture as the behavior that overlies, alters, and adds to existing patterns of activities and is unique from one society to another, but may influence other groups. Such behavior is not biological in origin, being neither inbred nor inborn.[10]

Rather, it is embraced, copied, or passed down from one generation to the next, with each succeeding generation modifying or customizing that behavior into their present culture. Culture becomes the sum total of knowledge and behavioral patterns taught by the preceding generation, and learned by their descendants, similar to animals reacting instinctively to a stimulus based on their prior experiences and conditioning. The very presence of culture on our planet, let alone its abrupt emergence after a global catastrophe, implies its existence as having been bestowed upon humankind as a gift from influences beyond Earth, apparently from the Ancient Ones. A brief examination of a few early settlements will reveal the existence of surprisingly advanced archaic cultures, substantiating outside intervention as the likely source for such progress.

One of the oldest permanent villages was established at Tell Mureybut, a site about 50 miles southeast of modern day Aleppo, Syria. That small but solidly built and fortified community dates to *c.*9000 BC. Its houses were built using wood framing that was filled-in with clay, then finished with a solid adobe shell exterior. Extant artifacts dated at 8000 BC indicated worship of the Mother Goddess cult at that time. The original culture apparently abandoned the site around 7500 BC after almost 1,500 years of continuous use, although numerous later cultures occupied that deserted village, inhabiting it at different times over the ensuing ages.

Jericho is another early city, located at Tell es Sultan in Israel/Palestine, dating to 8000 BC. This was not the Biblical

Jericho, but a vastly older one, with numerous later constructions that were built over prior ruins at the site, until the Biblical city of Jericho was built over roughly the same location some 6,000 years later. The original city was an oasis in a valley at the northern end of the Dead Sea. It grew quickly into a crowded trading center covering almost eight acres, housing about 3,000 inhabitants. A twenty feet high wall of stones, precisely cut and fitted without mortar, and a thirty feet by ten feet deep moat encircled the city. The complex also had public buildings including a community temple, indicating that some sort of central government existed. Private homes were constructed using brick, and featured clay ovens with chimneys.

The city was populated mainly with peasants laboring as sharecroppers or serfs, although they practiced modern crop rotation techniques. The original settlers' appearance might be revealed from their art, which included a few human skulls that had their features restored using clay, with shells used as eyes, creating an Egyptian-like appearance.[11] The culture of the original site continuously expanded over a period of about a thousand years, until it was abruptly abandoned or destroyed. The ruined site then remained unoccupied for about 700 years, until it was rebuilt and re-inhabited around 6250 BC.

Yet another settlement was the ancient city of Catal Hüyük in the south-central region of Anatolia, the modern day nation of Turkey. Catal Hüyük formed as early as 7400 BC, high in the center of a fertile agricultural plain along the edge of the Carsamba Cay River, at an altitude of 3,000 feet, about 185 miles south of modern day Ankara, Turkey. It became a major settlement by 6500 BC, and a prominent city in 6250 BC. By 6000 BC, it also became a significant trading center. All construction strictly adhered to an efficient but conservative urban layout, without a fortress wall surrounding the city for protection. However, the houses were all attached along one exterior wall without an external entrance, with those exposed solid walls essentially acting as a continuous fortress or barrier enclosing that city.

Entry to each individual but attached home was made through a roof opening. Travel around the city or to other houses occurred via the flat terrace rooftops, with ladders connecting the various differing roof heights. Carpet found in the ruins was of such high quality it compared with the most expensive and durable products woven today.[12] The number of inhabitants varied between 6,000 to 10,000 people, and comprised mostly peasants who labored as sharecroppers or serfs, with wheat and barley its main crops. The city also had public buildings, sanctuaries, and shrines where both the Mother Goddess and the Bull god cults were worshiped, a fact confirmed by statues and wall paintings. The double ax symbol was also found in Catal Hüyük, which is associated with certain earlier Cro-Magnon cultures and ancient Crete. Its culture featured durable pottery and woven fabrics including wool, all of which exhibited high artistic levels. In 5400 BC, the city was suddenly abandoned for some still-unknown reason.

The ancient settlement of Jarmo dates to 6800 BC, a village located along a drainage basin of the Tigris River in the Kurdish foothills near the northeastern borders of Iraq and Iran. It was a Neolithic farming community that apparently had little contact with other cultures, due to its rather isolated location. The site's multi-room houses were constructed using dried mudbrick built upon stone foundations, which were then equipped with ovens and a sunken-floor 'basin' that was used as a fire pit.

An olden settlement at Tell es Sawwan, an area about 70 miles northwest of modern day Baghdad, has been dated to 6000 BC. This relatively small city possessed a very advanced culture for its time, especially for one without advantages of a written script. It was an agricultural-based society, evidenced by its grain silos and designated areas for livestock grazing. Their culture possessed pottery, weaving, highly refined art featuring carved alabaster statuettes, and metallurgical expertise, as evidenced by their copper knife and bead artifacts. The people worshiped the Mother Goddess and buried their dead in tombs. Their culture exhibited many similarities with Catal Hüyük, and may have been one of its outposts or colonies. The original culture abandoned the city around 5000 BC, with their reason still remaining unknown.

A slightly later settlement was found in Europe, rather than in the conventional 'cradle of civilization' in the Near East. At Lepenski Vir, Yugoslavia, a little village was located in the Iron Gate gorge between the Carpathian and Balkan Mountains, at a small but protected valley forest near the Danube River. The village is dated to around 5450 BC, and had between 200 and 300 inhabitants that lived in a group or commune fashion, all interdependent upon one another. They were fishermen and hunters, living in an Old Stone Age tradition. Their detached houses were all identical in size and layout, and were not much more than tent structures with a central fireplace and altar, although author Charles Berlitz claims the houses had poured cement foundations with indirect central heating.[13] Such houses were precisely arranged in a prescribed pattern of mathematical proportions around an equally patterned grid system of streets. There were four larger structures that may have been public gathering places or temples. The people apparently worshiped a Water or Fish god, the first evidence of such a deity, and a divergence from the long-held Mother Goddess veneration previously seen elsewhere.

A subsequent settlement, Khirokitia, was found on the Mediterranean island of Cyprus. That community was constructed during the height of the Neolithic period, around 5200 BC. It contained about a thousand houses that were very similar to the earliest phase of Jericho. Those beehive-shaped structures were built using dried mudbrick, with openings and doors framed with wood. The houses featured below-grade sunken floors with a central hearth made from clay. Some homes were built with multiple rooms including kitchens, while others featured detached workshops located in a compound area around the main house. The paved streets of the city were elevated above the level of the houses, with stone ramps leading down to each dwelling. Although such a semi-subterranean layout provided privacy from the public street, it appears to be an unusual arrangement for such an orderly culture, since it would have left those residential homes quite vulnerable to flooding.

Returning to the Near East, the next major city was Tell Halaf, a settlement southwest of Lake Van near the northern Syrian-Iraq border. It formed about 5000 BC, in the territory that later became known as the Land of Hurri (the land of the Hurrian people). This culture flourished along the Northern Tigris and Habur Rivers, with its people serving as the nucleus for several other regional sites as they migrated from Tell Halaf. The inhabitants worshiped the Bull cult and also revered the double ax symbol. They conducted farming and herding duties, and also produced fine polychrome pottery.

The next prehistoric city (defined as without written records) to be established was Eridu, which emerged around 4900 BC on the huge mudflats and shallow lakes of the Euphrates Delta at the head of the Persian Gulf. This marshland was not habitable before 4900 BC, until the sea level had finally receded around that time. The first inhabitants were an advanced group of ethnically mixed people, with some arriving from the northern Caucasus Mountains, while others were believed to have migrated from the Persian Gulf in the south. This mixed group developed their own unique culture now known as Ubaid, named after one of their later settlements in the region that was called al'Ubaid.

Eridu's numerous private houses were built using sun-dried adobe brick, while its city government provided public buildings for meetings and worship. The Fish or Water god later became an object of worship, seen only once before at Lepenski Vir. Such worship was performed at a raised shrine built from wood, the first known elevated altar used by any culture. Farming was accomplished by constructing irrigation canals to reclaim land from the swamp and marsh areas. The settlement's greatest innovation may have been its spread of the Ubaid culture to other regions. That culture expanded to form other separate cities within surrounding areas, namely al'Ubaid, Urartu, Ararat, and Aratta; all forming the first city-states of Mesopotamia.

This brief review of a few extant olden cities is in no way a comprehensive or definitive description of such ancient settlements. Many scholarly works have been written further documenting these and other remarkable ancient sites, for those desiring more details. Rather, such descriptions were intended to demonstrate that prehistoric societies of numerous early human cultures were not necessarily primitive or savage, with many being highly evolved. Still other advanced enigmatic sites may yet be uncovered, adding to the ever-increasing evidence that suggests outside intervention with Earth's early development. This review further provides the necessary historic background from which to continue presentation of the *Elder Gods* theory.

Chapter 17

Post Diluvial Earth

Development of the *Elder Gods* theory resumes, with continuation of the previous chronological format, commencing shortly after the massive and devastating effects from the Great Flood event became apparent.

*c.*10,500 to 7000 BC:

Earth had been selectively evacuated, primarily to the moon base, with the approach of the ominous conditions that combined to cause the Great Flood. With the ensuing global demise of most life on Earth, our planet was once again facing the likelihood of an indigenous species vacuum. Without a planetary heir apparent, the outer planet humanlike beings, who were now sufficiently compatible with Earth's environment, petitioned for permanent habitation of our devastated world. For unknown reasons, the Ancient Ones denied their request, igniting the long-simmering animosity that the outer planet humanlike survivors on Mars had been harboring toward the genetically engineered *Homo sapiens* and the Ancient Ones.

The outer planet humanlike beings wanted greater freedom, with faster progress toward a replacement high civilization, and resented the imposed restrictions mandated by the Ancient Ones and the Cosmic Order. Not all outer planet humanlike survivors felt that same bitterness and impatience with the perceived slow reconstruction of their civilization. Those humanlike Helpers assisting the Ancient Ones, along with the descendants of the outer planet humanlike survivors living on the lunar base, were all supportive. But a majority of their brethren on the Martian base finally rebelled, breaking away from the Ancient Ones and most of the basic beliefs and concepts of the Cosmic Order, especially its restrictions.

The Cosmic Order strictly prohibited any forced retention within its membership. Only the forceful prevention of self-destructive acts that would threaten other worlds was ever allowed. Therefore, every outer planet humanlike inhabitant was allowed to choose either separation from the Ancient Ones, remaining with their like-minded brethren on the Martian base; or departure with the Ancient Ones, becoming permanent exiles from their present homeworld. After making their individual decisions, the split populace effectively created two distinct 'groups' of humanlike beings.

Ancient records seem to allude to just such a split. The Babylonian *Enuma elish* states that the Primordial Parents, Tiamat and Apsu, bore offspring who later destroyed them. This narrative, an allegory of the Near Eastern god Marduk splitting Tiamat into two parts, stated that a new world was created from the destroyed body of the parent.[1] The Hindu god Indra's deed of killing Vritra, the serpent-demon son of the goddess Danu (who was Tiamat's equivalent), was a similar separation-account contained in the *Rig Veda*.[2]

The *Urantia Book* revealed a discontent or dissatisfaction with the regimented universe administration dictates of the Joint Council,[3] the celestial planetary governance or guidance committee overseeing the universe.[4] A resultant split occurred due to a desire for greater freedom of choice and self-government, which also meant exclusion or isolation from that Joint Council administrative bureaucracy.[5] Such accounts resemble the separation of the outer planet humanlike beings from their caretaker, the Ancient Ones, an act that created a new splinter group from its original source.

As a result of this separation, the Ancient Ones relocated all 'loyal' outer planet humanlike inhabitants, those who chose not to break from their alliance with the Cosmic Order, to the base on Earth's moon. The breakaway outer planet humanlike dissidents were given full control over their sovereign world, their base on Mars. That included all the technology left by the Ancient Ones to run the technical aspects of their planet, and its implements of defense and commerce. They became a sovereign world, completely free and independent from the influence of the Ancient Ones forever. To differentiate this group from their genetically identical loyal followers who stayed with the Ancient Ones, those that relocated to the moon base; this text will refer to the rebels as the Breakaway Outer Planet Humanlike beings, the *BOPH* beings. The group living on the moon base will be referred to as the *Lunar Pitris*, Earth's ancient patriarchs,[6] as they were known in ancient Sanskrit texts. Both Pythagoras and Plato acknowledged those beings, with the great philosopher, Plato, referring to these 'ancestors' from the moon as the 'lunes populi.'[7]

The Ancient Ones avoided the Martian base, although they continued to monitor its developments, but without any direct intervention. On Mars, the BOPH survivors faced the prospect of fending for themselves without the assistance of the Ancient Ones. The BOPH beings had hoped to progress quickly on their own, leading to space vehicles capable of traveling to Earth to independently colonize the planet after the flood, before the Ancient Ones returned with their 'salvaged seeds' to repopulate the planet with the *Homo sapiens sapiens*. But their separation involved much greater adjustments and learning periods than anticipated; just to comprehend and utilize the technology left by the Ancient Ones.

Although they retained and used those devices left by the Ancient Ones, they did not fully understand the theory or science behind them. Hence, their use was somewhat limited. As those devices required repair, they became unserviceable to the BOPH inhabitants, and were eventually discarded or abandoned, with such technology lost to their subsequent generations. Eventually, some of the lost implements were ultimately reinvented, but at rudimentary and crude levels from their originals. Their earlier goal of reaching Earth prior to the return of the Ancient Ones failed. As flood waters receded between 9600 and 9200 BC and Earth approached habitable conditions once again, the Ancient Ones returned with some of their loyal Helpers, along with the descendants of the pre-flood *Homo sapiens sapiens*.

The prior flora and fauna preserved through DNA specimens was once again reintroduced to Earth, perhaps utilizing cloning methods. Indications in ancient texts suggest cloning was the procedure used, as implied in the Akkadian version of *The Epic of Gilgamesh*. In that narrative, the god Ea orders Utnapishtim, the 'Noah' hero of that account, to build a ship.[8] Ea then commands: "Aboard the ship take thou the seed of all living things."[9] Well over one thousand years later, that similar statement was recorded in Genesis 6:19-20. Note the original use of the term *seed*, rather than living creatures, indicating the 'essence' of such creatures, not the animated species itself. Realistically, if such an extensive salvage and preservation effort was actually conducted, it would have likely involved the use of DNA materials only, considering the vast space requirements necessary to store nearly all earthly lifeforms.

A small number of antediluvian *Homo sapiens sapiens*, along with perhaps even a few Cro-Magnons, would have likely escaped to the high mountainous regions of Earth, thereby surviving the Great Flood. Their descendants were the few wild primitive humans that inhabited the planet at the time of the Ancient Ones' return. With Earth's reclamation and repopulating efforts well underway, new settlements were established, such as those at Mureybut, Jericho, and Catal Hüyük. Once those settlements were established and a plan implemented for educating and civilizing humankind, the Ancient Ones once again departed, leaving their devoted outer planet humanlike Helpers to educate and watch over Earth's fledgling inhabitants.

It is possible that monuments would also have been constructed, to memorialize and record the occurrence of the Great Flood. Perhaps the unique stellar alignment that best immortalized that fateful date was determined to be the 'belt stars' of the Constellation Orion. The lowest 'altitude' of those stars during their processional cycle, in conjunction with their path through the Milky Way Galaxy, also depicted the exact course of the Nile Valley as it crossed the meridian at the same time of that momentous event. At least that is the theory postulated by the Belgian engineer, Robert Bauval.[10] That specific celestial formation date was determined to be 10,450 BC[11] by Mr. Bauval in his book *The Orion Mystery*, which he co-authored with Adrian Gilbert. Such an arrangement was supposedly then duplicated on Earth, in the physical arrangement of the three great Giza pyramids of Egypt, perhaps as a 'celestial date-stamp' of the Great Flood event. Several lower stone courses of the center pyramid had possibly been started prior to the Great Flood, and served as an inception point from which to duplicate such an arrangement on the ground.[12]

Back at the Martian base, the BOPH beings finally obtained their goal of space travel, albeit much later than desired. Their early success was reminiscent of Earth's own Mercury era 'space capsule' program, with limited travel capabilities. A more advanced version of such a craft would be utilized centuries later, for an emergency escape flight to Earth in the 6th millennium BC, which will be revealed in that era's discussion.

7000 to 6000 BC:

The breakaway from the Ancient Ones did not have the outcome desired by the BOPH beings. Their lingering dissatisfaction with their leaders, along with the lack of progress toward any real correction of the continually deteriorating living conditions on the Martian base had spread throughout the populace. Conflicts erupted, with some desiring to rejoin the splinter group, the Lunar Pitris, on their moon base. At that time, the BOPH ruler on Mars was only temporarily successful in appeasing both sides. The malcontents were first segregated from society, but as their numbers grew, the dissension and dissatisfaction erupted into open rebellion.

Eventually, as their space travel technology permitted, the group wanting to realign with the Ancient Ones fled to the lunar base in crude one-way ships, reuniting with the descendants of those that previously chose to remain loyal to the Ancient Ones at the time of the original schism. Meanwhile on Earth, the human population continued their steady progress under the oversight of the Ancient Ones and their Lunar Pitris Helpers. Established cities grew into major commercial and trade complexes, while new settlements were being continually established, such as the one at Jarmo during this time frame.

6000 to 5000 BC:

Some of the best remaining BOPH scientists were among those refugees that fled to the base on Earth's moon. That caused major concern that solutions to the environmental problems on Mars would never occur, further exacerbating the discontent harbored by the continually decreasing number of BOPH beings on Mars. It was further recognized that the BOPH beings' desire to occupy Earth would likely prompt a substantial conflict with its human population, which would be assisted by their Lunar Pitris Helpers. Moreover, the BOPH beings' space technology was not yet sufficiently advanced to reach Earth, engage in battle if resistance was encountered, and still have the ability to escape Earth's much greater gravity for return to their Martian homebase if necessary. However, similar concerns with an attack on the moon base of the Lunar Pitris did not exist. The BOPH leadership ultimately carried out a retaliatory attack upon the moon base, a target achievable within their technological capabilities, where they could do battle and still escape the weak gravity of the moon.

A brief war ensued, resulting in the annihilation of all the Lunar Pitris on the moon base who had remained loyal to the Ancient Ones. Dating of that event is difficult due to its occurrence on another world, as well as the obscure and detached nature of the account. It may have even occurred during a slightly earlier time period, perhaps as early as 8000 BC. That attack would later become known as the 'War of the Olden Gods,' and was perhaps the cause of the bombing pattern craters found on the moon. Further confirmation of such an attack may be indicated by the core samples secured during the Apollo 12 moon mission. According to Dr. Immanuel Velikovsky, those core samples showed anomalies resulting from thermal disturbances, and also displayed an increased level of radioactivity, suggestive of possible nuclear explosions as the source for such thermal abnormalities and radiation traces.[13]

Life support equipment left for use on the moon, along with other 'new' technology supplied by the Ancient Ones since the original schism, were plundered and taken back to the Martian base. However, subsequent reaction to the attack by the BOPH populace on Mars was negative. It was viewed as wasting limited vital resources and efforts on warfare, rather than on actual improvements to solve the home base problems. Also, technical devices seized in the war did not supply the environmental improvements sought by the rebel force. As a result, that BOPH ruler was then displaced by a peaceful, but ineffective leader. After his nine year reign,[14] another warlike ruler overthrew that king. It is unclear if that nine year period referred to Earth years or Martian years, which would have equated to about 17 Earth years. The new ruler, who was later identified as Anu,[15] believed that the only future left for the BOPH beings was one that would be found on Earth, since Mars was a dying planet beyond salvage.

187

The dethroned ruler and his immediate family escaped the ensuing turmoil, and sought refuge by fleeing to Earth some time around 5450 BC. That otherworldly visitor is later identified in several mythological accounts as Alalu, known from the Kumarbi myth commonly called *The Story of Alalu, Anu, and Kumarbi*, an account contained in both Hurrian and Hittite mythology.[16] Such narratives seem to serve as the starting point and very essence of the superb and fascinating Earth Chronicles book series researched and authored by Zecharia Sitchin.

The likely mode of travel for Alalu's escape was an archaic one-way rocket and space capsule, which the royal family had hidden away in a remote location populated with loyal supporters. That escape vessel later became known on Earth as the *Benben*. It became a sacred enigmatic object of worship in ancient Egypt,[17] the site where it landed. It resembled a conical-shaped projectile, sitting on top of a pillar-shaped base. Supposedly the Benben 'fell from the sky in ancient times,'[18] with legends claiming it was the upper part of the 'Celestial Barge' that came to Earth from the 'Planet of Millions of Years.'[19] The Benben's similarity with the early Mercury capsule sitting at the top of a Saturn rocket is readily apparent, and also represented an immense back step in technology from the Ancient Ones' far superior intergalactic craft used to reach our solar system. The original Benben shrine was built in Heliopolis (aka Innu and On), the City of the Sun, the modern day Cairo suburb of Al Matareya. Later, the pyramidal capstone placed at the top of pyramids also came to be known as the Benben.[20]

Alalu evidently did not remain in Egypt, most likely because of its low altitude location and excessive heat, with such conditions being 'foreign' to a prior inhabitant of Mars. Evidence suggests that Alalu and his family first relocated to Europe in an isolated area, and formed the primitive settlement at Lepenski Vir in the mountains of Yugoslavia. Perhaps such a secluded site was desired to hide from any pursuing BOPH authority, or to maintain a low profile with the Ancient Ones and their Helpers. A final move was made by Alalu approximately 50 years later, settling his family in the cool mountains around Lake Van, the ancestral home of the Hurrians and other advanced Caucasoid people of the region, perhaps at Tell Halif. Such movements and relocation paths are extrapolated from circumstantial evidence and excerpts from ancient myths.

One translation of the name 'Alalu' is 'man who oversees the waters,' connecting him with the first appearance of a Water or Fish god, with its initial emergence at Lepenski Vir, a most enigmatic site that mixed advanced attributes with primitive methods. Such a unique Water and Fish god then appeared at Tell Halif near Lake Van, a region that helped populate the mixed group that comprised the Ubaid culture of Eridu where Alalu was once again mentioned, an occurrence that will be discussed in the next chronological segment.

Efforts by the BOPH beings to develop more advanced space technology eventually allowed them to construct ships capable of reaching Earth sometime between 5300 and 5200 BC. That accomplishment accounts for the existence of both the Ancient Ones' vastly advanced, superior technology during the earliest primordial times of Earth, only to be followed by the 20th and 21st century technology of the BOPH beings during later 'ancient' times; a notable regression in technological abilities. However, both distinct levels of technology were apparently later lost to subsequent human generations, with limited rediscovery and reinvention only millennia later during our own 20th and 21st centuries.

A very small scout party had initially arrived by 5200 BC, lead by a person later identified as Enki from various myths. Their purpose was to evaluate the reaction of the Helpers to the arrival of BOPH visitors, and to also establish a small colony on Earth. Contrary to other popular assertions, the *Elder Gods* theory contends that although Enki landed near the head of the Persian Gulf, he did not immediately settle at Eridu. He initially established a base on the island of Dilmun, the 'Land of the Gods,' which is now known in modern times as the Persian Gulf island of Bahrain.

At the time of Enki's arrival, the Ancient Ones were not on Earth. Their usual procedure was to transfer the implementation of subsequent phases of civilization to their Helpers, once an appropriate plan had been established for each individual emerging planet. The Ancient Ones would then depart for other worlds, where similar efforts were implemented, with routine reviews of their prior contacted planets made periodically.

Since Enki and his small crew posed no immediate threat to the Ancient Ones' Helpers, no concerns were raised. The Helpers did not contact the Ancient Ones to request their return, but decided instead to closely observe and further evaluate the BOPH visitors' activities. After establishing his base in Dilmun, Enki quickly achieved an assembly of willing human followers under his tutelage, forming the nucleus of what would later become an empire. That base eventually sent its 'graduate' humans to migrate and mingle with settlements that had been established by the Helpers of the Ancient Ones. The intent was to spread discontent with the slow and restrictive progress allowed under the Cosmic Order policy, eventually converting those humans to the BOPH colonists' quick and unregulated growth option.

Chapter 18

Infiltration of Earth

Earthly humanity had become relatively self-reliant, progressing at a slow and measured pace. But that condition allowed humans to be tempted into 'shortcuts' by outside influences.

5000 to 3000 BC:

Enki apparently maintained a reasonably low profile at his Dilmun base and thus caused no immediate problems, so the presence of his scout party invoked no negative reaction from the Helpers. Around 5000 BC, Earth's Stone Age cultures were changing to a transitional one of copper and clay implements. Groundwork was being laid for the Lunar Pitris Helpers to initiate new settlements around Mesopotamia, where a modernized civilization could emerge and spread throughout the region.

As previously revealed, the humanlike Helpers established one of their main settlements at Eridu around 4900 BC. It was built on the valley marshes and mud flats of the Euphrates Delta at the head of the Persian Gulf after sea levels had receded and the region was enjoying a warm climate. Although essentially a swamp, it was also fertile, well watered, and quite suitable for irrigation, which made it ideal for farming.

It started as a small settlement in order to civilize and indoctrinate humans to the concepts of the Cosmic Order and its slow and regulated growth policy. The site progressed steadily, while also being augmented with imparted advancements and knowledge as its populace grew in enlightenment. On a limited basis, new immigrants were allowed to join the community, creating an ethnically mixed culture. Growth came from nomads and migrants from the various surrounding desert regions, providing steady growth. Such arriving groups brought their mature cultures with them, which became blended within the greater community. Together, those tribes comprised the Ubaidian people, forming the advanced and distinct Ubaid culture that spread to other early cities such as Urartu and Aratta, forming the nucleus for the first city-states of Mesopotamia.

One migrating group came from the northern Caucasus Mountains, combining with nomads from the north of Iraq and the highlands of Iran. A portion of that group traveled through the Lake Van area, while another band initially traveled farther west, evidently occupying the Tell Halaf settlement before finally moving into Eridu. Such migration may have even included some humans that had been influenced by Alalu at his mountain retreat near Lake Van.

This text previously revealed that sometime before 4000 BC, the Ubaid culture was the first to build a raised platform altar for worship, as if to imitate its location on a mountain. The earliest deity to be worshiped at that altar was a Water or Fish god.[1] However, that god was not Enki,[2] but more likely Alalu. Ancient 'royalty tablets' recovered from Eridu's early Ubaid period acknowledged the institution of Kingship, noting it was 'first lowered from heaven in Eridu,' and mentioned Alalu as the first king.[3] Another 'water or fish' connection can be detected from the writings of Berosus, the Babylonian historian who wrote extensively of Oannes, the "being endowed with reason,"[4] who appeared in the first year of the descent of kingship from heaven. Accounts contend he appeared from the Erythrean Sea (Arabian Sea) and brought agriculture and civilization to Mesopotamia from the Arabian Gulf.

Oannes was described as having a human head under his fish head, and human feet under his fish tail; a reasonable description by a primitive culture of a man in scuba gear, a deep-sea diving suit, or perhaps even a helmeted space suit. Or the legend may simply be an accurate description of an amphibious being. Oannes, the "Fishman of Nineveh," was also called Oan, Uan, or Ichthys in other accounts.[5] Most likely, such records are a distortion, combining numerous different beings into a single creature. Perhaps Alalu became a confused recollection known as Oannes by the much later Berosus. That early deity may have ultimately inspired the later Water god cult led by Enki, who was known as Ea by the Akkadians.

The Ubaid culture of Eridu prospered, introducing many cultural 'firsts.' They invented the pottery wheel, making earthenware articles from distinctive greenish-yellow clay, which they then decorated with geometric designs using dark-brown paint. The earliest known sailing ships also originated at Eridu. The city possessed the first known designated cemeteries, which were located at the outskirts of town. Most prior cultures had buried their dead beneath their houses, rather than at some formal designated area.

The earliest levels of the great city-states of Ur and Uruk are from the Ubaid period, and most likely include the Royal Cemetery (Tombs) of Ur, which Sir Leonard Woolley dated between 3500 and 3200 BC. Progress was neither rapid nor linear, with setbacks due to natural catastrophes, such as a regional but major flood around 4000 BC.

During the same time period, space technology had further advanced on Mars, allowing an additional small contingent of BOPH colonists to be sent to our planet. They stationed their mother ship in orbit around Earth as a space station, establishing a more permanent presence. That occurrence is recorded in the *Enuma elish*, which stated that 300 gods, the Igigi, were stationed in the heavens as guards.[6] Apparently, they were sentinels watching for the expected return of the

Ancient Ones, so the BOPH colonists could be quickly alerted.

Additional BOPH colonists continued to arrive on Earth during this time period, maintaining a low profile so as not to provoke any negative reaction. Their increased presence slowly allowed implementation of their plan to create dissension among humans, thus alienating them from the Ancient Ones, allowing the BOPH colonists to exploit the planet. At their Dilmun base, the BOPH colonists taught and trained humans more advanced knowledge, at levels beyond those that the Lunar Pitris Helpers were allowed to impart to humans under their influence. Around 3700 BC, Earth culture was undergoing a transition from the Copper and Clay Era to the Bronze Age, which may have been an introduction by the BOPH colonists. However, the metal did not become widely used until about 3200 BC, primarily around Mesopotamia, when that new alloy was used extensively to produce weapons of war.

Dilmun, the land also known in ancient texts as Kur.bala, Niduk.ki, and Tilmun,[7] eventually expanded to form the Dilmun Empire, which extended along the extremes of the Persian Gulf from Bahrain to the island of Failaka, which lies in the center of Kuwait Bay. There, the BOPH colonists established themselves as regional supreme rulers over their select human followers by means of their superior technology, while schooling them in advanced sciences, mathematics, and the written script now known as cuneiform.

Ancient records refer to a period between *c*.3800 and about 3150 BC as 'chaotic,' a condition possibly caused by the ever growing friction between the Ancient Ones' Helpers and the ever expanding influence of the BOPH colonists and the humans under their influence. By 3600 BC, the BOPH colonists had commenced their formal relocation of small groups of humans from their Dilmun Empire into established human cultures previously formed solely by the Helpers of the Ancient Ones. The first settlements to receive a few of those troublesome immigrants were the thriving Egyptian cultures

194

along the Nile Delta under the control of the humanlike Helpers of the Ancient Ones, who were then known as the Shemsu-Hor. Such infiltration into a previously model Cosmic Order settlement was likely the reason for the 'chaos' cited during this period.

The Shemsu-Hor, meaning the 'Followers of Horus,' were described in ancient texts as the mortal helpers and emissaries of the god Horus. According to Professor Walter Emery, the Shemsu-Hor formed a 'master race' or aristocracy that dominated all other cultures of Egypt during their reign. Such dominance was also due to their physical appearance, which comprised extremely large bodies with larger skulls that could not have developed from any contemporary people of the area. Their remains have been found in the northern part of Upper Egypt in graves dated to as late as $c.3150$ BC, when any further trace of this race and their culture also ended.

The Shemsu-Hor settled in Edfu (modern Idfu), the capital of Horus in Upper Egypt, and also in Tanis (the Biblical Zoar), the cult center of Horus in Lower Egypt. At various sites along the Nile, they introduced the next level of civilization during Egypt's pre-dynastic period, which may have started as early as 3800 BC. Professor Emery concluded that shortly after the arrival of the Shemsu-Hor, the high culture of ancient Egypt seemed to suddenly spring into existence from its prior Neolithic state without any transitional period, with most of its advancements occurring between 3500 and 3200 BC.[8]

Just after 3400 BC, another group of 'advanced' humans from Dilmun migrated to Eridu, a distance of over 400 miles, and later became known as the Sumerians. That event is known from archaeological evidence found on Bahrain Island that reflected the same later phase of the Ubaid culture, linking the two sites. The mixed Ubaidian culture at Eridu openly accepted the Sumerian immigrants, giving the BOPH colonists a foothold into another of the Helpers' model settlements.

The Sumerians were a dark-haired people, referred to as the 'Blackheaded Ones,' who were of unique ethnic origin, bearing no racial resemblance to any other Indo-European racial group in Mesopotamia, and thus were unique as the Sumerian people. They spoke a language unrelated to any other known Earth language, one so different that a British Museum brochure stated: "Sumerian...is an unclassified language which has so far resisted all attempts to relate it to any known living or dead language."[9] Their uniqueness may have been the result of interbreeding, as descendants from a parental mix of BOPH colonists and the humans under their influence.

The Sumerians brought their superior and mature culture with them, intermarried with the indigenous Ubaidian farmers, and quickly influenced the culture. More immigrants were sent from Dilmun over the decades, dominating Eridu. By 3350 BC, Eridu became a Sumerian city, with the region becoming known as Sumer (aka Sumeria). The Ubaidian people that resisted absorption into the Sumerian culture continually migrated to Egypt, where they joined with the humans overseen by the Shemsu-Hor Helpers. Such departure greatly increased around 3250 BC, until all had left by roughly 3150 BC. After the Sumerian take over, the area grew in power and riches, and dominated many other Mesopotamian city-states in that region.

The splendid Sumerian temple honoring Enki, their god of Water and Wisdom, was soon built over the original Ubaid temple previously described, shortly after achieving control over the city. Other gods were added later, creating the first known pantheon, which included An, Ki, Enki, Ninurta, Nannar, and Nannar's twins, Utu and Inanna. Surprisingly, they did not remove the Mother Goddess veneration or the Bull god cult, but merely demoted those followings. Such accommodation seems to indicate the continual underlying conflict or competition between two different ideologies, and perhaps even Alalu's or his descendants' influence, for control of Eridu.

The Sumerian culture exhibited a sophisticated economy, comprehensive legal codes, high levels of artistic achievement, rich literary traditions, and an advanced level of scientific and technical knowledge. Beside their written cuneiform script, Sumer had many other 'firsts' that included schools, a pharmacopoeia, law codes, chariots, astronomical star and planet charting, reckoning tablets (archaic 'slide rules'), and metalworking. They were also unsurpassed in the craft of goldsmithing and gem cutting, producing many fine works of art and jewelry.

However, the Helpers still sought to continue their spread of 'controlled' civilization, despite the severe competition from the human groups influenced by the BOPH colonists. But the unrestrained progress offered by the BOPH colonists to their humans was more attractive. The BOPH colonists did not impose the same safeguard restrictions on the implementation of their advanced technology, as did the Helpers. Humans began to increasingly choose an affiliation with the BOPH colonists over that of the Helpers, lured by promises for quick progress and its associated advantages. Without the safeguards provided from a slow technological introduction and a corresponding required increase in enlightenment and morality within each culture, such knowledge and devices imparted by the BOPH colonists began to be misused by the humans.

Although contact between the two groups was competitive, it was purposefully kept peaceful and cordial. About that same time, around 3250 BC, the Ancient Ones returned on one of their routine visits to directly check on the progress of their ongoing civilizing efforts that were being implemented through their faithful humanlike Helpers. The Ancient Ones were disconcerted by the orbiting mother ship/space station of the BOPH colonists upon their arrival to Earth, but the apparent lack of any hindrance or violence toward the Helpers' progress with their human students raised no immediate concern.

Additionally, the Ancient Ones recognized a certain 'prior claim' that the BOPH colonists possessed; based on their very remote ancient ancestors who had established small bases on Earth, prior to the destruction of Maldek. That commenced an initially strained but peaceful coexistence between the Ancient Ones, their faithful Helpers, the humans of Earth, and the BOPH colonists. That benign relationship eventually became strained with the arrival to Earth of Enki's half-brother, Enlil, during that same 3250 BC time period.[10]

Enlil was the Sumerians' ultimate authoritarian god who was prominent throughout its Jemdet Nasr period, which existed between c.3250 BC and c.2800 BC, when the cities of Nippur, Shuruppak, and Kish were settled. Enlil assumed control over the efforts of the BOPH beings to colonize Earth, and no longer followed the prior policy of maintaining a low profile approach, one without any confrontations with the Ancient Ones or their Lunar Pitris Helpers.

Around 2850 BC, near the end of the Jemdet Nasr period, the tradition of male kingship was revived at Nippur and Kish; once again 'lowering this custom of rule from heaven.' In Hurrian myth, Nippur was considered to be the capital city of their god Kumarbi, the son of Alalu, while Sumerian lore claimed Nippur as one of Enlil's capital cities. Such claims seem to indicate that some dissension existed between the royal families of the BOPH colonists, mainly those of Alalu and Enlil. Regardless, the impact of human kingship gave the appearance of allowing humans more personal control over their own development, although in reality such kings were merely a conduit for the agenda of the BOPH colonists. Such continued blatant interference with human development by the BOPH colonists greatly disrupted the mission of the Helpers, and threatened their efforts to control the rate of humankind's progress. That competition defied the deliberate and metered progress desired by the Ancient Ones. The resultant opposing doctrines of the two groups eventually divided the human population into hostile competitive factions.

As the BOPH colonists spread their dominance and control, their campaign to undermine the efforts of the Ancient Ones and their Helpers was succeeding. Such strained coexistence ultimately led to open hostility, erupting into the legendary 'wars between the gods' (aka the battle between good and evil, or the fallen angels' rebellion with God). Earth's first 'world war' was underway. The results would seem to be quite predictable, but perhaps the 'good guys' did not win. The BOPH colonists would appear to be no match for the far superior Ancient Ones and their humanlike Helpers. But a conventional war was waged, with the BOPH warriors using the humans under their influence as fighting pawns. Although humanity was allowed to pick their allegiance with either side, most did not possess the ability or all the facts to make a truly informed choice. Their alliance was established along 'religious' beliefs, with promises for quick growth and riches, following 'Masters' who were thought to be religious deities by many humans.

One might assume that the side of good would prevail, that evil would be defeated. But, as with all wars, the winners write the history books. Such winners are always depicted as the good and morally-correct side. Had the Axis powers led by Nazi Germany won World War II, history books would incorrectly reflect that the 'righteous Nazis' defeated the 'evil forces of the wicked Allies.' The difference between war criminals and war heroes is their allegiance with the ultimate winning side. Perhaps a similar scenario occurred in Earth's archaic past. Such an aberration could lead to false history, as well as the confused record of both 'good' and 'bad' gods.

Evidence of one such rewriting of actual history can be found in the *Rig Veda*, where the Ancient Ones are referred to as the Grand Asuras of Heaven, who in the beginning were the only 'Living Power.' They were initially described as the elder brothers of the Aryan gods, those who possessed the greatest magic and power of all the gods. Only later were they made into 'enemy demons,' the evil dark divinities of ancient times.

In some esoteric texts of India, such a transformation from 'grand-to-evil' was distinguished by a name change. The *Suras* were the earliest, greatest, and brightest gods, and became the 'evil demon' *Asuras* only when they were arbitrarily 'dethroned' by the Brahmans, the human priests associated with the later BOPH 'gods.'

Ancient temple accounts recorded an even more descriptive narrative by Ani, the Egyptian royal scribe of Thebes in *c.*1450 BC. Chapter 17 of the *Papyrus of Ani* refers to the "War in Heaven and Earth," where: "...the Children of Impotent Revolt...that night of battle...into the eastern part of heaven, whereupon there arose a battle in heaven and in all the earth."[11] Other confusing passages suggest that the 'Children of Impotent Revolt' might have succeeded in their 'impotent' effort and actually 'won' the war, or at least that battle.

So as not to prolong that 'War between the Gods,' as it later became known, the BOPH colonists resorted to nuclear weapons, using technology derived from both their own destroyed ancient ancestors, and the Ancient Ones themselves. Perhaps the BOPH colonists even threatened to exterminate all life on the planet if the Ancient Ones did not relinquish. Quite conceivably, the BOPH warriors likely concluded that a few strategic nuclear explosions would greatly concern the Ancient Ones, making them believe that the BOPH rebels would devastate the surface of the planet, thus creating an uninhabitable world. Regardless, the Ancient Ones were prohibited from utilizing such doomsday devices in such a situation, in accord with the Cosmic Order. According to the Cosmic Order, deadly force could only be utilized to protect other worlds; but never against a 'rogue' planet that was threatening only its own existence.

The decision by the Ancient Ones, which advised humans under their influence to suspend hostilities with the warring humans sponsored by the BOPH colonists, had yet another cumulative consequence. Although it spared further loss of human life on both sides, and negated the devastation of the planet from further threatened nuclear attack; it also allowed the majority of humans to vote for an alliance with the BOPH rebels. Such a rejection of the Ancient Ones by the indigenous population of a planet required them to cease contact with that world.

Since the decision to align with the BOPH colonists was a premature one, long before the developing humans were ready for such an important determination, the Ancient Ones agreed to a 'temporary' period of exile. That allowed further human contemplation toward such a final and important decision. With mutual agreement on the terms of this temporary exile, the Ancient Ones expected further human growth and enlightenment during their 'absence,' while the BOPH colonists anticipated that their influence over the earthly humans would only increase over time.

Such an altruistic act to save Earth further denied the Ancient Ones any direct involvement or influence within humanity's development during their exile, which encompassed some specific, but unknown time period. That time frame may have been based on some celestial cycle, such as the arrival of a specific Zodiac Age, or perhaps simply an indeterminate period that might last until the next unforeseen worldwide conflagration that would threaten Earth. If so, then the Ancient Ones would once again be allowed direct and open contact with Earth, in order to provide assistance in combating such a disaster while helping its victims, including those descendants of the BOPH colonists. Likely, the BOPH colonists truly believed that an adequate level of technology, one equivalent to the Ancient Ones, could be achieved before such a new disaster might occur, thereby negating any required future assistance from the Ancient Ones.

The Ancient Ones apparently accepted these terms and departed Earth sometime between 3150 and 3100 BC, thus sparing the planet any further harm. However, many humanlike Helpers chose to stay on our planet, considering Earth to be their 'adopted' home world. That momentous break between Earth and the Ancient Ones may have occurred in 3113 BC, a recurring and notable date that also marked the beginning of 'Ages' or 'Periods' in numerous olden cultures, as referenced in their ancient records. Day One of the Mayan *Long Count* calendar started on August 13, 3113 BC,[12] a date and event of some unknown significance. The Olmecs also used 3113 BC as a starting date, while other ancient cultures also noted the significance of that year.

That temporary exile from Earth evidently carried the requirement that the Ancient Ones could not have organized public contact with the planets' inhabitants, thus prohibiting their influence over the masses during the undisclosed, agreed upon time period. Numerous records refer to just such a 'separation' agreement. The *Enuma elish* specifically referred to the defeat of Tiamat, the primordial ancestor, as a separation between Earth and the Heavens.[13] The Hindu Indra's killing of the serpent demon son of the goddess Danu also separated the Earth and sky from the heavens, releasing the waters that then flowed for man[14] (the freedom from constraints imposed by the Ancient Ones). Still other accounts referring to such a separation of Earth from the heavens are found in the Bible, as well as in numerous ancient myths, where a dragon, serpent, or Leviathan is slain. Archangel Michael and his angels prevailed in their fight against that dragon, casting out and forcing the demon from the heavens. This is the same allegory that is associated with the 'Fallen Angels' account, when Lucifer and his hosts, a third of the heavenly population, were evicted from Heaven after losing their rebellious war.

Additional accounts of 'Wars in Heaven' are found in the Puranas, Greek myths, and the Norse Mythology known as the *Battle of the Flames*, where the sons of Muspel fought on the field of Wigred. Stanza VI, line 6 of the *Book of Dzyan* states: "There were battles fought between the Creators (the Ancient Ones) and the Destroyers, and battles fought for space."

Author Timothy Wyllie's interpretation of the religious beliefs of the Gnostic Christians is a somewhat depressing realization of Earth in opposition to the better judgment of older and wiser beings in the universe. That opposition was designed to seal-off any contact with that higher divine reality, and the knowledge they possessed.[15] Other descriptions of a separation between Earth and heaven are found in *The Secret Doctrine*, which stated that the Kings of Light departed in wrath...leaving their [celestial thrones] empty. Another reference is found in the Chinese *Shu Ching* (aka *Shu-King*), where the antediluvian race called the Maio (aka Mao, Miao, or Mao-tse) became evil, lacking virtue. Hence, the Divine King, Lord Chang-ty, cut off all communication between Heaven and Earth, resulting in no more 'going up and coming down.'[16] According to a later Chinese text, the *Kuo-yiu*, King Chao of Chu wondered in *c*.500 BC if that 'communication' had previously not been cut, whether humans might still be 'able to ascend into heaven.'[17]

Perhaps a related notion, one also dealing with a future occurrence, describes the Second Coming of the Messiah as an apocalyptic event, something ominous and dreaded, a very strange foreboding of what should be a glorious development. Such apprehension may actually be referring to the return of the Ancient Ones, per their agreement of *c*.3150 BC; with the BOPH colonists simply planting the idea that such an event is sinister, as well as a dreaded event to be feared. Portraying the Ancient Ones' return as a dire event could be compared to the practice of the winning side 'demonizing' their defeated opponent after a war.

After the Ancient Ones departed, the BOPH victors then established themselves as gods, and proceeded to rule over Earth and its human population. Perhaps the clearest example of such proclaimed divinity occurred with the emergence of the Dynastic Period of Egypt in *c*.3150 BC, a marked change from prior protocol. But humanity did not benefit from the 'victory' by the BOPH beings or their self-elevation to 'deity status.' As evidenced in Sumer, humans labored to serve such gods by tending fields and livestock, making luxury goods, brewing beer, weaving cloth, cooking and baking, and tending the temples; all for the sole benefit of the gods. Sumerians were essentially the sharecroppers or serfs of the gods, and paid taxes in the form of a percentage of their animal flock or farm crop to their ruling god.[18]

Such gods were described as physical beings of human form, possessing superhuman powers, believed to be immortal, but rarely seen by the populace. Their many exploits are memorialized within humanity's legends and mythology, where the ancient gods are credited with such deeds. The theocratic rule by the BOPH gods was in direct opposition to the Cosmic Order. Only their 'cousins,' the humanlike Helpers of the Ancient Ones that had remained on Earth, were left to offer a different development, outlook, and hope for Earth and humanity.

PART TWO

SUGGESTIVE & SUPPORTIVE

EVIDENCE

Chapter 19

Anomalous Artifacts

Evidence supporting the presence of advanced devices and knowledge possessed by the Ancient Ones, their Helpers, and the BOPH gods exists as relics discovered in Earth's ancient record over the ensuing millennia. Such articles date from times when those relics simply should not exist, according to orthodox beliefs. Yet such abundant bits of evidence do exist to support the *Elder Gods* theory. Alone, they are easily overlooked, but when compiled and considered in their entirety, such evidence fits together, becoming clear and conclusive. With this book's exposure of the known facts pertaining to the creation of the universe; the formation of Earth and our solar system; the evolution of planetary species; and the emergence of early cultures; the reader is now equipped to recognize those artifacts, fossils, and ruins that seem 'out-of-place'.

Only a small sampling of anomalous evidence is presented in this text, with an unknown quantity still awaiting discovery, previously destroyed or discarded, or simply misidentified and relegated to storage and obscurity. The following selective collections of artifacts, which conflict with present theories, have previously been reported in other accounts. This author has made no direct examination of any referenced anomaly, or endeavored to browse museum basements for any similar items. The intent was not to break new ground, but to expose known contradictions to the accepted paradigm, suggesting that additional aspects are apparently also missing. Merely one lone anomalous artifact creates some doubt with academia's prevailing orthodox theory.

Physical Evidence

Prior mention was made of a few aberrant relics and anomalous remains that dated from the most archaic ages of our planet. Artifacts from more recent Earth periods are equally perplexing. A mummy found in Cuzco, Peru, wore quartz beads that had been drilled with tiny holes, allowing them to be strung together.[1] It has only been in modern times that commercial drill bits have been manufactured to produce such miniature holes. During a 20th century excavation of a mastodon skeleton in Blue Lick Springs, Kentucky, at a depth below the internment level of the animal, archaeologists unearthed the prehistoric floor of a building that had been paved with cut-stone tiles.[2] Since mastodons vanished with the Pleistocene Extinction, any building found below the level of that known historic period would reflect its construction date before 10,500 BC.

A geode, a geological term used to describe a mineral specimen that contains an internal hollow space formed by a trapped gas pocket, was found in February 1961 about six miles northeast of Olancha, California, at a 4,300 feet elevation above the dry lakebed of Owens Lake. When this rock was split into two halves, a remnant described as an ancient device similar to a spark plug was discovered.[3] The partial remains of a hexagonal body surrounding a porcelain or ceramic insulator encasing a central metal rod remained, with the lower casing eroded away and indistinguishable as a result of the corrosion, but with its outline remaining.[4] Clearly resembling a modern spark plug, the remnant has come to be known as the *Coso artifact*, as reported by author Ronald J. Willis.[5] The geode formation has been dated as young as only 1,000 years, to as much as 500,000 years old by an unidentified geologist,[6] although either extreme would date the artifact long before the invention of the internal combustion engine.

Many inexplicable archaic metal artifacts date to times before their required metallurgical abilities were known to exist, as defined by orthodox beliefs. Iron ore mining has been dated to 41,000 BC in the Ngwenya Hills of the Hhohho district of northwestern Swaziland, South Africa,[7] and speculatively traced back to as long ago as 70,000 to 100,000 BC.[8] Yet scholars state that the earliest ironworking did not start until about 1400 BC in Armenia, an area far north of Mesopotamia and even further from South Africa. Hence, why would primitive Stone Age men labor in such mines, and how would they have known what to do with the ore once it was extracted? Identification of raw ore, let alone the smelting and refining of the metals from such deposits, requires expertise, considerable knowledge, and sophisticated equipment. Moreover, had the base metals been identified and extracted, an even higher level of skill and knowledge would have been necessary to produce the complex alloys that comprised certain ancient metallic relics. Yet anthropologists continue to claim that such technology and knowledge did not exist during the periods in which such artifacts were discovered.

According to anthropologist J. Alden Mason, molten platinum was used to cast ornaments and other similar items that were found on the Andean plateau.[9] Platinum melts at 3,224 degrees Fahrenheit and requires a blast furnace or other technical means to generate such high heat. Yet we are advised that such technology did not exist during ancient times. Additionally, artifacts made using an aluminum alloy were found buried with the personal possessions of the Chinese general, Chow Chu (265-316 AD).[10] But aluminum requires refining from bauxite ore, with the first extraction by Faraday through electrolysis in 1808, and from chemical means by Oersted in 1825. According to scholars, the use of aluminum was unknown to man prior to modern times.

Evidence has been found in Armenia of a metallurgical factory that utilized gloved workers, steel tweezers, and protective respiratory filters; all dating to *circa* 3000 BC.[11]

Such an operation would imply the existence of a miniaturized or delicate assembly process. Based on similar centers and the numerous high-alloy metal artifacts found, scientists now concede that ancient metallurgists had the ability to produce at least 6,000 degrees Fahrenheit temperatures as far back as 5000 BC.

Equally puzzling are the extensive ancient copper mines that extend for hundreds of miles along Lake Superior. They date to a period before 5000 BC, but abruptly ended around 1000 BC.[12] Author and researcher, Frank Joseph, believes that hundreds of thousands of tons of copper were mined and removed from those ancient open-pit mines between 3000 and 1200 BC. He also believes that some of the ore was refined on an island in Rock Lake or Moon Lake, Wisconsin, by white or fair skinned miners who were also associated with the Ancient Mounds in Minnesota. There were no permanent settlements that dated to the times of the mines, which were centered on Isle Royale in Lake Superior. The later Native American Indians of the region knew nothing about the mines, nor did they utilize or work them.[13]

The equally ancient copper mines of Rio Tinto in southern Spain are often dated to between 8000 and 6000 BC,[14] further verifying the antiquity of metals, which were not known to have been utilized by any human culture of those eras. Modern mining operations have consistently intruded upon ancient tunnels associated with coal, chalk, salt, slate, and various precious metal mines. Such archaic shafts are often so old that many ancient coal veins turned to dust upon inspection. Yet why would primitive, non-industrial natives expend effort to mine materials we are told they could not utilize, based upon the primitive nature of their cultures?

The use of bronze dates to as early as 3700 BC, with the Bronze Age attaining widespread dispersion by *circa* 3200 BC, but the use of plain copper prior to those times was not very prominent. True bronze is an alloy of 84-92% copper, mixed with 16-8% tin. Not only is bronze easier to cast than pure copper, it is also much tougher. But common bronze usage seemed to appear overnight, without an apparent 'learning curve.' Further, tin was relatively rare in antiquity, being found principally in Gaul, Spain, Cornwall, Bohemia, and around Lake Titicaca in Bolivia; areas that are not close to the Near East where the Bronze Age supposedly emerged.

An iron pillar at Meharauli, India, a site in the Delhi territory near the capital city of New Delhi, rises to a height of 22 feet.[15] This solid, tapered shaft of wrought iron has an average diameter of about 4.5 feet.[16] Such a fine wrought pillar would be a notable modern day achievement due to both its size and composition, but it has been dated by some to 450 AD. An even earlier date associates this pillar with Emperor Asoka, the ruler over most of northern India during the second century BC.[17] He is credited with the construction of a series of columns, which may have included the mysterious wrought pillar, although it would have been the only one of that group made from iron. Those posts were erected as national symbols for peace, resulting from the emperor's conversion to Buddhism. The one unique iron post appears to resist oxidation, remaining rust-free after many centuries of exposure to the elements, an achievement that continues to impress modern metallurgists. It is believed that the iron is so pure and free of contaminates that a thin layer of oxidation formed a protective coating that prohibited any further oxidation to occur. However, no reason is given why this one pillar is dissimilar to all the others.

Certainly the extraction of rare minerals, precious metals, and other raw materials would be a motive for extraterrestrial beings to visit our planet. The primordial memory of a Golden Age is common to most all early cultures, although gold was merely an attractive but 'useless' metal. Yet gold is a most useful material to an advanced culture, with numerous applications in electronics, since it is an excellent conductor of both heat and electricity, while also resisting corrosion. Thus, it is often chosen as a material used in the construction of space probes that are required to last a very long time, while perhaps encountering harsh or caustic environments.

The Caliphs of Baghdad, the early Muslim leaders of the Arabian world, initiated the Renaissance around *c*.650 AD. Their ample libraries were filled with confiscated records and manuscripts from all over the world. In 820 AD, Caliph Abdullah al-Mamun sent his men to enter the Great Pyramid, based on persistent rumors that hidden chambers contained great treasures and relics of an ancient civilization that had long vanished. Author Warren Smith wrote that legends claimed such articles would include precise maps of the world, celestial charts, math tables, scientific knowledge, and inventions such as malleable glass that could bend without breaking and metals that would not rust.[18] Yet historic records document that no treasures were found upon entry into the Great Pyramid.

But the Arabs perhaps did remove ancient archives and mysterious artifacts during their visit. The Arabian text, *Le Murtadi*, described some of the alleged discoveries that were supposedly removed from the King's Chamber. According to author Peter Kolosimo, those removed objects included two statues, both a male and female of a race very different from the Egyptians, and a mysterious vase that was reported to have strange powers over gravity, weighing the same when either full of water or when empty.[19] The *Khitat* (aka *Hitat*), written by the Arabian geographer and historian Ahmed al-Maqrizi (1364-1442 AD), stated that 30 secret vaults were located under the Great Pyramid.[20] Those vaults reportedly held maps and charts of the 'divine ancestors,' and contained iron tools that would not rust, and glass that could be folded without breaking. One small vaulted chamber supposedly contained a book written in an unknown language, along with a green stone statue depicting an unusual appearing male being.[21]

Numerous vases were found in the chambers beneath the step pyramid of Zoser at Saqqara, Egypt.[22] The vessels dated to at least the time of Zoser, *c*.2650 BC, but could be as old as

4000 BC, since ancient items were highly prized by the early Egyptians of that period.[23] The tall vases had long, thin necks that flowed into widely flared bodies that incorporated fully hollowed-out shoulders, producing a uniform wall thickness throughout.[24] But these vases were cut from solid stone! No machine tool has yet been invented that would be capable of carving such a hollow interior, yet narrow enough to pass through the small neck restriction, while being strong enough to cut, remove, and shape the smooth rock interior; all in some sort of collapsible and contoured fashion. It would appear to be an obvious impossibility to apply sufficient cutting forces upon such a delicate machine tool, in order to achieve the required removal of stone material, yet leave a smooth surface without tool marks. Such a feat would only seem possible if the stone had been made pliable by some unknown method, then molded into the final vase shape and resolidified. Yet numerous such vases exist, obviously made by some unknown and exotic process.

Prehistoric shoes are known to have been in use by 7500 BC, in the form of fashionable and durable footwear, with the earliest specimens found during 1998 within Missouri caves. They were as complex and well-made as much later shoes, indicating not only the sudden emergence of foot protection, but also a consistency in craftsmanship over the millennia.[25] A variety of different styles further indicated a fashion consciousness. A total of two hundred pairs of woven fiber sandals were also found within Lamos Cave in eastern Nevada. That footwear collection dates to 7000 BC and exemplified a highly stylish product of excellent workmanship.[26] Such a large quantity of shoes further implies a mass-production operation attributable to a high culture that possessed organized craftsmen and a division of labor.

Organic Anomalies

Human fossil evidence may represent the most amazing of all anomalies. Truly Modern man did not emerge until around *c*.11,600 BC, shortly before the Great Flood and the Pleistocene Extinction. Such older fossils may be further evidence of the earlier proto-Sapiens subspecies, which first appeared as early as 400,000 BC. Yet a much older find of an anatomically modern *Homo sapiens* skull was discovered in Buenos Aires, Argentina, which was dated between 1.5 to 1.0 million years old.[27]

Existence of such anomalies is not in question. Such discoveries, although few in number, contradict the conventional linear evolution of our species, thereby challenging the prevailing hypothesis. Unless one accepts that a time machine will be utilized sometime in our future to propel future-man back to those remote epochs, the more likely explanation would be visitations to Earth by extraterrestrial humanlike beings during past antiquity.

Anomalous Technology

Anomalies extend beyond the physical articles of antiquity, and also manifest within the technological levels displayed by numerous ancient cultures. One of the most stunning examples of advanced knowledge can be found in the vast extent of medical expertise that greatly exceeded the level of obtainment ascribed by scholars. In the Western world, Egypt is considered to have been the origin of medical science. Around 450 BC, Hippocrates, the Greek 'Father of Western Medicine' admitted that he learned much of his medical knowledge from Egypt, acknowledging that medical science had started there.

Egyptian records state that Imhotep was the first and greatest doctor. He was also considered to be the first architect and engineer. Two conflicting time periods are attributed to Imhotep. The first is around 4500 BC, while the second occurred during the reign of Pharaoh Zoser of the Second Dynasty, *c*.2650 BC, when Imhotep was reported to be the *Viser* or Prime Minister of the pharaoh. He is also credited with the design and construction of the first stepped pyramid, Zoser's ziggurat at Saqqara, along with a hospital outside of Memphis. His medical skills reportedly included the regrowth of severed limbs and even the resurrection of the dead. Egyptians considered Imhotep to be mortal, or at most a demigod, even though the written accounts of his many accomplishments were separated by about 2,000 years. Still, no record of his death or even his burial tomb has ever been found.

The evidence of the extent of Egypt's medical knowledge is reflected in the discoveries of prominent archaeologists. The *Edwin Smith Papyrus*, named after its discoverer, is a fifteen feet long scroll comprising 49 sections of medical knowledge.[28] It is considered to be the world's oldest extant medical textbook. It contains no magic or witchcraft, just modern approaches and logical treatments in a step-by-step method starting with the nature of the malady, examination of symptoms, diagnosis, treatment, and final prognosis. It dealt with the heart and circulatory system, along with wound and fracture treatment. It also detailed clinical cases of paralysis, citing the connection between the muscular and nervous systems with limb movement, and lists possible causes for paralysis. Another medical text, the *Ebers Papyrus*, deals with the surgical treatment of tumors and also lists 700 herbal and chemical compounds as pharmaceutical prescriptions for a wide variety of ailments, ones still considered valid for use in modern times.[29]

Another medical papyrus from the 11th Dynasty prescribes a specific fungus or mold that 'grows on still waters' for the treatment of wounds and open sores.[30] That would seem to be an obvious reference to penicillin, some 4,000 years before its discovery by Dr. Fleming. The Greek Alcmaeon, a student of Pythagoras, was the first person to dissect a human body, although he was already familiar with the circulatory system and able to distinguish between veins and arteries.[31] He also discovered the optic nerve, the Eustachian tubes, and further determined that the brain was the source of intellect.[32]

Ancient India also possessed advanced medical knowledge. A surgical text written in the 8th century BC, which became a part of the *Atharva Veda* of the *Samhita*, contained detailed and specific transplant techniques.[33] A later text, the *Sushruta*, which had also been based on Vedic knowledge dating from earlier times, lists diagnosis for 1,120 diseases. It details the surgical procedures for tumor removal, amputations, tonsillectomies, and reconstructive or plastic surgery, while also describing 121 different surgical instruments.[34] Indian doctors understood the functions of the circulatory system, the nervous system, metabolic functions, and how specific characteristics are transmitted by heredity. They performed cesarean sections, did brain surgery, used anesthetics, and knew counter-measures for treatment of exposure to poisonous gases.

Even older knowledge is reflected in an ancient Chinese text, the *Nei Ching* (*Book of Medicine*), which dates to 2650 BC and contains modern diagnosis and treatment plans.[35] Records state that the Chinese Emperor Tsin-Shi (259-210 BC) possessed what is described as a fluoroscope, a device referred to as the 'Magic Mirror.'[36] Later, that machine was reportedly kept in the palace of Hien-Yang in Shensi around 206 BC, and used to image organs and bones of patients who stood in front of its almost six feet by five feet large viewing screen to diagnose injuries and disease.[37]

Approximately 800 clay tablets taken from Ashurbanipal's 7th century BC library dealt with medical subjects. The Persian *Zend-Avesta*, *c*.600 BC, describes what it called a 'word doctor,' evidently a reference to a modern doctor of psychiatry, indicating a knowledge of psychosomatic origins for certain illness. The early Peruvians performed a brain surgery procedure known as *trepanation* as far back as 500

BC.[38]   Further evidence of neurosurgery is found at Talca, Chile, within the large number of skeletal remains found there that displayed recalcified openings in the skulls, indicating survival after the procedural access to the brain.[39]

Astronomy

Astronomy is another scientific discipline utilized by the ancients that exemplified advanced knowledge beyond their ascribed level of attainment.   Sumerian cuneiform tablets describe the precise location of one of our outer planets, along with the four largest moons of Jupiter, and knowledge of certain moons of Saturn.   Such wisdom would require the use of telescopes thousands of years before their invention by Galileo.   However, the manufacture of glass and mirrors dates to Sumerian antiquity.   Egyptians knew how to produce glass by 2500 BC, as verified from a rock drawing at Beni Hassan that depicts men making glass.[40]   Pliny further stated that glass had also been produced by the earlier Phoenicians.

Excavations at Pompei revealed several sheets of glass comparable to modern quality and composition.   Ancient concave mirrors, which rival our modern parabolic reflectors, were found in La Venta, Mexico,[41] dating to 1400 BC.   Author Charles Berlitz reported that a solid sheet of glass weighing about 8.8 tons was discovered in 1956 at Beth She'arim, an ancient Hebrew settlement.[42]   This glass slab was determined to be man-made, produced for some unknown purpose.   In 1853 at Bedford, England, Sir David Brewster, a British physicists and optical expert, displayed a lens optically ground from rock crystal that had been discovered among the temple ruins at Nineveh.[43]   Another convex lens was found in Nimrod, along with one found in a tomb in Helwan, Egypt.[44]   Others have been discovered in Mexico, Ecuador, Australia, and Libya.   Optical lenses were common artifacts found in most ancient cultures, but were often mislabeled as 'jewels' by archaeologists and museum curators.   The ancient inhabitants of Sicily were reported to have used a magnifying instrument called a *nauscopite*[45] to view the coast of Africa. The description of that device clearly reveals a telescope.

Ancient astronomical knowledge would have required the use of accurate timepieces, such as chronometers, in conjunction with their telescopes. The *Brihath Sathaka*, along with other Sanskrit texts, reference microsecond subdivisions of time called *kashtas*.[46] Science has no explanation for an ancient culture's need to differentiate such infinitesimal increments of time, unless for high technology use. Anomalous artifacts confirm that the components and knowledge existed for ancient cultures to construct sophisticated viewing and timing instruments.

In 50 BC, the Macedonian astronomer, Andronikos of Kyrrhos, built a model of the universe incorporating a complex clock.[47] That device was found in the 'Tower of the Winds' in Athens,[48] and may be a similar mechanism to one found by Greek sponge divers in 1900 off the small southern island of Antikythera.[49] This badly encrusted and corroded instrument consisted of a complex series of differential cog wheels, a 240 tooth crown wheel, and adjustable inscribed and graduated scales and dials; all set on a three-tier axis upon a bronze base plate. The device was dated to *c.*65 BC and believed to be an astronomical computer, one capable of calculating lunar, planetary, and stellar cycles; based on the examination and evaluation conducted by Dr. D. J. de Solla Price, a scientist at the Institute for Advanced Study at Princeton, New Jersey.[50]

Electricity

Abundant evidence exists to indicate that ancient cultures understood and utilized electricity. While exploring over a period of several years near Baghdad, Iraq, in the 1930s, an Austrian archaeologist, Dr. Wilhelm König, unearthed numerous earthenware jars about six inches high, containing iron rods set inside copper cylinders sealed with pitch around its top opening.[51] Those objects were dated to *c.*25 BC, with similar objects, some even larger in size, also found in the Berlin Museum. Such relics are typically cataloged and displayed as either religious objects or toys. In 1957, Willard F. M. Gray, a scientist at the General Electric Laboratory in Pittsfield, Massachusetts, examined these items and found them to be dry cell batteries.[52] A modern duplicate was then constructed with new electrolyte added, allowing the resultant assembly to produce a steady direct current flow of electrons.

Such devices may explain the numerous articles found throughout the Near East that were electroplated with gold and silver over base metals. Electroplating has also been found in the ancient Peruvian Chimu culture of Chan Chán, where copper articles were plated with gold and silver, and silver artifacts were plated with gold. Similar plated articles were also linked with the ancient Chibchas culture of Columbia.[53] Yet numerous such artifacts have been dated to 2000 BC, several millennia older than the König batteries, leading one to believe that the use of electricity may extend back to even more remote times.

An ancient Sanskrit text of India, the *Agastya Samhita*, actually contains instructions for constructing electric batteries, while concluding that: "a chain of one hundred jars is said to give a very active and effective force."[54] Such dry cell electrical storage devices may have had a number of uses in antiquity. Ancient classical authors have constantly mentioned ever-burning lamps, eternal flames, and glowing eyes of statues. An Egyptian papyrus depicts hands holding an orb over an insulator column, appearing to be an ancient equivalent of a Van de Graaff static electricity generator.[55]

The Danish inventor, H. C. Oersted, first understood the basis principals of electricity in 1820. Thomas Edison then used that knowledge to eventually develop the incandescent light bulb in 1871. The Egyptian Temple of Hathor at Denderah is located about 45 miles north of Luxor on the Nile shore near the city of Qena, Egypt. A tomb painting found in

Hall Number Five of that temple unmistakably depicts a huge five feet long light bulb, complete with filament and braided connector wires attached to what appears to be a transformer, all held in position by a large high-tension insulator.[56] Such an enigmatic object that resembled an electrical insulator is a common Egyptian symbol or depiction known as a *Tet*, which was also called a *Djed* pillar.[57] Those objects came in several variations and dated to early dynastic times. They were often connected with religious practices, with the Tet being associated mainly with the worship of Osiris. According to Egyptologist Sir Wallis Budge, such objects were made only from wood (an insulator) or from gold (a conductor).[58]

Two more of those large light bulb devices were also depicted in a petroglyph wall relief found in the basement crypt under the Denderah Temple in a room designated as Number XVII.[59] Those depictions may solve the lingering mystery of how tombs, pyramids, temples, halls, and tunnels were illuminated without leaving smoke on the walls and ceilings. The absence of smoke means fire or torches did not provide the light for such delicate work. But the many intricate multi-colored paintings and hieroglyphs could not have been made in total darkness.

The prevailing theory espouses a complex series of mirrors, set up to collect the sun's rays from outside the structure, reflecting the light from mirror to mirror while turning corners and descending levels, for final relay of the reflected rays to the gallery area being painted. Such an explanation requires constant repositioning of all the many collection and relay mirrors as the sun moves across the sky. That seems even more outlandish than the electric light bulb the ancient Egyptians depicted as their light source.

Aircraft

In addition to the unexplained electrical devices pictured on the walls of the Egyptian Denderah Temple, unknown symbols and hieroglyphs were also found, which have resisted translation. Similar markings, along with other strange depictions, were also found on engraved panels among the ruins of the Seti I complex at Abydos. One panel clearly depicts objects that should be beyond the attainment level attributed to ancient Egypt. Researcher and author Richard C. Hoagland scrutinized those figures, describing them as spaceships, or 'land-speeders' as made popular in the *Star Wars* movies, along with a depiction of a modern Apache helicopter. The panels also contain unknown hieroglyphs that defy translation. Those panels have yet to be fully explained by Egyptologists.

Ancient legends tell of flying gods in celestial chariots, boats, dragons, snakes, discs, and numerous other items; all supposedly made by primitive people without technical knowledge or an understanding of aeronautics. But airplanes, jets, rocket ships, and craft resembling modern day UFOs were clearly evident during archaic times. Numerous wooden models of glider airplanes have been found in Egyptian tombs. One example was found in 1898 at the Saqqara ruins and cataloged by the Cairo Museum as item #6347,[60] but misidentified as a 'bird.' That plane, which dated to 2000 BC, along with several others, were reexamined in 1969. They all incorporated a correct dihedral angle of wing attachment, with aerodynamically designed proportions that were ideal for flight.[61]

A solid-gold delta-wing aircraft, dated at 1400 BC, is displayed in the State Museum of Bogota, Columbia.[62] Analysis by the Aeronautical Institute of New York determined its design and proportions to be fully airworthy. A manual known as *Aeronautics*, written in ancient India, details aircraft construction and aviation 'secrets.'[63] It was reportedly based on an ancient Sanskrit manuscript, the *Vymaanika-Shaastra*, authored by the sage Maharishi Bharadawaja, further indicating archaic man's interest and understanding of air transportation. Other texts from India describe the latent power derived from a 'conversion-engine' fueled by mercury, which "sets the driving whirlwind in motion,"[64] clearly describing an operational turbine engine.

Circumstantial Evidence

Evidence of technology before its time can also be detected in the hard fossil remains from antiquity. Although the tools or devices utilizing such suspected advanced technology remain undiscovered, their end products or resultant effects from such artifacts are known. An extinct auroch (wild ox) skull, dated at hundreds of thousands of years old, is exhibited at the Moscow Museum of Paleontology. This fossil was found in 1962 west of the River Lena in the Republic of Yakutsk, in northeastern Siberia. The skull displayed a hole in its forehead, which could only have resulted from a high powered projectile such as a rifle bullet, since no radial stress cracks were apparent around the opening.[65] In fact, the hole had started to recalcify sometime after the impact, indicating the animal had survived the trauma. It would be unlikely that a natural phenomenon, such as a small pebble propelled by a tornado at the auroch's head, would have been the cause, since the ox probably would not have survived the tornado.

A similar sample found in the Broken Hill area of Rhodesia, Africa, involved the skull of a Neanderthal man that exhibited both entry and exit hole wounds.[66] Again, no radial stress-crack lines were evident around the holes, indicating the impact from a high velocity projectile. Knowing that Neanderthal man existed only between 150,000 and 26,000 BC, the wound would greatly predate the known invention of the modern rifle or pistol.

Chapter 20

Mysterious Monoliths

Some of the most baffling anomalous artifacts are also the largest. They are the mysterious ancient stone structures from deepest antiquity, called monolithic, cyclopean, or megalithic. Such unexcelled stone constructions seem to defy explanation, not fitting with the level of technology the historians ascribe to their primitive cultures. Yet their very existence proves a remarkable ability by ancient cultures to quarry, cut, transport, place, fit and finish massive blocks of stone that modern mechanization would be strained to accomplish. Certain anomalous rock formations have been determined as even being beyond the expertise of modern land-based abilities, and would require aerial assistance. It also appears that it would be impossible to position the required number of workers around many of the mammoth stones in order to move, place, position, and finally fit and finish them to the precision they display. Clearly, some sort of advanced mechanization or unknown process must have been employed in such construction, perhaps even using aircraft or some yet to be discovered enormous crane.

Such megalithic constructions are most often found along coastal areas, or on small islands. Many sites are in relatively isolated regions, primarily accessible only by boat or air, not by land routes. An island location provides an excellent place to develop a culture, or separate a race of people, with little or no outside interaction or contact with other beings. Massive stone walls often surround such ancient sites, perhaps as fortifications against any fierce or gigantic animals of the region, allowing the inhabitants to live in a paradise of isolation.

Perhaps such secluded locations represent the legendary Gardens of Paradise associated with many archaic cultures. Such legends may have a basis in reality, with each culture having their own regional 'divine being' that coordinated activities at each sacred land of paradise. The *Elder Gods* theory reveals such benefactors as the Ancient Ones and their humanlike Helpers. Such megalithic edifices are generally concentrated in five regions around the world that include:

1. The European sites in the British Isles, Spain, western France, Belgium, Portugal, Greece, Scandinavia, the Crimean peninsula, the Balkan Mountains, and the Mediterranean islands along with its numerous underwater sites.
2. Near Eastern sites including Turkey, Lebanon, Egypt, North Africa, Iranian uplands, and the Caucasus range.
3. Some Asian sites of Japan, Burma, and India (mainly Assam and the Deccan Plateau), including the earliest phase of construction associated with the Borobudur of Java.
4. Certain South Pacific islands, especially Easter Island.
5. The Americas, including areas in Mesoamerica, the Andes, and the United States.

Construction Types

A generally accepted estimate states that more than 50,000 megalithic monuments are known to still exist in modern times. Countless others have been destroyed by natural disasters, acts of man, as well as by sand, wind, and rain erosion. The stones are classified as menhirs, dolmans, blocks, or slabs; all used in part or in whole to build certain ancient edifices. Carved menhirs are probably the prototype of the later and more refined obelisks. A dolmen consists of two vertical menhirs, with a stone slab laid horizontally across their tops. A cromlech is a grouping of menhirs and dolmens forming various designs, such as the one at Stonehenge. Such structures appear to be grouped into three general construction and craftsmanship phases, exhibiting different builders and time periods.

The oldest are believed to have been built between 15,000 and 10,500 BC, which generally utilized the largest stone sizes and displayed the best workmanship. The stones are usually not uniform in size or shape, yet are precisely fitted to form seamless joints without mortar. Other rocks utilized during that earliest period include the massive slabs of stone that appear to have been 'sliced' from their quarry as if in a plastic state. An intermediate building phase followed between c.9200 and c.6000 BC, which utilized more uniform cube-shaped blocks that were perfectly cut and polished for precise fit without mortar, forming generally parallel seams. The last period occurred from roughly 4500 to around 1500 BC, after which megalithic construction essentially ended, with no explanation for its stoppage. While a few edifices may have been built after 1500 BC, most were merely repairs or additions made to prior existing structures.

That final construction period relied on irregular stones left in their rough state, joined without a uniform pattern or seam. Only the adjoining faces were crudely fitted to an approximate match, with gaps filled with a mud-mortar mix. Oddly, the earliest dated structures are generally the most complex and spectacular, creating even more mystery. All the largest and most enigmatic edifices were built on solid bedrock, insuring stability, longevity, and accuracy.

The age of such impressive structures is very difficult to establish. There are two types of dating generally utilized for such determination. Relative dating is accomplished by stratigraphic methods, where it is assumed that each stratum and its artifacts becomes older with each lower level of excavation. Absolute dating is accomplished by chemical or radioactive methods. The radioactive methods are based on the time required for half of the atoms of an isotope to disintegrate. The most widely used is the Carbon-14 method developed in the late 1940s, a process based on the 5,730 year half-life of the Carbon-14 isotope employed, but that procedure can only date organic matter.

Earth is steadily exposed to cosmic radiation bombardment from subatomic particles, which create a small quantity of Carbon-14 in the atmosphere. All living organisms contain carbon compounds that absorb Carbon-14 in the same known proportions found in the atmosphere, and maintain that same constant level throughout life. That absorption stops with the death of the organism. Its known level of Carbon-14 then starts to disintegrate at a constant and established rate, allowing calculations to determine the time of organic death, based on the amount of remaining isotope present at the time of testing. Carbon dating is generally considered accurate only to a limit of about 55,000 years, with time scale errors of 2,000 to 5,000 years expected when approaching that extreme limit, but with much less error within 'younger' ranges.

Even advanced new techniques for dating stone would merely indicate the age of the rock, not the date of the structure built from them. After abandonment by their builders, such edifices were inhabited over and over by later cultures, so dating by cultural epoch is just as unreliable. According to author Graham Hancock, Professor David Bowen is developing a new Chlorine-36 rock-exposure dating technique at the University of Wales.[1] Such a process would provide an estimate of the elapsed time since a cut rock face was first exposed to the atmosphere. However, even such dating techniques would be unable to distinguish original quarry cuts from any later periods of restoration, redressing, or repair.

Archaeoastronomy, the discipline of dating archaeological structures or monuments by their orientation with astronomical alignments or their seasonal focus on celestial phenomena and objects, appears to be as reliable as any other known dating method. The 19th century English astronomer, Sir Joseph

Norman Lockyer, demonstrated in 1894 that ancient complexes were oriented and aligned with astronomical events and/or celestial formations, often correlating with equinox or solstice arrivals. Later scholars including such notables as British professor Sir Fredrick Hoyle, Oxford University professor Alexander Thom, and United States astronomer G. S. Hawkins have also arrived at the same conclusions. According to author Erich von Däniken, Dr. Rolf Müller proved that megalithic structures were arranged according to the constellations.[2]

Such ancient alignments involved both astronomical and mathematical skills greatly beyond the ability ascribed to the people of its construction era. Professor Alexander Thom recognized that mathematical use of the Pythagorean theorem for right-angle triangles was employed to establish sighting positions, while Professor Fred Hoyle maintained that the builders must have known of the natural phenomenon described as the Precession of the Equinoxes. Such complex alignments demonstrated by these monuments were then used as celestial calculators or direct sighting aids to predict eclipses, solstices, equinox, and other cosmic events.

Similarities between construction styles can be seen in sites scattered around the world, yet separated by thousands of miles. Such connections are evident in the corbel-vaulted cave like tunnels found in New Grange, Gavrinis Island, Malta, and the connecting hall between the burial chamber and temple at Palenque. Further similarities can be found among the numerous structures built from polygonal interlocking stones fashioned in a jigsaw pattern, or the numerous sites that used precision cut, fitted, and stacked mortarless blocks. Still other sites display a common design, such as the familiar circular or fan-shaped arrangement found at many locations.

Two general layout plans were followed, the first being distinguished by a corridor ending with rooms that were square, oval, or round in shape at its final destination. The second plan had a similar corridor, but with rectangular chambers branching-off the hall before its conclusion. Certain entryways were secured with a stone slab that was perforated with a small porthole or round opening, which was a feature common with many megalithic tombs and chambers. While those openings are too small for humans, even children, they may have been accessible to the 'little people' of ancient legends.

Some megaliths were reportedly built using only stone tools, even when metal implements were available. The minimal metal traces that have been found on a few of the stones were deemed not to be associated with their original quarry work or final fitting efforts. It has long been thought that religious convictions prohibited metal implements from being used in some megalithic construction, as portrayed in the Biblical tradition prohibiting the use of iron tools during the building of the Jewish Temple under Solomon's reign. The absence of metal tool usage does not necessarily imply that stone tools were thus utilized in such construction. Perhaps other methods or advanced processes beyond our current technology, ones that were lost to later civilizations, may have been used in such projects. The BOPH gods or the Helpers of the Ancient Ones may have used modern processes such as laser or high-pressure water-jet cutters on those later structures. Extra-Biblical traditions claim that Asmodeus, the son of Tubalcain, used 'a certain stone that cut other stones as a diamond cuts glass.'[3] Another similar tradition claimed that Solomon used a device called a *shamir* to cut the temple stones.[4]

The accessible ancient megalithic sites were raided by subsequent cultures. Their structures were then used as ready-made quarries, with many original stones removed for later construction projects by the younger 'invading' cultures. Numerous ancient monolithic sites now only consist of the huge stones too large for the subsequent cultures to carry off, or those that were buried out of sight, deep in the ground. One is left with the obvious question of how older civilizations could cut, transport, and place massive stones of gigantic size that would eventually become too large for later humans to handle. The answer may be found in the technology of the Ancient Ones, who did not utilize smaller, more easily handled blocks simply because they could readily utilize large stones, seemingly with ease. Those larger stones allowed construction projects to be more quickly completed, while assuring longevity due to their massive size.

New sites were often built by later cultures over previous ruins, probably for the same reasons that the prior civilization chose that location. Such motives might include proximity to water, forests, wild game, or the ability to defend such an encampment site. Undoubtedly some ancient sites were built over even older structures buried beneath them, obscuring such unknown discoveries for fear of disturbing or damaging the known archaeology. Many olden sites are often combinations of several ancient structural remains that were then incorporated into the construction of even later buildings. One example is the Mayan crypt of Pacal, one of the structures at the Palenque complex in the state of Chiapas, Mexico. Pacal's (aka Halach Uinic, meaning 'true man') burial chamber is below the Temple of the Inscriptions stepped pyramid, connected by a corbel-vaulted stairway. The crypt is of an unknown but much older age than the pyramid temple, which was built around 450 AD, although Lord Pacal did not die until 683 AD.

Analysis of the site revealed several different levels of construction, with the temple being built above a stepped pyramid that had been erected over an even earlier stepped pyramid built on a lower level. That crypt contained the famous engraved limestone slab supposedly depicting a seated ancient astronaut in a spacecraft. That stone engraving served as the 12.5 feet long, five ton sarcophagus lid. Another structure that is thought to have incorporated several building periods is the Temple of Hathor in Denderah, Egypt. The architectural quality, construction, and artwork all appear to be in conflict, with some areas displaying the highest quality, while other areas are substandard. Such disparity within the same structure suggest that two very different time periods, as well as different builders, were involved with its construction and decorating process.

The Seti I Temple at Abydos, Egypt, is another site where a later edifice was built to incorporate a much older structure known as the Osireion. That construction will be reviewed in detail in the following chapter. Numerous other mysterious ancient sites were revealed to have been built over or combined with earlier archaic structures. Perhaps multiple ruins of even older construction lie buried deeper beneath many of Earth's ancient sites.

Ancient Symbols & Markings

The most archaic structures, primarily from the first construction period, were devoid of any markings. Only later, mainly during the second period of ancient megalithic construction, did it become somewhat common to display universal symbols such as spirals, snakes, crosses, mazes, axes, and the signs of the zodiac on such structures. A review of such symbols that frequently appeared within diverse cultures from vastly separated locations during ancient times follows.

The Spiral symbol is considered to be one of the oldest, believed to represent the universe or its infinity. It is thought to have also been used as a representation of our galaxy, exposing ancient humanity's knowledge that some galaxies were arranged in a spiral manner. The spiral symbol was also believed to represent creation, perhaps specifically the Big Bang event.

Snake pictograms are found on various ancient underground chambers and megaliths throughout the world. The serpent is considered to be the symbol of wisdom, science, and knowledge.[5] Initiates into the Ancient Mysteries used snakes during certain temple ceremonies as a symbolic sign of their reverence toward such wisdom. Numerous accounts in ancient texts allude to the serpent as the symbol of the 'eldest gods,' apparently referring to the Ancient Ones who were also known as the Serpent People, a term that later also referred to their followers. The coiled snake is believed to have represented the universe or the galaxy containing Earth, a derivation of the spiral form. Author Robert Charroux noted that snakes possess a unique movement, speculating that early humans might not have understood the propulsion device or mechanism employed with the ancient aircraft used by the gods. Hence, they may have equated such craft with serpents, since snakes also move without any obvious external means, such as legs. A rocket or an aircraft fuselage is also elongated, similar to that of a snake. That may also explain ancient references to flying or feathered serpents and winged dragons. Only in much later times did the snake evolved to become a symbol of evil.

The Caduceus, the winged staff surrounded by two entwined snakes, has been the symbol of physicians since antiquity. Such entwined snakes may symbolize the double helix of DNA, with the wings representing the ancient gods' ability to fly, while the staff represents the 'staff of life' or the scepter of kingship bestowed by the gods. The scepter was a symbol of kingship since earliest times, with engraved stone tablet depictions showing the tradition of the scepter being passed down by the reigning god to his appointed sovereign to rule over his people.

The similar and somewhat later three-pronged scepter, often associated with Poseidon, subsequently became a trident and eventually degraded into the pitchfork of Beelzebub, the devil. The trident was a prevalent symbol of Hindu gods, and also evolved to represent the Tree of Knowledge. That similar Tree of Knowledge symbol was found in numerous ancient cultures, with its most prominent display carved on the slopes of the Paracas Peninsula above the Bay of Pisco, along the Pacific shore of Peru. This unique design is also known as the 'candelabra symbol' and the 'Chandelier of the Miraculous Sign of the Three Crosses.'

The cross symbol can be traced to remote antiquity, long before its use by the Christian faith. The original symbol was believed to be a cross surrounded by a circle, which Ignatius Donnelly believed represented the capital city of Atlantis, with its three-ring circular irrigation moats as described by Plato. The cross has also been described as representing the four cardinal points of the compass, exemplified by the Mayan cross, which was believed to symbolize the Four Corners of the world. In a similar manner, the cross was also thought to designate the four winds. It is known that ancient cultures constructed a crude compass by placing a sliver of magnetized metal at right angles over a floating reed or twig in water, forming a cross.

The cross symbol was used in the Egyptian *Crux Ansata* (aka *ankh*) and the *Tau* in China. The Chaldeans, Mayans, Peruvians, and Phoenicians also utilized this symbol. Such crosses may have evolved from other forms such as the 'Jain Cross' also known as the hooked-cross, and later as the swastika, its oldest counterpart found on pre-Flood rock paintings. The earliest swastika is believed to have derived its form from the ancient Sun Wheel of India. The swastika symbol was also found at Tiahuanaco, Troy, Scotland, China, Crete, Sweden, India, and at the Indus Valley ruins. Its present negative connotation, associated with Nazi Germany, is strictly a modern convention. Its earliest symbolism was most benevolent, as signified with its use by the Hindus and the Jains, cultures founded upon love, peace, and harmlessness to all living things.

The winged sun disk was the universal symbol of the gods throughout the Near East. It signified the lofty position of the gods and their ability to fly. One legend of the winged sun disk is inscribed on an ancient temple wall in Edfu (modern day Idfu), Egypt, describing the landing of the god Ra and his crew between the city of Edfu and the Pechennu Canal. It tells of Ra's son, Hor-Hut, flying into the sky in a large disk-shaped craft 'as bright as the sun' to battle with their enemies. The ensuing loud and brilliant explosions from the aerial fighting left the enemy dead. After Hor-Hut's return from battle, his craft became known as the winged sun disk.[6]

The maze or labyrinth was another ancient symbol depicted on rocks, caves, and cliffs in North Africa, southern France, the islands of Crete and Malta, England, Scotland, southern India, and the Southwestern United States (mainly Arizona). The maze was believed to represent life's mysteries. It is further associated with the 'zigzag' or 'meander' patterns that were linked to the ancient gods.

The maze was also reproduced as a megalithic stone formation. The Great Labyrinth was known as one of the Seven Wonders of the Ancient World. Herodotus, Strabo, Diodorus, and Pliny described it in detail. After seeing the Great Labyrinth, Herodotus stated it was beyond description, and surpassed even the Great Pyramid. He described the twelve covered courtyards encircling the 3,000 rooms that were distributed evenly, with half at ground level and half as subterranean.[7] Their passages created a maze in which "no stranger could find his way without the aid of expert guides," according to Strabo.[8] Three similar but smaller labyrinths were also reportedly built, one on Crete, another in Lemnos, with the last one built in Italy.

The Double Ax symbol is one of the most obscure, linked with Cro-Magnon man who has been described as 'the man with an ax.' It is generally believed to be a religious icon. The double ax of the Etruscans was very similar to the one found at Crete. That same type of ax was also engraved on one of the megalithic pillars of Stonehenge. The Tibetan Buddhist monks told of a hand-held instrument called a *dorje*,[9] which was described as being 'double-headed' like an ax. The original dorje was believed to have been of celestial origin, and reportedly capable of great powers if used correctly. This device was also referred to as a *Vril rod*, and may have been

233

the origin of the 'magic wand' utilized by ancient wizards. Ancient Sanskrit texts credit the inhabitants of a lost continent, which existed prior to the Great Flood, with mastering a sidereal power called *vril*,[10] which reportedly was able to control the effects of gravity.

The origins of the Signs of the Zodiac can be dated to times long before the Great Flood of *c*.10,500 BC. The oldest known representation of the zodiac is found on a portion of the ceiling in the portico of the temple at Denderah, Egypt, which displays the vernal point in the sign of Leo (the Lion or Sphinx), signifying a time period generally between 11,010 - 8850 BC. Others date parts of the Denderah configuration to much earlier times. According to author W. Raymond Drake, the Zodiac of Denderah is believed to portray a cosmic configuration of stars as oriented around *c*.90,000 BC,[11] based on the depicted astrological symbols. Denderah is the only site in Egypt with a complete zodiac representation, including the 36 *decans* of the Egyptian year. The decans represented the ten-day periods of stellar positions, comprised of three periods per month, totaling its 36 celestial configurations.

Origen, the 3rd century AD Christian theologian who is considered to have been the leading Old Testament Biblical scholar of the early Church, believed that the constellations were divided and named before the Flood. Throughout remote locations of antiquity, the celestial signs and original names of such corresponding constellations appeared to have been consistent within cultures that had no contact with each other. Such an occurrence appears to be highly unlikely unless a common influence, such as the Ancient Ones and their Helpers, taught the same cosmic concept around the world.

Chapter 21

Old World Structures

A review of only a small sampling of impressive and enigmatic structures from antiquity reveals technical achievements far beyond the capabilities believed to exist on Earth during their time of construction. Such anomalous structures are found throughout the world, contradicting our prevailing belief system. The following brief review only highlights typical features and traits found in many archaic edifices, so the presented structures should not be viewed differently from other enigmatic ancient edifices not mentioned.

Structures such as the numerous magnificent Mayan ruins, the buildings of the Indus Valley, the Cambodian jungle structures of Ankor Wat and Ankor Thom, the Mesopotamian ziggurats, and the ancient Zimbabwe walls and towers will not be reviewed. Such edifices were able to be built by humans, one small brick or stone at a time, without any mechanization or aerial assistance. They are generally more ornate, with elaborate engraved details and stylized figures, and often possess written or pictorial scripts. Most megalithic edifices are devoid of ornamentation, or depict only simple archaic symbols, perhaps added by later primitive inhabitants of such complexes. It is the existence of such enigmatic megalithic edifices that suggest the intervention of advanced technology by otherworldly beings such as the Ancient Ones and their Helpers.

Europe

The now vanished legendary city of Tartessos is believed to have been located on the delta of the Guadalquivir River in Spain. Enormous ruins now exist at that site, according to author Charles Berlitz. It was described as a port city for ocean faring ships, and was called Tarshish in the Bible. It has been dated to 6000 BC, but some of the many megalithic ruins along the coasts of Spain and Portugal are believed to have been erected prior to the Great Flood of $c.10,500$ BC. The huge ruins near Niebla, Spain, are believed to have been part of the remnants of that past Tartessos Empire.

In nearby Great Britain, Stonehenge, an ancient structure that consists of four concentric stone arrangements, has been dated to $c.2800$ BC for Phase I, which consisted of most of its outer earthen trench, the Station Stones, the Heel Stone, and the Aubrey Holes. Phase II was comprised of the Bluestone Circle, the Altar stone, and the five Trilithons forming a horseshoe-shape, believed to have been built in $c.2100$ BC. Phase III occurred between 2075 and 1750 BC and may actually represent two phases, during which the Sarsen Stones and their curved lintels were added and arranged in a circle, along with the resetting of the previous bluestones.[1]

The source of the bluestones was from the southwest, within the Prescelly Mountains of South Wales, some 240 miles away. Stonehenge was utilized as a ceremonial and observational complex, with author Rupert Furneaux noting that its 56 Aubrey Holes were used to track the cycle of the moon every 56 years.[2] A link to other ancient cultures is found in the faded image of a Cretan double ax design carved on one of the menhirs, along with the unique shape of a Mycenaean dagger found on another stone at the complex. A similar ancient cromlech arrangement was also found at Avebury about 20 miles north of Stonehenge.

New Grange is about 50 miles north of Dublin, Ireland, and features one of the finest monolithic structures of Europe.

This turf-covered ancient mound structure lies in the Boyne Valley near the Boyne River. The site was perhaps an ancient astronomical observatory that was built before 3100 BC, but is generally believed to be much older. It was rimed with 38 huge boulders as large as eight feet high. Its entrance stones are decorated with a triple spiral pattern similar to those found on rocks in Crete, and also at Tarxien on Malta. Its main compartment can be accessed through a long 70 feet massive stone passage, which is topped with gigantic stone slabs forming a roof of about five feet in height. This passage leads to the main chamber or vault that opens up to a height of 20 feet. That vaults' cantilevered roof slabs were arranged in unusual horizontal layers that extended past the top edge of lower ones, with each stone held in place by the one above; a simple, efficient, and most ingenious design. Its numerous wall carvings of spirals, chevrons, and other geometric symbols are among the finest in the entire world.

Numerous vitrified forts exist throughout Scotland, with about 60 in the central and northern area alone. One of the most famous is Craig Phadrig in the Highlands, about 1.5 miles west of Inverness. It is a fort or citadel of roughly oval-shape, built from granite blocks featuring a basin-like depression almost nine feet deep at its center. This Celtic site displays massive areas where the granite blocks were vitrified, some consuming stones along the rampart walls as thick as five feet. Other areas exhibit melting from both sides, while others exhibit vitrification only on the outer face. Some vitrified areas remained standing while others were strewn as rubble around the site. A temperature in excess of 1,300 degrees Centigrade is required to vitrify granite rock. Similar forts found in other Celtic lands such as Whales, Ireland, and areas of northern France also show signs of vitrification damage; foremost being the forts on the Aran Islands, which are found off the west-central coast of Ireland at the mouth of Galway Bay.

Mediterranean

More than 200 sunken ruins are estimated to be under the Mediterranean waters,[3] including port cities off Cádiz, Spain, and Morocco, Africa. Massive underwater ruins were found off the coast of Morocco in 1958, where megalithic blocks formed enormous walls 26 feet long by 19 feet high. They continued for several miles, at depths ranging from 45 to 60 feet below the surface, and may be traces of ancient port cities that existed during lower sea levels. One of the most impressive ancient Moroccan port cities is Lixus, near Larache on the Lucus River, with its massive polygonal stone construction resembling that of Sacsahuaman in Peru. Volubilis is another site in northern Morocco that exhibits megalithic stone constructions similar to those found in the Andes Mountains at Tiahuanaco. Much later, the Romans built at Volubilis, ultimately leaving their ruins over those earlier constructions.

Other colossal underwater stone walls, made from massive blocks over 16 feet square, were found in 1968 by the archaeologist and anthropologist, Dr. J. Mason Valentine, off the small island of North Bimini, in the Bahamas. Portions of the wall were reportedly still perpendicular in orientation, branching off at right angles into two other perfectly straight walls that ran for over 600 feet.[4] Further exploration exposed a complex structure with stone quays and a double jetty, believed to comprise a portion of a wharf or harbor during some remote epoch.[5] This discovery coincided with one of Edgar Cayce's most famous predictions that a portion of sunken Atlantis would reappear in 1968.[6]

Other megalithic stones, apparently arranged to form steps, were found about 1,400 feet deep scattered around the Bahamas. In a similar manner, ancient Mayan roads originating in Belize and the Yucatan continue out into the sea for miles from the coast. Off the northern coast of Venezuela, an undersea wall extends for over 100 miles. Still other massive stone walls and structures are found as deep as 1.5 miles, in waters off the Peruvian coast in the Nazca Trench.

Far from the Mediterranean, a pyramid about 64 feet tall was found in 1987 at a depth of 80 feet in the waters off the coast of Yonaguni, Japan, a small island just off the coast of Okinawa. The sunken structure is described as half of a stepped pyramid, and is believed to be connected with the Jomon culture. This construction has been extensively studied by Dr. Robert Schoch, and dated relative to the periods when the area was believed to have been at or above sea level. That status was determined to have occurred during two different time periods, either between 8000 and 6000 BC, or an earlier period from 12,000 to 10,000 BC.

Malta

Additional megalithic ruins are also found on the islands within the Mediterranean, with Malta possessing some of the oldest known stone structures on Earth. Many geologists agree that Malta was once connected to the mainland, most likely with a link to Italy through Sicily. Further connections may have existed between the islands of Gozo, Comino, and Filfla, which formed a land bridge between Europe and North Africa until *circa* 100,000 BC. It is also believed that a land bridge once connected North Africa to Spain at the Straits of Gibraltar, making the Mediterranean a fertile basin at that time, with numerous individual lakes. The legendary Great Flood later broke that dam, allowing the Atlantic to create the Mediterranean Sea.

The megalithic oval complexes on Malta are among the most impressive ancient edifices, especially considering its isolated location. The temples were built using megalithic limestone blocks, some rough-hewn and others polished, though all were precisely cut and shaped to fit without mortar. Some stones had painted surfaces, while others were plain. Still others displayed intricate carvings of various designs. An underground tunnel system formed a network of catacombs on Malta, utilized for various purposes including mining and burials. Construction similarities exist between Mycenae, Hattusas, and the most ancient Egyptian monoliths at Saqqara and Abydos, linking them with techniques and designs found on Malta.

At Hal Saflieni on Malta, a subterranean labyrinth known as a *hypogeum*, a type of underground tomb cut from solid rock, housed the bones of 7,000 bodies. It was only during a much later period, toward the end of the Stone Age, when that hypogeum was used as a burial vault. Its corbel-vaulted roof was cut to resemble a cantilevered vault. A small antechamber, known as the 'Holy of Hollies,' is found off its main chamber. Spiral symbols painted in red ochre are found throughout the chambers, which were designed with unique acoustical properties where sounds echo from vault to vault with remarkable clarity, even to the smallest chambers.

Hagar Qim is an elaborate megalithic temple of Malta, found near the town of Zurrieq. A massive outer wall of stones exhibiting the ancient spiral pattern design protected the Hagar Qim structure. The complex was used in part as a temple for the Mother Goddess. As with numerous other ancient sites, portions of the complex are believed to have been built or rebuilt during various different periods of time. The Great Flood may have even destroyed portions of the original structure, a theory held by archaeologist David Hatcher Childress. He believed the flood waves came from the west, smashing the stones of its western wall, moving the massive blocks almost 40 feet to the east.[7] A three feet layer of silt was then deposited over the ruins, indicating that massive flooding ensued after the destruction of its outer wall.[8]

It was concluded that an earthquake or tornado could not have caused the displacement of those massive blocks, due to the directional manner and distance involved. Hence, the most likely source of such forceful waves was the Great Flood. If true, Hagar Qim must have been built before the Great Flood

240

of *c*.10,500 BC. Evidence indicates the complex remained unoccupied for a long time after that initial destruction, until Malta was repopulated by a different culture that repaired portions of the original structure and built certain known additions.

The Mnajdra Temple is another site of ruins also located in Zurrieq, near the edge of the sea cliffs. Its construction was in a fan-shaped layout, with a building style resembling the Andean site of Sacsahuaman. The ruins are badly eroded, due to the nature of the soft limestone blocks used in its construction. The circular stone ruins of the 'walled-city' on the Canary Islands resembles the Mnajdra complex, linked by their many similarities in both style and construction.

Tarxien is yet another ancient structure located near the village of Valetta, along the Great Harbor of Malta. Its complex consisted of three distinctly different periods or phases of construction. Its purpose remains unknown, although it was not a palace for the ruling class, or housing for the local inhabitants. Nor was it built as a fort, or used as a defensive structure against attacks; although it may have served as a refuge, to keep out large fierce animals.

Its massive stone gates pivoted open for entrance, utilizing round stones employed as ball-bearings, fitted to sockets cut in the bottom of its gate doors. The complex consisted of a maze of chambers and corridors, with some containing semi-circular shrines and raised altars decorated with spirals. One sanctuary featured a large statue of the Mother Goddess. The same three feet layer of flood-silt found at Hagar Qim was also evident at Tarxien, indicating their similar date of burial and origins perhaps before 10,500 BC. Its third and final phase of occupation occurred between *c*.4500 and 2550 BC, after which the ancient Malta culture vanished without a trace.

Gozo Island

Gozo Island is a small 'sister' island to the northwest of Malta, about fifty miles from Sicily. The Ggantija Temple, meaning the 'work of the giants,' is located at Zagra and is the most impressive site on Gozo. The ancient spiral design and snake motif are evident, along with the stone ball and socket employed to pivot massive stone entrance gates similar to Tarxien. The massive outer wall of tightly fitted limestone slabs stood as high as 26 feet, and is believed to have been used to keep out fierce animals. One massive stone reportedly measured 16 feet high, by 26 feet long, by 13 feet wide. An early expedition by a German university uncovered 100 skull-less skeletons buried among those megalith stone blocks. According to David Hatcher Childress, no trace of remaining Carbon-14 isotope was found within those bones during radiocarbon dating,[9] which he suggested could indicate their age as possibly exceeding 30,000 years old.

It is believed that those bones had been buried during the structure's initial construction, suggesting that the temple complex was also over 30,000 years old according to Mr. Childress, perhaps making it the oldest known structure on Earth.[10] The Gozo and Malta ruins are believed to share about the same construction type and age, perhaps making both islands the origin of megalithic construction in the Mediterranean, Europe, and the Near East. Similar to ancient Malta, the last phase of the ancient Gozo culture also suddenly vanished around 2550 BC without explanation.

Mycenae

Mycenae was situated about 47 miles southwest of Athens on the Greek mainland, in the area known then as Peloponnesus on the ancient Greek 'peninsula' known as Sparta. The man-made Corinth Canal now separates this region from the rest of Greece. Before the canal, that land acted as a bridge between the earlier Minoan civilization on the island of Crete and the classical Greek culture. The site was first excavated in 1874 by the respected German archaeologist, Dr. Heinrich Schliemann.

Mycenae was a megalithic citadel built of huge 50 ton boulders of polygonal shape, which were cut and fitted precisely to each adjoining block. This type of construction is very similar to that of Machu Picchu and other Peruvian sites. In fact it was Dr. Schliemann who first used the term 'cyclopean' to refer to the use of huge polygonal stone blocks that were precisely cut and individually fitted in a jigsaw manner without mortar. That type of construction is most impervious to earthquakes, since the walls may move and tremble, yet not collapse during the shock of a quake, but simply settle back into place due to their 'interlocking' nature.

The famous Lions Gate of Mycenae is located at its mammoth entrance, framed with a trilithon doorway, crowned with huge carvings of two lions facing a central pillar. This gateway utilized the same peg-and-socket joint used at Stonehenge. The doorway is framed with a gigantic lintel, raised more than 20 feet above the floor. This landmark is similar in motif and architecture to the Lion's Gate of Hattusas. The distinctive Mycenaean trapezoidal doorway design, which tapers inward toward its top, is identical to that found in the ruins at Machu Picchu, high in the Andes Mountains.

A large underground dome known as the Treasury of Atreus was accessed from the Lions Gate. That one room structure was attached through an antechamber, and was built using red granite blocks. It featured an arched ceiling constructed from overlapping stone courses, topped by a single monolithic slab. A similar construction method is found in the Palenque Arch at the Temple of the Inscriptions in Mexico.

Greece

The megalithic ruins found near Amoudia in northern Greece have been explored by David Hatcher Childress. Such remnants are clustered around Lake Acherousia on the western coast, an ancient but now dry lake bed. One of those ancient structures included the Nekromanteion of Aphyra, located along the River Acheron. According to Mr. Childress, the River Acheron is believed to be the legendary River Styx.[11] Its ruins consisted of massive polygonal megaliths, precisely cut and fitted to their adjacent stones. That type of construction is extremely similar to those found in the Andean Mountains at Machu Picchu, Sacsahuaman, and Ollantaytambo.

Mr. Childress also revealed a great marble quarry located near Pieria, approximately 12 miles north of Mount Olympus, in the forested mountains of Thessaly, south of Macedonia. The quarry contained megalithic blocks that were cut and stacked, but never transported or used.[12] Rather, they were abruptly abandoned during antiquity, for some unknown reason. Marble was utilized during the later generations of Greek gods, but was only used infrequently during the earlier megalithic construction phases.

The more recently discovered site of Dion, believed to have been a religious site for worship of the ancient gods, was found near that marble quarry, according to David Hatcher Childress. Evidence indicates that a sanctuary dedicated to the Egyptian goddess, Isis, existed on a portion of the Dion site.[13] Such a shrine seems to link the ancient Greek and Egyptian cultures, albeit through the cult figures of widely separated times and differing religious beliefs.

Turkey

Hattusas lies along a gorge in the central Anatolia Mountains near the small Turkish village of Bogazkale (aka Bogazkoy), about 95 miles east of Ankara. A massive stone wall that extended for nearly four miles protected this site that served as the Hittite capital. Some of its stones were 26 feet long, by almost 20 feet thick. Its main complex was built from perfectly fitted polygonal stones set over megalithic foundation walls, in a manner similar to Mycenaean and Peruvian constructions. Massive gates were located at the east and west extremes of its protective outer wall. Its east gate featured statues of kings, while huge lion statues flanked its west gate. Those massive gate doors pivoted on stone sockets, reminiscent of the temple gates on Malta.

The Hittites later occupied this site, restoring and expanding the facility during their reign, although it is unclear how much of the complex was already in existence upon their arrival to the area. The Hittites reached their height of power and influence around 1180 BC, when they suddenly disappeared. Their fortified capital complex was looted and burned, with massive areas of the stone structure left vitrified, as were the bricks of some houses inside the compound, which were found charred and fused together.

Like many others, that complex had apparently been originally constructed utilizing the advanced technology of the Ancient Ones. Later habitations tend to indicate that such prior technology diminished until it was lost sometime after the departure of the Ancient Ones around 3150 BC. Remnants of fierce battles indicate such sites were highly desired by the BOPH gods, perhaps for the devices and technology those complexes contained. Such battles were either waged by the BOPH gods against factions influenced by the Helpers, or perhaps with the descendants of Alalu and their human followers. The evidence of vitrification at those sites, and the apparent lack of occupation after such battles, may indicate remaining radioactive contamination left from nuclear weapons, requiring a long duration of abandonment until once again becoming safe for habitation.

Near East

Baalbek is a site about 44 miles east of Beirut, Lebanon, consisting of a number of catacombs and stone ruins. It contains some of the largest cut blocks of stone in the world, including three blocks of the enclosure wall known as the *Trilithon*, which are the largest extant blocks ever to be used in construction. Those megalithic giant stones were cut, removed from their quarry pocket, moved to the building site, then lifted almost 25 feet in height to be placed in position over foundation stones. An even larger companion stone, although cut and lifted from its quarry bed, was abandoned at its quarry less than a half-mile from Baalbek. That cut block is the largest single quarried stone known to man, measuring about 70 feet by 13.5 feet by 13 feet, with an estimated weight between 1,200 and 2,000 tons. No modern excavation machinery or crane could lift and transport this single block even today, yet we are led to believe that primitive people without mechanization somehow accomplished the task.

Baalbek's on-site quarry revealed an unusual technique used to cut such monstrous stone slabs. The stone's outer face, two sides, and both ends were first quarried in-place. That left the back of the stone to be cut as the last operation just before removal, requiring it to be lifted up and out from its place of origin. That is a most unusual method for processing stone, and is observed in only one other known location, that being Easter Island.

On Easter Island, one of the *moai* statues that guard its shoreline was discovered in the process of completion, lying in its quarry. While still in its quarry, its facial outline was first sculpted, then all excess rock was cut away to form the full monument. That left the cutting of a stone rib along the back of the statue as the last operation, prior to lifting the completed work from its original bed. Normally, an individual block of rough-cut stone is removed from its quarry, then carved and finished in the open, rather than the opposite process at Easter

Island and Baalbek.

A second quarry was located about 1.25 miles north of the Baalbek ruins. Both area quarries are believed to have also served as the source of the foundation ashlars used in the Wailing Wall and the Temple Mount in Jerusalem, the monolithic foundation stones of the Jewish Temple.

There are no Egyptian, Greek, or Roman records that mention the planning or construction of the Baalbek temple. The edifice was never completed, with work being stopped very suddenly and then buried. Clearly, the structure was partially built, with later additions made in various stages by different cultures, all separated by many years. An early temple, built between *c*.3000 and 2000 BC to worship the Ugarit god Baal and his goddess Astarte, was the earliest known addition made to the much older abandoned stone foundation that included the great Trilithon. Millennia later, the Romans built their temple over the Ugarit shrine to honor their god Jupiter. Ancient Arab records state that the earliest stone temple on that site was built by a group of giants, at the order of the legendary King Nimrod, the reported grandson of the Biblical Noah. That construction occurred sometime just before or just after the Great Flood, depending on which Arabian version is referenced.

Egypt

The Giza Pyramids, an arrangement comprising the Great Pyramid attributed to Khufu (known by the Greeks as Cheops), the middle pyramid ascribed to Khafre (the Greek Chephren), and the smallest or third pyramid, which is credited to Menkaure (the Greek Mycerinus); all appear to reflect different construction periods and methods. The Great Pyramid displays the best skills and quality construction exhibited by any pyramid in the world, and was built using between 2.3 and 2.6 million stone blocks, most weighing between two and three tons each. It has been quite extensively detailed in many other writings, for those wanting additional information and details.

The middle or Khafre Pyramid appears to have been built in two stages. In order to create a level construction platform for this middle pyramid, it was necessary to build-up the foundation elevation at its south and east faces, due to the irregular topography of its site. That was achieved by stacking megalithic 100 ton blocks as foundation stones, bringing those sides up to the desired level. The first several course levels of stone on those faces were also constructed using similar megalithic blocks, while the corresponding courses that formed the north and west faces were excavated or sculpted directly from the solid bedrock outcropping at the site.[14] Once surveyed, leveled, and started, the work evidently abruptly stopped. Construction resumed at some later time, using the more common but smaller two to three ton blocks, which were comparable to those used to build the Great Pyramid. According to Arabian records, the bottom stones of the middle pyramid came from Aswan, while its remainder was built using Kaddan stones.

A distinctive line of demarcation is evident between the two different construction methods, suggesting different builders who used different techniques, separated by some indeterminate period of time. It may well be that the Khafre (middle) Pyramid was actually the first one started at the site. It is the middle pyramid that is connected by a causeway to the Great Sphinx, the Sphinx Temple, and the adjacent Valley Temple of Khafre; perhaps linking all those structures in some unique way such as their construction dates, other than just their causeway connections.

The small Menkaure Pyramid was built using granite; not the limestone blocks used in the other two. Its blocks clearly reflect rougher quarry work and inferior masonry skills, with less precise placement and fitting. Such differences tend to indicate that all three pyramids may reflect their construction by different builders, during separate eras. As previously reported, there are no reliable data identifying their date of construction or their actual builders. Subsequent pharaohs often usurped the work of their predecessors as their own, either by claiming credit if the edifice was unnamed, or by removing prior dedications and adding their own inscription and tribute. Yet such a practice is not evident with any of the three Giza Pyramids.

Such uncertainty as to the builders and their methods used to erect such structures invites debate and controversy. Most Egyptologists discount any extraterrestrial connection with the building of pyramids, since humans were known to have constructed the later ones. The cemetery where the ancient stone masons and support workers were eventually buried has been unearthed, proving that man built at least some of the later pyramids. Ramps, hoists, and diorite stone balls used as quarry tools have also been found, further attesting to man's involvement.

The truth does not require a choice between opposing alternatives. A reasonable assumption points to some type of intervention, most likely by the Ancient Ones, as the builders of the oldest structures, while humans built the later ones, perhaps by attempting to copy the ancient pyramids as models. It becomes obvious from a review of the various structures that multiple methods and types of construction were used, along with differing levels of craftsmanship. The smaller, later Egyptian pyramids were greatly inferior to those at Giza. They were also of a much simpler design, as if the older master builders had disappeared, with their skills being hidden from those later inferior builders.

It is quite probable that certain ancient Egyptian structures, ones mistakenly associated with the much later dynastic period of the pharaohs, were actually built during an earlier epoch of Egyptian culture. The previously mentioned first several base-courses of megalithic stones used to start the Khafre Pyramid may be such a structure, along with the Sphinx, the Sphinx Temple, and the Valley Temple. All might belong to an earlier phase of construction at Giza. Such a period may have even preceded the Great Flood of *c*.10,500 BC. Such an early time frame, one perhaps reflecting the oldest phase of megalithic building, may also be the construction period for the main floor of the Osireion. That structure is much further south from Giza, located about nine miles west of Luxor at Abydos. These exquisitely archaic megalithic structures will be more extensively examined, beginning with the Abydos site.

The Osireion was the megalithic temple dedicated to the god Osiris, which was commonly known as 'The House of Millions of Years.' The edifice is incorrectly thought to have been a lower level segment of the Seti I Temple, located below and to the rear of that much later built structure, which was also known as the 'Great Temple of Abydos.' While the Seti Temple is known to have been built during the time of Seti I, around *c*.1300 BC, the much earlier Osireion clearly was not. It was constructed using megalithic limestone and granite blocks, the largest of any in Egypt. The structure embodies a central mezzanine surrounded by a moat, and may have been designed to depict an island surrounded by water. A rectangular wall of red sandstone enclosing that moat was at least 20 feet thick, cut and fitted in the distinctive polygonal shape of other ancient edifices, and exhibited no inscriptions or ornamentation anywhere on the structure.

Since the Osireion was a subterranean structure more than 50 feet below the level of the later temple, apparently the Seti Temple was deliberately built around and aligned with that much older existing structure. However, the style, masonry type, and quarrying methods link the Osireion more with the Valley Temple at Giza than with the Seti Temple. It also seems more reminiscent or comparable to certain aspects of the Great Labyrinth, as described by ancient historians. Graham Hancock has mentioned a 1996 stratigraphic sequence analysis of Nile silt covering the Osireion site, revealing a total of 22,000 layers. If an average of two Nile floods occurred each year over the millennia, the Osireion could be dated to *c*.9000

BC, although an even older date is equally possible.

The Sphinx, which was carved all in one piece from an outcropping of solid limestone bedrock, may have been built to signify the precessional advance from one 'Age' to the next. It might have indicated the change from the Zodiac sign of *Virgo the Virgin* to *Leo the Lion*, which would have encompassed the years from 10,970 to 8810 BC. The sculpting of the Sphinx may have been started prior to the Great Flood of *c.*10,500 BC, based on extensive research that focused on severe vertical erosion marks worn deep into the soft limestone body of the Sphinx.

Author Graham Hancock revealed such a 1992 study compiled by scientist John West, which concluded that the deep erosion marks were precipitation-induced weathering brought about by constant torrential rains over thousands of years, not from a wind-blown sandblasting profile.[15] Since the most recent period during which prolonged rains occurred was between 10,500 and 9500 BC, a logical conclusion requires the Sphinx to have been in existence *before* that time frame, in order to receive the full effects of such downpour. Professor Robert Schoch, a geologist and rock erosion specialist with Boston University, agreed with Mr. West's research data but tempered his chronology, believing the Sphinx dated to a period between 7000 and 5000 BC, although possibly even older.[16]

As with other exquisitely ancient structures, the Sphinx has no markings or inscriptions. It is known that Khafre and one of his later successors, Thutmosis, restored the Sphinx due to its deterioration over time. The argument that the face of the Sphinx is that of Khafre or any other pharaoh, thereby claiming it to be that pharaoh's construction, simply neglects the obvious. Any ruler who would have restored the Sphinx would naturally impart his own likeness to such a reconstruction project. Further, Egyptian oral traditions describe the Sphinx as a guardian over its surrounding sacred ground during the *First Time*, a time long before the known reign of any pharaoh. That period was a Golden Age when gods ruled and civilization was brought to humankind.

The oldest fragmentary records seem to indicate that the Sphinx was sculpted in stages, starting with a female face, while its rear lion's portion was carved during a later period. Such a connection with a lion perhaps alludes to some evolutionary path from a feline source, explaining the focus and fascination with feline deities during ancient times. The face of the Sphinx is often compared with the controversial Face on Mars. However, many disagree with that analogy, unable to detect much similarity, and cite the mingling of human, feline, and simian features in the Martian image. Its mouth features appear particularly simian, reminiscent of characteristics depicted in the classic movie, *Planet of the Apes*. Certain similarities are also cited between the Face on Mars and the 'Weeping God' likeness at Tiahuanaco, carved on its Gate of the Sun.

The Sphinx Temple and the Valley Temple are located at the Giza complex, with both being attributed as construction efforts by Khafre. The Sphinx Temple was built immediately in front of the Sphinx, with the Valley Temple constructed about 50 feet away, directly on its south side; which in turn was diagonally connected by its Causeway, rearward toward the middle pyramid of Khafre, far behind the Sphinx. The Valley and Sphinx Temples were built using megalithic limestone blocks ranging in size from 50 to well over 200 tons, with the majority weighing 200 tons. Many of their massive blocks were multi-angled stones of polygonal shape, fitted in jigsaw fashion without mortar, cut and removed directly from the site of the Sphinx quarry. Both structures are presently roofless, but sixteen support columns at the Valley Temple still remain, perhaps indicating pilings for massive ceiling slabs similar to those of the Osireion at Abydos and the Great Labyrinth, although with a sloping or wedge-shaped roof.

As was the case with all the other exquisitely ancient constructions, there is an absence of any ornamentation, inscriptions, dedications, or markings of any kind. The earlier mentioned Inventory Stele stated that the Valley Temple was built long before the reign of Khafre, or his predecessor Khufu. Oral traditions state that it was construction by the Neteru, the early or elder Egyptian gods, during the First Time; and explicitly referred to that structure as the 'House of Osiris.' At both the Valley and Sphinx Temples, many of the exterior blocks exposed to the elements have been reinforced with granite facing-stones, fitted into the severely eroded areas like a 'patch.' Such repairs are thought to have been conducted during the Old Kingdom, to compensate for erosion of the original limestone blocks over the ages. Examination of the underlying abrasion reflects similar water patterns to those associated with the Sphinx erosion marks. Such unique erosion evidence allows the three structures to be dated at roughly the same epoch, sometime before 7000 BC.

Ancient rumors and legends, which persist to modern times, state that there are subterranean passages cut into the solid bedrock beneath the pyramids, leading to the Sphinx. Between 1992 and 1993, a seismic survey of the subterranean bedrock at the Giza complex was conducted by Thomas Dobecki, a United States geophysicist. His results indicated the presence of a large rectangular crypt beneath the front paws of the Sphinx.[17] Apparently, the chamber was artificial, due to its squared-corner construction, and was made public by the 1993 NBC Network TV special, *Mystery of the Sphinx*. Such chambers have been speculated to be ancient repositories, and associate them with an esoteric knowledge that was lost during the remote past.

In late 1997 and early 1998, subsequent excavations by Dr. Zahi Hawass, then the Egyptian Pyramid Director, discovered other additional chambers. The Fox Network TV special, *Opening the Lost Tombs*, which aired on March 2, 1999, revealed those subterranean chambers on at least three different levels, accessed through a 20 feet deep shaft leading to the first level. About 40 feet further down, at about 60 feet, the shaft opened to a chamber on a second level. That chamber further descended through a deep shaft to a third level, about 100 feet below the Giza monuments. On that third level, a structure was found in a quarried depression, submerged under water. Upon being pumped-out, the structure was revealed to be a tomb that contained a sarcophagus covered with a stone lid, surrounded by a moat area with four pillars at its outer corners, a design reminiscent of the layout of the Osireion at Abydos.

A network or series of tunnels spread out from the area around that burial chamber, with some passages remaining yet unexplored. It is unknown where they lead, or what might be discovered in their depths. A similar complex of mysterious subterranean tunnels, all cut from solid rock and numbering in the thousands, was also found under the ancient burial tomb of Ti in Saqqara.[18] Many passages from their central corridors simply conclude at dead ends, with some housing massive stone chests estimated to weigh 100 tons. Yet those chests could not have been dragged manually into their crevices, since most abut the end of the tunnel, nor could they have been pushed into place, due to a lack of room necessary to house sufficient manpower that would have been required. Hence, some unknown method evidently was used.

Chapter 22

New World Structures

It appears that the origin of civilization in the New World emerged from a people referred to as the Ancient Peruvians. They, or their even earlier ancestors, were the builders of the numerous grand complexes hidden away within the Andes Mountains. Although the Incas are associated with many of those same sites, they were not the original builders. The Incas arrived much later, and merely occupied and restored the archaic structures left by those prior ancient builders.

Andean Mountains

The most enigmatic and oldest known site in the New World is the Tiahuanaco complex. Perhaps no terrain on Earth is more moonlike, icy, and desolate than that of Tiahuanaco. Yet it appears to be the cultural origin from which all later civilizations and settlements evolved in the Americas. One reason may be the world's largest deposits of tin and copper, which are found in Bolivia and Chile, including the area around Lake Titicaca and Tiahuanaco.

Tiahuanaco is located in Bolivia on a plateau high in the Andes Mountains near the southern shore of Lake Titicaca. The lake's islands may have been the nucleus for the earliest Tiahuanaco culture. The boarder between Peru and Bolivia bisects Lake Titicaca, with the lake split roughly in half between the two countries. It is the world's highest navigable fresh water lake, at an altitude of 13,861 feet above sea level. It is about 120 miles long, by as wide as 44 miles, with a 35 mile average width, covering about 3,210 square miles. Lake Titicaca is very frigid and quite deep, ranging from 100 to 1,000 feet in depth, and has been deemed by some to be the most remarkable body of water in the world.

The ruins of a sunken city are known to exist in its cold depths, consisting of high walls and paved paths that are visible at certain times of the year. Great palaces are reported to be visible just below the surface, during the area's occasional periods of severe drought. An underwater team explored the lake's depths and confirmed the presence of high walls that have deteriorated from the brackish water. An oral legend refers to the existence of the great 'Jeweled City,' which is now submerged in the middle of Lake Titicaca. Indigenous natives around Tiahuanaco also retain a distant legend that some of their most remote ancestors were sacrificed and buried under the foundation stones when the complex was being built, perhaps a parallel with the skeletal remains found under the megalithic stones on Malta. The sunken city, along with the various extant islands, may represent the remnants of the earliest Ancient Peruvian culture that might date to as early as 34,000 BC.

Tiahuanaco is the site of a complex comprising several ancient ruins, covering an area approximately one by two miles in size. Its inhospitable height has a very thin atmosphere, and only eight pounds per square inch air pressure. Despite its high altitude location, sea shell fossils and ocean sediment are found around the site. That suggests the area was once only a few feet above sea level, or was affected by some past cataclysm that subjected the area to immense wind, rainfall, and flood waves that projected sea level beach soils and debris to its lofty region.

Stone docks and quays built around the ruins indicate its prior use as a port, probably in conjunction with Lake Titicaca. The ancient shoreline of Lake Titicaca has been established to within 600 feet of the Tiahuanaco complex, surrounding it on three sides, essentially making the original compound a peninsula. That port complex likely provided supplies to the sacred islands dotting the lake, which are covered with farming terraces. That prior proximity to the lake occurred during one of the earliest phases of the complex, when the level of Lake Titicaca was about one hundred feet higher, but before tidal waves and winds from the Great Flood affected the area. The two areas are now separated by about eleven miles, although lake levels vary, depending on the region's precipitation, drought patterns, and other conditions.

The complex was built using hard andesite stone blocks that came from a peninsula of Lake Titicaca near the village of Copacabana about 20 miles away, as well as from Kiappa, an aerial distance of 40 miles. Transports involved both water and land routes. Other quarries for the limestone, basalt, and red sandstone blocks also used in the construction were taken from various regional sites, some up to 200 miles away. Transportation of such large stones over the imposing terrain would pose a monumental, perhaps impossible problem, even with utilization of modern equipment. Yet such blocks retained their crisp, sharp corners, as if cut with a laser, and show no signs of rough handling, which would have rounded corners. The ancient builders obviously accomplished such transport tasks without the use of any intrusive force.

One indigenous legend states that those stones were carried through the air by 'gifted beings' to the sound of a trumpet. Another legend passed down by the Ancient Peruvians tells of giants living around Lake Titicaca who were eventually pushed to the south by the natives. Tiahuanaco was then built over the ruins left by those 'Fair-haired Giants' that had built the original structure at the site, supposedly between 250,000 and 200,000 BC, according to legend.

At the center of the Tiahuanaco complex is the Kalasasaya, meaning the Standing Pillars, and is sometimes called the Temple of the Sun. The Kalasasaya was an ingenious astronomical and calendarical observatory, built from enormous 200 ton stone blocks of polygonal shape, locked together with molten bronze cleats poured into key-depressions cut into the stones. When resolidified, the cleats hold adjoining stones together. The use of such metal cleats to connect or hold polygonal stones is believed to have been employed to withstand the effects of earthquakes.

Sculptures originally located in the Kalasasaya include the Monolith (aka Giant), which is the largest stone idol of Tiahuanaco, standing nearly 24 feet high, with an estimated weight of 20 tons. It was sculpted from fine gray andesite, and displays indecipherable, enigmatic symbols. Its same likeness was reproduced in other locations throughout Central and South America, but in smaller sizes. A more humanlike statue, believed to be the god Viracocha, was carved from red sandstone and stands almost nine feet high. A six feet tall statue, the Friar, was cut from red sandstone and once stood in the southwest corner of the Kalasasaya.

The Akapana (aka the Hill of Sacrifices) is located directly behind the Kalasasaya, slightly to its southeast. It is an immense man-made hill, built as a truncated pyramid 170 feet high, which was carefully aligned with the cardinal points. Its complex earthen stepped-pyramid structure resembles the ziggurats found in the Near East, but with underground chambers and monuments similar to those of Mayan design, comparable with the early earthen edifices built by the Mound Builders of North America. Originally its outer surface was faced with huge rectangular stone slabs; a feature reminiscent of the casing stones that initially covered the Great Pyramid of Giza. Even with such similarities, its original purpose still remains unknown.

A sunken open-air courtyard is located east of the Kalasasaya, where three red sandstone menhirs were erected near its center. That structure also features a prominent display of carved stone representations of 'faces' or 'heads' that protrude from the surfaces of its surrounding walls. That elaborate array showcases virtually every known human race on Earth, and even some of an unidentifiable race.

An olden Peruvian fable claimed that their god Viracocha had designed and sculpted a great stone monument at Tiahuanaco, which contained all the nations (races) he intended to create. He reportedly formed each race from clay, imparting distinctly different features to each before bringing them to life and establishing Tiahuanaco as a sacred place. Those carvings display obvious facial differences in the eyes, noses, mouths, and foreheads, along with other characteristics, creating a virtual 'gallery of humankind.' The varied facial features displayed in that courtyard gallery seem to be reminiscent of Viracocha's legendary work. Such sculpted heads were carved from red sandstone and were held in place on the walls of the courtyard with stone spikes.

Such a display is also reminiscent of an ancient shrine identified as Grotto 58, found in the Buddhist monument known as the Grottoes of the Thousand Buddhas, located about ten miles north of Tun-huang, China. This site was carved directly into the mountain, forming small caverns that were connected by a corridor leading to a central hall with several large meeting rooms. In the grotto identified by archaeologists as number 58, a sculpted scene is found that displays a Buddha sleeping on an altar surrounded by an assortment of worshipers who clearly represent numerous different races, including Native North American Indians in full feathered headdress.[1] Other races are depicted that remain unidentifiable, or perhaps are from some lost or unknown race that no longer exists on Earth.

A gateway called the Puerta del Sol, the Gate of the Sun, was originally located in the northwest corner of the Kalasasaya. This entrance stone is extremely similar to the Persepolis Gate in ancient Persia. It was carved from a single block of volcanic andesite, weighing over 100 tons. This archway depicts the 'Weeping god,' a face carved with three tear drops on its cheeks, a common motif found at other ancient South American sites. But closer scrutiny may indicate a mechanical device similar to a magnifying glass or monocle.

Perhaps that device was an individual eye-piece, lens, or shield that could be positioned for each eye, allowing it to pivot at its lower end for rotation to an out-of-the-way position when not in use. This same image was later reproduced on numerous artifacts, mainly vases and cloth pieces, throughout the remote regions of Peru, Bolivia, and Chile. This carving was previously compared to the Face on Mars for similarities.

A 'calendar frieze' was engraved on the eastern side of the upper lintel, just below and on either side of the Weeping god figure. Similar figures thought to represent the god Viracocha comprise the majority of the frieze, and are reminiscent of Mayan stylization. Less distinct images were carved along the base of the frieze. Author Graham Hancock deciphered those badly faded geometric designs and forms, identifying them as depictions of prehistoric animals, such as toxodons and other extinct elephant like and equine creatures.[2] Such depictions of Pleistocene animals add further credence to the preflood dating of the complex.

An area known as Puma Punku (aka Puma Puncu) is situated nearly a mile southwest of the other structures found at the main complex, and is considered to have been the site of the oldest Tiahuanaco ruins. It was built during a time when the waters of Lake Titicaca had 'cradled' that ancient complex with extended 'canals,' creating the site's original configuration as a peninsula. That represented a time when Lake Titicaca had been much larger in surface area, and estimated to have been more than 100 feet deeper than present. Puma Punku was first believed to be a separate site, but is now known to have been an integral part of the original greater complex, believed to have been the principal harbor when Tiahuanaco was a port city.

Although Puma Punku contained some of Tiahuanaco's largest edifices, ones built upon immense foundation slabs as large as 440 tons, researchers believe that it had been violently and completely destroyed by seismic disruptions that caused flood waters from Lake Titicaca to crash into its structures during the eleventh millennium BC.[3] Its resultant ruins then formed a jumbled heap, as if tossed about like dominos, although some of the strewn blocks are a massive 26 by 16 feet in size, cut from the Lake Titicaca quarry. Found among that rubble was a series of partially sunken enclosures made from perfectly cut and shaped blocks. Those structures had been built using huge red sandstone slabs that were ultimately broken into three or four pieces by the previously mentioned but unknown calamity.

The actual design of the original structure or structures located at the Puma Punku site still remains a partial mystery, due to the scattered condition of those massive slabs and blocks. It has been suggested that such a jumbled array of intricately shaped stones had been components forming four complex main structures along the eastern edge of the site, with numerous smaller auxiliary buildings surrounding them. Others claim merely a single main structure existed at the site, with the balance of the precisely cut blocks that were found within its ruins utilized merely as individual components that comprised various complex dies or molds, perhaps used to produce enormous cast machine-elements for some unknown purpose.

It is thought that such a single main structure once had a massive roof that was supported by long cylindrical columns, which were fitted into receptacle depressions cut directly into the mammoth foundation stones. The slabs, blocks, and cylinders that once comprised such a structure all displayed indications of having been precisely machined, with tight tolerances and surface flatness that was true and accurate over their entire length. Receptacles for columns, alignment holes, and other joining and layout features, as well as their physical dimensions and proportions, all reflected the use of machinist's tolerances, not masonry ones. Such cutting operations and their subsequent construction and fitting was thoroughly precise in every aspect. Similar cut and prepared stones still remaining at the quarry across Lake Titicaca indicated an apparent sudden interruption of work by their mysterious builders, who were either destroyed by some unknown conflagration, or abruptly abandoned the area and simply never returned.

The German scholar Arthur Posnansky, one of the foremost authorities on the Tiahuanaco complex, dates the ruins as old as 15,000 BC. His calculation was based on the astronomical orientation and layout used for sighting and recording cosmic and solstice events, the very purpose for which its advanced observatory was built. Dr. Rolf Müller, an astronomer from the Potsdam Observatory, another acknowledged expert on the Tiahuanaco site, further confirmed Arthur Posnansky's dating.

Professor Posnansky moved to Bolivia around 1910 to devote his life's work to the examination of the ruins. He found three distinct cultural phases evident at Tiahuanaco. The oldest phase dated from 15,000 to 10,500 BC, ending with the Great Flood. The megalithic construction, including the Gate of the Sun, was from that earliest period. The next interval was from c.9200 to 6000 BC, followed by its last ancient phase that occurred between c.4500 and 1500 BC. Examination of the archaeological strata actually revealed remains of five different periods of construction, resulting in five distinct cities, some overlapping their prior level, with every level ending in tangled confusion and disaster.

Arthur Posnansky had concluded that the terrible natural disaster that destroyed Puma Punku occurred during the eleventh millennium BC, which is also the time frame during which the Great Flood of circa 10,500 BC occurred. Professor Posnansky thought such a cataclysm had been due to seismic disturbances, which resulted in Lake Titicaca overflowing its waters in a tidal wave fashion, accompanied by numerous violent volcanic eruptions. The climate also abruptly changed afterward, producing a colder and harsher environment at the site.

It has been suggested that following such a cataclysmic destruction, much later settlers to the site chose to restore only those structures located at other areas of the complex, which were originally built utilizing somewhat smaller stones. Such later repair and reconstruction work apparently avoided the Puma Punku area, rather than attempting to wrestle its massive stone slabs that weighed 300 or 400 tons.

The Tiahuanaco area is mineral rich, but was not fully exploited. The region contained abundant platinum, iron ore, mercury, and petroleum deposits that apparently were never utilized; although numerous tin, copper, silver, and gold mines in the area were regularly worked. Even with plentiful copper and tin, the metals necessary to produce bronze, no Bronze Age ever existed in South America. Sophisticated dies or molds sculpted from stone were among the ruins, which could have produced intricate cast parts for some unknown use.

A unique owl-head vase design associated with the area is now in the Louvre Museum of Paris, and is identical in size, shape, and design to one found by Heinrich Schliemann during his excavations at Troy. The discovery of such uniquely identical artifacts, located on different continents, is a most unlikely occurrence, unless both cultures shared some common source, such as the benefactor Ancient Ones and their humanlike Helpers.

The Tiahuanaco area also provided one of the world's greatest mountain retreats, with nearby boating on Lake Titicaca. Such a secluded mountain site would offer maximum privacy and solitude from which to conduct numerous genetic experiments or engineering projects. The nearby islands would also offer an excellent quarantine area for the resultant 'inventions' or 'creations,' providing a protective containment from which to study, educate, and monitor each new subspecies or race. The many enigmatic features associated with this complex suggest that the Ancient Ones did take advantage of such seclusion to conduct their work.

Due to the inaccessible location of Tiahuanaco and its high altitude, which makes the oxygen-poor air very 'thin' for breathing, it would have been nearly impossible for any ancient natives to build the complex. Estimates claim that 100,000 people would have been required to construct the site, but the Andean plateau could not have produced the animal and plant resources to sustain such a large number of people during construction. No known records identify its original builders, occupants, or purpose of the complex. Archaeologists offer no explanation for this site, and disagree on the age of the ruins, with the 'youngest' guess at 1000 AD, while others believe a much more ancient construction date, with its abandonment by the original inhabitants sometime between 10,000 and 8000 BC.

It was further determined that all its construction was done by genius builders and planners of some unknown origin. The more modern Inca armies, moving south from Cuzco, came upon the Tiahuanaco ruins in *c.*1200 AD. The Incas merely performed some repair work at the site, after which they occupied the complex. The Incas later copied portions of the Tiahuanaco architecture and duplicated certain of its features and aspects into their own great structures.

Satellite Sites from Tiahuanaco

Apparently the original Lake Titicaca culture expanded beyond Tiahuanaco, settling new sites that were built using similar megalithic techniques. Although the first expansion location was planned for Machu Picchu, earlier structures were strategically built along the route to that site. It is likely that Cuzco was the first of those locations, located about 300 miles northwest from Tiahuanaco, high in the Peruvian Andes. This was not the much later Inca's Celestial City of the gods, the 'Navel of the World,' but a major rest stop or way station used as a protective sanctuary and storehouse for supplies to replenish the travelers. According to legends, Viracocha did not establish that great complex until the third period of Tiahuanaco, sometime after 4500 BC.

Rather, it was during a much early period when the massive megalithic constructions around Cuzco occurred. Construction at Cuzco during that early period consisted of great refuge walls, such as the semicircular remnants of the Coricancha, and massive repositories, all built using megalithic polygonal stones perfectly fitted without mortar. Just north of Cuzco, on a hill overlooking that city, the nearby fortress of Sacsahuaman served as a *pucara*, a defensible fort that was used as a sanctuary if ever under attack. The complex covered more than several hundred acres, featuring three massive outlying walls, all over 1200 feet long by 60 feet high, arranged in a zigzag pattern. The walls were built using highly irregular polygonal boulders, some consisting of 36 surfaces, precisely cut and fitted without mortar. The largest boulders weighed between 300 and 400 tons each, quarried and transported from their source several miles away. The Pisac complex also loomed over Cuzco, on the very edge of a steep cliff. It served as another pucara or defensive encampment against attacks from the east, but was also a city unto itself, with shrines, palace gathering halls, and even hanging gardens.

Further north and directly east of the final destination of Machu Picchu, the huge astonishing monolithic walls of Ollantaytambo were erected. This site lies in the valley of the Urubamba River, between the Andes and the Amazon basin at the summit of a steep mountain spur, and served as a fortress that guarded the mouth of the Urubamba canyon along the route from Cuzco to Machu Picchu. There, a retaining wall was built using rough polygonal fieldstones. A gateway was cut into one stone as a passage to a platform, which itself was supported by a second retaining wall built using even larger polygonal slabs of stones. An attached enclosure, using that retaining wall as one of its sides, featured the unique trapezoidal shaped openings for both its two doors and ten window-openings, and was believed to be the main garrison.

The polygonal blocks also utilized cast metal cleats to hold the mortarless stones together, similar to the technique found earlier at Tiahuanaco 300 miles to the south.

The gigantic red granite stones used at both Sacsahuaman and Ollantaytambo were quarried from the mountainside on the opposite bank of the Urubamba River valley; requiring stone transport down one mountainside, across the river, and up the opposing side of the mountain opposite from the quarry. Such effort seems like an impossible task for primitive natives.

Complex geometric shapes were cut into the cliff faces throughout the nearby plateau areas. Such precise rock carvings were either sockets or receivers for now-missing keystones, or some unknown machinery that could fit into those receptacles during their utilization. In most all directions from Cuzco, similar stones can be found, cut into freestanding forms and shapes with no readily apparent use or recognizable purpose. Most consist of multiple shapes including intersecting compound planes, simple steps, precise grooves and hollows, basin depressions, multi-level tiers and platforms, rib and post projections, and right-angle pockets.

While simple solar or lunar alignments have been observed utilizing small portions of those sculptures, it makes no sense to add such elaborate and extraneous elements to the carvings if their only intent was for celestial sightings. They do not seem to reflect any aesthetic expression as sculpted art pieces, to justify such a massive expenditure of labor. The most logical explanation involves their use as dies or molds, used to cast massive machinery components.

Such 'dies of stone' were often clustered in galleries, set high on the mountainside. They may have once been a set or series of highly polished, irregular surfaced, progressive molds, all precisely cut from solid granite; apparently to cast intricate, geometric-shaped machine parts. The 'dies' display master craftsmanship, incorporating back draft, undercut, and die-lock areas, along with right-angle surfaces and sharp inside right-angle corners. They may have also utilized loose-piece cores to produce even more intricate and massive metal castings for some unknown purpose, perhaps as spare or replacement parts for advanced machinery or spacecraft.

The ancient journey from Tiahuanaco concluded at Machu Picchu. That complex was a fortified citadel city covering about five square miles, approximately 65 miles northwest of Cuzco, Peru. It was located at 10,300 feet above sea level, precipitously high in the Andes Mountains, almost 2,000 feet above the Urubamba River. It lies in a basin or hollow of two Andean peaks in total seclusion, a virtual hidden paradise. The city consisted of more than fifty farming terraces built around a central plaza, with each level linked by numerous stairways, all reflecting fine craftsmanship and engineering skills throughout its construction. Widely different construction phases are apparent, separated by long time spans between each distinct period.

The oldest cyclopean constructions at Machu Picchu presumably occurred during the early part of the second megalithic building period, which existed between 9200 and 6000 BC. Those structures were made from perfectly cut and dresses polygonal stone ashlars, all precisely fitted without mortar. Those stones came from two quarries, the nearest was about 15 miles away at Muyna, while the other stones came from beyond the Yucay River about 45 miles away. The lower walls around the complex were built in the same manner as Sacsahuaman, and keyed with bronze tendons like those found at Tiahuanaco.

Other megalithic construction included the Principal Temple and the famous Temple of the Three Windows, which were adjoined by the Sacred Plaza. The Temple of the Three Windows at the eastern edge of the Sacred Plaza had only three walls, with its open side to the west, which overlooked a seven feet tall stone pillar. The main or Principal Temple, located on the northern edge of the Sacred Plaza, also consisted of only three sides, which reached a height of 12 feet in some areas. Its white granite stones were transported a great distance over rough terrain up and down mountain sides, through valleys, and across dangerous rivers. The distinctive trapezoidal doorways and 'window-openings,' which tapered at the top, were common features associated with Machu Picchu's oldest structures. The much later 'simple' houses, which were built using fieldstone and mortar, were of noticeably lesser craftsmanship and quality.

The Torreon, which is also known as the Tower of the Sun, is a semicircular structure whose outer wall followed the natural curvature of the rock cliff at the edge of its basin plateau. It was accessed using seven steps leading from the terrace area. That semi-circular open area featured a Sacred Rock that was carved with intricate shapes like the previously mentioned stone dies. An opening behind the Tower lead to a small cavern lined with precision-cut stone forming the 'royal mausoleum,' which also contained a throne and a number of alcoves cut from solid rock.

Northwest from the Sacred Plaza, steps led to a flattened hill where the Hitching Post of the Sun, the *Intihuatana*, was sculpted. There, the sun's rays caused the shadow created from that 'rock post' to exactly fit within a 'measured area' of the stone marker during the summer solstice.

Chavin de Huantar

Chavin de Huantar was likely the next major satellite complex established by the Lake Titicaca culture. It was located far to the northwest of Machu Picchu, in the northwestern Cordillera Blanca mountain range of the Peruvian Andes, at an altitude of 10,000 feet. It consisted of a series of platforms and hillside temples with corbel arched corridors, which displayed fine stone sculptures and relief carvings. Its premier structure was the Castillo, the central temple on the southwest corner of the complex, built using enormous stone blocks. It comprised several rectangular structures, forming partitioned rooms and passageways. The Castillo had three terraced levels reached by steps through a gateway that was flanked by cylindrical columns and rectangular pillars supporting a mammoth one-piece lintel 30 feet long. An outer wall nearly 500 feet long by almost 40 feet high encompassed three sides of the site, with its eastern open end adjoining a river. All its buildings were aligned with the cardinal points.

The original inhabitants also possessed mining and advanced metalworking skills, although nearly nothing is known of those people or their culture, which produced their own unique style of stelae and other unusual monuments. The Raimondi Monolith is a carved stone slab depicting some sort of creature that appeared to be half-man and half-bull, reminiscent of the fabled Minotaur of Greek legend. Another, the Tello Obelisk, is a bas-relief stone carving depicting strange human creatures with feline features, grotesque animals, unknown geometric shapes, and god-like creatures apparently exhibiting some type of propulsive device. Some of the fantastic carved shapes are described as cosmic engines or rockets, and have been compared to the figures that adorn the Gate of the Sun at Tiahuanaco. A third stone carving, the El Lanzon, depicts a composite creature that appears to have the head of a wild boar, on a distorted humanoid torso.

Intricately complex stone key-slots or receptacle sockets, which are similar to those scattered around the plateau areas north of Cuzco, are also found in the Chavin region. The Chavin culture is believed to be the prototype or nucleus for all the people of north central Peru that eventually followed. Such sites may have included the early phases of the stone ruins found at Chimbote, Pisco, Pachacamac, and Cajamarca; as well as areas around the Casma, Rimac, and Nepana valleys. The ruins of Cajamarquilla are found outside Lima, in a side valley of the Rimac River, on an amphitheater plain high in the hills. The ruins consist of three groups of buildings and stepped pyramids, connected by streets and narrow passageways that contain subterranean vaults. According to oral traditions, Pachacamac, a site along the Pacific coast of

Peru, was a sacred city where the Ancient Peruvians worshiped the Creator. Its ruins consist of large stone walls and adobe brick buildings, many of which remain buried under the sands of the desolate region.

Central America

Moving further north into Central America, gigantic stone platforms are found at Monte Alban, the ruined capital of the pre-Zapotec culture of the ancient Olmecs and Mayans. Its complex is located on an excavated plateau between two hilltops overlooking the Oaxaca Valley in the foothills of the Sierra Madre del Sur Mountains, about seven miles from the city of Oaxaca, Mexico. Its massive stone platforms, one to the north and the other at its southern end, are considered to be the Western Hemisphere counterparts of the Baalbek megaliths. The purpose of such massive stone slabs remains unknown. Monte Alban dates back to at least 3000 BC, and only later became an Olmec site. Its 55 acre complex consisted of a central plaza, underground passages, pyramids, temples, an observatory, and an elaborate series of vaulted tombs, in addition to its two megalithic platforms. Those structures were carefully arranged according to a precise orientation. The quarry site for its massive stones is believed to have been in Mitla, Mexico.

North America

It was suggested in Chapter 15 that the Ancient Peruvians may have been the original ancient builders of the enigmatic earthen mounds found scattered around the United States. Although not constructed using megalithic stones, the earliest mounds would have still required efforts beyond the ascribed levels of primitive natives. Based on the complexity and massive size of certain mounds, aerial assistance would be indicated in order to accomplish their construction.

A few megalithic sites are found in the United States, in New Hampshire, Connecticut, and in upstate New York. A state park in eastern Oklahoma contains a series of megaliths covered with Norse Runes, similar to the Kensington Rune Stone carvings in Minnesota. Such markings are usually dismissed as a hoax, since they contradict orthodox belief, although there is no proof of any deception. At Casa Grande, south of Phoenix, Arizona, an ancient three story skyscraper was built using concrete. The site was once an ancient city with concrete-lined canals, ones that are still in use today. David Hatcher Childress revealed that the site is speculated to be connected with an ancient city within the Grand Canyon, which is reported to contain vast catacombs and tunnels forming an Egyptian-like complex, according to a 1909 article published in the *Phoenix Gazette*.[4]

Abundant evidence exists that the Ancient Peruvian's Lake Titicaca culture sponsored by the Ancient Ones ultimately spread to the United States. It apparently reached the northeastern extremes where megalithic stone slabs were found, penetrated the north, reaching the copper mines of Lake Superior in Michigan's upper peninsula, and also expanded all the way to the Mima Mounds in the northwest. A path from those sites in the Pacific Northwest, as well as directly from ancient Peru, can be traced to the numerous islands of the Pacific, according to Thor Heyerdahl.[5]

Easter Island

The tiny and mysterious Easter Island displays evidence of at least three construction periods. Its finest megalithic structures were built during its oldest period. Huge platform altars called *ahus* were built in numerous locations around the island. The island's most precise altar walls, ones thought to date to its oldest period, are found at a small site known as Tahira Ahu, a location near the southeastern coastal village of Vinapu. Its walls consist of mortarless, perfectly cut and fitted stone blocks, identical in style and craftsmanship to those found at Machu Picchu and throughout the Cuzco area.

The 19th century American naval officer and explorer W. J. Thomson described an area of ancient ruins found at the southern end of the island. He revealed those ruins as consisting of about 80 to 100 stone shelters, built in a row along a natural rock terrace. All those houses were constructed using huge five feet thick irregular stone blocks.[6] Some rocks found within an adjacent area to that site were carved as monuments, displaying images of fish, turtles, and birds. At the opposite end of the island along its northern coast, strong magnetic disturbances have also been recorded.[7] Similar magnetic anomalies have also been observed along the Nazca plateau, as well as on the Canigou Mountain in the Pyranees' Range, and in the Moroccan frontier at the edge of the Algerian Sahara.

The prevailing belief surrounding Easter Island's famous *moai* statues claims that brute force was used to carve, move, and raise those stone monuments. A modern re-enactment using better equipment still required 500 men to lift one statue a little over eight feet in height. A noticeably greater number would have been required for each stage of statue construction, from its quarry to final erection. Such manpower usage would have monopolized the entire work force of this small isolated island, precluding farming efforts necessary to feed the moai sculptors and their support population. Its society, whose maximum population never exceeded 10,000 inhabitants, is believed to have been a closed one, with no known origin and no known demise. The original inhabitants simply appeared, lived their isolated lives building moai, and then vanished. The reason why the islanders engaged in such intensive work, and exactly what process or method they used in such effort, still remains unknown.

At the location of the oldest alters, those located along the western coast of the island in a bay near Ahu Tahai, a bust was found depicting an image very different from the classic moai statues that overlook the island. That head was carved from red volcanic stone, and dated to a far older time period of the island. No theory has yet been formulated explaining that statue or the being represented. Perhaps it represented one of the Ancient Ones.

Easter Island was considered to be one of the ancient 'navels' of the world. Legends claim that the first men to live on Easter Island were survivors of the world's First Race. Ancient texts and legends described that First Race as an antediluvian people who: "...possessed a superior knowledge of an entirely different world," which "...existed amongst the stars,"[8] according to native accounts. Other records also referred to such beings as 'Long Ears.' Later legends state that a bearded, white god, Hotu-Matua, came from Peru to Easter Island in 475 AD with 300 men and performed marvelous acts. Oral histories of the modern natives state that the moai statues were transported around the island by spirit force, as if by magic. Numerous similarities are found between the Peruvian and Easter Island statues, as well as their numerous comparable construction styles, all further linking Easter Island in certain specific ways with Tiahuanaco.

Polynesian Islands

It is believed that Easter Island was the origin or center from which other Polynesian megaliths evolved. Author Peter Kolosimo reported that the scholarly researcher Serge Hutin detected similar ruins to those of Easter Island on Mangaia Island, an area south of Cook Island.[9] Numerous connections and similarities are also cited by archaeologists in support of that belief.

Inhabitants of other Polynesian Islands also transported and used similar massive stone objects. Generally, only the Marquises group, Pitcairn, Raivavae, and the extreme portions of Polynesia used large stones for buildings and statues. Most of the megaliths of Polynesia, Melanesia, and Micronesia were not dressed or polished, although they were precisely fitted, all without mortar. Some finished stones can also be found in those areas, such as the famous gateway or trilithon cromlech at the town of Mua on Tonga-tapu Island, where its lintel is estimated to weigh 30 tons. In the Marquises, ten ton stone slabs were transported along mountain slopes, in an effort to reach their final destination for some still unknown purpose.

According to author Eklal Kueshana (pen name of Richard Kieninger), immense ruins of an ancient city called Metalanim were found on the southeastern shore of Pohnpei Island,[10] the island formerly called Ponape in the Caroline Island group. The massive city was built using megalithic stone blocks as large as 15 tons each. The city's architecture and engineering is equivalent to modern levels, and is quite different from the more primitive cultures of Oceania. Artificial waterways intersect with the city, large enough to accommodate ocean liners.[11] The number of inhabitants associated with the ruins has been estimated as high as two million people.[12] The nearby site of Nan Madol was built on a coral reef, located off the southeastern point of Pohnpei and the tiny island of Temuen (aka Temwen), where approximately 90 great buildings were enclosed by a massive walled fortress that was constructed during ancient times.[13]

Some 3,400 miles away, the remnants of 40 stone temples that resemble the Ponape Island architecture are found on the otherwise barren Malden Island.[14] Roads built from massive basalt blocks extend from those temples in all directions, and continue into the ocean, according to Mr. Kueshana.[15] Some believe that one section of those ancient roads once connected with streets found on Rarotonga Island. Remnants of similar architecture can be found on many of the mountainous Pacific islands, and are often regarded as sacred sites by the native inhabitants.

Chapter 23

Stone Legends

Amateur archaeologist David Hatcher Childress revealed strange quarry marks were associated with some ancient stones. Certain stones in the quarry near Mount Olympus at Pieria, Greece, show a rounded corner fracture that may indicate a routing or milling process used to 'score' the rock during its quarry process. Mr. Childress references the work of the Greek writer, Konstantinos Zissis, who describes those unusual markings as 'parallel grooves.'[1] Those tool marks display a slightly wavy track or groove, which tends to rule out a machining process as their likely cause. The worked-areas also exhibited small, crater-like holes or pores, aligned along the depressions of the grooves. Mr. Zissis described those anomalies as perhaps evidence of a melting or liquefying process that once affected those grooved areas, softening the rock and allowing it to be torn away from its bedrock base during the quarrying process.[2]

Other evidence further indicates that some form of mechanization was likely involved with such quarry work. Archaeologist Friedrich Ragette believes that marks left on stones used as late as the Roman restoration of Baalbek conform to a pattern of concentric circular swings made by some unknown quarrying machine.[3] The radial arc exhibited by such an unknown device also exceeded the swing and force that could have been produced by manual human labor alone. Mr. Ragette believed such a quarry machine had an adjustable and weighted arm that could extend to a radius of 13 feet, as evidenced by the largest radial marks left on some of the rocks.[4]

Some stones may have even been sawn using jeweled blades. The one-piece stone chest or sarcophagus found in the King's Chamber of the Great Pyramid would have required saws at least eight feet long to cut it from the bedrock. The final finish and quality of those cuts could not be surpassed even with the best ceramic or diamond-tipped cutting tools of modern times. The noted archaeologist and surveyor, William Matthew Flinders Petrie, did find evidence indicating the use of long copper saws,[5] some over nine feet long, unearthed at the pyramid builders village west of Giza. Ancient texts tell of the 'Awesome Saw' and the 'Olden Copper Lance,'[6] both able to accomplish great tasks, although no description of either actual tool or their operation accompanied such reports.

Sir Flinders Petrie also found evidence indicating the use of copper or bronze chisels and drills.[7] Certain holes drilled in some granite blocks found at Giza were carefully examined by Sir Flinders Petrie. He concluded from the steep angle of the residual spiral tool marks that jeweled-tipped bits must have been used, involving very high feed rates and massive pressure forces.[8] Such indicated speeds and feeds, used for any sustained period, would be beyond the limits of even our modern day industrial bits.

According to author Erich von Däniken, Professor Joseph Davidovits, a chemist and director of the Institute for Applied Archaeological Science at Barry University in Miami, Florida, hypothesized that the pyramid stones may have been cast.[9] He theorized that the blocks were poured right at the construction site like concrete, concluding that such blocks were of artificial composition. A 1979 analysis, conducted by mineralogist Dr. D. Klemm on stone samples taken from the Great Pyramid, revealed that those blocks contained far more moisture than normal for a 'natural' rock.[10] While natural stone formations usually display a uniform density throughout its composition, the pyramid stones reportedly exhibited a more dense distribution at its bottom, as compared to its top, where a higher incident of entrapped air was said to exist.[11]

The *Famine Stele*, found by Egyptologist C. E. Wilbour in 1889, reportedly described the manufacture of artificial stone.[12] An olden legend also disclosed that some 29 mineral and chemical ingredients supposedly could be used to make artificial rock, along with the binding agents and the methods necessary to fuse such a composition.[13] Still other legends refer to stones being 'cast as if by magic.' The artificial cast pillars previously mentioned in Chapter 15, found on the islands of Oceania dating as old as 10,950 BC, may have been attempts to reproduce such a lost formula and ancient technology; one that existed only as an incomplete remnant of the past.

Other legends reveal the knowledge and ability of ancient civilizations to utilize the hardest rock with ease for their construction purposes. A sample of those legends, along with their location of origin, will be further examined, revealing additional anomalous evidence from ancient times. A granite rock on a butte called Windy Mound in Marshall County, South Dakota, has hand prints imbedded into its surface. This rock is commonly known as 'Prayer Rock,' and also contains markings that resemble Chinese characters imprinted on its surface. Those markings have been dated to at least 2500 BC, and also exhibit similarities with an ancient Alaskan Eskimo culture.[14]

The Sioux Indians attribute Prayer Rock to the power of the Thunderbird, their Great White Father, whose home was alleged to be less than two miles from that mysterious boulder. Myths claim that an old Sioux chief prayed for rain at that rock, and afterward his hand prints were left embedded in its surface.[15] The legend of the Great Thunderbird god is nearly universal among the indigenous Indian tribes of North America. Common tribal accounts describe such a god as a Caucasoid-trait humanlike being, who brought civilization to humanity upon his arrival from the heavens in a loud flying craft.

At Amelie-les-Bains in the Pyrenes-Orientals District of France, imprints resembling small hands being pressed into soft clay are evident in a sandstone rock displayed in a public park.[16]   A granite rock in Zazliai, Lithuania, bears the impression of footprints on its surface.[17]   Granite blocks with distinct hand prints are also on display in the museum of Cochabamba, Bolivia.[18]   Many stones bearing such foot and hand prints are found throughout Peru. In most cultures, such unique rocks are called 'touched stones.'

Ancient Peruvian legends tell of a plant whose juices caused the surface of rocks to soften, allowing precise fits between adjacent stones by rubbing together the mating faces while pliable, then allowing the stones to harden in place. Other legends stated that ancient builders knew of an herb that could be used to soften any type of stone, making it malleable, which would later reharden in the sun.[19] The use of such a plant extract to soften stone was often the native's explanation for the intricate fit of ancient polygonal stone constructions.[20]

The British explorer, Colonel Percy Fawcett, reportedly had first hand experience with such a vegetation extract. Around 1922, he supposedly observed the discovery of a sealed jar containing a liquid that had been enclosed in an ancient tomb located somewhere in Brazil, although another account states its location somewhere in the Andes of South America. Upon opening the container, a small quantity of the liquid was reported to have fallen on a rock, which softened where the liquid had pooled, but later rehardened to solid rock.[21]

Author Charles Berlitz reported that the plant extract that Colonel Fawcett found was even described by some as being radioactive.[22] Reportedly, the extraordinary liquid was derived from a special foliage that the local natives had described to Colonel Fawcett as being a type of plant that grew "low to the ground with thick red leaves."[23] Such rare plants supposedly existed either in dense forests, or in high locations on cliff ledges and rock faces of mountains.

Colonel Fawcett failed to learn the secret of the unique liquid supposedly derived from such exotic vegetation, or explain its properties before he was forever lost in the Amazon Jungle in 1924. Paracelsus, the 16th century AD German physician and chemist, along with his 17th century Flemish counterpart, van Helmont, reported the existence of a 'universal fluid solvent' that could reduce all materials into their original elemental composition; dissolving stone, gems, glass, and metals.[24] Reportedly, such fluid could make glass and stone malleable, while also allowing for reversal of the process, with the rehardening of the items by some method.

The Hebrew Temple in Jerusalem, built under the direction of Solomon, reportedly was built without the use of an ax, hammer, or any other metal tool. Previous mention was made in Chapter 20 to a certain stone that could cut other stones, along with an enigmatic cutting device called a *shamir*, which was used as a cutting tool. That device allegedly disappeared after the Temple was built. Another mechanized device reportedly used to soften and cut stone was the 'Measure Marker.' Author George Andrews suggests that such an apparatus might have caused the mysterious 'cup marks' or 'Devil's Hoofprints' that are embedded in stones found in the Near East, India, North Africa, China, Europe, and much of the Americas.[25]

The four huge stone idols found at the Tula complex, known as the Atlantes, grip an unknown weapon or tool in their right hand. A Toltec bas-relief carving, which was found on a supporting roof column, depicted that same device being used by a worker wearing a backpack, utilizing the instrument to blast away at a rock face.[26] It is unknown if the depiction was meant to portray the engraving of the stone, a rock cutting process, or the shattering of stones into usable pieces of ore.

The lifting, transport, and placement of huge stones by ancient builders have defied rational explanations. Legends tell of sound being employed to accomplish such tasks. Some ancient texts state that Babylonian priests were able to raise heavy rocks into the air, "which 1,000 men could not have lifted."[27] Coptic writers state that blocks used to build various pyramids were elevated and transported into place by chanting incantations. Later Chaldean texts reported that priests used magic wands to create storms and move stones for temple construction. The Bible states that the walls of Jericho were brought down by the use of trumpet blasts. Egyptian mythology refers to their god Thoth as the 'Great Lord of Magic' who could move objects with the power of his voice. Numerous other accounts also describe the employment of sound to either build or destroy stone structures.[28]

It seems logical that some sort of advanced technology or mechanization was used to manipulate the enormous blocks of stone used during remote antiquity. It is also reasonable to note that heavy machinery such as cranes, helicopters, and wenches produce great noise, and often raise clouds of dust similar to that of a storm; conditions often associated with legendary accounts of megalithic construction. Modern science seeks to develop a device or technology that defies or overcomes gravitational forces, based on theories that vibrational frequencies of extremely high cycles might be employed to create a state of temporary weightlessness. The specific combination of molecular vibration and sound may some day be used to achieve such control over gravity. Ancient machinery not yet extant may one day be found, which might help to answer such mysteries. In any case, it is probable that such devices or advanced technology was once used on Earth, but was later somehow 'lost' to subsequent cultures.

Such accounts suggest that some type of technology still unknown to modern science existed during the times of megalithic stone construction. That knowledge apparently involved the use of sound waves, utilized in some manner yet to be understood by present humanity, perhaps along with some unknown advanced technological device. Although lacking any hard evidence for confirmation, the source of such prior technology was likely the Ancient Ones.

Although many great structures were later erected after the Ancient Ones' temporary exile from Earth, only a few included cyclopean stones. Such edifices may have merely incorporated existing monolithic blocks that remained from prior constructions, or perhaps such advanced ancient devices associated with megalithic building eventually became inoperable, or their underlying technology merely expired during some later time. The cyclopean constructions that were built with apparent ease during the distant past were simply discontinued during later generations. The many grand structures built by the olden but later cultures of Babylon, Greece, India, Egypt, and the Romans all utilized smaller more manageable-sized construction products after the departure of the Ancient Ones, although many magnificent edifices still resulted from such human labors.

Chapter 24

Cave Paintings & Rock Drawings

Yet another form or type of anomalous evidence can be found within the pictorial histories and glyphs left by our predecessors' art. Cave paintings, along with the fossil evidence those inhabitants left, help to provide an accurate history of their era. Artifacts have been found in caves located in France, Spain, Belgium, Germany, Italy, and Great Britain; all providing further insight into the lives of our early ancestors. Objects of bone, which included sewing needles, necklaces, harpoons, spears, knives, and pendants, were often carved with intricate designs. One stunning collection of such engraved art was found at La Colombiere, France. Interspersed in their carvings and rock depictions are mysterious creatures and objects that defy explanation.

Wall paintings and engravings have been found in over 200 caves, dating from *c*.35,000 to 10,500 BC, with heavy concentrations in Spain and France. The Grimaldi caves, located three miles west of Ventimiglia, Italy, date to 33,000 BC, while caves in the Pyrenees, where many exceptional ceiling and wall paintings are found, date between 32,000 and 10,500 BC. Fine etchings and multicolored paintings dating to 31,000 BC are found in the Chauvet caves of southern France in its Ardeche region. Such drawings depict geometric signs and symbols, animals, and occasional humanoid figures.

The paintings are often located deep inside the cave, such as at Lascaux, France, where the highest level of multicolor animal art can be found. In the Alta Mira caves of Spain, vivid colors made from mineral pigments mixed with animal fat produced masterful paintings of prehistoric bison, mastodons, and other animals. Yet no trace of soot can be found on the cave's ceilings, questioning how the work surfaces were adequately illuminated for such highly sophisticated art.

The complexity of depictions often increases with their more remote locations within the deepest passages farthest from the entrance. Other art is found on walls of the largest chambers, indicating the cavern's use as a religious or ceremonial room, while other paintings are practically hidden in narrow passages. Many caves served as community gathering places for surrounding regional groups, providing ceremonial centers acting as temples for some unknown spiritual role.

Humankind's earliest identified spiritual veneration or belief focused on the Mother Goddess image or icon that first appeared in the early Stone Age Gravettian cultural epoch around 24,000 BC. Such veneration was practiced throughout Europe and the Near East. Stone figures carved to form the Mother Goddess have been found at La Gravette, Laussel, and Lespugne, France; as well as in Cukurca, Turkey; Willendorf, Austria; Kostyenki, Ukraine; and Petersfels, Germany.

Cro-Magnons are often incorrectly perceived as primitive, wild cavemen. The mere existence of their sophisticated cave and rock paintings implies leisure time for the arts, and a specialization of workers, demonstrating high levels of skill and talent. Such specialization may imply other divisions of labor not yet extant. Their high artistic accomplishments, requiring considerable thought and planning, was not equaled until the Renaissance period, tens of thousands of years later. Further, the sculpting of ivory, bone, and soapstone requires use of extremely sharp and durable engraving and carving tools, not the stone tools attributed to humans of that period. The stone bas-reliefs at Laussel, along with the statuettes and figurines recovered from Willendorf and the Grimaldi Grottos could not have been made using crude stone implements. The historic perspective of those early times appears to clearly be distorted.

The Cro-Magnon cultural era is commonly divided into three periods. Its oldest European segment was the Aurignacian Period from c.35,000 to 20,000 BC. The bulk of that period's art, which reached a peak in c.23,000 BC, was found in the grottos of Aurignac, France. That period reflects the second highest level of primitive art accomplishment, and consisted mostly of semi-human gods and animal paintings. The second division was the Solutrean Period from 19,000 to 15,500 BC, which reflected a regression in both talent and output throughout its era. That could have been the result of a natural catastrophe or a severe climatic change, which preoccupied the people with survival. The last era was the Magdalenian Period from 15,500 to 10,500 BC, with its artistic apex reached between 12,000 and 11,000 BC. That peak represented one of the greatest periods of prehistoric artistic attainment.

Main locations for such art were in the Dordogne Valley of France, the Pyrenees Mountains, and along the Biscay Coast of Spain and France. The refinement of both Aurignacian and Magdalenian art was sudden, reaching definable peak periods after which they abruptly declined. Many archaeologists agree that numerous early periods reflected better and finer levels of art than some later intervals. That may imply a possible regression of skills within Cro-Magnon man during various times, perhaps as the result of major climatic or cataclysmic Earth changes, or the brief removal of an outside influence watching over and guiding those early human ancestors.

Author Andrew Tomas disclosed astronomical charts made by ancient cultures, believed to depict the constellations of Ursa Major, Ursa Minor, and the Pleiades.[1] Such charts reportedly were arranged as clusters of small cavities or depressions cut into rock faces found in the caves of Pierres Folles, La Filouziere, Vendie, and Brittany. Evidently, our ancestors intended to record and convey their celestial observations for the benefit of subsequent generations.

Certain caves in the Andean and Patagonian provinces of Argentina, the Territorio de Neuquen and Territorio Nacional de Santa Cruz, both exhibit the so-called meander symbols, the drawings of mazes or labyrinths. Identical symbols are also found in Africa and Europe. The caves of La Pileta, Spain, which were inhabited between 30,000 and 10,500 BC, had walls covered with unusual stylized symbols and signs that were carefully fashioned and repeated.

Similar markings are contained within the paintings at Lascaux, France, which display more complexity as one proceeds further and deeper into the cave. Those strange script characters have never been deciphered, although it has been speculated that such markings may have been a form of early written notation. Perhaps an ancient form of record keeping, one that still remains unknown to Modern man, existed concurrently with the earliest spiritual veneration practices.

Scholars have detected other patterns in certain archaic bone carvings and rock and cave markings that date from the Pleistocene epoch. Such possible script markings comprised of vertical lines and wavy symbols may be the earliest extant form of notation by man, although yet indecipherable. Remember that cuneiform writing was considered to be 'chicken scratchings,' random marks, or decorative designs, prior to recognizing its true communicative purpose.

In addition to such precisely spaced spiral grooves and parallel wavy lines, another potential ancient notational script, which consisted of vertical line and dot sequences, was painted or engraved on stone and bone found scattered throughout Spain, while also spreading all the way into Ukraine. Thousands of those markings have been found, with the script duplicated repeatedly from 35,000 to 8000 BC, all without any distinct interruption. The indecipherable signs and symbols located in the deepest cave tunnels of Lascaux, France, may be the earliest prototype or examples of such early notation.

Author David Hatcher Childress revealed conclusions from a study conducted by René Noorbergen,[2] who had examined a piece of reindeer bone found in a cave near Rochebertier, France, which dated to *c*.10,000 BC. That bone was covered with markings that were determined to be more than just simple decorations, and may have represented a form of proto-notation.[3] Mr. Noorbergen further determined that such bone markings were very similar to those used in the later periods of Tartessos, the Biblical Tarshish, reportedly with certain characters being identical between both scripts.[4] Other bone carvings, believed to be calendar markings, were also found in the caves of Dordogne, France, with some dating to 30,000 BC.

Linguist Charles Berlitz referenced a similar study released in 1971, conducted by Alexander Marshack,[5] an anthropological researcher associated with the Peabody Museum of Archaeology. His research reexamined the linear carvings made on numerous deer antler and mammoth bones that were housed in various European museums, which dated between 33,000 and 15,000 BC. His findings revealed that the similar series of scratches, incisions, markings, and notches were a form of record keeping or proto-notation, believed to be used to track the phases of the lunar cycle, serving as a type of calendar.[6]

Another proto-script might be evidenced from the pebble and stone notations found at Mas d'Azil, France, which are similar to the markings discovered in the caverns of Spain and North Africa. Additionally, the reindeer bone carvings removed from caves at Mas d'Azil and La Madeleine reportedly resembled Phoenician icons. A controversial stone tablet found in 1924 near Vichy, France, in the small village of Glozel, displayed a collection of symbols and signs thought by some to be a form of symbolic notation, even though the artifact was dated by some prehistorians to the Magdalenian period.

Rock Drawings

In addition to the ancient universal symbols previously discussed in Chapter 20, the depictions found on various rock surfaces are equally intriguing. They include petroglyphs, engravings, ideograms, and paintings of enigmatic images. A brief review of some of the more perplexing depictions follows, starting in Europe. Rock drawings that date to 13,000 BC at Lussac-le-Chateau, France, show modern day dress styles and haircuts, while featuring fashionable hats, jackets, trousers, petticoats, boots, and shoes.[7]

A drawing found in the Pech Merle Cave of France depicts a hairless humanoid figure possessing a large head with a pointed chin, elongated and upward-slanted eye slits, but without any ears.[8] The creature is shown pierced with spears, evidently an act committed by the natives of the area. This drawing depicts the recognizable shape of what is known as a small 'Gray' alien associated with modern UFOs. Numerous ancient rock carvings of humanoid figures, either in space suits or as tunic-clad beings with antenna headgear, can also be found throughout the surrounding valley at Val Camonica, Italy,[9] an area about 62 miles northeast of Milan.

Similar unusual petroglyphs are also found in the Americas. At a site near Three Rivers, New Mexico, petroglyph paintings of hands with six fingers can be found. Such depictions are dated to at least 1300 AD, but are considered much older by others. It is unknown if these glyphs represent 'normal' mutations in *Homo sapiens*, or if they are intended to portray appendages of an unknown being. In Toro Muerto, Peru, a rock drawing of a humanoid is depicted as receiving what appears to be a chest X-ray, complete with an exposed view of the ribs.[10] Another jagged stone carving also at Toro Muerto is dated to *c*.12,000 BC. It is a pictorial of the helical DNA molecule, drawn near a crude disc-shaped spacecraft being launched from a larger mother ship.[11]

According to Peruvian legends, rock drawings displaying zigzag symbols are believed to represent their olden gods. Similar geometric patterns are also found on the massive Gate of the Sun at Tiahuanaco. Other figures on that gate share a resemblance with the 24 symbols that surround the 'rocket ship' depicted on the stone slab found at Palenque, Mexico, in the Mayan Temple of the Inscriptions. Some researchers believe such designs represent spacecraft or automated vehicles that were operated by ancient astronauts. Nearby at Monte Alban, Mexico, helmeted beings that appear to be wearing space suits were found carved on the rocks.[12]

Equally intriguing rock drawings have also been found in Asia. Cave paintings found near Bombay in Ajanta, India, are quite unique. While the art displays the highest skill levels, it is the luminous paint that makes those murals unique. In the darkness, its figures appear as three-dimensional forms, portraying special effects created by their artist.[13] Professor Tschi Pen Lao of the University of Peking found carvings on the side of a mountain in the Hunan Province of China. Those carvings depict beings with elephant-like trunks, thought to represent a breathing apparatus, even though they have been dated to c.43,000 BC.[14] Professor Lao also found similar drawings on an island in Lake Tungting in China.

Other beings apparently also using some type of breathing apparatus were found on drawings scattered throughout the Tassili Mountains of the Sahara Desert,[15] which are generally dated between c.8500 and 6000 BC. In the various cave areas around the Tassili Mountains, strange beings are commonly depicted. A space-suited one-eyed being, which was found in 1956 on the n'Ajjer plateau, is commonly known as the 'Great God of Mars.'[16] This one-eyed being, along with smaller humanoids, are shown surrounded by horned giants that stand almost 11 feet high. Other area rock paintings show humanlike beings exiting from a domed disc resembling a UFO 'flying saucer,' along with other humanoids that are wearing gear resembling a spacesuit.[17]

Similar designs and themes to those found in the Sahara are also depicted in caves and on rocks in Australia, mainly around the Woomera area where depictions of space-suited creatures are numerous. A rock painting in the Central Kimberley District of Australia features a portrait of Vondjina (aka Vonjinda), their mouthless large-eyed mythical god of prehistory.[18] That god was considered to have been the personification of the Milky Way and one of the most revered gods, according to ancient traditions. Such a being is somewhat similar in appearance to the modern UFO little 'Gray' alien. An Ice Age diprotodon, a giant marsupial about the size of a rhinoceros, was painted on a rock in an area north of Cairns, Queensland. The animal is depicted with a rope around its neck, perhaps indicating its domesticated status.[19]

Another Australian bush cave drawing depicts two space-suited beings with rays emitting from their heads, which culminate in star-like points. The painting is known as the *Two Creators* or the *Star Gods*.[20] Another Australian petroglyph depicts a crude spacecraft on a tripod with an astronaut inside.[21] A somewhat similar rock drawing is found in Navoy, Russia, which dates to *c*.3000 BC. That representation also exhibits what appears to be an entity inside a spacecraft, being attended by other creatures wearing some sort of breathing apparatus outside the ship.[22]

Chapter 25

Ancient Records

Prevailing conventional belief claims that writing did not exist before the cuneiform script of *circa* 3500 BC. But dispute lingers over which culture was ultimately responsible for its introduction, which is most commonly attributed to the Sumerians. It is known that the prior Ubaid culture utilized a form of pictograms that may have evolved into cuneiform. However, most artifacts displaying the earlier Ubaid pictograms were made of wood and have since mostly decayed, leaving minimal evidence for study. It is unknown if wandering Sumerians from the early Dilmun Empire introduced the script while visiting or traveling through the Ubaid city-state of Uruk during that 3500 BC time frame, or if they influenced the Ubaidian culture to refine their existing pictogram notation, which then developed into the cuneiform script.

In either case, when the Sumerians permanently immigrated to Eridu around 3350 BC, they possessed a refined cuneiform script. This wedge-shaped script has been inscribed on tens of thousands of pieces of pottery, clay cylinder seals and tablets, along with hundreds of inscriptions on statues, foundation stones, stelae, vases, and bricks. The ability to write and document events reflected the official start of humankind's recorded history.

The Sumerians considered writing to be a gift from the gods, and thus must be used in an acceptable and wise manner. Its vast majority, between 90 and 95 percent of all early writing, consisted mainly of administrative and business records, receipts, legal transactions, inventories, deeds, and similar documents necessary to conduct commerce.[1]   The remaining small balance of texts recorded scientific knowledge, major historical events, and celestial observations. Writing was not used for myths, legends, or epic stories until about 2200 BC when they first appeared, although many of the later written narratives were based on earlier oral histories and traditions passed down over the ages.   While the Sumerian texts are the oldest known narratives, most of the extant original Sumerian records are merely incomplete fragments. Most Sumerian stories and historic records were pieced together mainly from duplicated texts later written in Akkad and Babylonia, which were copied from the Sumerian originals.

While no extant text is known to exist from the period before the Great Flood of *c.*10,500 BC, numerous ancient texts allude to such antediluvian records.   Ashurbanipal, the Assyrian king of Babylon between 669 and 627 BC, claimed to have found certain ancient stone tablets that were believed to date from a period before the Great Flood, which his translators ultimately deciphered.   Such records were reportedly <u>written</u> in a dead language no longer used during Ashurbanipal's time.[2] The Druids also believed in books that predated the Great Flood, referring to them by name, mentioning *The Writings of Hu*, *The Books of Pheryllt*, and *The Writings of Pridian*.[3]

Around 1000 AD, the Arabian historian and Coptic writer, al-Masudi, revealed that an ancient Egyptian king, who had reigned 300 years before the flood, allegedly built two of the Giza pyramids.[4] He was King Surid, the son of Salahoc, who reportedly ordered all Egyptian wisdom and knowledge, including their understanding of different arts and sciences, be compiled as <u>written</u> records and sealed in the Great Pyramid to preserve such knowledge from an impending flood destruction. Surid's stated intent was to preserve such wisdom "...for the benefit of those who could afterwards comprehend them," according to al-Masudi.[5]

It is unlikely that the referenced flood was the universal one of *c*.10,500 BC, since the Giza pyramids appear to have been constructed after that date but before 4000 BC. If the account is true, it may have been a precautionary action to safeguard records if another flood should occur, although still referencing ancient written records that predated the conventionally accepted start of writing. Numerous other cultures also allude to a secret repository or ancient 'Hall of Records' where archaic wisdom was stored, although such archives have yet to be found.

If such antediluvian records ever existed, the flood likely destroyed them. Those records, along with possible earlier predecessor texts, would have been buried deep within the Earth, and most likely lost forever, due to deterioration and decay. Yet one ancient record associated with the Great Pyramid is known to be lost. According to many archaic reports, some of the polished white limestone outer casing stones apparently contain inscriptions, with confirmation made by Herodotus who personally saw such writings during his Egyptian visit.[6]

Reports indicate such inscriptions evidently contained more than 10,000 words in content. No extant record of that inscribed composition is known to have survived into modern times. However, an unknown, secretly hidden record may exist somewhere, since accounts claim that copies were made "in a number of languages" that still existed as late as the 14th century AD.[7]

Strabo, the Greek historian and geographer, stated that *written* records from the great seaport of Tartessos, a site located in southwestern coastal Spain, dated to as old as 7000 BC.[8] Berosus, the Babylonian historian, stated that Oannes, the creature who brought civilization to ancient humans, *wrote* about the lives and ways of humankind generations before the Great Flood.[9] Herodotus stated that he was told by Egyptian priests that Egypt's *written* history dated back to nearly *c.*11,800 BC.[10]   Archaic Sanskrit manuscripts referred to a 'very old book' or a 'parent doctrine' that was reportedly written in *Senzar*,[11] supposedly a sacred language dating to the most remote times, dictated directly by the Divine Beings,[12] and known to all adepts of early cultures.

Such a root-text was presumed to be the source for the much later works that included the primitive Chinese Bible, the *Book of Shu Ching* (aka *Shu-king*), meaning the *Book of History*; the Puranas of India; and the Chaldean *Book of Numbers*.   It is also thought to have been instrumental in compiling the occult Hebrew books, the *Siphrah Dzeniouta* (*Book of the Concealed Mystery*), the *Sepher Jezireh* (*Book of Creation*), the *Sefer ha-Bahir* (*Book of Brightness*), and the *Sepher ha-Temuna* (*Book of Image*).

The previous chapter alluded to certain rock markings and bone engravings that some researchers claim may be an early form of notation.   The numerous series of regularly spaced lines, swirls, notches, dots, and other similar markings have been speculated to be forms of an ancient notation.   The Tuatha Dé Danaan (aka the Dana or Don people) were a mysterious mining and naval people that were said to possess magical powers when they landed on the shores of Ireland.   An Irish oral tradition claims that Og, the supreme ruler of the universe, guarded the Tuatha Dé Danaan. Og reportedly gave his people a prehistoric script called *Ogham*, a series of dots and dashes similar to a visual Morse code.[13] Reportedly, the original ancestors of the Tuatha Dé Danaan eventually left Ireland for a land on the other side of the Atlantic, where they were associated with the earthen structures of the ancient Mound Builders.[14]

Another suspected form of ancient writing is associated with the mysterious archaic 'cup marks.' Researcher Charles Fort described cup marks as "strings of cup-like impressions in rocks,"[15] which were sometimes surrounded by rings or semicircles. Such markings appear throughout the world, except in the far north, according to Mr. Fort.   They were mostly concentrated in Italy, Spain, France, India, the Americas, the British Isles, Algeria, and China, with many appearing on rock cliffs. They were usually arranged in regularly spaced rows, according to an 1883 article by Professor Douglas that appeared in the *Saturday Review*.[16] Such markings are believed by some to be an archaic form of inscription, perhaps comparable to the Braille system or Morse code.[17]

While no extant ancient text conclusively proves that Earth was influenced by otherworldly beings, the many similar accounts that allude to such contact seem to offer solid circumstantial evidence suggestive of such visitations. Humanity's inability to find the surviving ancient texts referenced in our oral traditions, myths, and legends certainly does not preclude their prior existence. Indeed, the many ancient anomalous artifacts, which reflect exceptional levels of technology, point to the existence of an advanced society, one that certainly would have possessed written texts in some form. Such a belief is indirectly supported by the complexity of numerous ancient structures that would have required written detailed designs and preplanning.

All extant ancient texts are dependent upon an accurate translation into later contemporary languages, and therefore can become a product of the preconceived notions of those numerous subsequent translators. Hence, they are susceptible to differing interpretations that could result in possible distortions of the original author's meaning and intent. Such content may be deemed pure fantasy and dismissed as mere legend or myth due to each text's advanced knowledge and capabilities, which could be incorrectly assessed as being beyond the perceived scope of such archaic authors. A reevaluation of certain ancient documents will be undertaken, in order to appraise their scientific content and message, when assessed from our modern understanding.

However, the reader should also be made aware of the many manuscripts and records that have been lost due to natural catastrophes, as well as through the many ill-conceived, deliberate interventions by humankind. The many documented natural disasters involving fires, volcanic eruptions, tidal waves, and earthquakes that have occurred since the Great Flood have destroyed many written records. Those eradicated texts might have supplied the missing segment or lost revelation providing answers to the many mysteries surrounding Earth's history and humanity's origins, as well as the true nature of the 'gods' of antiquity. The lingering echoes from such long lost archaic texts perhaps endured through oral histories and legends, complemented by the few written fragments that have survived.

Known Archives

Libraries are not a modern invention, with repositories of knowledge and records being common since the emergence of civilization. The library at Nippur, the once religious center of Sumer and Akkad, dated to around 3000 BC. It housed 30,000 tablets, mostly of clay, with the balance being inscribed on stone. Another center of knowledge was created by King Ashurbanipal around 660 BC. Since his early youth, Ashurbanipal was a scholar who sought knowledge. After he was appointed king and ruler of the world by the Assyrian god, Ashur, he attempted to amass the entire known knowledge of his time. He sent his scholars and scribes throughout the lands to obtain original tablets or their copies, preserving those transcripts in his extensive library at Nineveh. That great receptacle of knowledge eventually contained a total of about 26,000 texts[18] pertaining to philosophy, mathematics, religion, medicine, and astronomy. It also included dynastic lists, art, poetry, historical accounts, songs, hymns, and great epic literature such as *The Epic of Gilgamesh*.

Many of the great libraries of antiquity, including Rome, Athens, Alexandria, Pergamum (aka Pergamon), Carthage, and Syracuse, were often attacked, resulting in the destruction of records to various degrees. Although some of those lost documents were restored to a limited extent, they endured a constant threat of subsequent assaults. While many of the destructions were major, they were not complete in most cases. While natural disasters can be accepted as fate, the deliberate destruction of records is unforgivable, with valuable and irreplaceable knowledge being lost forever. Such deliberate acts eradicating many olden texts were the result of both religious censorship and political rivalry. It was also part of a plan by the BOPH gods to eradicate all knowledge of the Ancient Ones, removing them from the memory of humanity.

Ancient artistic statuary was also attacked, after being branded by the Church with 'heathen' or pagan labels. The *Abodah Zarah*, one of the books of the Hebrew *Talmud* written in the fifth century AD, lists ways to destroy the 'power' of pagan idols by knocking off the nose or the tip of an ear of such statues.[19] That is one of the main reasons why so many works of ancient art are found mutilated in such a manner.

The earliest mentioned man-made destruction of written knowledge is attributed to the army of Alexander the Great, which burned the Persepolis Library in 330 BC, resulting in the loss of many of the sacred books comprising the Avesta (aka Zend Avesta) of the Zoroastrian religion. It is highly unlikely that non-religious texts were actually destroyed, due to Alexander's personal thirst for knowledge and records, although their buildings may have been. His great Library of Alexandria later stood as testimony to his devotion for such texts.

At its height, the Alexandrian main library and its annex reportedly contained several million rolls of texts. Some were originals, while others were copies compiled by scribes Alexander sent throughout his empire, in his attempt to record all known knowledge. Even after repeated massive destructions, it was believed that the library never contained less than 700,000 rolls before its final demise. The library featured a 120 volume catalogue of authors, along with a brief biography of each, according to historic accounts.

The following summary consists of only major acts that led to the significant destruction of ancient records and textual accounts, realizing that many more confiscations and devastations took place on local levels, which were never widely documented.

In 213 BC, the Chinese Emperor Shih Huang Ti (aka Che Hwang-te), who reigned from 221 to 206 BC as the first emperor of the Ch'in dynasty, ordered all science, astronomy, historic, and literary texts to be destroyed. Some copies of those books were reportedly saved in the Ch'in Imperial Library, while Tibetan monks saved others by hiding the manuscripts from the emperor's men. The sketchy history of China was a result of that act, although some details were handed down verbally, and were eventually rewritten by later intellectuals such as Confucius.

In 146 BC, the Romans were reported to have destroyed the half million volume Library of Carthage, forever losing many Phoenician books.

Sometime in 83 or 82 BC, the original *Cumae Text*, and perhaps other Greek *Sibylline Books* were destroyed during a natural, not man-made fire in Rome. Those works were the collected prophetic teachings of the god Apollo, as uttered through his prophets, the Sibyls; although some fabrications of pseudo-Sibylline texts were also written during the 2nd century BC. The Sibyls were the ten inspired women who, in a state of ecstasy, revealed both future occurrences and past historic events, mentioning the Great Deluge and the Tower of Babylon. The two most famous were the Sibyl of Erythrae in Ionia, and the Sibyl of Cumae in southern Italy. Their revelations were recorded by the high priests of Apollo, and contained Greek, Babylonian, Persian, and Hebrew prophecy.

In 47 BC, Julius Caesar ordered the first burning of the Alexanderian Library, apparently to diminish Greek influences from the Roman Empire. Fortunately, less than ten percent of the records were destroyed as a result.

Around 1 AD, Emperor Augustus, who reigned over Rome from 27 BC to 14 AD, ordered the destruction of over 2,000 volumes of the Greek prophesies, along with all advice provided for humans by the gods Zeus and Apollo, which they had supposedly transmitted to the oracles.

In 54 AD, Saint Paul ordered the burning of all books dealing with pagan rituals and occult dealings at Ephesus.

In August 79 AD, the Roman Herculaneum Library was destroyed by a massive eruption of Mount Vesuvius, burning and burying 1,800 to 2,000 papyri scrolls, carbonizing those texts.

In 272 AD, the Roman Emperor Lucius Domitius Aurelian, who reigned between 270 and 275 AD, was at war with the Queen of Palmyra. As a result of one battle during those hostilities, the Alexandria Library suffered collateral damage, with a portion of its texts lost.

In 296 AD, Emperor Diocletian, who reigned over the Roman Empire from 284 to 305 AD when the capital was moved from Rome to the Eastern capital in Asia Minor, undertook a campaign to persecute Christians. Diocletian, along with other Roman leaders, ordered the burning of all Christian libraries, including their Greek and Egyptian documents.

In 298 AD, the Western Christian emperors ordered all pagan texts to be destroyed, along with any remaining 'Wonders of the Ancient World.'

In 389 AD, Emperor Theodosius I, who reigned between 379 to 395 AD, again burned the *Sibylline Books* that had been reconstructed from memory and rewritten.

Then in 390 or 391 AD, Emperor Theodosius I also ordered Christian armies to burn down the Alexandrian Library, which had become a world repository and learning center, comprising a 700 year collection of records. Numerous one-of-a-kind original documents were destroyed, thus loosing some valuable and irreplaceable manuscripts forever.

In 395 AD, the Visigoth king, Alaric I, destroyed the Greek cities of Eleusis and Athens in Attica. That also ended the *Eleusinian Mysteries*, a religious tradition that included festivals, ceremonies, and a vast esoteric collection of knowledge. Its tradition was based on the revelations of the Grain Goddess Demeter and her daughter, Persephone, taught to the initiates of its secret cult. Previously, the Eastern Roman Emperor Julian, who ruled between 361 and 363 AD, reestablished paganism after rejecting Christianity, and was initiated into the *Eleusinian Mysteries*.

In 405 AD, Stilicho, the consul and acting ruler of the Western Roman Empire between 395 to about 408, destroyed all of the once-again restored copies of the *Sibylline Books*.

In 410 AD, the Visigoth king, Alaric I, then sacked Rome, destroying the Roman Libraries. That loss included the Great Pergamum Library, originally founded by Attalus I (241-197 BC), at the capital of the Pergamum Kingdom in northwest Asia Minor. It was given to Rome as a gift in 133 BC, at a time when it contained over 200,000 scrolls, and was also the site of operation for a college of advanced learning.

In 439 AD, the Vandal king, Gaiseric, subjugated the city of Carthage, which had previously fallen under Roman rule, destroying a great portion of the texts in its great library. At its height, the Carthage Library was reported to have contained as many as 500,000 documents, many being original texts that were lost to humankind forever.

Around 598 AD, Pope Gregory I burned the Library of Apollo, located on the Palatine Hill overlooking Rome.

In *circa* 625 AD, Irish monks burned 10,000 runic texts, destroying much of the history and traditions of the Celtic civilization.

In 641 AD, Caliph Omar I, the Arabian leader who ruled between 634 and 644 AD, burned the Alexandrian Library for a final time, ending nearly a millennium of document storage.

In 698 AD, the Arabian seizure of Carthage resulted in further destruction of texts contained in its great library.

In 789 AD, Charlemagne ordered the destruction of all pagan articles and manuscripts throughout the world.

Starting in 1219 and continuing through 1222 AD, Genghis Khan attacked the Turkish Empire, first sacking the city of Bukhara, and subsequently assailing the city of Samarkand in 1220. Both cities were almost completely destroyed, which resulted in the loss of most all manuscripts and written records of the empire. Genghis Khan then continued his march into Russia, plundering much of its territory, destroying most learning centers and their associated texts and records, along with much of the high culture of the Orient.

During the 14th and 15th centuries, the Inquisition ordered the burning of all heretical manuscripts. That was the culmination of the suppression and distortion of science and knowledge, which started in the 5th century AD with the advent of the Dark Ages, the period of cultural stagnation now known as the Middle Ages, which lasted for a thousand years. This oppression was brought about by the Church filling the vacuum of power left by the splintering of the Roman Empire between the Eastern and Western rulers during the 5th century, when the political control collapsed in the West. The Church teachings and writings began to depict the ancient gods as diabolical at that same time. During that thousand year period, scribes hid most authentic historical documents, suppressing such knowledge as heresy and enforcing censorship compliance through the use of the death penalty.

In the 16th century, the Spanish conquistadors, under the Christian Bishop Diego de Landa (the second Bishop of the Yucatan from the Franciscan Order), destroyed nearly all the manuscripts of the Mexican and Mayan peoples. Fewer than twenty original scrolls and codices remain of the once numerous ancient written records of those early Central American cultures. All Mayan texts were destroyed except for the three codices now in our modern museums. These three volumes consist of fragments totaling 208 pages, some of which still resist deciphering. The *Popul Vuh*, the sacred book of the Quiché Mayans of Guatemala, was completely rewritten from memory, after destruction by the Christian invading armies. It is also reported that the enormous Russian library of Czar Ivan the Terrible (1530-1584) simply disappeared during the 16th century without any remaining trace.

Since its earliest times, the Church had issued edicts or decrees banning 'objectionable' writings. In 1559 the Catholic Church published its first official *Index of Forbidden Books*, releasing its last revision in 1948, while not ultimately discontinuing this Index until 1966.

Throughout the 17th, 18th, and 19th centuries the Church continued its suppression of scientific knowledge and forced conformity of beliefs. Such censorship is best exemplified by the permanent house arrest of Galileo, which was ordered by the Church in 1633 for his failure to denounce the correct Copernican teachings of a round and orbital Earth, and publicly embrace the false Biblical belief in a flat and stationary world. Numerous scientific books and concepts were often suppressed by censorship edicts issued by the Church. Even as late as the Victorian Period, the Church feared that the advancement of science endangered religious beliefs.

Considering all the suppression and destruction of records by both rival religious and political factions, the startling realization should be that any ancient texts survived at all. One of the main reasons modern man has many of the archaic texts we now possess emerges from the fact that those records laid buried and protected for thousands of years, under layers of debris and soil during times of repeated destructions. Only within the 19th and 20th centuries have those records been unearthed, such as those at the ancient Babylonian Library of Nineveh, and the Sumer/Akkad Library of Nippur. Other ancient records survived by being hidden with the help of secret sects, such as the Tibetan monks who religiously guarded esoteric texts from harm and destruction, even during modern times.   Their large and wealthy mountain lamaseries contain subterranean crypts known as *guptas*, along with secret cave libraries that were cut directly into the cavern's rock surface.

The Tibetan lamaseries reportedly rival any other archive elsewhere within our world.   One such lamasery is in the Karakoram Mountains of western Tibet, in the Kunlun (aka Kuen-lun) pass.   Another is located near the Okhee region of the Himalayas.   Their records are alleged to contain esoteric scientific information pertaining to the concepts of anti-gravity, the use of cosmic energy, and application principals used in the telekinesis process.

Still other reports state that the Vatican in Rome contains a basement library whose contents consist of such a vast quantity of manuscripts they would span the equivalent of seventeen miles, with still another account claiming the equivalent of 57 miles of texts.   One can not know when some new edict might be proclaimed that would outlaw the reading or ownership of specifically targeted materials, or when global unrest might ignite another period of massive destruction of records through various acts of war or religious censorship.

Due to the manual copying of originals, the rewriting of lost texts from memory, and the preservation of accounts by oral tradition; it is no wonder that contradictions, inconsistencies, errors, and gaps exist in some of those ancient texts.   By reevaluating ancient manuscripts utilizing the filter of modern scientific knowledge, it becomes clear that the vast technical understanding possessed by people of certain archaic civilizations was much more advanced in the fields of astronomy, science, mathematics, and medical knowledge than historians yet admit.   Until science had finally obtained the levels of technological proficiency that were achieved by the mid-20th century, many written accounts from antiquity would have certainly appeared to be pure fantasy.   Seemingly, such accounts would naturally be labeled as myth or legend during any prior and less informed age, as will be demonstrated within the following chapters.

Chapter 26

Ancient Commentators

Before examining these archaic records, a brief review of the people responsible for much of what is known of the ancient world will be presented. Such accounts provide insight into the ancient life and beliefs held by those cultures, which was the direct result of laborious efforts by those early historians, chroniclers, geographers, and scientists.

Sanchuniathon

Sanchuniathon (*c*.1250-*c*.1190 BC, although some sources incorrectly place him during the 7th century BC) was the Phoenician historian who resided in the area now known as Beirut, Lebanon, where he wrote his *History of Phoenicia* around 1193 BC. He believed the gods to be mortal humans who possessed great knowledge and powers. His work is believed to be based on a combination of oral traditions, ancient texts, and secret writings of the Ammonians; with his main source coming from the writings of Jerombal (aka Jerubaal), a high priest to the god Jeuo (aka Iao). Jerombal had apparently incorporated ancient wisdom and historic accounts into his writings, which he then dedicated to Abibal, the King of Berytus (*c*.1300-1250 BC). Reportedly, Sanchuniathon (aka Sanchoniatho and Sanchoniathon) further claimed to have derived some of his information from the Egyptian god Thoth, or at least from his records and wisdom.

The Biblical *Book of Genesis* is believed by some scholars to be based on Sanchuniathon's written work, as pointed out by author Robert Charroux.[1] He reported that Porphyry, the 3rd century AD Greek philosopher, had openly claimed that Moses had copied essential parts of *Genesis* from Sanchuniathon.[2] Sanchuniathon's original historic work is lost, but a translation into Greek during the first century AD by Philo Byblius was widely known during his time. That translation was later also lost, although Porphyry, along with various other historians and writers, quoted from its later Greek version. Such quoted references, along with the few extant fragments from Sanchuniathon's original, provide the remaining knowledge of his historic work today.

Hesiod

Hesiod (8th century BC, around 710 BC) was the Greek poet who compiled the genealogy of the gods in his *Theogony*. His vast reorganization and reinterpretation of the mythical Greek gods' tradition, which was originally copied from the Egyptians, accounts for many discrepancies and contradictions found in the various accounts and chronologies of the gods. His narration of the olden gods' activities and deeds tended to describe repeated cycles of atrocities, followed with acts of revenge; while a more favorable account of the younger gods, who he considered more just, were portrayed as being superior to their ancestors. Such a belief may represent the success of the BOPH gods, Hesiod's younger gods, to demonize the olden gods, the Ancient Ones.

Hesiod believed that hard work and effort spent in overcoming obstacles was a blessing, not a curse, an essential tenet of the reincarnation belief. His published *Works and Days* further concluded that such challenges and strife taught lessons that were necessary to eliminate known faults, leading to self-improvement; a concept he deemed necessary to achieve true excellence.

Pythagoras

Pythagoras (*c*.582-*c*.507 BC) was the Greek mathematician, scholar, scientist, teacher, and astronomer who made his home in Samos, an island of Ionia. Around 530 BC, Pythagoras moved to a Greek colony in Crotona, Italy, where he taught classes at the college located there. He taught concepts including the orbital motion of a round Earth and theorems of geometry, based on prior Egyptian knowledge he had acquired. He was believed to have had access to an esoteric science and secret knowledge, from which a new religious belief ultimately emerged. That belief was in the transmigration of the soul, and of a mathematical basis or relationship that was employed throughout the universe where natural laws were obeyed by all celestial bodies everywhere in the universe; perhaps a reference to the Cosmic Order. His spiritual following, known as the 'Pythagorean Movement,' was similar to the *Orphic Mysteries* of Orpheus, which propagated the conviction that the soul was the immortal part of humankind.

One of his teachers was Psonchis of Sais, considered to be the wisest Egyptian high priest, who instructed him in the sciences. Pherecydes, a scientist of the 7th and 6th centuries BC who was self-taught from ancient, esoteric Phoenician manuscripts, along with Oinouphis of Heliopolis, also instructed him. His extensive travels, especially throughout Egypt, provided him with much historic knowledge, which he shared with his pupils. The many accomplishments made by Pythagoras clearly depict his genius and recognized status as a man ahead of his time.

Herodotus

Herodotus (484-425 BC), the Greek historian known as the Father of History, was recognized as the first historical authority. He was born in Halicarnassus, a southwestern Greek region of Asia Minor, but lived on the island of Samos.

He confirmed that the Greeks learned all their ancient scientific knowledge from the Egyptians. Herodotus is considered to be the most accurate of all ancient historians, with his geographical data and precise descriptions of Egypt and Asia Minor being exact to the smallest detail. Marveled by Egyptian accomplishments and knowledge, he visited Egypt in July of 459 BC and spent ten years learning its many secrets. In 448 BC, he then wrote about those travels in his book, *The History of Egypt*.

In that work he described his visit to the Great Labyrinth, which was already in ruins at the time of his exploration. He stated that it was even more marvelous than the Great Pyramid, comprising 3,000 chambers built from megalithic stone slabs. His detailed description of that ancient wonder is one of the most complete records of that now lost complex.

Herodotus reported that the gods lived with the Egyptians as physical beings during their first generation, then returned to their celestial homes. Their departure was then followed by 12,000 years of priestly rule. He was one of the first historians to record the actions and events of mankind, as well as the gods. He wrote his most prominent book, *The History of Herodotus*, in *circa* 435 BC, which was an all-encompassing historic account of the world, in nine parts.

Valmiki

Valmiki (4th century BC) was a Hindu sage, historian, and hermit; considered to be India's equivalent of Herodotus. He wrote his epic *Ramayana* poem around 300 BC, which was the narration and history of the Hindu deity Rama and his wife Sita. Rama was an Indian prince believed to be the seventh incarnation of the Hindu god, Vishnu. Valmiki's historic facts and research used in the *Ramayana* reportedly was based on the oldest temple records at Ayhodia, India, believed to have been handed down since *circa* 18,000 BC. That ancient information, along with other later temple histories and accounts including much earlier Vedic records, were dictated by the temple priest Narana, a Rishi, to Valmiki. Valmiki's works also incorporated extensive and detailed accounts of verifiable ancient Indian history, recorded in Sanskrit.

Berosus

Berosus (*c*.300-230 BC) started as a Babylonian scribe and became a high priest and astronomer at the Esagila Temple, serving the god Marduk (aka Bêl and Belus) around 275 BC. Berosus had access to extensive temple records, reportedly encompassing 200,000 years of knowledge.[3] He compiled his *History of Babylon* on thousands of clay tablets that were added to the Temple Library, which had been started centuries earlier by King Ashurbanipal (*circa* 640 BC) in his capital city of Nineveh. He later traveled west to Athens, where he taught astronomy and the sciences.[4] Berosus translated his cuneiform writings into Greek, and wrote a combined historic and astrological narrative called *Babyloniaca*, which also included predictions of future events revealed to him by the god Marduk. He also invented an improved model of the sundial.[5]

He additionally authored *The Babylonian Legend of the Flood*, with Xisuthrus as the Noah hero. In the 3rd century BC, Berosus expanded the list of eight pre-flood kings (known from the Weld-Blundell Prism, believed to have been compiled during the 3rd Dynasty of Ur) to ten kings, lengthening each king's reign to a longer duration. Alexander Polyhistor, the 1st century BC historian, wrote extracts from Berosus' works that have since been lost. Knowledge of his work continued through Eusebius (270-340 AD), who wrote *Chronicon* from Polyhistor's extracts, but reportedly distorted some of the facts from that earlier document.

Berosus knew that the Earth's *ecliptic*, its 'Great Year,' required about 25,800 years to complete one full revolution through the 12 Zodiac 'Houses of Heaven.' The Great Circle period is a result of the phenomenon known as the Precession of the Equinox, which science credits to Hipparchus in 128 BC as its discoverer. Modern calculations reveal the actual completion of one great revolution to be just under 25,779 years.

Manetho

Manetho (3rd century BC) was a high priest in Heliopolis, and acted as a temple scribe during the reign of Ptolemy II Philadelphus (r.285-246 BC), writing in the Greek language. He was also reported to have been both a member and promoter of the Serapis (the Sacred Bull) cult of Egypt. Manetho was born around 300 BC, on the west bank of the Nile at Sebennytus. His access to olden esoteric temple and priestly records, which he claimed contained 36,525 books of Ancient Wisdom written by the god Thoth,[6] prompted his work as an Egyptian historian, authoring his *Aegyptiaca* (*History of Egypt*), a three volume work, in *c.*270 BC. The original is lost, but extracts, essential passages, and specific citations are known from the works of numerous later historians and chronographers. Some of his material was included in the first century AD works of Josephus and the third century AD Greek historian Julius Africanus, who referenced much of Manetho's work in his writings around 240 AD. Additional fragments were also referenced in the works of Eusebius around 300 AD, with later citations made by Georgios Syncellus about 800 AD. Some of the enlightenment derived from Thoth was also incorporated within the Gnostic religion.[7]

Manetho also recorded the chronological reigns for all the Egyptian Pharaohs, organizing them into the successive thirty one dynasties of ancient Egypt from *c.*3150 to 332-304 BC (which included the Ptolemies), along with the chronological order of rule by the gods and demigods that preceded them. His chronology and *Kings List* is the accepted one used even today, although the portion dealing with the reigns of the gods and demigods is dismissed by scholars as 'mythical.'

According to author Andrew Tomas, the only known papyrus of Manetho's Dynastic List existed as merely broken fragments of 'junk' in a storage room of the Turin Museum, until the great French Egyptologist, Jean François Champollion (1790-1832), discovered it.[8] Best known for his work with the Rosetta Stone and its value as a translation tool, Professor Champollion then salvaged those bits and pieces of 'junk' papyri and reconstructed them in the manner of a jigsaw puzzle, eventually restoring the only known copy of Manetho's Dynastic List.[9]

Diodorus

Diodorus of Sicily (*c*.102 or 80-*c*.28 BC) was a Greek born in Agyrium, Sicily, who traveled throughout North Africa, the Near East, Asia, and Europe, spending his final 30 years living in Rome during Julius Caesar's and Emperor Augustus' reigns. He was considered a leading Roman historian and wrote his *Library of History* (aka *University History*), a world history comprising 40 volumes, around 30 BC. Only 15 volumes are extant, with fragments of 20 other volumes also in existence. Much of his work was based on the earlier 5th century BC Greek historian, Hecataeus of Abdera.

Diodorus stated that the gods taught humankind about the arts, agriculture, tools, mining, and metallurgy. He also reported that the Egyptian god Osiris established a number of cities in India. He further wrote that 10,000 years had elapsed from the time of Osiris and Isis, until the reign of Alexander the Great, while acknowledging another account that stated such a time lapse encompassed just under 23,000 years. Those two accounts would establish the Osiris reign in either *c*.23,300 BC or *c*.10,300 BC. Diodorus also claimed that some of the gods were buried on Earth, although admitting that such information contradicted numerous other records.

Strabo

Strabo (*c*.64 BC-*c*.21 AD) was a renowned geographer, explorer, world traveler, cartographer, and historian. He lived in the Greek city of Amasei on the Black Sea, and wrote in Greek. Strabo first compiled a 47 volume collection titled *History* that no longer exists, although the expansive appendix of that work is extant, making it a highly detailed reference of the original compilation. He extensively used material from earlier Greek sources to support his accounts, thereby preserving certain records that would have otherwise been lost. He also compiled a 17 volume work titled *Geography* during his later years, detailing the world from Britain to India, as well as from Ethiopia to the Baltic; providing great details of those visited lands. He revised much of the earlier Greek geography, which was often based on reports by Roman soldiers during their conquests of the West, rather than from more reliable historians and cartographers.

Pliny [The Elder]

Pliny (aka Gaius Plinius Secundus, *c*.23-79 AD) was the foremost Roman authority on science, writing extensively on history, geography, nature, and various sciences. His great encyclopedia, *Historia Naturalis* (*Natural History*) consisted of 37 volumes derived from about 2,000 sources, and contained an estimated 20,000 facts or findings regarding such topics as astronomy, zoology, botany, medicine, anthropology, and metallurgy. Those volumes are the only remaining ones from his approximately 100 volume writings.

He is perhaps one of the earliest scientific authors to acknowledge what are now known in modern times as UFOs. He described such craft as 'strange shields' and 'fiery shields,' stating "a burning shield rushed across the sky."[10] He also described what modern UFO researchers once called 'angel's hair,' a sublime substance with the appearance of cotton candy that was often found around locations of reported UFO sightings, referring to such material as 'heavenly wool.'[11]

Content and Accuracy

Written historic accounts have only occurred since roughly 2000 BC, but commented on many older events long before that date. The resources that could have been used to determine the factual accuracy of local information and its sources did not exist during ancient times, creating suspicion with some chroniclers and their accounts. Both Herodotus and Diodorus claimed they merely reported information provided them by their 'esteemed' sources. The facts they relayed pertained to both the builders and ages of the pyramids and other 'wonders,' which were supplied by Egyptian priests and other reliable authorities. Herodotus reportedly commented that his duty was to record what people said, but that he was not bound to believe it. Neither historian claimed to have researched the factual basis or nature of the accounts provided to them, substantiating only the 'reporting accuracy' of such records presented from the data they were told.

The known and identified instances of contradictions and inconsistencies found between numerous historic accounts made by different ancient historians could simply be attributed to the antiquity of their subject matter. The very nature of such topics, whether reporting on a structure, event, or person, often involved some unknown remote time, during which no contemporary written record existed. Such monuments and events of vastly archaic periods simply transpired during times long before the then-present epoch of the ancient reporters, as well as their sources, either in Egypt or any other ancient country. Hence, no one could have known with any certainty the true history of specific occurrences and/or structures about which such inquiries were made. That reality may have prompted some sources that were interviewed by historians to augment any vague or missing account 'gaps' with legends or fictional stories, further distorting the real truth and the historic facts behind such topics.

Chapter 27

Source Documents

Much of the knowledge known about ancient cultures has been derived from the surviving manuscripts recorded by the previously mentioned historians and commentators. A select group of cultures and their texts will be examined, allowing an evaluation and better understanding of the knowledge and wisdom contained in such documents that were revealed by those authors.

Egypt

Early Egyptians seemingly recorded everything in a desire to preserve and share their vast history and knowledge. As previously stated, they inscribed virtually all objects in their zeal to share their wisdom with the world. There was no apparent intent to hide any truth or knowledge they possessed. Their oldest continuously preserved and recorded form of literature consisted of the *Pyramid Texts*, which were carved on interior walls of temples and tombs of ancient structures. All such texts were engraved in hieroglyphic script, and thought to be recorded between 2800 and 2175 BC. However, its content is believed to represent information, sacred wisdom, and esoteric knowledge handed down orally from the most remote Egyptian epochs. A possible even older date is its association with the Shemsu-Hor, a group of Helpers that disappeared around 3150 BC, but had reportedly compiled the earliest records found in Heliopolis.

Later scribes who copied the earlier textual versions from their original form often did not understand the words or meanings they were transcribing, according to Egyptologists such as Sir Wallis Budge. The construction of certain sentences contained in those texts are unfamiliar, as are the precise meanings of a large number of glyphs, with some script remaining completely unknown, leaving many lines untranslatable. They further incorporated mythical accounts that often focused on religious rituals, incantations, and formulas, as well as hymns and prayers to the gods, especially Osiris. Such texts also disclosed the archaic existence of a vanished culture, one that possessed a high level of scientific achievement and astronomical knowledge.

The oldest and largest source comprising the *Pyramid Texts* is found in the tomb chamber associated with the pyramid of Unas, which is located at Saqqara, a site directly across the Nile from Memphis, about ten miles south of Giza. The walls and ceilings of that repository are covered with magnificent hieroglyphics, artistically carved into the solid limestone, then painted over with blue and gold colors. Although that account represents the oldest known portion of the *Pyramid Texts*, additional Saqqara documents, along with others recorded by the high priests of Heliopolis, are also included within this record.

The portion of the *Pyramid Texts* referring to the prior mentioned vanished advanced culture also discussed a special ladder, one similar to that of the Biblical Jacob. Such an Egyptian ladder was occasionally a rope ladder, but usually one made from wood or iron, which hung from an 'iron plate' suspended in the sky.[1] Its purpose was to provide a means for select people, including dead pharaohs, to ascend into the sky where a "doorway to the stars" would be opened for them.[2] That doorway was referenced as an "aperture of the sky-window where the gods greet you," known as the *Duat*.[3] The use of iron to construct special ladders or an iron plate in heaven is puzzling, since the ancient Egyptians never possessed an Iron Age. The earliest date that Egyptologists have established for the use of iron in Egypt was *c*.650 BC. Their main implement or tool material was obsidian, a volcanic glasslike stone. But descriptions of iron thrones and vast iron plates that conveyed people into the sky were common, with iron often referred to as the Metal of Heaven, or the Divine Metal.

The *Coffin Texts* from the Middle Kingdom replaced the earlier *Pyramid Texts*. They were painted on coffins and also inscribed on stone slabs, obelisks, and stelae. Many were written records of earlier oral traditions, while others were simply newer copies made to replace older, damaged records. They consisted of historical accounts, literature, and hymns written between 2175 and 1675 BC, with many 'addendum' stone posts and stelae being continuously engraved throughout Egyptian history, either as new records or duplicates of prior deteriorated ones.

The *Mortuary Texts* of the New Kingdom then replaced the *Coffin Texts*, which were written continually after 1675 BC on rolls of papyrus. Papyrus was a durable and long lasting product made from a secret Egyptian process that rivaled the finest white, glossy muslin paper of today. *Mortuary Texts* consisted of wisdom and religious texts, historic accounts, instructional manuals, hymns, and scientific data that included mathematical, astronomical, and medical knowledge.

The Book of the Dead is a collection of various religious records that the Egyptians generally titled as the book of *Pert em hru*, translated as "Coming forth by day." Since this compilation is essentially an anthology, there is no known single record comprising all the texts that are sometimes included within this work. Although *The Book of the Dead* (aka *The Book of Going Forth by Day*) is usually included within the *Mortuary Texts*, much of its content actually originated during much earlier times, either in some unknown written form, or as ancient oral tradition. It was an evolving work, with continuing variations and additions made over ensuing years, with three known versions. The oldest being the Heliopolitan recension compiled by the priests at the

College of Anu from *Pyramid* and *Coffin Texts*. The Theban recension is the middle version, compiled roughly between 1500 and 1000 BC. The youngest version is the Saite one, which covers an approximate period from 700 to 100 BC.

Hence, *The Book of the Dead* is a compilation that is composed of numerous parts, portions, and groupings of different records by unrelated authors. In the 19th century AD, it was arranged into 165 chapters, with additional ones included later to total 192 chapters.[4] No known original or individual source was responsible for the entire compilation, although some chapters are ascribed to certain authors such as the Egyptian god Thoth (the Greek god Hermes), who is often credited as one of the main inspirations for *The Book of the Dead*. Fragments pertaining to Thoth's teachings and revelations also formed the basis for the later esoteric *Egyptian Mysteries*. The fragmentary record of Thoth's writings and teachings, known as the *Thoth* or *Hermetic Fragments* (also the *Trismegistic Literature*, the *Corpus Hermeticum*, and the *Collectum Hermeticum*), were highly revered by early Church Fathers of the Christian faith, including Origen, Augustine, and Clement; and were also central elements within Gnostic beliefs.

References clearly show that *The Book of the Dead* existed in some form before 3100 BC. Author Warren Smith reported that the 64th Chapter is attributed to Thoth, with one reference made to an inscribed copy dated around 4250 BC, with the original work being derived from an even earlier unknown date.[5] *The Book of the Dead* stated that the Earth was spherical, recording its approximate length of orbit, circumference, and the equatorial distance to its poles. It also described its equatorial bulge and flattened condition existing at its poles. Other data indicate its authors understood sophisticated map projection that required the use of higher mathematics.

Additional chapters were engraved in various locations, with some duplications as well as dissimilar versions of the same stories being produced at different source sites. Supplemental vignettes were also added, further confusing this record. Thus, its age and origin can not be accurately assessed, due to its many variants. Independent partial versions of certain chapters, as well as continuing additions, were also later written on papyrus starting around *c.*1500 BC. An important portion of *The Book of the Dead* is comprised within its 175th Chapter (or its 17th Chapter as organized in other versions), written by the scribe Ani.[6] That segment is also supplemented by various conflicting vignettes, and also exists separately as the *Papyrus of Ani*, which originated as a 78 feet long scroll of the 18th Dynasty, dating to around 1450 BC.[7]

Another individual work, the *Emerald Tablets*, which is commonly attributed to Thoth, is dated to *c.*2500 BC by Dr. Sigismund Bacstrom, an 18th century scholar. The term *Emerald Tablets* actually refers to the *Smaragdine Tablets* (aka *Tabula Smaragdina*) attributed to the Greek god Hermes (the Egyptian god Thoth). The legend surrounding this record claims its origin as being an emerald slab inscribed with Phoenician characters that Alexander the Great reportedly discovered clutched in the deceased hands of Hermes as he laid in his burial tomb (supposedly a dark cave in the Valley of Ebron). This same record has also been attributed to an Egyptian adept, perhaps a king, who reportedly lived around 1900 BC. Only a few fragments of this archaic record are known to remain after its reported later destruction by Emperor Diocletian during the late third century AD.

One excerpt from this record stated: "All things owe their existence to the Only One...."[8] This may be a reference to the unity of matter just before or during the Big Bang event, prior to the formation of elementary particles; or perhaps a reference to the Creator who conceived and brought forth physical existence. Such comprehension reflects abstract reasoning far in advance of the mental abilities that are ascribed to ancient man.

India

The Egyptians and the Hindus of India often shared knowledge between their cultures, as evidenced by the numerous similarities in their records. However, the Aryan culture that intruded into India by 2500 BC and continued until 1300 BC, had an equally formative impact. The Aryans are generally credited with bringing Sanskrit writing to India, and perhaps even the *Vedas*, or at least a portion of them. But prior Indian cultures of the Dravidians and the Nagas had already initiated the *Vedas* in an early form of Sanskrit, long before the Aryan intrusion.

The Sanskrit language is derived from the Indian term *Sanskrita*, meaning "polished or complete"; and is considered to be an ideally constructed language, consisting of fifty characters, each possessing a constant and inflexible pronunciation.[9] Its script is called *Devanagari*, literally translated as "divine abode."[10]   Ancient seals written in Sanskrit prove that the language was not derived or borrowed from Semitic or Aryan influences, although its earliest origin still remains unknown. Sanskrit is considered to be the predecessor from which all Indo-European languages emerged, according to Panini, the great philologist of ancient India.[11]

The *Vedas*, or Knowledge Books, are the most ancient known sacred wisdom texts of India. They are revered as being 'not of human origin,' but divinely inspired; believed to be 'revealed texts' from an unknown age, originating from the time of the gods. Often called India's Bible equivalent, the *Vedas* were originally handed down orally by the sages or Rishis from generation to generation, through chanting of their verses. They were believed to be first recorded in written form around 1500 BC, composed in Vedic, an early form of Sanskrit. The oldest extant copy is dated about 220 BC. There are four *Vedas*: the *Rig Veda*, *Sama Veda*, *Yajur Veda*, and the *Atharva Veda*. Collectively, all four *Vedas* are known as the *Samhita* or the *Mantra*.

320

The oldest *Veda*, the *Rig Veda*, was an invocation to the gods. The *Rig Veda* is of epic length, containing 1,028 hymns of about ten verses each, divided into ten books containing 10,800 stanzas. It speaks of advanced cosmology, other inhabited worlds, the 33 gods of Manu, and the sacred Soma plant that produced a drink favored by the gods. The second *Veda*, the *Sama*, contained the instructions for the tunes used to chant the *Rig* hymns. The *Yajur Veda* contained sacrificial formulas and spells. The *Atharva Veda*, the fourth *Veda*, is the main source for magical incantations, chants, and spells. It is also considered to be the oldest medical text of India, and identifies 107 types or species of healing herbs.

The *Vedas* have also been interpreted as describing rocket engines, aircraft design, atomic energy, space travel, and television. They reveal astronomical knowledge of the Earth rotating on its own axis, the correct cause of eclipses, and awareness that the sun was the source of the reflected light from the moon. They also describe a missile known as Indra's 'thunderbolt,'[12] and a golden aircraft with three engines and landing gear. A three-step process that separated Heaven and Earth was also identified, resulting in a two-part universe comprised of Earth and the 'Upper Dwelling' place. The *Vedas* further speak of seven divine sages, with seven being a recurrent sacred number throughout the *Vedas*, as well as in numerous other religious texts.

Other Sanskrit writings include the *Puranas*, the 'ancient tales,' which are comprised of 18 *Great Puranas* and multiple 'subordinate' *Puranas*. They were also written in the early form of Sanskrit called Vedic, first recorded between 1500 and 1400 BC. These sacred scriptures speak of four Earth 'Ages' totaling 432,000 years, matching the 432,000 years assigned to the reign of the Mesopotamian gods recorded by the Babylonian historian Berosus. Dr. R. Cedric Leonard, an archaeologist and anthropologist, reported the oldest *Purana*, the *Vishnu*, mentions "the chariots of the nine planets,"[13] perhaps an indication that the ancients were aware of the nine planets comprising our solar system (at least before Pluto was 'demoted').

This group of writings also includes the *Mahabharata*, a great epic poem of about 200,000 lines, consisting of 18 'Major Books,' which were first started around 1500 BC, with additions made over centuries until its final form emerged around 300 BC. It was based on temple records, oral tradition, and histories handed down from much earlier times, reportedly reaching back to 20,000 BC. It begins with an account of Creation, chronicles the epic story of the 'War between the Gods,' describes the Great Flood, writes of the life of Krishna, and includes the historical Bharata war between the Kurus and the Pandavas of *c.*1400 BC.[14]

The *Mahabharata* discusses life on other planets, stating: "Infinite is the space populated by the Perfect Ones and gods; there is no limit to their delightful abodes."[15] It also reveals a weapon called the *Agneya* (aka Agneyastra), which may be a nuclear missile, described as an iron projectile alleged to have all the power of the universe and the radiance of 1,000 suns. It was known as the Mighty One, the 'destroyer of worlds,' and was credited with the complete annihilation of two races of peoples, the Vrishnis and the Andhakras. It describes the vaporization of people from a mighty blast, and the loss of any survivor's hair and nails.[16] A similar weapon was also referenced in a collection of ancient records generally known as the *Old Commentaries*, contained in *The Secret Doctrine* written by H. P. Blavatsky.

The Secret Doctrine is the English collection of archaic revelations extracted from thousands of Sanskrit manuscripts found in Brahminical, Chinese, and Tibetan temple archives; coupled with certain oral traditions that comprise the essence of Hindu, Chaldean, Egyptian, Islamic, Buddhist, Gnostic, Jewish, Zoroastrian, and Christian religious theology.

The *Ramayana* is another epic poem believed to be initially authored by Valmiki in the 4th century BC. It is the story of Rama and his wife, Sita, contained in 48,000 lines. Valmiki used temple records at Ayhodia, writing in poetic verse, to compose the *Ramayana*. Neither the *Mahabharata* nor the *Ramayana* remained in their original forms, with numerous alterations and additions known to have been made over the years.

The *Sutras*, meaning 'string of rules,' comprise another collection of Hindu texts, which are collections of rites, laws, and ritual ceremonies. They are also condensed manuals that seem to describe advanced devices. The *Samarangana Sutradhara*, an early Sanskrit technical work, deals with architecture, temple and palace construction, and city layout; according to both Dr. R. Cedric Leonard and Charles Berlitz. One such chapter on mechanical devices detailed the construction, operation, maintenance, and traits of aircraft that were called *vimanas*.[17] According to that text, "By means of these machines, human beings can fly in the air and heavenly beings can come down to Earth."[18] The *Ramayana* described the vimanas as 'double-deck' circular aircraft, with portholes and a domed top.[19] Some vimanas were reportedly even capable of leaving the atmosphere of Earth,[20] sounding much like modern UFOs.

The *Samarangana Sutradhara* also contained blueprint-like drawings depicting turbines and expansion chambers similar to modern jet engines, including fuel and power sources, and aircraft limitations. The text further described takeoff and landing procedures, extended preparations for flight, and possible collisions with birds.[21] It also discussed other engines capable of producing very strong propulsive forces, using fire and mercury as its fuel source.[22] The text required its construction and propulsion secrets to be guarded, with certain details deliberately withheld for sake of secrecy rather than ignorance, fearing certain people might wrongly use such machines.[23]

Dr. Leonard also discussed the *Surya Siddhanta*, an ancient Sanskrit book believed written by Prince Asura Maya, an early scientist, astronomer, and genius of India. Dated to the 1st century BC, the *Surya Siddhanta* is a technical work dealing with astronomy, trigonometry, and higher mathematics. The text claimed that "the Earth is a globe in space,"[24] and accurately calculated its diameter, as well as the distance from Earth to the moon. It further stated that the moon only reflected light from the sun, and did not emit its own. It warned the Siddhas, the high priests of science, to guard the mysteries of the gods, so ordinary people could not abuse such power, as indicated in its sixth chapter, stating: "This mystery of the gods is not to be imparted indiscriminately."[25] The *Surya Siddhanta* also referred to a long ago epoch when scientists could orbit the Earth "below the moon but above the clouds."[26]

Certain foreign influences and texts were also brought into India, such as the *Avesta* (aka the *Zend-Avesta*), which is the Zoroastrian religion's collection of its holy scriptures, ancient beliefs, and record of its customs. Although that doctrine originated in ancient Persia under the great religious teachings of Zoroaster (aka Zarathuštra), that belief lost followers after the conquest of a vast majority of the Persian Empire in 327 BC by Alexander the Great, as a result of relentless persecution. Many believers fled to India for refuge, taking only a portion of their sacred texts and writings, causing the balance of Zoroastrian records to be permanently lost.

The Zoroastrian religion flourished in India, where it found a permanent home. It is widely thought that the original doctrine resembled the composition found in the *Rig Veda*, so the two texts may share a common source. In modern times, its believers in India far outnumber those followers in Iran (Ancient Persia) of this olden religion, where a few of the faithful had remained hidden during ancient times, keeping that faith alive over the ensuing millennia.

China & Tibet

Only a relatively few archaic Chinese texts were believed to have escaped the 213 BC destruction of records ordered by the Ch'in Dynasty. The *Shu Ching* (aka *Shu-king*), meaning the *Book of History*, is the oldest known book of China, dated to at least 2150

BC. The *Shih Ching* (aka *Shih-king* and *Shi-Ching*), translated as the *Book of Odes*, is the second oldest, followed by the *I Ching* (*Book of Changes*). All are believed to be based on much older records and oral tradition dating to at least 3322 BC.[27] The works are spiritual manuscripts of divination, acknowledging an intentional and orderly creation of the universe, along with a moral plan for humans to live life in harmony within such a structured universe. It is unknown how many other ancient 'hidden' texts may also exist in the secret lamaseries of Tibet that survived the 213 BC destruction, as well as all the other subsequent record confiscations.

The *Book of Dzyan* (aka *Stanzas of Dzyan*) is reportedly an ancient Tibetan text that was eventually translated into Sanskrit during archaic times, which consists of at least 51 known stanzas.[28] It is often considered to be one of the oldest chronicles from ancient India, passed down by oral tradition until it was eventually recorded once writing was developed. It reportedly originated in the remote reaches of the Himalayas, with no known date as to its true age, or if its original version might still exist. Allegedly once written on palm leaves, such an early text was purported by some to possess supernatural properties that allowed communication by non-conventional means, through mere physical contact with the book. It was reported to have first been written in the *Senzar* language, the divine language of the ancient gods, which was known to the high priests and adepts of the early Mystery Cults. It is believed to have been hidden away by Tibetan priests in archaic times, thereby preserving its 'sacred' content.

The complete work reportedly contained the history of the primordial ancient world, the evolution of humankind over millions of years, sacred symbolic signs, and the formula of Creation, which is contained in its *Seven Stanzas of Creation*. Those *Seven Stanzas* are an abstract description of the formative stages of the universe, as a result of the Big Bang event. The stanzas are also believed to be the inspirational source for the

Seven Creations contained in the *Puranas*, as well as the Bible's *Seven Days of Creation*. The *Book of Dzyan* is often described as a puzzling and conflicting book of abstract ideas, although its purpose and meaning may become more apparent when evaluated with modern scientific understanding and an open mind. The Creation hymns found in the *Rig Veda* are quite similar to portions of the *Book of Dzyan*, making it unclear which ancient manuscript is older, although the *Dzyan* stanzas are believed to predate the *Vedas*. Further similarities from this text also exist within the *Mahabharata* and the Hebrew *Cabala*.

The *Book of Dzyan* is known to the Western World through an English translation from the Sanskrit language by Madam H. P. Blavatsky, which was contained in her 1888, six volume epic, *The Secret Doctrine*. Modern printings produce that writing now as a two volume work. Helena Blavatsky was reportedly shown a copy of the *Book of Dzyan* written on palm-leaf pages while living in India. Her later works reflected many if not all of the complete *Dzyan* stanzas, along with its ancient commentaries, accompanied with explanations and insights by Madam Blavatsky.

The *Old Commentaries*, also called the *Ancient Commentaries*, are interspersed throughout her work to clarify, elucidate, and expand on the mysterious meanings within her text. Those commentaries were also based on Tibetan Sanskrit translations derived from the initial archaic *Commentaries* written in Senzar, which accompanied the original *Book of Dzyan*. But certain commentaries are still considered to be as confusing as some of the original stanzas themselves.

Helena Petrovna Blavatsky (1831-1891) and an American lawyer, Colonel Henry Steel Olcott, her occult and social partner, founded the Theosophical Society in New York City after living in India for a number of years. That Society was formed between 1874 and 1875 as a philosophical and religious system. Theosophy is the examination of the nature of God, the revelation of the knowledge of God, and the relationship of the universe to

God through philosophical inquiry or mystical intuition. It is a system of occult philosophy based on doctrines of Oriental religious teachings; metaphysical Sanskrit treatises based on ancient Hindu texts and the later Upanishads; and other secret or esoteric texts, including the *Book of Dzyan* and China's *I Ching*. Its doctrine purports that all souls are essentially equal and same, differing only in their degree of enlightened development toward perfection.

H. P. Blavatsky's *The Secret Doctrine* was compiled from select sacred scriptures, oral traditions and histories, esoteric texts such as the *Book of Dzyan*, and numerous legends and myths from many cultures. It reveals ancient cosmological knowledge that parallels modern findings, and disclosed that Earth was inhabited by non-human beings 18 million years ago, claiming humans evolved from a series of different Root Races or species over the eons.

The Secret Doctrine also revealed the arrival many thousands of years ago of a small group of visitors from the heavens that apparently orbited Earth several times before landing. Once on Earth, those visitors stayed to themselves, but were worshiped by humans that knew of them. Rivalries emerged between the visitors, eventually splitting them into two groups. One group moved away from the original site of arrival, and subsequently found a new human following at their resultant location. The two separated groups of visitors eventually engaged in war, fighting battles in the sky with their crafts, using weapons of incredible power. One such weapon was described as a great shining lance that rode on a beam of light and burst over the city of its enemy, burning all its inhabitants and those of nearby villages.

More distant survivors that looked at such a blast were blinded. People later entering the destroyed city became sick and eventually died, as if even the dust of the city was poisoned. The city eventually crumbled to dust and was forgotten by later humans. The winning side reportedly was saddened by what they had done to their fellow beings and left Earth, never to return.

Such a conflict seems to describe nuclear warfare with ensuing fallout from radiation poisoning. That account is quite similar to an Akkadian one that described the destruction of the city of Ur. Note should also be made of the 'separation' into two groups of the visitors from the heavens, perhaps a direct reference to the schism between the BOPH gods and the Lunar Pitris.

Mayan

The *Popul Vuh* is a collection of Mayan beliefs and legends passed down orally through the centuries. It is the sacred holy text of the oldest branch of Mayans from Guatemala, also called the Quiché Mayans, who utilized both the snake and swastika as their religious symbols. These Mayans worshiped humanlike gods who presumably came from other worlds, referencing 'white men who came from the stars and from the sea,' alluding to some mysterious land in the East where they resided, perhaps the legendary Atlantis. The *Popul Vuh* further implies that mankind was created to serve the gods. The advanced knowledge possessed by the Mayans was reportedly imparted to them by the First Men, their forefathers, who eventually became separated from the gods. All the knowledge and wisdom possessed by those First Men was later taken away by the gods. The Quiché Mayans also recorded an ancient conflict between two groups of beings that possessed superhuman powers and abilities, perhaps referring to the 'outer planet schism.'

The books of *Chilam Balam*, referring to the Mayan prophet Balam of the late 15th century AD, had a number of versions or supplements based on each village or town that recorded its content. They represent the religious texts and history of the Mayans of the Yucatan, a later branch than the southern Quiché tribe. Reportedly, the first inhabitants of the Yucatan were the 'People of the Serpent,' who came from the East in boats lead by Itzamana, who was known as the Serpent of the East. Such titles or epithets appear to be direct references to the Helpers of the Ancient Ones, who were also known as the Serpent People. The *Chilam Balam* also seems to allude to otherworldly visitors, claiming that the white gods who 'reach the stars,' arrived from the sky on flying ships.

Hebrew

The Jewish *Cabala* (aka *Kabbalah*), meaning 'received tradition' in Hebrew, encompasses the many forms of Jewish mysticism. It is generally considered to be one of the most comprehensive but puzzling secret doctrines in the world. The *Cabala* is thought to have been imparted at roughly the same time as the *Torah*, and is regarded as a second oral law. It is an esoteric work that was initially revealed to merely a few select high priests that handed it down to only certain mystics. Its text contained prophecy, Greek and Egyptian science, numerology, Zoroastrian beliefs, interpretations of mysterious pronouncements within the Old Testament, and elements of Gnostic dogma that were considered by some to be heresy. It links occult knowledge and facts with the mystical power of various gods. The *Cabala* also speaks of 49 'divine names,' although some appear to be duplicates, perhaps indicating a total number smaller than 49 separate beings.

The seven volumes forming the *Cabala* were comprised mainly from a combination of two books. The first source was the *Book of Formation* that dealt mainly with the ecstatic experience of God, secret formula, signs, and symbols. This work was first written down and released to the public in the 8th century AD. However, the majority of data contained in the *Cabala* came from the *Sefer ha-Zohar* or the *Book of Zohar* (aka *Book of Splendor*). That work represented more than 1,800 years of oral tradition, from c.600 BC to 1286 AD, including the extensive research, teachings, and beliefs of Rabbi Simeon bar Yohai during the 2nd century AD. It was finally written down between 1280 and 1286 AD by Moses de Leon (1250-1305), and was only later printed for release to the public for general consumption.

The *Cabala* is primarily considered to be an occult encyclopedia of metaphysical speculation on science, the universe, and God. It professes that Earth's redemption and reunification with the Godhead is humanity's task on Earth, a goal accomplished through good acts, observance of the Laws (the commandments), and prayer. It contains symbolic language, magic formulas, and the nature of the divine world. Author Erich von Däniken disclosed that the *Cabala* revealed the existence of seven other inhabited worlds in the universe, namely: Geb, Nesziah, Tziah, Thebel, Erez, Adamah, and Arqa.[29] Two of those worlds, Adamah and Erez, were represented as being populated by relatives of the Biblical Adam, while the world of Thebel was reported to be inhabited by an amphibious race.[30]

However, Dr. Tamar Frankiel, a *Cabala* scholar, wrote of four worlds, including Atzilut, Beriah, Yetzirah, and Asiyah;[31] and also mentioned the 'lower worlds' of Chochmah, Malkhut, Yesod, Chesed, and Binab.[32] Other interpretations believe the *Cabala* contains indications of another seven worlds that remained unnamed. But the *Cabala's* inherently confusing manner may merely be referring to the previously named seven worlds, rather than to an additional seven.

Another ancient Hebrew book, the *Book of Enoch*, is equally enigmatic. The book has several versions, with some portions found with the various texts comprising the *Dead Sea Scrolls*. Enoch was presumably a high priest or priest-in-training, and a scribe in one of the temples of the gods. This allowed insight into the functions and inner-workings of the gods, as well as the opportunity to observe and record their deeds and accomplishments. He evidently was singled out by his mentors, and was allowed special privileges and freedoms, according to his later written accounts.

Little information on Enoch is found in the Bible, merely listing him as the seventh patriarch after Adam, and the father of

Methuselah. However, extra-Biblical texts report that Enoch was taken into the heavens on two separate trips to Aravoth (Olam in another version), the celestial home of the gods. Further, he did not die on Earth, since he was granted immortality by the gods during his second trip into space, and allowed to reside on their home planet in the heavens.

Much more is known about Enoch from ancient records that were deliberately excluded from the Bible. Some of those excluded records are contained in the *Book of Enoch*, but the original manuscript, of an unknown age, did not survive from antiquity. Nor is it known if an actual recorded version existed before the Great Flood, when Enoch was alleged to have lived, or if the text was only transmitted orally across the vastness of time until written down during the ancient historic times of the Hebrews. The subsequent eventual Hebrew manuscript was later copied and translated into both Greek and Latin. Those translations, along with fragments and excerpts of the Hebrew text, were continuously preserved over the ages. They deal directly with Enoch the man, his activities, and his life; rather than merely his role within the patriarchal lineage recorded in the Biblical narration. Although excluded from the Bible, the *Book of Enoch* was included in the canon of the early Abyssinian (Ethiopian) Church.

Three versions of this presumably pre-flood text exist. One is an Ethiopian account known as *1 Enoch* that was translated from the Coptic language. It is generally believed to be the oldest version, predating the others by about 200 years. Portions of this version are known to have been based upon even older records, including the lost *Book of Noah* and *The Book of Adam and Eve*, both known mainly through fragments. This was the version accepted by the Abyssinian Church canon. The second variation is a Slavonic translation known as *2 Enoch* or *The Book of the Secrets of Enoch*. That rendition is the one included with the apocryphal manuscripts that were excluded from the Bible. The Slavic version contains additional passages missing from the

Abyssinian Church account. That variation exhibits scientific knowledge associated with the teachings from the Egyptian culture centered at Alexandria during *c.*50 BC. A third version is a translation by Hugo Odeberg, published by the Cambridge University Press in 1928. That variation is known by scholars as *3 Enoch* or *The Hebrew Book of Enoch.*

When Enoch was 365 years old, the Watchers invited him on a trip, flying him upward into the heavens. Enoch described those Watchers as two very tall men with radiant faces that he had never before seen on Earth. Once Enoch was anointed with a special ointment (in *1 Enoch*, he shed his earthly garments, and was clothed in the 'robes of splendor' of his hosts), there was no longer any difference in their appearance. That flight, which reportedly lasted 60 days, originated from a place on Earth called Ahuzan, with God's home planet, Aravoth, as the final destination. That world was referred to as the 'tenth heaven' (in *1 Enoch*, it was the 'seventh heaven'). Enoch described a number of other 'heavens' he either passed by, or had actually visited as a 'secondary stop' during his voyage.

The first part of his journey entailed a layover on the fifth heaven, perhaps Jupiter or one of its moons, where Enoch encountered 'fallen angels,' which were referred to as Grigori (Rephim in *1 Enoch*). He also observed a number of 'wonders' involving flying creatures. In Chapter IV, Enoch is brought before the 'elders,' the "rulers of the stellar orders...who rule the stars and their services to the heavens...."[33]

While on the home planet, the tenth heaven, he encountered God and was instructed in the secrets of nature and man; how the Earth formed; and the secrets of the planets and stars. It was the Archangel Pravuil (Archangel Uriel in *1 Enoch*) who showed Enoch the secrets of all the workings of the heavens, the Earth, the seas, all the elements, and cosmological understanding. The Archangel also gave Enoch 'Heavenly Tablets' containing great knowledge, and instructed him to record their wisdom. From those tablets, Enoch wrote 366 books (360 books in *1 Enoch*) documenting those revelations, which he gave to his descendants upon returning to Earth. Those 366 books of knowledge have never been found, and either vanished, or perhaps never existed.

Enoch personally imparted some secret wisdom directly to his son Methuselah before leaving again on his second celestial trip, which occurred shortly after his initial return. His subsequent voyage was made with the intent of staying on another planet, presumably the home world of the gods where he first visited. No record ever reported Enoch's return to Earth. Later, Church editors and censors changed those narratives and the 'nature' of Enoch's trips, making them merely 'dreams' or 'visions' that he once experienced, hiding the real truth of those visits.

On his trip, Enoch was supervised directly by the *Azazels*, who were also called Watchers, the select intermediaries or representatives between mortal humanity and the divine gods. According to the *Dead Sea Scrolls*, the father of Noah was not Lamech, but rather a Watcher.[34] One of the kings of Babylon, Nebuchadnezzar (r.651-604 BC), had a vision in which "a Watcher and a Holy One came down from heaven."[35] Apparently Watchers, Holy Ones, and gods were all different beings, which could be distinguished by the indigenous humans of Earth.

The name Azazel (aka Azael, Azaeil, Azarel) has been used to indicate numerous beings other than 'God's Helpers' or Helpers of the gods, although such intermediaries were also called '*Sadaim*,' according to author George Andrews.[36] Other accounts refer to Azazel as the 'Goat god' of the Hebrews, to whom animals, mainly goats, were sacrificed. Azazel was also used as a reference to demons, specifically desert demons. The name also referred to six different beings, each believed to be the leader of a group of Helpers during various distinct periods of time on Earth. According to the *Cabala*, Azael was a 'fallen god' who came down to Earth during the time of Tubal Cain. Such negative attributes show the success of the BOPH gods' plan to demonize the Helpers who remained after the Ancient Ones

333

departed.

According to the Hebrew *Talmud*, the *Law of the Azazel* included those laws that man's intellect could not understand. Extra-Biblical texts further indicate that the Azazels brought civilization to Earth and taught men to make such items as swords, knives, shields, breastplates, and mirrors. One extra-Biblical text claimed that the Azazels taught men to make 'Magic Mirrors,' which "allowed men to see distant scenes and people clearly through them."[37] Similar devices were also called 'Animated Stones' by Sanchuniathon.[38] Other texts referred to them as Dark Crystals or Black Stones, describing them as pedestals formed from a radiant substance resembling glass, where deities appeared to 'select viewers.' Perhaps those objects, although described in a primitive but accurate manner, simply referred to the modern device we now know as television.

In his later works, author Erich von Däniken referred to Japanese texts that describe special mirrors that could be interpreted as being devices resembling a television. The malevolent Central American god, Tezcatilpoca, meaning 'Smoking Mirror,' defeated Quetzalcoatl in Tula, the ancient legendary Toltec city of Tollan. Tezcatilpoca is reported to have used a mysterious device also called the Smoking Mirror, to view mortals and gods from a great distance,[39] thereby providing Tezcatilpoca with an ability to eventually defeat Quetzalcoatl. Based on mythical descriptions, some scholars believe such devices were fabricated from obsidian.

In olden times, obsidian was called *tezcat*, and was used to make crude mirrors that were utilized by wizards to aid them with their 'visions.' The manufacture of such occult gadgets appears to be an attempt by later primitive people to copy or duplicate a vague or remote memory from the distant past that was based on such a Dark Crystal or Smoking Mirror; devices that were apparently once used by the ancient gods. Such instruments may have been similar to our modern cathode ray tubes, viewing screens, or surveillance monitors.

Chapter 28

Religion & Law

The earlier chapters in Part One of this writing revealed the emergence of religious belief before the development of laws or true civilization. The origin and reason for the initial formation of religious or spiritual belief has never been revealed or adequately addressed. It may have first occurred due to the superstitious nature of humanity, in response to the forces of nature. Still, some anthropologists have noted a metaphysical spirit as an underlying element associated with ancient beliefs, one accepting a superior order to which all matter in the universe is subjected.[1]

Such a concept produces a form of constraint, or law unto itself. Religion is also an excellent way to control groups of people, while shaping their agenda and actions. It is a method used to manipulate others, through selective disclosure of knowledge and enticement of rewards. Since ancient times, politics and religion were one and the same, providing a method of control over the masses by the few. Religion works as an indirect method of control, utilizing the 'honor' system. It also forces a prescribed discipline or way-of-life from which core values of right and wrong, or good and evil are instilled.

At its simplest level, religion employs 'rewards' to motivate and control actions. Violations of accepted precepts carry the threat of a loss or decrease in those rewards, either in the present life or in an afterlife, with the intent to compel strict adherence to the prescribed path. Fellow colleagues reinforce this method by encouraging one another to remain in conformity with the rules. Such methods work whether others are watching, or if one is alone when 'suspect actions' might be conducted, since a Supreme Deity is believed to be ever observant. Religious control or conformity is the best 'first step' in establishing rule, discipline, and order within a society. It further teaches a moral or value system within each person, creating core beliefs. Such a plan is intended to work with minimal oversight or extraneous control, as when a small group is attempting to control a much larger one. It can be either good, as in the case of the Ancient Ones' efforts; or detrimental, as was the case with the BOPH gods' basic enslavement of humanity.

When belief alone no longer fully controls actions or produces the desired responses, laws become inevitable. Laws are a direct, observational enforcement method of control. They establish rules dictating certain actions while prohibiting others, with any enforcement only resulting from direct observation of violations. Laws are intended to control humanity's actions in the present, rather than the afterlife, dictating what behavior is unacceptable, and the resultant contemporary punishment for violations. It requires constant oversight and quick enforcement. It can not be effectively employed by a small group attempting to control a larger one unless intermediaries are used, or some advanced technical surveillance devices are employed.

Perhaps ancient Watchers acted as such intermediaries, while the 'dark crystals' discussed in the previous chapter were the equivalent of closed circuit monitoring. Civil laws can produce a sense of orderliness and harmony when applied justly and uniformly. A combination of religious belief and civil laws would cover all aspects of cultural control when fully implemented. Total control can be achieved with a combination of religion and law enforcement. Such control results in predictable behavior, and hence a known outcome from future events. It creates the *order* and *harmony* required by the celestial forces described in many ancient texts. It would also be precisely the outcome desired by a group of advanced beings concerned with a chaotic and undisciplined species, which could eventually construct future instruments of mass destruction.

Laws

The God of the Hebrews reportedly gave the Adam-to-Noah generations a set of seven laws, the Noachide Laws (aka Noachian Code). They consisted of prohibitions against murder, idolatry, blasphemy, theft, sexual immorality, eating the flesh of living animals, and a mandate to establish a secular rule-of-law, including a civil and criminal court system.[2] Such Hebrew Law is reminiscent of the Akkadian *Seven Tablets* of the Anunnaki.

According to the *Book of Exodus*, when God inscribed the Ten Commandments (the Moral Laws), He further issued a similar edict instructing Moses to write a set of secular laws to govern the Hebrews. Those Laws (the Health Laws) are reportedly contained in the first five books of the Bible, known as the Pentateuch, which consists of *Genesis*, *Exodus*, *Leviticus*, *Numbers*, and *Deuteronomy*. These five books also comprise the written portion of the *Torah*, God's revealed instructions and will, consisting of Jewish law, customs, and practice. While the Noachian Code was binding on both Jews and Gentiles, the Mosaic Laws were binding only on the Jews.

The Jewish sages, the rabbis, believe that the Hebrew God revealed both an oral and written law. The instruction or collection of their oral Jewish Law is known as the *Mishnah*, which forms the basis of the *Talmud*. The *Talmud* is the interpretation of the *Mishnah*, or more correctly the 'study of that study.' It can not merely be read, but also requires researched study eventually leading to understanding and insight. Essentially, it is considered the 'commentary on the written commentaries,' which were faithfully transmitted through the ages from master to disciple, thereby leaving oral Jewish Law open to infinite individual interpretation. The

Hebrews believed that by submitting to God's Will and obeying His Laws, humankind could become a harmonious part of the cosmos, a part of what they perceived to be a *Cosmic Order*.

The Levites were reputed to be descendants of Levi, one of Jacob's twelve sons, comprising the twelve tribes of the Hebrews. Moses and his brother Aaron were the leaders of the Levites after the Exodus. The Levites were the high priests of the Hebrews, and were entrusted with both the written and oral traditions, comparable to the Brahmins of India.[3] They were the exclusive group that created Jewish Law, and became the only group within a community to possess, interpret, censor, change, and judge such Law.[4] The Levites ruled with supreme authority as aristocrats over all other Hebrews.

The quantity of Ancient Ones and their accompanying Helpers were few in number within their mission to civilize and educate infant species, and establish order throughout the universe. Likewise, the later BOPH visitors were also limited in their numbers. Ancient accounts, both written and oral, state that the total number of gods, Watchers, White Fathers, or any of the other names used to identify those extraterrestrial visitors, always comprised only a small quantity of beings. Mesopotamian records indicate that such later visitations started with only one family, that of Alalu, followed later by Enki and his six followers.

Fifty additional visitors were soon followed by yet another 300, which eventually joined that group.[5] Another subsequent 300 visitors later arrived on Earth, joined by 300 in the heavens[6] (the 300 Igigi referenced in ancient texts, perhaps on an orbiting space station or mother ship guarding Earth); totaling just under 1,000 visitors comprising the first phase of colonization by the BOPH visitors. Egyptian records indicate that by *c*.2750 BC more than 2,000 gods were on Earth.[7] But, it is believed that there were never more than 2,500 total 'gods' at any one time on Earth, with no further references made of those physical gods after *circa* 500 AD.

Anthropologists estimate that Cro-Magnons numbered about one million by 22,000 BC, increasing to over 10 million prior to their demise by the Great Flood. Yet not until after 3150 BC, once the Ancient Ones had departed, did strict supervision by the gods become the norm. Certainly the BOPH gods would have realized they were vastly outnumbered by humankind, and therefore found it necessary to exert tight control over them. While total control through slavery might have been their ultimate goal, as depicted by later human kings all having human slaves, various methods short of imprisonment and bondage was tried first. Almost universal in every ancient culture was a detailed list of laws under which all humanity must abide. Government was the vehicle utilized to achieve that rigid control, administered at the direction of the prevailing political-religious governance of each city-state. New laws and ever tighter religious requirements were continuously enacted, further tightening the BOPH gods' grip over the masses.

A closed mind is often prevalent when considering religion and prehistory, with only the traditional orthodox version being advanced for consumption. The discovery of long lost records reveals that our modern prevailing version is a distortion of those ancient facts. Certain ancient texts had the good fortune of being preserved through their prior burial, thus remaining hidden during the numerous times of later document destructions over the ages. Such manuscripts tend to portray a different perspective of humankind's association with celestial divine beings and supernatural forces. Since the average person has not extensively researched the many different religious doctrines existing today, they are unaware how much has been withheld or excluded from their originally intended teachings. Censors feared such material could result in different interpretations from their own 'orthodox' explanations, perhaps even raising reasonable doubts with their promoted interpretations and subsequent authenticity. In earlier cases, such alterations were originally an orchestrated campaign by the BOPH gods to remove all references of the Ancient Ones and their efforts to benefit Earth and humanity.

Theology is ultimately politically inspired, providing the means through which a desired behavior can be achieved, all in an attempt to control the development of the masses and influence their beliefs. Through the use of religion, which often harbors political motives and agendas, Sacred History was spawned. That allowed historic events to be reinterpreted and redefined (perhaps distorted and reshaped) in an effort to conform to a prescribed way of thinking, fulfilling the political agenda of each city-state god, as well as the later Church leaders. Such distortion was common during ancient times, and included the later gods' usurpation of prior deeds and accomplishments made by earlier beings, usually those of the Ancient Ones.

The same stories contained in 'pagan' mythology are also contained in the Bible, but the Biblical accounts are viewed as historic narratives and often elevated to the level of Sacred History. Duplicated mythology from prior sources thus became the Sacred History of another. It is known that the Bible edited and condensed older texts from other nations, co-opting and combining multiple different gods into a single supernatural deity. It further dismissed the ancient gods as being imaginary or merely the pagan beliefs of savage and primitive men, labeling such earlier similar tales and narratives as being 'mythical.'

Moreover, the description of fantastic exploits attributed to the deity of an 'accepted' religious belief were deemed true and sacred, with those exploits becoming the miracles and mysteries of its faith. Conversely, the same deeds by a rival 'god' were simply rejected as mythical fantasies. Yet the narratives of both the 'accepted religion' as well as the pagan ones are essentially identical, with the pagan source often being the older, original version. The 'surviving' religion thus reduced the 'conquered' religious accounts to ones of myth and fantasy.

Such thinking is evident even during modern times. Pagan fables are often described as the product of uneducated primitives who lacked the knowledge, truth, and intellect of our Judeo-Christian believers. But, if such pagan accounts reflected the ignorance of primitives who lacked the enlightenment and knowledge of more modern beliefs, how does one account for the superior advanced scientific knowledge of those pagans, compared to the 'stationary flat Earth' belief that dominated the Judeo-Christian theology for over 1,400 years?

Sacred History & The Bible

A modern and common misconception, one perpetuated by Hollywood, is that the Hebrew God, the God of the Bible and Moses, did not have a name or a physical countenance of being; that He was an invisible entity. But that was not the case. The personal name of the Hebrew God was *Yahweh*; not the inaccurate but more commonly translated 'Jehovah.' Since the ancient times of Moses, continuing through the Hebrew Dynasties of Kings, Yahweh was recorded as 'YHVH' throughout the Old Testament, since the Hebrew language had no vowel symbols in their written script until the 1st century BC.

By 250 BC, the name of Yahweh or YHVH was considered to be so sacred that the word was forbidden to even be pronounced. Hence, the term *Adonai*, meaning Lord, was substituted for Yahweh. The word *Elohim*, meaning Divine Beings, was also substituted for God; but Elohim is the plural form meaning *gods*. However, certain grammatical usage and/or contextual arrangements can confer a singular meaning to this generally plural word. The term Elohim may have originated with the earlier Phoenician historian, Sanchuniathon, who referred to the allies and assistants of the god Cronos (aka Kronus) as the *Eloim* (aka *Eloeim*).[8] There are many references to gods in the plural, and to Yahweh

341

taking His stand in the Divine Assembly among the other gods. Yahweh is reported to have issued decrees to the Israelites, per Psalm 82: "God takes his stand in the Divine Assembly; In the midst of the gods he gives judgment." Such a statement resembles the exact manner in which the 'Unalterable Decrees' were comprised and issued by the earlier Sumerian and Akkadian gods within their seven member Divine Assembly.[9]

The Hebrews thought of the Earth as belonging to Yahweh, with humankind its caretakers, gardeners, and tenant farmers. The Hebrews were materially dependent on Yahweh, believing He controlled the rainfall upon which their harvest depended. Thus, they were obligated to pay offerings of gratitude, and sacrifice livestock to Yahweh, as a type of city-state tax. Yahweh used affliction to test His people, with any failure that affected the Israelites deemed to be a punishment from Yahweh. But as long as the people remained faithful to Yahweh's Law, He would not allow them to be defeated by their enemies.

Yahweh was considered to be the God of the 'Land East of the Jordan,' the God of both the Hebrews and the Nabateans. Yahweh worship has been traced back to Enosh, the pre-Hebrew patriarch in the Adam to Noah lineage, but may refer to a title or position, rather then a specific physical being or deity. The God Yahweh was most probably a composite of different beings or numerous gods over the ages. In the most arcane literature, Yahweh was originally a Lord of Mars,[10] according to author Brinsley Le Poer Trench. Beside the Hebrew texts, Yahweh is also mentioned in Amorite and Ugarit records.

Yahweh was not the only God that was worshiped by the Israelites. Baal and Ishtar were also worshiped, often with dual alters side by side, one for each god.[11] While Yahweh was the nomadic God of the Exodus and the one who issued the Ten Commandments from Sinai to the 'Chosen People of Yahweh,' that was not the name used by their earlier Hebrew ancestors when they referred to God. However, certain later written texts may have been revised, substituting the name of Yahweh for the earlier mentioned God or gods.

The continuity and constancy of God's name is a disputed one, with conflicting Biblical and extra-Biblical passages. Statements made by prominent patriarchs such as Joshua, along with some early Hebrew records, indicate that Yahweh was not the God of the prior Hebrews.[12] God was often referred to by His epithets, such as The Awe of Isaac, or the Mighty One of Jacob.[13] Yet Exodus 3:4-6 quotes Yahweh saying, "Moses, Moses...I am the God of your father, the God of Abraham, the God of Isaac, and the God of Jacob," combining numerous prior gods into a single being. The God of Abraham was perhaps the Akkadian god Sin, who was a Semitic god, with his cult center in Ur; rather than the earlier Sumerian god Enlil, or the much later Nabatean god Yahweh. This is likely since Abraham was an Aramean, the Semitic people from the west of Assyria who lived in Ur, the capital of the Sumer and Akkad Kingdom during Abraham's time. The Semitic god Sin, who had his cult center in Ur, fits logically; even more so when Abraham later migrated to Harran, following the god Sin who relocated his new cult center to Harran.

Numerous Biblical accounts depict God as a physical being. The *Genesis* tale describes God with a white beard, seated on a golden throne. God physically appeared to Abraham, Job, and Moses on numerous occasions, and personally presented Moses with the Tablets of the Ten Commandments. God is described as taking walks in the afternoon to enjoy the sea breezes, while other accounts refer to Him sleeping, eating, and visiting; as well as numerous additional activities that are routinely conducted by any other physical being. Elijah once held a contest between Baal and Yahweh on Mount Carmel, which Baal apparently won. In fear for his life, Elijah fled to the hills of Mount Horeb and hid in a cave to escape Baal's wrath, and had to later be rescued by Yahweh in person.

Evidently during ancient times, humans, gods, and angels intermingled freely. Abraham was sufficiently intimate with God to negotiate with Him in person for food, clothing, and shelter, agreeing in return to worship only Him as his God. Abraham evidently also influenced God's politics and His policies, dealing with Him as a personal friend. Many olden texts refer to Abraham as the 'Friend of God,' who bargained with Him on behalf of the Sodom and Gomorrah people, persuading Him to reduce the required number of 'righteous inhabitants' from fifty to ten, in order for those people to escape destruction.

God's messengers and assistants, the angels, were also portrayed as physical beings. Genesis 19:3 describes two angels who visited Lot in Sodom. Lot prepared food that those angels ate, indicating their physical status. In Genesis 32:24-25 & 29, Jacob wrestled with an angel (or perhaps Yahweh) all night, finally defeating him, even though the angel used his supernatural power to dislocate Jacob's hip.

Jacob also viewed angels ascending and descending a ladder touching the Earth, whose top reached to heaven, per Genesis 28:12. Biblical censors later changed that account to a dream. Angels reportedly came down from the heavens to regularly visit on Earth, and were even known to intermarry with humans. The concept of angels as spiritual or ethereal beings did not appear in religious teachings before the sixth century AD.[14] Angels were first named in the *Book of Daniel*, the last book of the Old Testament, naming Michael as the guardian angel of Israel, sometime around 500 BC. The religious leaders prior to that time generally considered angels to be corporeal beings who were the messengers of Yahweh.

Originally only cherubim and seraphim had wings, not the Biblical angels. Only the later Christian artists depicted angels with wings, apparently indicating their ability to fly. The concept of demons also accompanied the belief in angels. The notion of the devil emerged after the Persian conquest of 539 BC, when Satan (aka Lucifer or the Persian Iblis who reportedly was an 'accuser' in the court of Yahweh), was portrayed as the enemy of Yahweh. The emergence of demons also introduced the concept of good and evil, a notion borrowed from Zoroastrian belief. That time period also introduced another new belief, the resurrection of humans into an eternal life in heaven, or their everlasting damnation in hell. Prior afterlife belief had merely consisted of a nondescript, inactive, dreary, and eternal existence in a shadowy place called *Sheol*.[15]

Chapter 29

Judeo-Christian History

One might conclude that Jewish written history started somewhere in the middle of its narrative, commencing about 4,000 years ago when Abraham had an encounter with a God who would later be known by the name Yahweh, meaning 'the Self-evident' or 'He that is.' Abraham is reported to be part of the tenth generation within the Noah lineage, evidently descending from Noah's son Shem. Very little is known of Abraham's prior ancestors after the time of Noah, until the Biblical account of him meeting Yahweh. Abraham and his immediate ancestors were believed to be Arameans, a Semitic group of semi-nomadic people who lived west of Assyria, centering on Nisibis, east of the Habur River in the central Tigris Valley of Mesopotamia.

Abraham's family was living in the Sumer and Akkad city of Ur, which was the capital of the combined kingdom during that time, but was undergoing political and physical attacks from other city-states for control over its empire. Many people incorrectly refer to Abraham's city as the Ur of the Chaldeans. But Chaldean rule over Ur did not occur until about 1,400 years later, during their period of control over the Empire of Babylonia, which took place between 612 and 539 BC, the period comprising the Babylon captivity of the Hebrews.

It was shortly before 2000 BC when Abraham, his wife Sarah, and his father Terah left Ur, moving the family 600 miles northwest to the Hurrian city of Harran in the southern part of modern day Turkey. Harran was situated around several Aramean states, located northeast of Canaan in the foothills of the Taurus Mountains, believed to be under Amorite rule at that time. Harran was a major crossroads, controlling the northern trade and caravan routes to the lands of western Asia. By their mere act of leaving the Sumer and Akkad city of Ur, Terah and his family became the first 'Hebrews,' meaning "those who pass from place to place," or "the ones from the other side,"[1] referring to their crossing of the Euphrates River. Hence, the term *Hebrew* simply refers to their status as 'nomads.' Abraham's migration did not create a race or ethnicity, but rather a culture or lifestyle.

Terah, a descendant from the lineage of Shem, seems to suddenly continue the Biblical *Genesis* story after a 'silence' or gap of almost 8,500 years, following the Great Flood of *c.*10,500 BC. In actuality, the Biblical flood of Noah was most likely the regional flood of *circa* 4000 BC, which buried the city of Ur, but was depicted as the Great Flood of the Pleistocene Extinction in Biblical accounts. It is believed that Terah was a military expert or leader, migrating to Harran under the orders of the priest-governor of Ur, or perhaps the Akkadian city-state god himself, Sin (aka Nannar in Sumerian). About that same time, Akkadian texts recorded that the god Sin also moved his capital city from Ur to Harran, where his great temple of Ur, the Ekishshirgal, was duplicated at his new capital. Shortly after Abraham's departure around 2004 BC, the city of Ur was destroyed at the end of King Ibbi-Sin's reign, along with the Canaanite cities of Zoar, Sodom, and Gomorrah.

Speculation has emerged that nuclear weapons may have destroyed those cities, citing the *Lament for the Destruction of Ur*, an Akkadian account that stated: "Evil Winds covered Ur like a cloth, enveloped it (a mushroom cloud?)...bodies dissolved, like fat left in the sun."[2] Areas of vitrified sand that show traces of radioactivity have been found in that region. The destruction of other cities, by what would appear to modern observers as nuclear warfare, was also depicted in other written accounts from surrounding nations and cultures.

In the Hurrian city of Harran, Yahweh and Abraham eventually encountered each other. It was Yahweh who reportedly first proposed a covenant to Abraham,[3] as a contractual agreement between Yahweh and the Hebrew people. Hebrews would acknowledge Yahweh as their ultimate king and legislator, agreeing to obey His laws, and circumcise all males as a sign of that covenant; while Yahweh would acknowledge the Hebrews as His 'particular' or chosen people, and be considerate of them. It is quite likely that Yahweh deliberately singled out Abraham, since he had inherited control of his father's army, and Abraham's prowess as a military expert was renown. Genesis 14 relates that the small but powerful army of Abraham had defeated the great forces of the Confederation of the Five Kings from the East.

Abraham did God's bidding, extending the territory under Yahweh's control through the use of force. For the following few centuries, up to 400 years by some accounts, Abraham and his descendants continued to wander as nomads throughout the land of Canaan. Around 1720 BC, the invading Hyksôs army conquered Egypt, and enacted their own rule and pharaoh. They invited surrounding nomadic tribes to enter Egypt, to work in various endeavors. Joseph was the leader of the Hebrews at that time and accepted the Hyksôs' invitation, moving his people to Egypt as free-men. His decision was made necessary due to famine from extended drought and crop failures in Canaan. Under Hyksôs rule, the Hebrews prospered in Egypt. The Hyksôs reign ended in 1555 BC, when Egyptians retook power and ousted the invaders, with some fleeing back to Asia, while others sought refuge in Canaan.

Not much is known about the Hebrews between their arrival in Egypt and their Biblical Exodus under Moses. Their 'welcome status' and living standards under the new Egyptian rule deteriorated greatly from its prior level under the Hyksôs, but evidence is scarce as to the duration of their freedom versus slavery, or if indeed they were ever enslaved at all. At that time, Moses was living in the house of Jethro, his father-in-law, who was a priest in Moab, perhaps in the temple of the god Chemosh or that of Baal-zebub. That area, near the Horeb Mountain, is where Moses initially encountered 'The God of Abraham,' identified at that time as Yahweh. Yahweh makes the same covenant with Moses that He made with Abraham, and commands Moses to lead the Hebrews from Egypt to the land of Canaan.

Many non-Biblical historians now compute the date of that Exodus from Egypt as having occurred sometime around 1440 BC. Evidence from Professor Garstang's excavation of Jericho concluded that the city fell under Joshua's siege in *circa* 1400 BC. Based on the Hebrew's own recorded occurrence of that event, which was stated as being just after the 40 years of desert wanderings, that would date the Exodus as having occurred in 1440 BC. Also, chronological notes contained in the *Book of Kings* state that Solomon started building the Temple 480 years after the Exodus, further establishing the 1440 BC date. The Exodus is further reported to have occurred 400 years after the arrival of Abraham's great grandson, Joseph. With typical Hebrew longevity, his birth would have occurred during the 15th century BC, also supporting the *c*.1440 BC date. While extant artifacts do substantiate Biblical accounts, the chronology remains somewhat unsure. Such events apparently did happen, but 'when' still remains a topic of debate.

Under the leadership of Joshua, the Jews had finally entered the land of Canaan, the modern day area comprised of Lebanon, Israel/Palestine, and parts of Syria. Yahweh ordered the Hebrew armies to depopulate the existing inhabitants, including all children and animals, claiming the people were 'wicked.' Perhaps the defeated inhabitants had become disobedient to their patron god, with that god utilizing a newly found 'loyal' populace to exterminate the old. Genocide has been used to create rapid political and social change throughout history, although Yahweh's commandment forbidding 'killing' was apparently disregarded.

The Hebrews reached Jericho around *c.*1400 BC, which was a fortified Hyksôs city at the time, protecting and dominating the entrance to the Jerusalem plateau. It became the first city to fall under Yahweh's incursion. Other cities were attacked and destroyed, giving the Hebrews a foot-hold in the land of Canaan. Some Indo-Europeans, primarily Hittites and Hurrians, had migrated from the Caucasus Mountains into the far northern boarder region of Canaan known as Ugarit, the modern day Syria, over the preceding 500 year span. While Ugarit was not a Hebrew city, Hebrew culture blended with those of the Philistines and Palestinians, creating a strong influence on Hebrew life, according to Biblical scholar Dr. R. K. Harrison.

Canaan was a land separated by rivers, and divided by mountain ranges in the north. Those natural geographical barriers worked against unifying the land, which was fragmented into little city-states. Although those individual city-states would temporarily unify against a common enemy, they remained rivals during other times, each vying for power and land. At that time, the Hebrews were merely a loose confederation of tribes, united by a common loyalty to the Sinai covenant, while their neighboring peoples were bound by monarchies or very strong city-state governments. Those Hebrew tribes that settled in the northern regions of Canaan eventually banded together, and became known as the Israelites.

During the forty years of wandering in the desert, many Jews had rebelled against the strict and rigid discipline of Yahweh, and went back to worshiping their olden gods. At that time, all gods were visible, physical beings who had personal names. While the official religion of the northern Israelites was the one faithful to Yahweh, the religions of Baal and Astarte were also worshiped in other regions. Such multiple worship continued from around 1400 BC until about 600 BC, when monotheism eventually became the rule.

The first Jewish monarchy arose when Saul was anointed king of Palestine, but in name only. The first actual king was the legendary David of Goliath-fame, who extended the kingdom by warfare. The last reported Yahweh contact was with King David. According to Cornelius Loew, a professor of religious studies, that meeting reportedly created an eternal covenant, establishing the Davidic Dynasty at Jerusalem on Mount Zion as the permanent center of Israelite faith.[4] A great temple was planned for construction, to worship Yahweh and signify that agreement. The task of building that temple in Jerusalem ultimately fell to his son, Solomon.

As the second king, Solomon solidified the kingdom through order and prosperity, forging peace. Upon the death of King Solomon in 931 BC, the Jews further split into two separate nations. A southern state of Judah was formed, with its capital in Jerusalem; while the northern kingdom of Israel made its capital in Samaria (Bethel). In 722 BC, the Northern Nation of Israel was the first to fall, after being conquered by the Assyrians, led by King Sargon II. The victorious Assyrians then repopulated the land with people loyal to them.

The Southern Nation became well established, and flourished over the years. It changed from a political nation into a church state, with new religious tenets under the reforms of Josiah, which occurred between 638 and 608 BC. The ensuing covenant of 621 BC reaffirmed their original contract, binding the Hebrew people and their king with Yahweh for all time. Afterward, Yahweh was no longer considered to be a city-state God, but became a world God.[5]

Several decades later, the Southern Kingdom in Jerusalem was ultimately conquered by Nebuchadnezzar of Babylon, starting with attacks in 597 BC, with the final destruction of Jerusalem occurring in 586 BC. Nebuchadnezzar brought the Hebrew people into captivity, allowing some of them to remain in Judah, while others were forcibly moved to Babylon. That deportation occurred over three distinct periods, the first starting in 597 BC, followed by another one four years later, with the last occurring in 586 BC. Judah's survival was thus assured with its remaining Hebrew population, allowing a place for the exiles to someday return. The exiled group included Jewish artisans, soldiers, and scholars; chosen to exploit their skills in Babylon. The prophet Ezekiel believed that the exile was a punishment inflicted on the Hebrews by Yahweh for their sins, an event that also marked the end of the Davidic Dynasty.

The captivity occurred during the New Empire period of Babylonia under Chaldean rule (612-539 BC), when its capital city, Babylon, became the most magnificent city of the ancient Near East. The Chaldean culture greatly influenced the Jewish people, who enjoyed much freedom and exercised a considerable amount of self-government, according to the *Book of Ezekiel*. Jeremiah also stated that Hebrew life under the rule of Nebuchadnezzar was not oppressive, with the Jewish exiles enjoying a better living standard in Babylon than in Jerusalem. During that time, the chief deity over the divine pantheon was the god Marduk (aka Bêl or Belus), whose cult center was established in Babylon where his splendid ziggurat temple, the Esagila, was later rebuilt by Nebuchadnezzar II.

Following the reign of several weak kings after the death of Nebuchadnezzar II in 561 BC, Nabonidus became ruler of Babylon in 556 BC. He restored the Temple of the Moon Goddess, Ningal, at Ur. Nabonidus' Babylonia Empire was then conquered by the Persian King Cyrus in 539 BC, supposedly with the help of the god Marduk. An act of clemency by Cyrus in 538 BC liberated all captives throughout Babylonia, and also restored the prior status of their gods, recognizing and honoring the God of Israel, Yahweh. However, many prosperous Jews stayed as citizens of Babylon, rather than returning to Jerusalem.

Starting in 538 BC, some liberated Jewish exiles, led by Sheshbazzar (Babylonian Sin-ab-usur), chose to return to Jerusalem, which had become a part of the Persian Empire. Ezekiel emerged as a great prophet during that exile return. He

353

became one of the architects of the Jewish restoration, helping to map out the construction for the Second Temple, and the regulations of the priesthood. Between 520 and 515 BC, Zechariah headed the new rebuilding of that Temple and the restoration of Jerusalem's walls, all with the support and approval of Cyrus.

With the death of King Cyrus in 529 BC, a more autocratic rule was enacted under his son, Cambyses. Cambyses died during an ensuing revolt, which was eventually suppressed by Darius, a son-in-law of Cyrus. Darius subdivided the Empire into administrative provinces, with each district allowed a measure of autonomy, usually under local rule. Under Darius (521-486 BC), his enlightened rule was largely a result of his belief in the Zoroastrian religion, which had been started by the Persian prophet, Zoroaster, around 600 BC when he reportedly first began to receive revelations from the god Ahura Mazda (Lord Wisdom).

The Israelites who stayed in Babylon after its liberation by Cyrus flourished in business and government. It was Ezra who then led a second exodus of about 1,800 Jews from Babylon back to Jerusalem in 458 BC. Ezra organized and regulated religious affairs of the community under the auspices of the Persian central administration. He also instituted a religious reform and revival based upon the *Torah*. In 445 BC, Nehemiah, a high ranking Jew in the Persian court, was appointed civil governor in Jerusalem over Judah. The two worked closely together, and Ezra was able to push his reforms with the forceful administrative backing of Nehemiah. As part of those reforms, only the High Priest was to have direct contact with Yahweh, thus acting as a mediator between God and His people.

In retrospect, both Yahweh and history have viewed the Jewish people as a select group, due to their intelligence, high potential, business expertise and success, their ability to overcome adversity, and their commitment to contractual matters, such as their religious covenant. The Jewish religion did not exclusively survive because of its doctrine, but also in large measure because of the extraordinary nature of the Jewish people themselves.[6]

The Greek conquest of the Persian Empire by Alexander the Great then followed in 332 BC. The creation of the splendid city of Alexandria in Egypt brought the Greek influence into the Near East. Upon Alexander's death in 323 BC, his Empire divided into four Kingdoms. One of his generals, Ptolemy, took over Egypt and Palestine, forming the Ptolemic Empire. With Alexander's empire fragmented, the desire to dominate the world became a common desire of many other ancient nations.

Rome is alleged to have been formed in 753 BC by the brothers Romulus and Remus, although significant expansion did not occur until the later period between 500 and 338 BC. As Greek influence began to gradually diminish, Roman influence filled that void, with the final fall of Sparta to Macedonia in 222 BC. True Roman influence started around 215 BC, with Macedonia as their target, resulting in their first war. After three wars, Macedonia finally became a Roman province in 148 BC. A period of instability followed, with civil wars fought until Julius Caesar ultimately became dictator, and reunified Rome in 48 BC. But his warfare and treachery was brief, peaking within four years after he declared himself dictator for life, resulting in his death at the hands of his 'friends' on the Ides of March (March 15) in 44 BC. Civil war once again ensued, with Augustus finally taking control in 27 BC, signifying the start of the mighty Roman Empire.

Rome patronized the pagan religions and fully accepted and tolerated the Jewish faith as one of the 'Ancient Religions.' Pagan gods were worshiped and kept supreme mainly due to their mortal human priests who perpetuated such cults. The main question shared by many of the cults was the identity of the 'living god' at any given time.[7] Christianity as a religious belief started years after the death of Jesus, when the Apostle Paul converted from Judaism after experiencing a vision of

Christ during a trip from Jerusalem to Damascus. Paul then defined and solidified the ensuing Christian belief, and spread its influence from *c*.51 to 62 AD, by employing the language and concepts of the Mystery Cult religions, with an essentially Jewish conviction of God. Since Rome considered early Christianity to be part of the Jewish sect, it was thus granted acceptance and protection under the 'Ancient Religion' tolerance mandate.

The early Christians were not unified, with numerous splinter sects in competition with each other. Adding to that division, its ultimate separation from Judaism started when the Christians refused to support the Jews in their second war with Rome, which lasted from 132 to 135 AD. During that time, the competing Christian sects had wanted to purge all Jewish influence from their religion, thereby creating a new and separate belief. Shortly after the Roman victory, the Christians succeeded in splitting from the Jews, with their various different beliefs remaining in competition with each other. Their separation from the Jewish faith caused the Christians to lose their 'protected' status provided by Roman Law under their tolerance for Ancient Religions. Christian sects were then considered to be only a 'superstition,' not one of the ancient religious beliefs. However, any Roman persecution of Christians at that time was extremely rare, usually undertaken only as a personal or political vendetta.

Such unofficial Christian tolerance continued until a turning point was reached around 250 AD. By that time, Christians had grown strong in both numbers and political influence. That concerned the Roman government, fearing Christians would gain political power. An active persecution of Christianity then ensued for a period of about fifty years until *c*.300 AD, when a shift in Roman government occurred. Christianity expanded after Constantine became one of the Emperors of Rome in 306 AD, with its followers eventually comprising the majority population of Rome between 310 and 320 AD. With Constantine becoming sole Emperor of the

Roman Empire in 324 AD, all persecution stopped, with Christianity becoming the accepted religion of Rome. Over the four year period from 326 to 330 AD, Emperor Constantine moved his capital to Constantinople (modern Istanbul, Turkey) in the Eastern Roman Empire of Byzantium.

It is not clear whether Constantine eventually converted to Christianity or merely tolerated and accepted that belief, allowing the Church to expand even further beyond the Empire. However, he did allow powerful Christians belonging to the largest fellowships to combine and persecute the remaining Christian splinter sects that did not include Old Testament teachings in their beliefs. That edict was an attempt to consolidate or force all the numerous fragmented sects into a single and cohesive universal Christian belief. The ensuing relentless persecution of such sects particularly harmed the Christian Gnostics who did not include the Old Testament Books within their doctrine.

Chapter 30

Composite God & Borrowed Beliefs

As previously stated, many of the customs, practices, miracles, stories, symbols, and tenets of Christianity were strongly influenced by the earlier pagan Mystery Cult religions. As far back as 250 BC, the sacred Attis Festival was observed by the Cybele Cult, with several variations of Attis as the young lover of the goddess Cybele. Attis was a shepherd who was tied to a tree on a Friday, died, was buried, and on the third day rose from the dead on Sunday, bringing salvation with him. The rites, customs, and beliefs of the Mystery Cult of Attis and Cybele were brought from Anatolia to Rome by eunuch priests before 50 BC, and enjoyed uninterrupted worship until 286 AD. Both Claudius and Augustus practiced and promoted the Cybele Cult, allowing it to flourish as one of the main religious beliefs of Rome.

Its eunuch connection is believed to be the inspiration for the custom of celibacy observed by the later Christian priesthood, which is still practiced by the Catholic faith today. Cybele is believed to have been a later version of the much earlier sun goddess, Arinna, who granted authority to the Hittite kings of Anatolia to rule its people, starting around 1900 BC. It is believed that Arinna became known as Cybele about 1000 BC. Cybele is also closely associated with the Greek goddess Rhea, the mother of the god Zeus. That goddess was later known as Ma Rhea (Maria) in Rome. Hence, Cybele is also the likely prototype for Mary, the mother of Jesus.

However, the most important Oriental religious forerunner of Christianity was the Mithra cult. It started in ancient Persia (Iran) and spread throughout the Roman Empire, becoming firmly established by the second half of the 1st century AD. The Persian god Mithra was the God of Light, associated with the sun disk, and was the chief intermediary between the Supreme God of the universe and humankind. The sacred texts of Mithraism are now lost, but some knowledge remains. There were seven grades or levels of initiates, but only the last four levels were thought to have been exposed to the sacred mysteries and secret knowledge of this cult. By the end of the first century AD, Mithraism became Christianity's strongest competition. Both beliefs include baptism, eternal life, a messiah sacrificed as atonement for sins, religious suppers, resurrection, a final judgment, a reward in heaven or a punishment in hell, and ethical requirements; with both observing Sundays and December 25 as special worship days.

The Gnostic religious belief formed from the Jewish faith, emerging as an early Christian sect. It used terminology derived from Mystery Cults, and incorporated certain concepts from Eastern religions. It was based on hidden mysteries and secret wisdom, reportedly divulged by Jesus to only a select few who had attained 'maturity of thought' and had also undergone an initiation into a secret doctrine of God.

A total of 52 texts comprise the extant Gnostic written record, which were found in 1945 among the cliffs of the mountains near the town of Nag Hammadi in Egypt. While the gospels of the New Testament are dated between $c.60$ and 110 AD, the versions of the Gnostic gospel date to a slightly earlier period from $c.50$ to 100 AD. The Gnostic documents consist of some gospels that are unknown to the New Testament, and others that differ or contradict with certain accounts of Jesus, as reported in the New Testament gospels. This early branch or sect of Christianity flourished from $c.80$ until around 250 AD, when orthodox Christians denounced it as heresy. Gnosticism survived that persecution, and managed to preserve their secret books by hiding them from planned destruction.

The spread of Gnosticism by the Greek philosophers Valentinus and Marcion provided great credibility to this sect. Gnosticism was also taught by Theodotus between c.140 and 160 AD. Its connection with Greek philosophy further provided a link between the Divine Logos and the mind of the adept, in the form of 'mystic education.' Such revelations allowed certain select initiates access to a 'secret wisdom,' which reportedly revealed answers to many mysteries. Such esoteric knowledge was a secret level above that of the priests and bishops, who were limited to offering only 'common' Church tradition. Around 140 AD, Valentinus claimed that he had learned those secret teachings from Theudas, one of Paul's disciples. That esoteric insight included a belief in two divine gods, the highest being the Creator God who was the 'God beyond God,' while referring to the lesser second God as the Chief God who ruled over Earth.[1]

Valentinus described the Creator God as "The root of the All, the Ineffable One who dwells in the Monad."[2] He further clarified the distinction between the two supreme gods, stating that the lesser divine being served as the instrument of the higher powers. The lesser god of Earth only reigned as king and lord, acting as a military commander who instituted laws and judged those who violated them.[3] He was identified as Yahweh, the God of Israel. Dr. Elaine Pagels, a noted Gnostic scholar, quoted the disciple Justinus who described the Lord's shock, terror, and anxiety "when he discovered that he was not the God of the Universe."[4]

Gnosticism contains fantastic elements of mythology, and a cosmology that consists of multiple levels of heavens, each assigned to a different god. It involves mystical speculation and practices, equating the serpent with the Divine Instructor. According to reports compiled by author Richard Dempewolff, Gnostic texts were also the source of the word *abracadabra*, which was used not as an incantation, but as a magical formula to ward off misfortune and disease.[5] Mr. Dempewolff further reported that records indicated the term 'abracadabra' was associated with Abraxas (aka Abrasax),[6] one of the Christian Gnostic deities. Abraxas was the god depicted with a human body, the head of a hawk, and legs ending as serpents. Other depictions show him with two bodies, one as a man, another as a bird. His face was often represented with the likeness of Bes, the dwarfed Egyptian god.

The Gnostics believed that the gods had civilized and instructed infant races, according to Professor G.R.S. Mead, whose extensive research of Gnosticism allowed him to write *Fragments of a Faith Forgotten* in the early 20th century. Professor Mead also stated that the founders of all the great Mystery Schools were either gods, or select initiates taught by the gods. It was also thought that such gods were descendants of highly developed beings that possessed knowledge of natural powers learned from prior-perfected beings not of Earth origin.[7] Mystery Schools were prevalent throughout most parts of the ancient world, for the purpose of introducing skills, art, knowledge, and civilization to emerging races. It was further thought that the divine teachers of those Mystery Schools gradually withdrew from Earth, as our infant human race developed the faculty of 'reason,' and were therefore deemed to be strong enough to function independently.[8]

There is evidence that Zoroastrian religious beliefs strongly influenced Judeo theology, and therefore also Christianity. Zoroastrianism was started by the Persian prophet, Zoroaster (aka Zarathuštra, 630-550 BC), around 600 BC when he began receiving revelations from the god Ahura Mazda (Lord Wisdom). Those revelations were compiled into a doctrine that was recorded in the form of psalms known as Gathas. Those Gathas later comprised a major portion of the sacred scripture known as the Avesta or Zend Avesta, the bible equivalent of this religion. Its belief contains certain 'magic' rituals, but no myth, formal priesthood, or divination.

Zoroaster was one of the first prophets to preach apocalyptic doctrine and monotheism, worshiping only Ahura

Mazda, who had six assistants. Zoroastrian belief embraced an opposing duality of 'truth and lie' or 'good and evil,' which permeated everywhere in the universe. Beside this dualism of right versus wrong, it also employed truly ethical laws with highly intellectual dispensation of rules, justice, intent, devotion, integrity, and morality. It could be described as a cause-and-effect religious philosophy or way-of-life. Its belief proposed a non-physical 'spirit' realm, which provided an afterlife reward in a paradise, or a punishment in hell. Zoroastrian customs required exposing a deceased corpse to vultures so it could be devoured, prohibiting burial as a pollution of the land. The *Manual of Discipline* found among the *Dead Sea Scrolls* contained many direct similarities with the Zoroastrian creed, and influenced the Judeo-Christian belief in the concept of demons and angels. Many Greek philosophers, including Plato and Aristotle, strongly embraced Zoroastrian beliefs.

Polytheism, the belief in many gods, flourished during the historical times of most ancient cultures. Usually, one god was elevated ahead of all others, making that deity the 'chief god.' Certain cultures expanded on that concept, subordinating those lesser gods as manifestations of their reigning god. In contrast, monotheism is the belief in a single God. The early Hebrews were neither monotheistic nor polytheistic, but henotheistic; the worship of only one god while also acknowledging the existence of other gods. The early Hebrew history elevated Yahweh as their chief God, but not the only god of their time; acknowledging the existence of other nation's gods, certain of whom were even worshiped by some of the Hebrew people.

While many Hebrews worshiped only Yahweh, numerous Jewish religious sites were built with dual altars, allowing Baal worship alongside Yahweh. That was a common practice during the reign of King Solomon. Additionally, Ashim-Bethel and Anatyahu were also worshiped alongside Yahweh, forming an Israelite/Canaanite Trinity; imitating the concept of the Egyptian Trinity.[9] According to Dr. Leonhard Rost, a scholar of the Old Testament, the cult of Zeus was introduced to the Jerusalem Temple in December of 168 AD.[10] Dr. Rost further revealed that a second Zeus temple was reportedly also built on Mount Gerizim.[11]

According to the *Pyramid Texts*, the earliest Egyptians initially recognized only one Supreme Divinity, an unnamed Force that created the universe. In later times, that Ultimate Force became known as Atum, and was joined by other gods. It was not that the Egyptian faith eventually 'evolved,' but rather that the BOPH gods elevated themselves to divine status, creating the commonly known broad spectrum or pantheon of gods. The Egyptian people were then forced to encompass a belief in the multiple gods of polytheism. Still later, the Egyptians again experimented with a single god concept, the Sun Disk or Sun god known as Aton, perhaps as an attempt to acknowledge the existence of a sole Creator. That brief experiment was initiated during the reign of Amenhotep III (1386-1349 BC), and became the mandatory religion under his son, Amenhotep IV (1349-1334 BC), the pharaoh who then changed his name to Ikhnaton.

Under Ikhnaton's rule, the capital was moved to the desert city of Akhetaton (modern day Tell el-Amarna), where a magnificent temple was built in the shape of a cross to worship Aton. The reigns of Ikhnaton and his father comprised the Amarna period of Egypt, known from approximately 377 cuneiform tablets called the *Amarna Letters*, through which both pharaohs maintained regular contact and alliance with Canaan and Babylonia. After Ikhnaton's death, the nine god pantheon, the Ennead, was restored, with the Egyptian capital brought back to Thebes.

According to author William Bramley, Manetho claimed that Moses was schooled by the Egyptian high priests at Heliopolis in philosophy, science, magic, and mysticism during the reign of Pharaoh Amenhotep. Moses' knowledge of Egyptian occult teachings is thought to have been one source for material contained in the *Cabala*. It should be noted that these dates do not fully agree. If the Exodus occurred about 1440 BC, the pharaoh referenced by Manetho would have been Amenhotep II, who reigned from roughly the mid-15th century BC to about *c.*1420 BC.

Since the Hebrews were so closely tied to Egypt during the start of the Ikhnaton experiment, its concept would have certainly influenced the later Jewish adoption of monotheism. According to Dr. Immanuel Velikovsky, true Hebrew monotheism did not occur until the time of King Josiah, the grandson of Manasseh, around 600 BC,[12] shortly before the Jewish exile to Babylon. The Persian conquest of Judah in the land of Canaan undoubtedly helped to solidify the Hebrew's monotheistic belief, due to the strong influence of the Zoroastrian religion on the entire region.

By embracing monotheism, the Hebrew Bible had to compress the actions of multiple deities into a single God, often combining contrary views and actions. Conflicting accounts resulted, sometimes describing a loving, helpful, righteous, and ultimately fair God; contrasted with other accounts of a vengeful, warlike, angry, wrathful, jealous, and judgmental God. Such extreme personalities are due to the merging of multiple different gods, portrayed as a single entity or being. The Great Flood legend is a prime example, with God deciding to exterminate humanity due to their irreverence, only to take compassion on humankind by sparing a few people to repopulate Earth. The original source of the universal flood legend was evidently the *Sumerian Deluge Myth*, an account that clearly depicted two distinct gods, with Enlil in the condemning role, and his half-brother Enki as the compassionate god.

According to the *Secret Doctrine*, it is believed that the earliest Hebrew religious faith was quite different from that which developed many centuries later in Egypt, Canaan, and Babylon. The original Hebrew belief did not worship the gods, but only honored them as beings that were superior to humans.[13] The early Hebrews chose one of the Elohim, perhaps the Akkadian Sin (the Sumerian Nannar), as their patron god, not *vice versa*. Even the esoteric religion of Moses was evidently altered several times, with worship of a physical Yahweh prevailing. The name of Yahweh was then used to reference all those prior gods, combining them into a single deity.

Their belief in a physical deity would occasionally change, as reflected with Yahweh being worshiped by King David in 1000 BC, followed by the reign of his son, Solomon, who revered other gods. That trend then reverted back to Yahweh worship during Hezekiah's time. But it was King Josiah in 624 BC who stopped the idolatry of all other gods, and also diminished the influence of the Zodiac on Hebrew beliefs.[14]

Even later, God became an unseen spiritual Being. Such a similar cyclic acceptance also affected the beliefs held by the high priests regarding the teachings of Moses. Although the 'Law of Moses' was embraced by the high priests of Judah, the supposed 'Books of Moses,' those comprising the Pentateuch, were not initially accepted, according to H. P. Blavatsky.

The Hebrew Bible usurped the qualities, epitaphs, and deeds of many other gods, of both earlier and contemporary times, as the accomplishments and glory of Yahweh. The all-knowing and wise 'creator god' who fashioned Adam was clearly based on the Sumerian god Enki, and his formation of Adapa. The god of the Garden of Eden where Adam lived was borrowed from the account of the Sumerian god Enlil, taking Adapa to tend his fields, in his paradise land of E.Din. The wrathful god who ordered the destruction of man by bringing on the Great Flood was the Sumerian god Enlil, while the benevolent god who warned the Biblical Noah to build the ark was Enlil's older half-brother Enki, who instructed Ziusudra to build his ship. Clearly, the singular Yahweh of the Bible would have had to possess a split personality to portray both roles, as described in the Biblical narration of the Great Flood.

Yahweh was often reported to be a 'Hidden God,' usually unseen by the public. Such seclusion reflects the reclusive nature of Enlil, who stayed in his temple and chose not to associate with 'lowly humans.' In the Apocryphal texts, Jesus was the son of the 'secret and hidden God.' The secret god of the *Cabala* was Ain-Soph. In Mesopotamia, Anu was the concealed deity, while Dayus was the 'Unrevealed god' of India, and Amon (aka Amen or Ammon) was the Egyptian concealed god, the Hidden One who resided in a secret place. The Hebrew Yahweh reportedly told Moses that 'no one could see him and live,' while a similar statement was also attributed to Enki's oldest son, Marduk, who reportedly claimed that 'no one could sustain his gaze.' Numerous other Biblical similarities exist between the attributes of Yahweh and the numerous gods of Sumer, Akkad, India, Babylonia, Canaan, and Egypt.

Yahweh, God the Father, made his throne in heaven, and is Lord over all the angels in heaven and on Earth. The Akkadian Anu (the Sumerian An) was god-the-father, the god who lived in the heavens, and the god over the Anunnaki of heaven and Earth. Anu reportedly lived in a temple surrounded by golden gates, reigning from a throne of gold. He was depicted as having a white flowing beard, dressed in the finest flowing robes, surrounded in splendor, and flanked by the hosts of heaven; the same description attributed to God the Father of the Judeo-Christian belief. In the holy psalms, Yahweh is supreme over all the Earth and the angels under him, just as Enlil was the supreme lord over Earth and all other gods during his reign.

Earlier speculation identified the God of Abraham with Sin, the Akkadian Moon god. The position of moon deity was considered a high rank within the pantheon. Yahweh was originally considered a lunar god by early Church Fathers such as Origen and Clemens of Alexandria, stating that the moon was God's living symbol.[15] Origen (aka Origenes, *c*.185-*c*.254 AD) was a Christian layperson, writer, teacher, and theologian who was recognized by the early Church as its most accomplished Biblical scholar. He specialized in the Old

Testament, and developed the concept of Christ as the Logos, or Incarnate Word. Iao, the Gnostic 'mystery god' and one-time leader of the gods, was also known as the Regent of the Moon, according to Origen. Later, that position went to Ildabaoth (meaning child of the egg), who is generally identified as Yahweh.

The earliest identified indigenous people of Jerusalem were the Jebisites, who are credited with settling the area as far back as 3000 BC. Prior to 1000 BC, their chief god in Jerusalem was El Elyon, a god of righteousness. Abraham was reported to have met a Canaanite priest of El Elyon around 2000 BC, about the time he made his covenant with Yahweh. Ugarit was a Semitic settlement whose texts are the most similar to the literature of the Hebrew Bible. The Bible has compared Yahweh with El, the Ugarit head of their pantheon. Asherah was the goddess wife of El, although some contemporary citizens of Jerusalem claimed she was the spouse of Yahweh.

El's son was Baal, both a universal god and a national one, who competed directly with Yahweh for followers. Reportedly, King Solomon simultaneously worshiped both Yahweh and the god Baal throughout his reign. It would appear that attributes from many different local gods of contemporary archaic cultures helped to define the Hebrew Yahweh, apparently creating a composite god, who later evolved into an unseen, ethereal or spiritual deity.

Chapter 31

Bible & Sacred Writings

The eventual merging of the Northern and Southern Jewish kingdoms, along with various adopted foreign cultures brought back by returning captive exiles, ultimately formed a mix of ideas and ethnic traditions that covered a broad cultural range. Those different Jewish cultures and their conflicting stories and events describing numerous different gods were eventually merged into one account. Such an act of unity created the Hebrew 'sacred history,' from which their supreme God emerged; the God that Western religions now worship. After much editing and redacting of that combined Hebrew history, the final nucleus of the Judeo-Christian religious belief emerged.

Even Yahweh evolved, going from a God of one nomadic tribe, to the chief God of a region, to the God of the heavens, to the supreme God, to the God of the cosmos, to an invisible God beyond the universe...the Creator of All. But such an evolution merely ended where it started, with the knowledge of an unknowable sole Creator, a concept originally revealed by the Ancient Ones during the most remote times. Yet such a convoluted evolution and its many variants of past humanlike gods ultimately did not alter the factual existence of the true Godhead, just as the belief in a flat Earth did not alter the reality of a spherical world. Regardless of the divergent and laborious evolutionary paths taken, from primitive gods to the cosmic Godhead, the Judeo-Christians, along with numerous other religions, ultimately ended up with the correct concept.

Such a borrowed and blended religious belief was not written down until centuries after the Exodus, which became the basis for the Hebrew Bible. Based upon differences in vocabulary, style, and perspective, along with numerous duplications and repetitions, scholars have determined that the narratives of the Bible are composite works. The finished result was derived from several different sources by anonymous authors, written at different time periods, having undergone many changes over the centuries before they were preserved in their final form.

Biblical scholars believe that the material chosen for inclusion into the Bible was based on a variety of earlier written works from various cultures. Since the Hebrews had a nomadic background, starting in the Sumer and Akkad Kingdom, followed by periods in Hittite and Hurrian lands, then later in Egypt, Canaan, and Babylonia; there can be little doubt as to the influence those many varied cultures had on the Hebrew tales and records. A direct connection can be made between the Aton Hymns of Egypt and the Biblical Psalms. The same sources are also apparent between the Egyptian text known as *The Wisdom of Amenhotep* and the Bible's *Book of Proverbs*. Some of the same phrases used in the description of the 'Day of Judgment' contained in the New Testament are also found in the Egyptian *Book of the Dead*.

The flood story of Noah is derived from any number of earlier narratives. The Biblical *Genesis* is often described as being copied from the much earlier *History of Phoenicia* by Sanchuniathon.[1] Biblical stories were chosen from a large body of sources and oral traditions. After which, they were condensed, rearranged, and at times combined into a single account. That task was accomplished by a group of editors who brought those documents into their final form, comprising the 39 Books of the Hebrew Scriptures, although manipulating their Hebrew ancestors' traditions with considerable freedom. Many Biblical scholars believe that the Old Testament is composed of four major narratives, which are identified as follows:[2]

1. The *Yahweh Documents* (wherein God is called Yahweh) are considered the oldest, believed to have first been written during the 10th and 9th centuries BC. These texts comprise the creation, prehistory, patriarchal, and covenant accounts. The name Yahweh was apparently used to identify all the prior gods and their accounts, combining them into one God, to maintain consistency with monotheism. Perhaps past accounts of earlier gods were simply bestowed on a being that was known as Yahweh, who apparently existed around the time of Moses.

2. The *Elohim Documents* (which refer to God as Elohim, the plural noun meaning 'gods') were first recorded during the 8th century BC. The Elohim (aka Elhim or Alhim) were first called Echod, meaning 'one of the divine many'; the 'great men'; or the 'Heavenly Men.' The term signified the category of divine beings not of Earth origin, while their offspring, who were born on Earth, became known as the 'giants.'

3. The *Book of Deuteronomy* reflects writings that date to the 7th century BC.

4. The *Priestly Documents* were written during the 6th and 5th centuries BC by priests who added their own comments and interpretations. Some of these narratives are thought to have been plagiarized, and are referred to by some detractors as being 'Pious Fraud.' Certain of these passages reference God as 'Yahweh Elohim' (Lord God).

The balance of the Old Testament books chronicle events that occurred around 200 BC, and represent the 'youngest' accounts included in the Old Testament. Thus, the Bible consists of written records spanning a period from *c*.1000 to 200 BC. Prior to recording the first Yahweh Documents, surviving Hebrew historical narratives were maintained only as oral traditions. Such isolated, episodic events were likely distorted to some degree over the ensuing years, prior to being recorded, even though the stories were presumably rooted in actual historic fact. The Old Testament does supply some

371

important historic information regarding the period in which they were written, but does not necessarily reflect accurate accounts of the events reported. Scholars believe that the authenticity of any historic event before *circa* 1000 BC must be suspect.

In the 6th century BC, the Jewish leaders canonized parts of the Yahweh and Elohim Documents, making them the 'Word of God,' and hence the first sacred history of the Hebrews. The covenant *Book of Deuteronomy* was accepted as authoritative under Josiah in 621 BC,[3] its first step toward canonization. Ezra, the leader of the Babylonian Exodus in the 5th century BC, teamed with Nehemiah and a select group of priests to revise the *Book of Deuteronomy*, claiming Moses as its author. They also added the four books of *Genesis*, *Exodus*, *Leviticus*, and *Numbers* allegedly written by Moses, with the revised *Book of Deuteronomy*. Their action created the compilation known as the *Pentateuch*, the first five books of the Jewish Bible.

In 444 BC, Ezra and Nehemiah declared those five books to be 'sacred texts,' canonizing them as the 'Word of God,' and forever closing then to any further change or interpretation. This grouping, known as *The Law* (the written *Torah* or *Pentateuch*), is considered to be the first of the Hebrew Bible's three parts, and is also common to both the Catholic and Protestant Christian Bible as well. The second Biblical part consists of the *Nebiim*, the prophetic literature that was canonized around 210 BC. Then in 70 AD, the last stage of canonization occurred for the *Ketubim*, meaning 'the remaining writings,' which comprises the third part of the Bible.

Ezra released a total of 24 books for publication but kept secret another 70 texts reportedly revealed to him.[4] The *Book of Ezekiel* was originally written entirely by Ezekiel, but the version accepted for inclusion into the Bible was revised and edited by the men of the Great Assembly (aka the Great Synagogue), because they believed the original words seemed to contradict the teachings of the *Torah*. That rewritten version was then sanctioned by the men of the Great Assembly, making Ezekiel's account a 'vision' rather than an actual physical encounter. Beside the *Book of Ezekiel*, the men of the Great Assembly also revised or wrote *Daniel*, *Esther*, and the *Twelve Prophets*. The Biblical editors' version of the past was then also sanctified and sealed, after declaring it to be Sacred History, thereby closing it to any future reinterpretation.

None of the original Biblical texts are known to exist, most probably being destroyed during the Babylonian conquest. The oldest Hebrew copy of the Bible, prior to the discovery of the *Dead Sea Scrolls*, was the Masoretic text that dated to 1088 AD, with the oldest partial Hebrew manuscripts dating back only to the eighth century AD. The *Septuagint*, the Bible's first Greek translation, occurred during the 3rd century BC in Alexanderia. Some fragments from later copies of that Greek version are extant, which date to the 5th century AD, making them the prior oldest known Biblical record until the *Dead Sea Scrolls* discovery. Note that only *II Maccabees* and the *Wisdom of Solomon* were originally written in the Greek language.

The Protestant Christian Bible is comprised of two parts, the Old Testament consisting of the 39 Books of the Jewish Bible (although arranged differently) and the 27 Books of the New Testament. The Roman Catholic Bible consists of seven additional books in the Old Testament account, for a total of 46 books, plus the same 27 New Testament books. While the original gospels of the New Testament are dated between *c.*60 and 110 AD, the New Testament editing process did not begin until 325 AD during the First Council of Nicaea. According to Voltaire (1694-1778), "By the end of the first century there were some thirty gospels, each belonging to a different society, and thirty sects of Christians had sprung up in Asia Minor, Syria, Alexandria, and even Rome."[5] Author R. L. Dione reported that the Church Fathers, lead by Augustine, convened the 397 AD Council of Carthage in North Africa to decide which books were to be deemed the actual 'Words of God.'[6]

That editing process continued into the 12th century AD, resulting in its final form known today. The foundation for the Christian belief is built around three basic elements: the cannon of the New Testament, the acceptance and profession of the Apostolic Creed, and the institutional structure of the Church; all emerging in their present form around 185 AD.

Author Brinsley le Poer Trench noted a puzzling aspect found in the Bible, derived from its specific references to a female deity. He detected the structure of the original Hebrew account in *Genesis* 7:1-4 and *Genesis* 15:1 used the feminine form 'Anochi' instead of the masculine form 'Ani' for the personal pronoun 'I' when referring to God speaking a directly quoted statement. The Ezekiel passages are also filled with Hebrew words in their female form, instead of their male form, when specifically referring to God.

Numerous Gnostic texts, found within the 1945 Nag Hammadi documents, contained quotes spoken in the voice of a feminine divine being, along with specific references to a female deity. One text, the *Hypostasis of the Archons*, describes the creation of the first man, Adam, by the Mother god;[7] perhaps linking that passage with the oldest known divinity of Earth, the Mother Goddess cult. Another text, the *Trimorphic Protennoia*, quotes the Divine Mother stating: "I am Protennoia the Thought that dwells in the Light...she who exists before the All...I am the Invisible One within the All."[8] This divine Mother is also called *Wisdom*, the one who empowered the God of Israel as her agent. Another text describes the divine Mother as part of an original couple, the 'Mother of the All' and the 'Primal Father,' reminiscent of the Babylonian primordial couple, Tiamat and Apsu.

Babylonian and Kassite texts stated that the first divine being on Earth was Tiamat, the mother of the earliest gods and the one who possessed the Tablets of Destiny. Perhaps the Mother Goddess was the prototype for Tiamat, or may have merely symbolized the primitive distinction between male and

374

female roles, or their positions of power within a community.

Most previous Near Eastern shrines or temples after the Great Flood had 'worshiped' the Mother Goddess, sometimes referred to as the Divine Ancestress, who was occasionally revered in combination with the Bull cult. The Mother Goddess was not worshiped, a common misconception, but rather 'venerated' by those archaic cultures. It is more likely that the Divine Ancestress was a female Helper of the Ancient Ones, with honor and respect displayed for her important contributions to civilize and educate humans, much as we honor our founding fathers and prior great leaders. The Mother Goddess cult was a divine reverence that had a continuous following since before the Great Flood, one that lasted until 500 AD when the Christian Emperors of Rome and Byzantium finally succeeded in closing down its temples.

Another lingering concern with Biblical content is associated with the selective editing of materials that were excluded from its final text. Such content included the Pseudepigrapha, the Apocrypha, and other similar extra-Biblical writings. Those texts were somehow deemed 'less holy,' but demonstrate no acute distinction between their content and that of the 'accepted' Holy Scriptures. Some of the known texts rejected for inclusion in the Old Testament consisted of two apocryphal books and the fourth *Book of Ezra*, although ten other chapters from the *Book of Ezra* were included. Other excluded content included the reincarnation belief professed by Jesus, which Emperor Justinian ordered removed during the Second Synod of Constantinople in 553 AD. The doctrine of reincarnation was then banned, along with the belief in past lives, with any future advocate that might profess such reincarnation doctrine threatened with excommunication.

The Pseudepigrapha texts profess to be Biblical in character, but are not considered to be 'inspired' or canonical. Such texts include specific Jewish scriptures from the century before and the century after Christ, which were anonymously written by authors using false or fake names. The earlier Apocrypha (the hidden writings) were comprised from both Jewish and Christian supplementary writings, dating from the 3rd century BC through the 1st century AD.

The extra-Biblical apocryphal writings also included the genealogy of Mary's parents, her mother Anna, and Joachim, a Hebrew temple priest. It was reportedly an angel who caused Anna to become pregnant with Mary, with the understanding that Mary would be raised by priests with assistance from angels at a temple in Jerusalem once she reached the age of three. When Mary was about fourteen, the temple priests then picked Joseph, a much older man, to become Mary's husband. Joseph was a wealthy architect, not a carpenter, who was widowed after the death of his first wife. He was left with two daughters and two sons, Thomas and James, from his earlier marriage. His Uncle, Joseph of Arimathea, was reportedly one of the wealthiest men in the entire world at that time.[9]

During a visit to her parents in Galilee, while preparing for her marriage, the Archangel Gabriel impregnated Mary with the Messiah, according to the Bible. Such a two generation cycle of possible 'artificial inseminations' would have likely increased the purity of the final product, the baby Jesus, who reportedly had red hair, was small in stature, and 'plain' in appearance; born sometime between 7 and 4 BC. Separately, the potential use of artificial insemination to produce hybrid humans who were as closely related to the outer planet humanlike species as possible might have been attempted from time to time. But it would be difficult to determine which group, the Lunar Pitris or the BOPH gods, might be responsible for any individual attempt.

There has been much speculation over the 'lost' years of Jesus, those years between age thirteen and his thirtieth birthday. Author William Bramley and other researchers believe that Jesus, perhaps using the name 'Issa,' moved to Tibet where He was tutored by Eastern masters in Hinduism, Buddhism, and the occult.[10] Author David Hatcher Childress stated that Jesus attended an ancient college of India, then traveled through Greece, Persia, and the Himalayas during his early adult years before returning to his mother's home.[11] It is believed that Jesus then commenced his ministry between 25 and 30 AD, culminating in his crucifixion between 27 and 33 AD. Such a range of dates produces a life span for Jesus comprising between 30 and 39 total years, remembering that no year 'zero' BC or AD ever existed.

Glenn Kimball, a modern lecturer and author of a book on the childhood of Jesus, dated the birth of Jesus in 7 BC, based on the cosmic conjunction of Jupiter and Saturn that occurred then, perhaps creating the 'Star of Bethlehem.'[12] He also dated Jesus' crucifixion as occurring in the year 33 AD,[13] resulting in an age of 39 years at the time of Jesus' death.

With the modern discovery of the *Dead Sea Scrolls*, which represent the oldest extant Biblical texts, scholars now know of additional documents excluded from the Bible. The *Dead Sea Scrolls* comprise a collection of Hebrew and Aramaic texts consisting of eight complete scrolls, and tens of thousands of fragments. The Aramaic language of the Aramaeans had become common in Canaan by 600 BC, and was the prevailing written script used when the *Dead Sea Scrolls* were being compiled. Most of the documents were written during various dates between 250 BC and 68 AD. The rolls of leather and papyrus, which were wrapped in cloth, were then secured in jars. They consisted of fragmented copies of every book in the Old Testament except the *Book of Ester*, plus prior unknown records and numerous hymn books.

Also found with those 'sacred' scrolls were Apocrypha and Pseudepigrapha books written in Hebrew, including fragments of the *Book of Enoch* and a substantial portion of the *Book of Jubilees*. The *Book of Jubilees* was written about 100 BC by an unknown sole author, most likely a Levite priest. It is a commentary on the *Book of Genesis*, and consists of a history of the world supposedly revealed by an angel to Moses on Mount Sinai, but its history is considered to be legendary, not factual. This book is also known as *The Lesser Genesis, The Apocalypse of Moses,* or the *Testament of Moses.*

Bedouins discovered the initial documents, the eight principal scrolls, which were found in caves at the northwestern hilly shore of the Dead Sea in Khirbet Qumran, Jordan. Later, in neighboring caves, tens of thousands of fragments and nearly complete texts were also recovered, all thought to be part of a Jewish brotherhood library, or perhaps a religious storage house. The religious group responsible for such scroll storage is referred to as the Qumran Brotherhood, who are generally believed to be related to the Jewish Essene sect, although specific differences were apparent between the Qumran branch and traditional Essene beliefs, which might indicate it was a splinter group.

The Qumran Brotherhood consisted of a group of priests and laymen living in a communal-type setting, all dedicated to serving God through strict emphasis and observance of Mosaic tradition. The Brotherhood was lead by the Teacher of Righteousness (more properly 'Right Teacher' or 'Orthodox Teacher') who interpreted and preached Mosaic Law, announced prophetic mysteries revealed by God, and believed in eternal salvation through a sacrificed Messiah. None of its members thought that their Right Teacher was the Messiah. The Teacher of Righteousness died between 65 and 53 BC, reportedly killed by the 'Sons of Darkness' almost a century before the death of Jesus, which occurred between 27 and 33 AD.[14]

It is known that the Essenes lived in the Qumran area during the period in which the writings occurred, and are further credited with formulating and promoting beliefs that were harbingers of the later Christian ideas, serving as the predecessors of the Christian movement. They believed in salvation through a sacrificed Messiah, resurrection, immortality of the soul, and eternal punishment in hell or a reward in heaven. Both John the Baptist and Jesus were believed to be members of the Jewish Essene sect. Christianity is known to have originated from one or more of several competing Jewish reform ideologies.

The *Holy Bible* is certainly one of the most respected and revered books of humankind. Yet it is a selective compilation of numerous different tales that were rearranged, revised, and edited by man, with companion portions deliberately excluded. It was not a contemporaneous recording of the events it described, but rather a narrative that was first saved more than a thousand years later, only to be knowingly altered, at least in part. While its intent is certainly noble, it can be argued that it may be no more credible than the sacred scriptures of other olden cultures. While such works were apparently based on revelations provided by divine beings, perhaps the Ancient Ones, their message and knowledge of the Creator was later suppressed and altered by the BOPH gods, prior to humans also eventually editing and changing those revelations even further.

Chapter 32

Creation Myths & Lost Lands

The events and revelations contained in various 'sacred' texts of numerous ancient cultures are viewed as merely mythological and engaging tales that were concocted only for entertainment by uneducated and unenlightened people, to teach lessons through the use of allegories. Yet certain mythologies appear to have a foundation rooted in actual historic events, perhaps altered by later transcribers who embellished certain metaphorical aspects. Modern translations of ancient texts can certainly transform and distort its author's original intent, or the factual elements of the event being discussed. Still, many discoveries of ancient artifacts and cultures have been made by amateur archaeologists who were not misled or limited by the constraints of traditional teachings and beliefs held by their professionally trained counterparts. Such freedom allowed those amateurs to go beyond established orthodox boundaries, thereby expanding potential findings.

Perhaps one of the most successful 'amateur' archaeologists was Dr. Heinrich Schliemann, the man credited with discovering Troy, a city previously thought to be mythical. He achieved his goal by following routes to lands described in Homer's *Iliad* and *Odyssey*. He viewed Homer as a reporter of condensed history, believing he had no reason to lie. Dr. Schliemann actually uncovered at least seven olden Troy cities at the noted Hissarlik, Turkey, site; each built on top of an earlier city ruin. The legendary Greek city of Trojan War fame known as Troy VI, dating to *c.*1190 BC, was not the oldest. An earlier grand city known as Troy VII was also uncovered that dated to 1300 BC. Such discoveries prove that myth and legend can have a factual historic basis.

Scholars could learn from the diligent work of Heinrich Schliemann, realizing some element of truth apparently exists in most folk tales. The following brief and superficial overview of ancient mythology and legend merely exposes certain common shared beliefs, which strongly influenced the development of human cultures during antiquity. It should be understood that any collective study of myths and legends represents an epic undertaking, so this brief review is not a comprehensive attempt to address all its many aspects. Select oral histories and traditions are also included, with some accounts considered to merely be mythical, although such inclusions should not be considered as being accepted or confirmed by this author. The intent is to expose available data that could further substantiate the *Elder Gods* theory, thereby also clarifying events that might explain Earth's true historic past.

Any review should naturally start at the beginning, with the 'creation accounts' themselves. Creation mythology can be divided into two groups, one of world creation, and another defining humankind's origin. World creation, or the formation of the universe from nothingness, is a belief shared by Greek, Egyptian, Australian, Judeo-Christian, and Mayan cultures.

The best known tale is contained in the Biblical *Genesis* account. Such a concept may have a basis in fact. Theories postulated by modern physicists contain evidence and indications that our physical universe may have actually evolved purely from a thought process. Such a unique and provocative hypothesis proposes that the entire reality of the physical universe may have derived its presence as a result of 'thought' produced from a pure energy source. Such a process of construction credits both physical existence and material reality as products created merely from 'thought,' by an unseen force envisioned as an energy-only consciousness. That 'thought' was further implemented through the 'Word' assigned to each conception, creating the material reality we know as our physical world.

Numerous ancient texts state that the whole cosmos sprang from *Divine Thought* that became the *Word*, which manifested from the *Voice* spoken by the Creator. From that process, the 'spores of creation' generated the universe. The Creator's command, the 'Voice of the Will,' was known as *Memrab*[1] in some ancient texts, while the Hebrews referred to it as *Dabar*,[2] and the Greeks called it the *Logos* or simply the *Word*.[3] The early followers of *Cabala* referred to 'thought' as a primordial act integral with the process of creation.[4]

That same concept of universal creation from thought-formation through verbal conveyance was also the Hindu Brahmin tradition of uttering the sacred sound *AUM*. Another reference is found in the New Testament Gospel according to Saint John, stating: "In the beginning was the Word, and the Word was with God, and the Word was God."[5] Such a statement has been interpreted by many as the belief in mere thought having produced all of reality; creating physical matter, corporeal life, and cosmic order.

The Egyptian god Ra was commonly credited as the Divine Intelligence that created the universe from the sound of his voice alone. Numerous other gods reportedly claimed that same accomplishment. Sir Wallis Budge cited a creation story from the *Papyrus of Nesi-Amsu*, which stated: "...before the world and all that therein came into being, only the great god Neb-er-tcher existed, for even the gods were not [yet] born."[6] The Egyptian Creator god, typically considered to be Atum, is also quoted as saying: "I [fashioned] my mouth, and I uttered my own name as a word of power...Nothing existed on this earth [before me], I made all things."[7]

The Akkadian Creation Epic, the *Enuma elish*, is known from the later Assyro-Babylonian account, a collection of seven clay tablets that dealt with the struggle between *Cosmic Order* and *Primeval Chaos*. The earlier Akkadian concept stated that physical creation was accomplished through utterance of the divine word. The creating deity had formulated a thought-plan that envisioned physical matter, then merely pronounced the word of each object to usher in its creation. Ultimately, *Order* was created from *Chaos* by such creation acts. To keep this cosmic order and maintain harmony, the gods devised the *Me's*, a set of divine and unalterable laws that governed the universe, which all creation was obligated to obey.[8] Anthropologists have detected just such an underlying metaphysical spirit that was apparent in many ancient cultures, which is discernible as a belief in a superior order to which all matter in the universe is subjected.[9]

Author and scientist Carl Sagan cited a first century quote attributed to Huai-nan Tzu of China, stating: "When heaven and Earth were joined in emptiness...then without having been created, things came into being. This was the Great Oneness. All things issued from this Oneness, but all became different...."[10] The *Rig Veda* also supports a similar belief in a creation-from-nothingness by some thought process. From its tenth book, Hymn 129, verse 4 (10.129.4): "Desire came upon that one in the beginning...Poets...found the bond of existence in non-existence." Yet another *Rig Veda* hymn (10.72.3) states: "In the first age of the gods, existence was born from non-existence."

The force that emanated from the 'Cosmic Word,' which converted ethereal energy into matter, was also known as the 'Messenger of the Creator's Will.' Through such a productive force, the ideas and thoughts of the Godhead were impressed upon matter and became physical reality. It was called *Fohat*[11] in Sanskrit texts, and was known as *Toum*[12] by the Egyptians, according to the *Book of the Dead*.[13] That entire creation process was known as *Kriyasakti*[14] in Sanskrit, the mysterious power of thought; a process from which its own inherent energy produced external, concrete results within the physical world.

Thought and imagination have no bounds. A time may have existed when a single source or origin of awareness once prevailed. Such a sole source of pure energy may have brought into being all the elements and structures of the physical universe we now know. Such a central source of thought, a Universal Consciousness, may have been the origin of all subsequent ensuing thought. Such portrayal could be a simplification of the event that occurred at the time of the Big Bang, with its energy release being orchestrated and balanced through a pure-thought process. The ensuing basic formation planned from 'prior thought' provided a code of order and physical laws from which matter would form, utilizing the non-matter essence of pure energy.

The physical universe then emerged through the modification and conversion of energy into matter, with its eventual return to energy; following some plan of perpetual recycling, perhaps as a mechanism for subsequent or continuing improvements. From such a fundamental creative thought process, tangible forms would first be conceived and later condensed into ethereal souls, further evolving into astral bodies, and finally taking solid form as biological creatures. Sentient, intelligent life would eventually ensue, allowing thought and consciousness to inhabit a mortal vessel, one that would also be 'recycled' through the process known as reincarnation.

Other world creation myths involve the work of physical gods during ancient times. As with numerous myths, accounts recorded at different times within a specific culture may vary in their narrative facts, contradicting their own earlier versions. Chinese mythology alludes to a primordial era when their creator god, P'an Ku, is reported to have traveled the cosmos around 2,229,000 BC;[15] a time calculated from accounts of Chinese periods based on assumed ages of certain mortal men. Carl Sagan revealed a *circa* 3rd century AD Chinese manuscript discussing P'an Ku, which stated: "First there was the great cosmic egg. Inside the egg was chaos, and floating in chaos was P'an Ku, the Undeveloped, the Divine Embryo."[16] Upon the birth (emergence) of P'an Ku, he reportedly then fashioned the world using a hammer and a chisel.

The ancient Sumerians held a similar belief that the world was created by the gods. In their account, that feat was accomplished by a primordial divine pair, Tiamat and Apsu. Tiamat was the goddess of the watery chaos, who, along with her consort Apsu, the god of the sweet (fresh) waters, were responsible for creating Earth and the ensuing gods; starting with their first born son, Mammu. A similar Pelasgian creation myth stated that Eurynome, the Goddess of All Things, emerged from *Chaos*. She then created the seven planetary powers from which other worlds emerged, setting a Goddess (a Titaness) and a Lord (a Titan) over each.[17]

Not all the beliefs from antiquity credited the gods with world creation. Various texts stated that the ancient Hindus did not attribute such planetary creation with the gods. Per the *Rig Veda* (10.129.6): "The gods came afterwards, with the creation of this universe"; clearly stating that the universe, resulting from the Big Bang event, was already in existence when the gods arrived to develop the Earth. The Greeks also did not believe that the gods created Earth, but merely built upon and managed the planet, which was already in existence when they first arrived.

The creation of humankind is also divided into two groupings. The first set of beliefs center around the Cosmic Egg concept, which was the belief in Africa, China, the South Pacific, India, Japan, and Greece. It is universally portrayed as a process wherein humankind broke forth from a fertile egg. In a Dogon myth, the cosmic egg is referred to as the 'placenta of the world.' Hymn 121 in Book Ten of the *Rig Veda* refers to "The Unknown God, the Golden Embryo." It speaks of the golden egg that separates, with the unknown god as the Golden Embryo or seed of that egg. Once born, this unknown god 'was the one lord of creation' who held the Earth and sky in place. Later, that same egg, but not that god, separated Earth from the sky. This Golden Embryo is also discussed in another *Rig Veda* hymn (10.82.5): "That which is beyond the sky and beyond this Earth, beyond the gods and the Asuras...." The Chinese also believed that their first man was born from an egg that the god Tien dropped from the heavens into the waters of the Earth.[18]

The cosmic egg concept may have a basis in historic fact. Such an event may have been the opening of a hatch on a spherical (egg-shaped) spacecraft, followed by the emergence of a humanoid being. A few rock drawings and certain cave art have been interpreted by some as depicting an egg-shaped craft, with beings emerging from what they identify as an opened hatch.[19] One ancient South American legend indicated that the first Peruvians were born from a bronze, gold, and silver egg that fell from the sky.[20] A cliff drawing in the Sahara seems to represent a similar belief, depicting a man emerging from an egg-shaped object decorated with concentric circles, found near the famous 'Martian God' figure.[21] It is likely that primitive people who might have viewed a strange being emerge from the hatch of an elliptical spacecraft would naturally believe the creature was actually being 'born' from such an 'egg' that fell from the sky.

A second classification of myths pertaining to the ancient origins of humanity consists of a set of beliefs portraying mankind as having been created directly by the gods. Some ancient texts describe a time when inhabitants from other worlds visited Earth during an age when humanity did not yet exist. Not until some later time did humans emerge, through specific action taken by those gods. Such beliefs were common in China, Egypt, India, Mexico, Greece, Peru, and throughout the Near East. Ancient Indian and Tibetan myths tell of the first humans on Earth being created by the gods during remote primordial times. Those First Men had the ability to fly in the air like their makers, but later lost or had that power taken away.[22] Olden Tibetan records claim that the first seven kings of Tibet came from the stars and were able to 'walk in the sky.'[23]

Such mythologies also affirm that there was a time when the gods reigned over humankind. Ancient traditions of India claim that all life on Earth was created by the 'Lunar Pitris,' the patriarchs of the moon, upon their descent from their lunar home;[24] evidently referring to their off-world base on the moon, which was loyal to the Ancient Ones. The Judeo-Christian belief in the *Genesis* creation account states: "Let us make man in our Image..,"[25] referring to God creating Adam. But, this statement does not account for the plural reference to God, or the existence of humanoids prior to Adam, such as *Homo erectus*, Java man, or Neanderthal man.

Such an act mirrors the Akkadian account of the gods, led by Ea in Eridu, creating Adapa as a 'model' of man intended for use by the gods as a servant. The *Adapa Story*, which vastly predates the Biblical *Genesis* account, was recreated from portions of tablet-accounts found in the ancient library of Ashurbanipal, as well as from passages in the *Amarna Letters*. Note that Adapa was not the 'first man,' but a 'model-of-man,' a prototype upon which others would be based. That statement parallels Egyptian accounts where their god Khnoum (aka Khnemu) was known as the 'Modeler of Men,' who fashioned humanity from the Mundane Egg.[26] *The Secret Doctrine* confirms similar claims by stating that the Watchers, the beings known as either assistants or messengers of the [BOPH] gods; God's angels; or the Lunar Pitris, the humanlike Helpers of the Ancient Ones; were identified as the 'Divine Prototype,' or modern copies of the 'archaic prototype.'[27]

The Babylonian *Enuma elish* epic also states that the gods created humans as their servants. Many Mesopotamian carvings and reliefs depict naked humans working in the employment of large, fully clothed masters or gods. Such olden humans went from being the sharecroppers of the gods, to eventually managing Earth,[28] perhaps with such gods becoming absentee landlords. Egyptian creation myths state that the gods, using their own DNA 'seed,' created man. The sudden appearance of *Homo sapiens* as a separate species occurred as early as 400,000 BC with the proto-Sapiens, very near the end of *Pithecanthropus* apemen. Evolution does not act that quickly, so the mutation from apeman to man evidently employed some other method. It may have occurred just as the ancient texts explain, as a genetic intervention performed by the gods.

Numerous legends reveal that prior civilizations of Earth were destroyed by cataclysms for various reasons, usually due to the decadence of humanity. Olden cultures of the Aztec, Hopi, Mayans, and Chinese kept track of such prior times, referring to them as *Suns*, *Worlds*, or *Ages*. Those periods also tracked the type of destruction, revealing it to be a result of fire, ice, or water.

The legendary reign of the Chinese Emperor Yao clearly documented that the Earth befell a calamity that 'lit the sky,' creating intense heat that destroyed harvests, and turned lakes into boiling water. Repeated hurricanes and other storms then ensued. Yao called upon his divine archer, Tsuyu (aka Tzu-yu), who contained such upheavals by flying into the sky.[29] Once nature was brought under control, Tsuyu then reportedly flew away to the moon. Other cultures record similar disasters in their written records, such as those found in the Bible, the *Mahabharata*, and the *Koran*. After those destructions, the records indicated that a New World was created, one inhabited by a new people who became humanity's next hope for a better future.

Native Canadian Indian legends tell of a great catastrophe or havoc in the land now known as the United States, one that convulsed its territory during a most distant epoch. Mayan legends also confirm such convulsions within the lands of the United States during its remote past, referring to that territory as the 'Kingdom of the Dead.'[30] That destruction was not the result of the Great Flood, but was caused by another disaster that occurred long before the flood. Author Peter Kolosimo wrote that an ancient human race, believed more civilized than other people of that era, inhabited that land (the United States) before its massive devastation.[31] That civilization reportedly vanished after suffering a massive natural conflagration.

Ancient Egyptians believed the Earth was divided into three parts, identifying one as *Amenti* (aka Amentet and Amento), the 'Paradise of the West,' with other hieroglyphic records referring to it as the 'Abode of the Dead,' the land in the West where many dead people reside.[32] It was also known as the 'region of darkness,' the domain of Osiris, mentioning it as part of the Divine Sunboat,[33] a reference to the 'afterlife journey.' Others have identified this land as the island of Copacabana in Lake Titicaca.[34] But that ancient burial ground most likely referred to the United States, based on descriptive similarities among the Egyptian accounts and later Canadian and Mayan legends of their 'land of the dead,' which is now identified as the United States.[35]

Numerous cultural legends preserve the memory of a Golden Age of mankind, when they lived among the gods in true peace, harmony, and fairness. The Zoroastrians of ancient Persia believed in a fabled paradise called *Airyana Vaejo*,[36] which was created by their supreme god, Ahura Mazda. That region prospered during its First Age, but was later destroyed by ice.

During Egypt's mythical First Time, the *Zep Tepi* (also *Tepi Zep* and *Tep Zepi*), a great primordial Island of Creation emerged from the flood waters of the Nun.[37] That island paradise, the Garden of the Gods, was called *Ta-Neteru*,[38] the location where the gods, the *Neteru*, physically lived on Earth while overseeing that Golden Age of true harmony, peace, and justice. It was much later associated with the Egyptian Ra, a BOPH god, after that idyllic island land was lost through humankind's decadence, and was subsequently destroyed by a natural cataclysm.

The native Creek Indian god of creation was Esaugetuh Emissee, who made his home on the island of Nunne Chaha in the primeval waters.[39] On that island, he built a house encircled with a great wall, which directed the waters into circular channels. The Iowa and Dakota Indians also claim an early homeland on a similar great island in the Atlantic.

Similar memories appear universal among ancient cultures, which vaguely recall a great empire that sank suddenly and violently into the ocean, followed by a resultant worldwide holocaust that killed most life on Earth. Such a destructive force also altered the face of the planet's land masses and ocean shores. Such legends are found in the Near East, Hindu India, Europe, North Africa, and throughout the Americas; all dating to a time before written records.

The *Book of Genesis*, along with early Mesopotamian texts, portray the Garden of the Gods as having a temperate climate, with God taking afternoon walks along its shore to enjoy the cooling breeze. It was a land of rich soil for farming and orchards, drawing its waters from a network of four rivers that were depicted as forming a cross. High mountains at one end of the land served as protection over that paradise.[40] The epic *Mahabharata* of India names such a 'land of the gods' as being Mount Meru, a land similar to Mount Olympus, the highest peak in Greece where the Greek gods resided. Many accounts associate the gods with mountain residences, including the Biblical Yahweh who was associated with several different mountains.

The concept of a mountainous island paradise where the gods resided is the popular legend of Atlantis. The early barbarians living along the Mediterranean coast reportedly regarded the civilized people of Atlantis as gods. Ignatius Donnelly wrote that the residents of Atlantis were described as a people having extraordinary strength, who: "...could move through space without the loss of a moment of time. They were wise and taught knowledge to men."[41] Author Martin Ebon states that there was only one known reference to Atlantis prior to Plato's famous account. That reference occurred when the historian Marcellus wrote of Atlantis in his now lost *History of Ethiopia*. That work stated: "...the inhabitants of several islands in the Atlantic Ocean preserved a tradition from their ancestors of the prodigiously great island of Atlantis which was sacred to Poseidon and held dominion over all the islands in the Atlantic for a long period."[42]

Further descriptions reveal that the region consisted of seven small islands and two medium islands, which surrounded one large main island, totaling ten islands within its chain. Proclus, who had access to Marcellus' work prior to its loss, retold those excerpts from his *History of Ethiopia*. Almost 20 years after Plato, the philosopher Crantor was reported to have examined the series of inscribed columns and stelae in Egypt that described the sinking of Atlantis, which reportedly agreed with Plato's version of Atlantis.[43] Some time later, those columns were either destroyed or had deteriorated and were never 'copied' or replaced, allowing the details and memory of Atlantis to eventually fade.

Diodorus wrote of a fabulous Atlantic island possessing great cities, which was identified as the birthplace of the gods. Diodorus believed that the account of the war between the gods and the titans was a history of the wars of Atlantis.[44] Diodorus stated that the known knowledge of Atlantis indicated its intended purpose was to be a dwelling place for gods, rather than men.[45] The few humans who lived there were either servants or mortal spouses of certain gods.

The Toltecs of Mexico claimed to be from Atlan or Aztlan, while the later Aztecs also claimed Aztlan as their ancestral homeland. Many have associated the Aztlan homeland with Atlantis. Author L. Sprague de Camp wrote that Strabo believed Atlantis to be factual, with one of their colonies located on the southwestern coast of Spain, believed to date back to 6000 BC, with its major city being Tartessos.[46]

Atlantis was likely a 'concept' rather than a location. Its name may have referred to any number of secluded sites used by the Ancient Ones and the Helpers where they could conduct work in private, away from the interference of indigenous humans and wild animals. As climatic changes occurred or destructive natural calamities happened, its site would occasionally change, with its relocation to a new region. While its actual geographic location may have sporadically changed, the name Atlantis, referring to the headquarters of the Ancient Ones, continued to identify the place where they instructed select humans in the ways of civilization.

The descriptive narrative of Atlantis provided by Plato may have been an accurate description of the Ancient Ones' headquarters at the time just before the Great Flood. That base was apparently located on a chain of ten islands between the Azores and the Bahamas.

The legends of Atlantis appear to be consistent throughout the records of Sumer, Akkad, Babylon, Chaldea, India, Media, Greece, Scandinavia, China, Guatemala, Peru, and Honduras. A similar version is equally universal among the Hebrews, the Celtic tribes of the British Isles, and most North American Indian tribes. Its eventual loss as the central headquarters where the Ancient Ones and the Helpers conducted their work is usually attributed to a flood disaster.

About 600 deluge legends are thought to exist around the world. However, Egypt contains only a single 'secondary' flood account, which likely was not the Great Flood. That minor version was contained in a funerary text discovered in the tomb of Seti I, the pharaoh who ruled from *c.*1305 to *c.*1289 BC. The Egyptian *Book of the Dead* contains a chapter, reportedly written by the god Thoth, referencing a flood that destroyed a disobedient and chaotic humanity.

According to researcher Ignatius Donnelly, Manetho attributed that Egyptian account as being taken from a Greek translation, one made by a younger or second Thoth (the Greek Hermes), based on an ancient stele credited to the original Thoth.[47] The Egyptian priests, when questioned about the Greek version of the Great Flood in which Deucalion was the hero, stated that the Egyptians were preserved from that disaster, although their records did indicate that world wide changes ensued as a result of such a flood.

The oldest narrative of the Great Flood is the Sumerian account where Ziusudra, the mortal governor of Sumer, was saved from that disaster. Other Mesopotamian versions include Berosus' short account where Cronus is the god, and Xisuthrus is the hero. A longer version is contained on the 11th of the 12 tablet account forming the *Epic of Gilgamesh*, with the god Ea assisting the hero Utnapishtim. Utnapishtim was later granted immortality by the gods, and allowed to live in Kur.Bala, the Land of the Gods. The Sumerian Kur.Bala was also known as the island of Tilmun, from its repeated mention in early Assyrian tablets that were recovered by Sir Henry Rawlinson in 1880.[48] That island land was further known as Ni.duk.ki in Akkad, and as Dilmun in Babylonia.

Archaeologists Geoffrey Bibby and Henry Rawlinson both identified that land as being the modern day Persian Gulf island of Bahrain,[49] where the great Dilmun Empire once existed. It expanded all along the extremes of the Persian Gulf, extending into the center of Kuwait Bay to Failaka Island. That empire was associated with the eternal home of the immortal ancestors of humankind, the home of the gods, and was the place where Gilgamesh went to search for eternal life. Dilmun was previously identified as Enki's earliest settlement and the original base for the subsequent BOPH colonists, as well as the initial 'training camp' for their later loyal human followers.

When Enki migrated to Eridu around 3350 BC, he appointed one of his daughters, the goddess Nin.sikilla, to be the guardian of Dilmun. Later, Inzak became the tutelary god of Dilmun, the god also known as Enshag or Enzak in Sumer.[50] Inzak has also been identified as the god Nabu (aka Nebo), the grandson of Enki, from a Babylonian tablet listing the gods and their protected regions during the time of Ashurbanipal.

Chapter 33

Ancient Gods

Many cultures claim that the gods, the demigods, and the god's Helpers or Watchers brought both civilization and knowledge to its people. Those educational leaders behind such civilizing efforts were known by numerous names, including Osiris in early Egypt, then later as Thoth, followed finally by the younger Horus. Similar gods were also known as Oannes in Mesopotamia, Rama in India, and Orpheus in Greece. Other comparable gods were known by various different names throughout Central and South America. The Sioux Indians claimed that their Great White Father brought livestock to them. Nearly all the indigenous North American Indians believed corn and coca were gifts from their spirit gods. Much earlier, the Sumerians held a similar belief, claiming that wheat and barley were presents from the gods, which were freely bestowed upon humanity.

Those cultures believed that such gifts were brought to Earth from elsewhere in the cosmos. No original wild plants of the Earth grains of rye, wheat, oats, maze, and barley now exist. Such grains either came from an earthly lost land, or from another world;[1] unless they were originally domesticated during the most archaic periods of our planet's antiquity, by some unknown lost civilization. The hieroglyphic writing of the Egyptians, along with the cuneiform script of the Sumerians, were both stated to have been gifts from the gods, not the inventions of man; its misuse, therefore, was prohibited. Japanese legends and oral traditions tell of extraordinary beings that came from the sky in shining boats, claiming they taught the people many 'wondrous things,' while also bringing 'marvelous objects' with them.[2]

The Roman poet Virgil (aka Vergil) referenced the 'last age of the Cumaean Prophecy' in his circa 37 BC work, *Eclogue IV* (*Pollio*). That writing has undergone numerous translations from its original Latin version, with one passage essentially stating that a new race descended from the celestial realms.[3] That statement referred specifically to beings arriving from the cosmos that were on a messianic purpose to civilize and guide humankind. It further predicted and venerated the future birth of a child who was destined to usher in a new Golden Age,[4] perhaps a reference to Jesus.

But evidently not all 'celestials' were humanlike in their appearance. Berosus wrote of Mesopotamia's remote past, long before the splendor of Babylon, when the first inhabitants of the land were people of a foreign race that were visited by a being called Oannes who came from the sea, perhaps an amphibious species. He brought civilization to the region, accompanied by six other beings of his species. Oannes taught the people knowledge, but lived alone and was never seen eating food, and eventually departed into the sea, although others of his species reportedly returned during later times.[5]

Additional reports of other alien appearing beings also exist, describing them as small in stature; green, blue, yellow, or gray in color; and often accompanied by humanlike beings acting as guards or assistants. Others seem to be hybrids between alien and humanlike beings that arrived from the sky to bring civilization to Earth. The 'goddess' Oryana (aka Orejona) of Tiahuanaco, the Great Mother of the Earth and the First Mother of Mankind, appears to be one such hybrid. She was described as a humanlike being, but with four fingers on each webbed hand, along with webbed feet. She supposedly arrived at Tiahuanaco in a vessel 'brighter than the sun,' which is claimed to be depicted on the Gate of the Sun.[6] Oryana, or a very similar goddess, was likely the Nazca Goddess, Orichana, who also arrived from the sky in a craft as bright as the sun.[7]

Such alien beings may have reflected the various species collectively known as the Ancient Ones. They had limited contact with infant races, preferring to remain in the background and devise the methods of implementation and the educational lessons to be taught, along with determining an 'acceptable rate' of civilization. It was primarily their assistants, the humanlike Helpers in the case of Earth, who guided and administered those civilizing plans for each world. Thus, most mythical accounts of civilizing gods arriving from the heavens describe beings that were humanlike in appearance. While most were the outer planet Lunar Pitris, some may have also been hominoids from distant worlds, perhaps the blue or green hued beings of certain myths. Such beings would have been specialists in a required discipline, recruited for a specific project.

Most Central and South American cultures describe a massive, heavily bearded, tall white man who possessed a large head, as the benefactor who brought art, knowledge, farming, religion, architecture, metallurgy, and civilization to their ancestors during ancient times. The primitive cultures receiving such gifts consisted of non-white races devoid of facial hair, and thus were clearly of a different ethnic origin from that of their benefactor. Those white gods were known by numerous different names, including Quetzalcoatl by the Toltecs and Tezcatlipoca by the Aztecs, both Nahuatl language tribes of Mexico. The white god of the Quiché Mayans of Guatemala was called Gukumatz, while the earliest god of the later Yucatan Mayans was Itzamna (aka Itzamana), followed later by their god Kukulkan. However, the related Tzendal tribe, which settled west and south of the Yucatan, called their god Votan.[8] However, such benefactors were sometime females, such as the young and beautiful white woman who came from the sky and built a palace in the city of Cealcoquin,[9] according to a Central America Honduran myth.

In South America, the Quechua language natives, including the Inca, called their white civilizing god Viracocha.

Some records indicate that Viracocha was not a person, but rather a race of people. Ancient Peruvian legends and oral tradition describe a period on Earth when Viracocha, the 'good spirit from space,' brought civilization and knowledge to the people,[10] and presided over a time on Earth of 'life without death.'[11] The tribes of the eastern extremes of the Andes called their god Zume, while Ayar Cachi was the Cuzco Valley god, who reportedly traveled by air on great wings.[12] Reportedly, some of those gods (or perhaps the same god) eventually departed by sea, usually from a port in Ecuador, promising to return someday.

The Native American Indians of Canada and the United States talk of the Thunderbird, the Great White Father, who traveled in "a bird which flies with the sound of thunder."[13] That 'bird' was further described as going up "in a big flame."[14] The Haida Indians of British Columbia, Canada, believe that their "great sages descended from the stars on discs of fire."[15] The Navaho Indians describe "creatures who came from the sky and stayed a long time on Earth but finally returned to their world."[16]

Most ancient texts tell of quarrels, dissension, and outright warfare between the gods; the gods and the titans; God and the devil; or the gods and a dragon or leviathan. Such 'Wars in Heaven' are found in the Puranas, Greek myths, Biblical accounts, and the Norse mythology known as the *Battle of the Flames*, where the sons of Muspel fought on the field of Wigred. Those struggles were fought for supremacy and control over Earth's inhabitants. Ugarit texts describe Baal's victory over a dragon called Lotan (aka Leviathan or Lawtan in other texts). In Isaiah 51:9, Yahweh fought and destroyed Rahab (Leviathan, the serpent) during a time in Earth's distant past. A similar battle, fought by Archangel Michael, is recounted in Revelation 12:7, "And there was war in the heavens: Michael and his angels fought against the dragon...." Stanza VI.6. in the *Book of Dzyan* states: "There were battles fought between the Creators and the Destroyers, and battles fought for space."

The Egyptian *Book of the Dead* recounts a conflict between Horus, aided by the 'sons of light' and his uncle, Seth, who was assisted by the 'sons of the dark.' The heroes, the 'sons of light,' were associated with the 'serpents of the clouds,' according to author Peter Kolosimo.[17] Another Egyptian account found in the *Book of the Dead*, which was originally taken from temple records preserved by the priests at Thebes, described the victory by the god Ra over the serpent monster Apep. The story was later greatly enlarged, becoming a manuscript called *The Book of Overthrowing Apep*, written during the Ptolemic dynasty. The monster was vanquished by piercing its head, splitting its face into two halves, and finally crushing each half on Apep's own land. Apep's body was then smashed into pieces and dismembered.[18] Such an account is similar to Marduk's defeat over Tiamat, which is found in the Babylonian *Enuma elish*.

Biblical researchers George Johnson and Don Tanner wrote that Isaiah believed Lucifer was the head of the pre-Adamic civilization.[19] Lucifer was referred to as the 'Majestic Angel of Light,' a king who reportedly lived in Eden, from where he protected his assigned domain and sanctuaries. He was described as being full of wisdom and perfect of beauty.[20] Judeo-Christian accounts claim that Yahweh's angelic army expelled Lucifer from his high position in heaven. A parallel account is found in Hurrian mythology, where their first supreme god, Alalu, was dethroned by Anu.[21] It is also similar to the Egyptian and Greek accounts of the Atlantian god, Poseidon, being relegated to a lesser position by the younger god Zeus.

Poseidon worship appeared as a widely held tradition during the Age of the Golden Race, prior to the younger gods' reign during the Age of the Silver Race. Poseidon was a Water god who was usually depicted wearing a trident crown and carrying a three-pronged scepter. Those same symbols were also associated with the Hindu gods. Later, the scepter was degraded to a trident, then to a pitchfork that was associated with the devil. Such denigration follows a familiar tradition of enemy demonization, one in which the victors of wars or political battles write the 'accepted' history, portraying their vanquished opponent as demons, and their acts as evil deeds.

Chinese legends parallel many descriptive narratives of the Hindus of India. Both detail similar devastating weapons and aerial battles in heaven. The rival groups that fought for Chinese rule were assisted by celestial beings utilizing fantastic weapons described as 'Dragons of Fire.' Such Chinese conflicts reportedly occurred in the remote past, during the 'Age of Miracles.'[22] Researcher Peter Kolosimo wrote that Chinese professor, Tchi Pen-lao, had dated such an age to about 45,000 years ago.[23] Such legends of war in the heavens may have a basis in fact. The previously reviewed craters found on both the moon and Mars were recognized as resembling patterns similar to modern saturation bombing or strafing. Author George Andrews concluded that such definite geometric patterns of crater distribution could not have been produced entirely at random, and therefore all could not have been created solely by chance.[24]

Other ancient mythological concepts focused on the celestial realm, revealing a knowledge and comprehension of outer space that vastly exceeded the level attributed to them by modern historians. The c.2800 BC *Epic of Etana* referred to outer space as 'the Heavenly Great Depths,' and described an ever diminishing Earth as if viewed from a departing space flight, precisely as it is now known to occur from our modern exploration of space. Boats always played an integral part in ancient cultures, especially in Egyptian narratives. The *Pyramid Texts* describe the great 'Waters of the Abyss' and the celestial boats that were used to traverse them. The celestial waters of space, as described in the Egyptian *Book of the Dead*, stated: "This place has no air, its depth is unfathomable and it is black as the blackest night,"[25] referring to this celestial abyss as the *Noot*,[26] while other Egyptian records called it the

Nun, 'which completely filled the universe.'[27]

In ancient India, the celestial waters were known as *Abhvam*, the monstrous abyss, which was described in the *Rig Veda* (1.92.5) as: "...dark, formless, enormous, and terrifying." The cosmic ocean was the source and domain of the gods, while the earthly oceans were the resting place of the gods. The Earth's atmosphere separated those two 'waters' according to the *Rig Veda* (1.185.2), which stated: "Sky and Earth guard us from the monstrous abyss." The Aztecs referred to the heavens as the cosmic ocean or the godsea. Both Sanskrit and Chaldean records refer to the army of the Lord of Hosts (aka the *tsabaoth*) as 'the crew of the sky ship of the Upper Ocean.'[28] The Hindu Puranas spoke of 'seven islands separated by seven oceans' that surrounded and encircled the Earth.[29]

In a time when distant travel was accomplished over the water in ships, often stopping at islands along the way to replenish supplies, the 'Universal Sea' was an excellent means by which to explain outer space to 'primitive' people. Planets could be described as islands, reached only by 'aerial ships,' as they traversed the waters of the 'Upper Ocean.'

Such cosmic descriptions made by 'primitive cultures' are very accurate representations of the nothingness and vast expanse of outer space. Those same 'primitives' also understood that a vehicle such as a 'celestial boat' was required to traverse those heavenly waters. In reality, such boats were space ships, the method of travel used by the Ancient Ones and their Helpers, as well as the BOPH colonists; although their vehicles were vastly dissimilar. In addition to boats, 'discs' were also used to traverse the celestial waters, according to ancient texts. The legends of China, India, Persia, and Japan speak of shining shells and golden discs, with similar craft in Egypt described as winged plates. Babylonian texts referred to their space craft as the '50-spoke solar wheel,' reminiscent of Ezekiel's vision of a 'whirlwind.'

Valmiki described a self-moving celestial car, the *Puspaku* car (aka Pushpa Chariot) of India, as: "The sky chariot which has a wonderful power and wings for speed, is gilded and lustrous...leaps above the hill, ...winged like lightning...lethal...covered in smoke...."[30] Another Hindu description detailed Prince Maya's "circular chariot of gold that measured 12,000 cubits in circumference (over 6,000 feet in diameter, or more than a mile across) and was able to reach the stars."[31] Archaic cultures commonly reported observing such aerial vehicles, including the Biblical 'cloud' that transported Yahweh through various Near Eastern lands. Additional descriptive names for such airborne craft included: chariots of fire, sky coaches, solar discs, reed floats of the sky, fire circles, whirlwinds, aerial cars, serpents of the clouds, winged globes, flying wagons, sky dragons, fiery winged wheels, sky boats, and the 'metal horse of the sky.'

The numerous 'winged disc' symbols found throughout the Near East refer to a vehicle, not the 'sun shining in the sky' as many scholars prefer to interpret that icon. This fact is evident by the many depictions showing both the winged disc and the sun as separate items, but pictured together in the same scene. One such example is found in Persepolis at the royal tomb of Nacch, which pictured Darius I and the god Ahura Mazda in a winged disc craft, while the sun was clearly positioned in the sky above those figures.[32]

Accounts of ancient gods are often dismissed as merely pagan beliefs of primitive men, with their tales and exploits likewise classified as fictional fantasies or myths. Yet similar accounts of fantastic deeds and accomplishments recorded by accepted religious beliefs are often embraced as 'gospel' and deemed to be 'sacred history,' with their exploits viewed as 'miracles' or 'mysteries of faith.' Similar ancient tales should be treated uniformly, especially when based upon a known common origin, regardless if from a pagan or an 'accepted' religious belief. But the enduring religions of victorious cultures are often allowed to diminish the 'conquered' ideology of a competing society's narratives, dismissing them as mythical fantasies.

Since the existence of Yahweh is accepted, the other ancient gods apparently also existed. The accounts of those other gods should be granted the same credibility as the exploits of their contemporary, Yahweh. Clearly, those gods were humanlike physical beings, with frailties, faults, and superhuman powers. The Greek gods were also depicted as having humanlike appearances with human faults. They lived in mountain sanctuaries, and possessed material goods and wealth. Hesiod stated that the gods were a Golden Race of men that were holy wisemen; benefactors and guardians of mortal men, but that fate closed over their race.[33]

Many myths convey the fact that the gods were readily and easily identifiable. Such a situation would apparently require a visual difference between humans and those 'gods.' That differential might be due to physical size, with gods being much larger than mere mortals. The Biblical Enoch's first encounter with such beings described "exceeding[ly] big" men who were unlike any men he ever "saw such on earth" before.[34] Many ancient depictions show gods as being much taller than mortal humans. Present day scholars have explained such a custom as representing or reflecting the respect and high reverence in which those gods were held.

The recognizable characteristic of the gods might be other than size. Prior NASA scientist Josef Blumrich's research of the *Book of Ezekiel* concluded that the Lord and His angels were similar in appearance to humans of that Biblical time, within normal variations of size, shape, weight, skin color, and physical features.[35] Such a conclusion then suggests something beyond mere physical stature as the possible identifying feature used to distinguish such gods.

Another often described characteristic of the gods was their 'radiance,' depicted as rays of light emanating from around their heads, indicating a 'brilliance.' Religious figures were depicted in later times with a halo around or over their heads. The *Book of Ezekiel* describes the occupant of the 'whirlwind' he saw as wearing a bronze or gold colored suit, perhaps of a metallic fabric,[36] since it reflected light in a 'flame-like manner.' The Hindu *Vedas* also referred to certain gods as being either golden or 'shining.'

Moses, after long durations in the presence of God or the 'burning bush,' developed a noticeable 'glow,' as described in Exodus 34:29, "the skin of his face shone." Jesus underwent a similar metamorphosis shortly before his crucifixion, when he and three apostles journeyed to a high mountain top where Elijah and Moses appeared to them, along with the voice of God speaking from a dense cloud. During that experience, the face of Jesus glowed, and his garments became luminescent, while Jesus: "...was transfigured before them: and his face did shine as the sun, and his raiment was white as the light," according to Matthew 17:2.

Chinese poetry written from 241 to 223 BC in the Chu Court of Southern China told of a god of Radiant Splendor who soared around the sky in his dragon chariot.[37] The Egyptian *Book of the Dead* makes reference to: "The Shining Ones who live in rays of light."[38] The olden gods of certain cultures, especially the early Egyptians, were depicted as having a red or reddish-bronze color. That might have been their actual skin coloration or the glow or radiance of their countenance. Gudea described one god as "a man that shone like heaven...by the helmet on his head."[39] Enoch described being awakened by two tall men whose: "faces were shining like the sun, their eyes...were like a burning light...from their lips was fire coming forth...their wings were brighter than gold...."[40]

Such portrayals describing the radiance of the gods may have degraded over time, resulting in the later Judeo-Christian practice of depicting God, as well as other holy figures, with 'beams' or 'rays' of light emanating from their physical likeness or countenance. Alexander the Great was often depicted with rays surrounding his head, prompting his Arabian epithet, 'the one with two horns.' Certain figures depicted on rock and cave drawings have rays emanating from around their heads. Such depictions are found in the Kimberly Range of Australia, the Tassili Mountains in the Sahara, and also on the plains of Nazca, Peru.[41] Other etching sites also exist near China Lake, California; and near Fergana, Russia;[42] although no extant record conclusively provides an answer for the reason or practice associated with such 'radiance' depictions.

Biblical records tell of angels blinding sinners who were menacing them. Numerous accounts describe gods, or their emissaries, blinding or even killing mortals by utilizing the power of the special headgear they wore. Babylonian myths stated that Marduk was not to be looked upon by mere mortals, 'since they could not endure his gaze.' A similar comment is made regarding Moses and his people, prohibiting them from gazing upon the Face of God. Specific Mesopotamian records describe the powers of a special headgear called the *Shugurra* or the Shu.gar.ra, also known as the Crown of the Plain.[43] Such a crown was reported to impart a radiance or glow to the countenance of its wearer.

The Atef crown of ancient Egypt was another headdress that was reported to impart special powers. It consisted of a conical shape, ending with a sphere or ball at its top, and incorporated the figure of a cobra on its front. Author Graham Hancock disclosed that such a crown is known only from the numerous engravings and reliefs depicting a god or pharaoh wearing such a device.[44] No crown, or even fragments from one, has ever been found within the numerous excavations of Egypt, according to Mr. Hancock. One legend stated that the god Ra gave an Atef crown to Osiris, who wore it for only a single day. That action resulted in great discomfort for Osiris, which was attributed to the heat of the crown swelling his head.[45]

Perhaps that device, or one similar to it, created the appearance of radiance associated with the gods. Such a device might allow the gods to focus their own higher state of energy (if so possessed) into some form of photonic beam, utilizing it as a protective barrier. Or, perhaps such devices simply emitted some type of energy force from an accompanying power source that was associated with the apparatus. The use of such an instrument would provide an effective means to control crowds, or perhaps may have served as a self-defense weapon.

The feature of radiance was a description often used in ancient Egyptian and Sanskrit texts when referring to the Ancient Ones, who were often called the Shining Ones. It is inconclusive if they had the ability to 'glow,' or if they utilized some advanced device to produce their 'radiance.' Such ability may have been utilized as a type of 'shield,' generated around the Ancient Ones as a barrier of protection from attack or harm. Indications support the use of some apparatus that was used as a weapon or protective device by the Helpers of the Ancient Ones. The BOPH gods evidently also used such devices, providing them with similar protection or perhaps some other intended function.

Chapter 34

Giants & Little People

The presence of giants on our planet during the Acheulian Age, Biblical times, and sporadically during the later Native American cultures in the United States, may reflect long-suppressed genes that occasionally resurfaced during later generations. Such genes may have originated with the DNA material contributed by the survivors of the outer planet humanlike beings. It is even quite likely that an individual subspecies indigenous to that outer planet might have been giants, or perhaps all the outer planet humanlike beings were originally giants. Genetic manipulations intended to create a compatible dual-planet species may have deliberately switched-off such a gigantism gene. That would appear to be an effort by the Ancient Ones to produce a practical-sized offspring to more efficiently utilize the dwindling resources of the Martian base. Such genetic suppression might resurface occasionally, producing giants in both the humanlike beings and in their distant earthly human 'cousins.'

Many myths and legends from ancient cultures documented the deeds and accomplishments, as well as the devastation and ravage, caused by giants. In Southeast Asia, scientists have found bones and teeth of enormous early-Pleistocene apemen called Giantanthropus and Meganthropus. Since giant apemen were once possible from natural evolution, then giant humans were likely also possible. A medical abnormality called *acromegaly* or *gigantism* is known to exist. The tallest known and acknowledged modern man was Robert P. Wadlow, who was born in 1918, and stood eight feet, 11.1

inches in height.[1]

Many ancient writings reference the existence of such giants, including the Bible, the Koran, the *Book of Dzyan*, ancient Hindu records such as the *Mahabharata*, and the sacred texts of Ceylon. Many ancient cultures possessed myths and oral histories concerning giants or titans. Such folk tales are an integral part of the Native Indian cultures of Peru, the United States, and Canada. Giants are also found in the legends of the Irish, Egyptians, and the Basque. Those accounts depicted only a few good titans, with the vast majority portrayed as evil, doing ruthless acts against normal-sized humans.

The numerous carnival sideshows of the past, along with the proven hoaxes perpetrated for fame and fortune, provide reasons for skepticism toward the existence of such a lineage or race. Although confirmed specimens remain rare, other legitimate discoveries were likely discarded when misidentified by the local medical provider or undertaker during olden times. It is likely that true relics of humanlike giant beings were dismissed as bones of extinct animals, such as mammoths and archaic apes, just as fake relics were touted as the real thing until proven wrong. In pre-modern times, it was only the town doctor or local undertaker who usually examined such unusual artifacts when found, with neither being a trained anthropologist.

The likelihood of misidentification would have been great, either for dismissing true finds, or authenticating false finds that anthropologists would later refute. Such misidentified 'real' remains would have then been discarded, never to have another chance at a second opinion. The following examples are but a few of the numerous reported specimens of giants found over the years, and represent the possibility that such beings once actually existed.

One of the foremost gigantism experts was the English researcher, John T. Battle. Mr. Battle referenced numerous giant *Homo sapiens* skeletons that were disinterred from their ancient burial sites around the world. Many of those finds came from the Near East, Siberia, remote Asian locations, and the United States, mainly in the Southwest and the Midwest Mississippi River Valley. Such specimens stood from eight to 13 feet tall, and possessed enormous jaws, usually set with both an upper and lower double row of teeth.

Mr. Battle observed that the older the skeleton, the more powerful and taller they appeared to be, while the youngest examples diminished in height to only about seven feet tall. While the oldest specimens appear to be beyond the range of carbon dating, indicating an age in excess of 50,000 years, the youngest finds dated to *c.*1 AD. If such giant specimens were products from the outer planet humanlike race that was genetically engineered by the Ancient Ones, perhaps their crossbreeding with indigenous normal-sized humans not only diminished their height, but may have also resulted in birth defects creating the 'monsters' recounted in many folk tales.

Ancient texts and legends described the reality of giants living during the Acheulian Age, placing them in South China, Morocco, Java, Syria, and South Africa. Author Warren Smith stated that Native Indians living in the Eastern Territory along the Allegheny River told of eight feet tall giants who were known by two names, the *Alhegewi* and the *Telligewi*.[2] The Delaware and Iroquois Indians overcame those giants, forcing them westward to an area around Chatfield, Minnesota, where they eventually became extinct.

The cannibal giants of the Penobscot Indians of Maine were called *Kiwakwe*. The Wyandot and Huron Indians knew similar giants as *Strendu*, while the Algonquin (aka Algonkin) Indians knew them as the *Windigo*. The red-haired, cannibal giants of the Piute Indians of Nevada were called the *Siwash*. The Native Indians around Mount Shasta know the Bigfoot giant or Sasquatch as *Matah Kagmi*. The Eskimo Inuits called their giants the *Tornit*. The large white hair giants led by Xelua were known as the *Tzocuillixeco* in Aztec legends. The Cholula natives of Mexico believe their Great Cholula Pyramid was built by an ancient race of deformed giants known as the *Quinames*. That pyramid was reportedly intended to eventually reach the heavens, in a manner similar to the Tower of Babel. Numerous legends state that many ancient megalithic edifices were also built by giant beings.[3]

Reports of physical evidence supporting the past existence of giants have been documented. A 300 pound stone ax was reportedly found at Birchwood, Wisconsin, which measured 28 inches long, by 14 inches wide, by 11 inches thick.[4] Another stone ax 17 inches long by nine inches wide was also found. A copper hand ax weighing 38 pounds, which measured 22 inches long, was found in an Ohio earthen knoll attributed to the Mound Builders.[5]

Numerous fossilized huge footprints have been found throughout the Southwest United States in Nevada, Texas, and New Mexico. Teeth and the lower jaw bone of a humanoid named *Gigantopithecus blacki* were found in central China by a Dutch paleontologist, Professor von Koenigswald. Weng Chung Pei found a total of 47 teeth belonging to the same type of creature in a cave in Kwangsi, a southern Chinese province.[6] Other skeletal remains of *Gigantopithecus* have been found in the Siwalik Hills of India. Such creatures are believed to be large anthropoids, estimated to range from nine to 12 feet in height, dating between 500,000 to one million years old.

In Java, remains of a nine feet tall giant *Homo erectus* named *Meganthropus*, commonly called the Java Giant, were found that dated between one and two million years old. That specimen was either a humanlike creature, or a primitive type of man believed to be an early forerunner of Java and Peking man, members of the later *Pithecanthropus* genus. Fossils of a humanoid dating to 700,000 years ago were discovered in Algeria, North Africa, and named *Atlanthropus* (aka Ternifine man),[7] believed to also be from the *Homo erectus* genus. The similar Transvaal Giant, a gorilla-like apeman, was discovered in South Africa. Fossil remains of giants ranging from eleven to just over twelve feet in height were reportedly found in the

Caucasus Mountains by several Soviet anthropologists.

More specific accounts have been reported by authors Frank Edwards and Warren Smith, with many of their examples found in the United States. In 1920, two huge molars, three times as large as those of a modern adult male, were found in a coal mine called 'Eagle Number 3,' at Bear Creek in Montana.[8] Those teeth were found in a geological strata that dated to 30 million years ago. A burial vault found in an abandoned Indian cliff dwelling in an area south of Winslow, Arizona,[9] contained a gigantic human skull of unknown age. In 1891, a twelve feet tall *Homo sapiens* was discovered in Crittenden, Arizona, interred in a stone sarcophagus.[10] That tall human reportedly had six toes on each foot. In July 1887, four miners found a broken human leg bone embedded in quartzite rock in Spring Valley near Eureka, Nevada.[11] Based on its 39 inch length from knee to heel, the height of its owner was extrapolated to have been about 14 feet. Doctors who examined the bone determined it to be of human origin.

A 1912 excavation of a cave near Lovelock, Nevada, by the University of California at Berkeley, discovered between 20 and 30 eight feet tall giant mummies possessing red hair that extended to their waists.[12] Reportedly that cave is now part of a state park. A photo is known to have been taken of at least one of those giants, propped-up next to a normal height human.[13] Artifacts including duck decoys, boomerangs, and footwear sandals were also found. All traces of the mummies, photos, and assorted artifacts are now hidden or lost. The University never released any test results to establish the time period during which the giants would have existed.

In 1833, soldiers uncovered a grave in Rancho Lompoc, California, which contained a stone casket covered with indecipherable writing. It held a 12 feet tall human skeleton, with a double row of both upper and lower teeth.[14] In 1925, amateur explorers unearthed eight prehistoric human skeletons in Walkerton, Indiana, all between eight and nine feet tall. All the remains were reportedly buried with their massive copper armor. Similar discoveries were made in 1960 at Tura, India, where the skeletal remains of an ancient humanoid standing 11 feet tall were found. The remains were not of a giant ape, since the deceased was found buried with a metal cup.[15] In 1969, the remains of 50 humanoid skeletons, measuring seven feet tall, were found in tile coffins that were buried in Terracina, Italy, about sixty miles from Rome.[16]

The Bible and related apocryphal texts contain numerous references to giants. Perhaps the best known was the c.1050 BC account of David's defeat over the Goth giant, Goliath, who was described as standing about 9.5 feet tall.[17] An even earlier account had Joshua's army defeating the Bashan kingdom ruled by its giant King Og (the Amorite king of Bashan and Gilead, reported to be about 13 feet tall), in the land of Canaan sometime around 1400 BC.[18] Hindu texts also reference a giant named King Og.[19] The familiar Biblical passage of the 200 'Sons of God' descending on Mount Hermon, at the southern edge of the mountains in Lebanon, reveals additional giants, as stated in the King James version of *Genesis* 6:1-2,4:

"And it came to pass, when men began to multiply on the face of the earth, and daughters were born unto them, that the sons of God saw the daughters of men that they were fair; and they took them wives of all which they chose....

There were giants on the earth in those days; and so after that, when the sons of God came in unto the daughters of men, and they bore children to them, the same became mighty men which were of old, men of renown."

The original Hebrew translation is slightly different, as revealed from a translation by the Biblical scholar and linguistic expert, Zecharia Sitchin:

"The Nefilim were upon the Earth, in those days and thereafter too, when the sons of the gods cohabited with the daughters of the Adam, and they bore children unto them. They were the mighty ones of Eternity...the People of the shem."[20]

The Hebrew Nefilim have been translated as giants, brilliant ones, or workers of wonders. According to the Hebrew scholar J. M. Vaschalde, the Nefilim were called marvelous beings, giants, and makers of wonders.[21] The use of the term 'giant' may have originally meant Earth-born, from the two forms of the Greek words *gyges*, meaning 'born of Earth,' and *gigas*, meaning giant. After the Exodus, Moses warned the Hebrews about the Nefilim, referring to them as gods who were strangers to the Hebrews, gods that their forefathers did not acknowledge or worship, according to Deuteronomy 32:16-17. The Hebrews had considered the Nefilim either 'new' or 'foreign' gods,[22] perhaps indicating some type of change within the 'divine' control over Earth.

Mr. Sitchin translated the term Nefilim as "those who were cast down upon the Earth."[23] He referenced the noted nineteenth century Biblical commentator, Malbim, who explained: "...in ancient times the rulers of countries were the sons of the deities who arrived upon the earth from the Heavens, and ruled the Earth, and married wives from among the daughters of man...."[24] Malbim further stated that those visitors called themselves Nefilim, defined as 'Those Who Fell Down' to Earth.[25] The most accepted linguistic translation of 'Nefilim' (aka Nephilim) is "those who are fallen". Such terms as 'cast down' or 'fell down to Earth' do not necessarily connote a voluntary act. An even earlier text might shed further insight on this intriguing, but apparently often-misinterpreted passage.

The *Book of Enoch*, a part of the earliest known Qumran Apocryphal writings, told of Enoch's first trip into the heavens of outer space and referenced what he saw in the 'Fifth Heaven' (the place some researchers claim could be planet Jupiter or one of its moons). Enoch viewed a group of perpetually silent giants with withered faces, who were referred to as 'fallen angels,' the *Grigori* or *Rephims*, by Enoch's host companions on that voyage. They may have been a small group of discontented humanlike exiles who left their Martian base between 7000 and 6000 BC, relocating to a base on one of Jupiter's moons, rather than the Lunar Pitris base on Earth's moon. Chapter 18 of the *Book of Enoch* described an encounter on Earth that was probably the original form of the later translation of the 'Sons of God' passage found in *Genesis* 6:1-2,4:

> "[The Grigori]...broke through their vows on the shoulder of the hill Ermon and saw the daughters of men how good they are, and took to themselves wives, and befouled the earth with their deeds, who in all times of their age made lawlessness and mixing, and giants are born and marvelous big men and great enmity."[26]

Hence, the statement 'cast or fell down to Earth' may refer to some form of social exile, where undesirables from another world that broke laws (their vows) escaped to Earth, perhaps from a prison planet or moon where they were exiled. Or such 'giants' may have simply made a visit to Earth, after being prohibited from doing so by leaders of their home world.

A number of tribes referenced in the Bible were races of giants, including the Rephaims, Grigori, Emims, Zamsummims, Horims, Anakim, and Gibborim. Those races or groups of giants reportedly occupied lands in Canaan, Bashan, and the kingdom of Og. The second chapter of Deuteronomy discusses the Rephaim, a band of giants defeated by King Chedorlaomer. The surviving Rephaim were reportedly imprisoned under the sea. Rephaim texts are contained in both the *Legends of Aqhat* and Genesis 14:5, which stated that Rephaims are inhabitants of Palestine and other lands. The Rephaim are also mentioned in Ugarit administrative documents, indicating that they lived in Canaan during the Amarna Age. Giants were often stated to be a distant and inferior kin of the Nefilim.

Other religious texts also discuss giants. According to the Islamic Koran, Dhu'l-Qurnain built a wall of brass as a defense against the giants Gog and Magog. The Hindus called their giants Rakshasas, while *The Secret Doctrine* believed such giants, or mighty primitive men, to be Atlanteans.[27] By associating giants with the 'Fifth Heaven,' perhaps their origin was on the 'fifth planet,' Maldek, that once existed in that orbit prior to its destruction. Some speculate that a planet with gravity lower than Earth's would produce larger beings. The much lower gravity of Mars or Earth's moon might have had that effect on beings relocated from a larger home world, especially if those indigenous beings were previously of a normally massive stature.

Little People

No discussion of ancient giants would be complete without their counterpart, the dwarf. Most folk lore contains tales of little people, mentioning them as gnomes, fairies, trolls, leprechauns, elves, imps, goblins, changelings, oafs, genies, sylphs, undines, or dwarfs. Such beings were often described as diminutive, deformed, and shriveled old men who possessed very large heads. They were uniformly thought to have lived underground. Such beings stood between eighteen inches high, to as tall as four feet. Gwyn was reported to be the king of the fairies who lived in Glastonbury, England; either in or on a mysterious hill or 'tor,' commonly referred to as Glastonbury Tor.[28] Many little people were also associated with megalithic sites. The Celts of Brittany, Wales, and Ireland attributed their megalithic stone structures to the 'little people' who could 'lift any amount of weight.'

According to author Daniel Cohen, the Penobscot Indians of Maine called such small beings the *Wanagemeswak*. The Eskimos called their friendly little people the *Kingmingoarkulluk*, while the Aztecs called their fearsome dwarfs the *Tepictoton*. The little people of the Ojibwa Indians of northern Minnesota were called the *Memegwicio* or *Memegwesi*. The Cree Indians knew them as *Memegwecio*. They were the diminutive humanlike creatures described as being about the size of a 10 year old, fully covered with hair, with a very flat nose. The Ural Mountain Turanian people called their dark, round-headed dwarfs the *Dwergar*. Many accounts link those dwarf beings with a companion race of giants, with both living side by side.[29]

Ancient Egyptians and the high civilizations of ancient Central America all held and displayed a high reverence for little people. Those advanced cultures believed dwarfs were directly connected with the gods. Bes, the small Egyptian god, was also worshiped by the Hittites and the Phoenicians. Bes was depicted as a dwarf with a thick black beard and a hunchback.[30] In addition to the Near East, his likeness has been found on rock paintings in the southwest regions of the Unites States, Greece, and Central America.

The 'Pyramid of the Magician' is located within the Mexican Yucatan at Uxmal. This necromancer's castle is also known as the 'House of the Dwarf,' derived from the Mayan legend of a dwarf with great powers who constructed the building during one night's work.[31] Mayan legends also assert that such grand construction was easy for dwarfs, since they could just whistle, and the heavy blocks would move into place. Belief in the awesome powers and abilities of dwarfs was common in early Central American cultures. As with certain ancient construction feats attributed to giants, numerous megalithic sites were reportedly built by dwarfs using their magical powers.

The UFO researcher, Jacques Vallee, drew a connection between the little people of folklore and extraterrestrial aliens. He noted that descriptions of both are similar, with fabled actions of the little people corresponding with certain strange phenomena associated with UFOs, such as abductions or kidnapings, especially the night abductions of children mentioned in folk tales.[32]

Like giants, physical evidence of diminutive beings has also been found. According to *The Natural and Aboriginal History of Tennessee*, written by John Haywood in 1823, the

416

skeletal remains of eight feet tall giants, along with thirty four inch tall midgets, were found buried in mounds near Sparta, Tennessee, in White County.[33]   The remains of the midgets were medically determined to be those of adults.   Another enigmatic discovery occurred in October 1932, in the Pedro Mountains, about sixty miles west of Casper, Wyoming.   Two prospectors exposed a small cave after blasting a rock formation in search of gold.   Inside that cave they found a fourteen inch tall mummy.[34]   Medical X-ray examination revealed a skeletal structure very similar to that of a normal-sized human, including a full set of adult teeth,[35] but all in miniature size.

Dr. Henry Fairfield, a member of the Wyoming State Historical Society, named that being *Hesperopithicus*.[36] Further medical examinations by Dr. Henry Shapiro of the American Museum of Natural History, along with several anthropologists from Harvard University, concluded that the being was about sixty five years old at the time of his death.[37] They further concluded that the mummy was of an unknown type and stature that had existed during the Pliocene Age. That required the diminutive being to have lived sometime between 2.5 and 12 million years ago, perhaps even during the mountain's formation. However, others have claimed that this mummy was a deformed infant that merely appeared to be older, which would be highly unusual since the mummy had a full set of teeth.

Author Robert Charroux reported that in 1942 (1938 in another account), a wall depiction was found in a cave of the Baian Kara Ula mountains, a remote region between China and Tibet. The rock carvings depicted the sun, moon, and stars, all attached to the Earth by various routes, shown as a series of dots.[38]   In the same cave, precisely aligned graves were reportedly found that contained the skeletal remains of beings about four feet, three inches tall.[39]   Those unusual remains reportedly could not be classified within any existing category of human species. The local natives associated them with an

417

ancient Dropas race, although the present Dropas are normal, full size natives. According to Chinese legend, ancient members of that race were short, yellow-skinned beings, with very large heads and a spindly body.[40] They were alleged to have come 'in peace' from the clouds between 11,000 and 10,000 BC, but were killed by local warriors who feared them.[41] Folk tales from ancient China associated such predominantly yellow skin beings with ancient royalty. Their description is very similar to the little 'gray' aliens reportedly associated with the modern UFO phenomenon.

Little people were also depicted as having green skin, much like the leprechauns of legend. Ireland was known as the 'Green Island' in ancient times, and is still referred to as the Emerald Isle. Perhaps such beliefs survived into modern times with tales of 'little green men from Mars.'

Such little people may also help explain the oddities found in some of the ancient megalithic stone structures located around the world, since they are often credited as being their builders. At Sacsahuaman, Peru, small tunnels with miniature stair steps were carved into solid rock.[42] Such diminutive stairs and tunnel systems reportedly honeycomb the entire fortress structure, and could only have been used by very diminutive beings, since the tunnels are described as being too small, even for children.

In Exeter, New Hampshire, a similar complex was also found that contained very small tunnels. The ancient ruins at Raica, Chile, appeared to be an entire city that was built exclusively for dwarfs. The monolithic ruins of Monte Alban in Oaxaca, Mexico, also contain an extensive network of tunnels cut from solid rock, near its tomb site. That site's miniature tunnel complex measures only twenty inches high by twenty five inches wide, and reportedly contains several miniature stone stairways,[43] all that were too small for use by normal-sized humans.

Chapter 35

Modern Legends

Certain aspects derived from ancient accounts remain a part of modern day beliefs. One can trace the evolution of Yahweh, the Hebrew God, from regional deity to His present day status as the Judeo-Christian God of the universe. Another intriguing example of ancient belief that survived into modern times can be found with the North African Dogons, specifically in their link with the star system Sirius. The cliff-dwelling Dogons, a tribe within the Berber family, are part of the Mandingo population of the West African Republic of Mali. They live in the cliff ridges and hilly uplands of the Bandiagara and Hombori regions, neighboring to the west of Algeria where the Sahara Desert runs through the northern part of their country. The Dogons are known for their construction of thick-walled houses built using red clay, resulting in their unique 'soft-sculptured' architecture noted for its rounded corners.

The Dogons have known for a long time that Saturn has rings and Jupiter possessed at least four moons. They also realized that distant stars were part of our Milky Way Galaxy. For centuries they further preserved a legend, memory, or belief that is connected with Sirius, the Dog Star. Sirius, the brightest star in our sky, is 8.7 light years from Earth. The Dogons knew that Sirius has a 'Dark Star' partner, a companion star, but one that is invisible to the naked eye. They also know that this Dark Star has an elliptical orbit of 50 Earth years and is 'the heaviest thing in the universe,' composed of a metal they called *sogolu*.[1] The Dogons claim that eons ago, amphibious visitors from the Sirius star system had brought civilization and knowledge to Earth, bestowing their celestial knowledge upon ancient humans. Olden tribal rituals were used to transmit such knowledge through oral histories, passed down from generation to generation. This belief is further detailed in Robert Temple's intriguing book, *The Sirius Mystery*.[2]

From modern astronomy we now know that Sirius, situated in the constellation Canis Major, is a binary star system. It is comprised of a visible main star, Sirius-A; and Sirius-B, a companion star that is a collapsed white dwarf star with an elliptical orbit. These stars take about 50 years to circle each other, being separated by 3.72 billion miles, almost 40 times the distance between Earth and our sun.

The ancient Egyptians also had a fascination with the Sirius star system, although no record implies that they knew of its 'dark' companion star. The Egyptians closely observed Sirius, associating the flooding of the Nile with the rising of that 'Dog Star,' also believing it to be connected with the hot 'dog days' of summer. Similar ancient beliefs in such prior human contact with 'otherworldly beings' and the Sirius star system are held by the Hopi Indians, the Australian Aborigines, and the Chinese who called this star *Tien-Kou*.

Other North African curiosities are evident throughout the Tassili and Ahaggar Mountains. The intriguing cliff and rock drawings found in those areas were previously examined, perhaps linking that region with 'strange beings.' Speculation has been advanced that the post-Flood survivors, including those from Atlantis, may have fled to the high elevations of the Atlas Mountains of North Africa, as well as the mountain ranges in the Sahara, forming that area's enigmatic ancient mountain cultures. Legends even refer to the Ahaggar Mountains as 'islands' during the time of the Triton Sea, the ancient inland lake of the Sahara valley that was formed by the Great Flood. Another Berber speaking people, the Tuaregs, also inhabit that region. They are a fierce tribe of the Sahara, also known as the Veiled People. In ancient times, the Tuaregs controlled the Trans-Sahara caravan routes.

The Tuaregs are a caste system society comprised of serfs, vassals, and nobles. They follow a matriarchal-determined social status where the men, not women, wear a headdress with a veil. The earliest Tuareg ancestors were likely a sea faring people that controlled the Triton Sea from their ports and trading settlements within their mountainous home lands, thus linking those early mountain cultures on both the north and south sides of the Triton Sea.

Statements by Herodotus, along with numerous Sahara rock drawings, connect that region with the Atlantis legend. The Tuaregs even refer to themselves as descendants from Atlantis, with some of their songs linking their culture with extraterrestrial worlds, specifically mentioning the Pleiades.[3] According to ancient legends, the inhabitants of Atlantis were sometimes referred to as the 'Blue People.'[4] During the later days of Lake Tritonis, the subsequent remnant from the Triton Sea, certain ancient inhabitants had also been referred to as the 'blue-clad people,' which included the Nigerians, the Tunisians, and some of those Atlas Mountain tribes.

As with the previously mentioned yellow, gray, and green colored beings of legend, blue was linked directly with the ancient gods. Many of the archaic divinities of India were depicted as having skin that was blue in color, or having blood that was blue. That was the origin of the term 'Blue Bloods,' used to describe royalty.[5] Information collected by the Roman Empire, based on oral traditions, stated that the natives in the central inland areas of Britain dyed their bodies with *woad*, in order to impart a blue color to their skin.[6] The belief was that such a blue appearance would scare their opponents during a battle, based on some belief linking blue color with olden 'superior beings.' Such unusual blue-pigmented ancient beings reportedly displayed supernatural powers. The term 'blue people' or the 'blue-clad people' may have had other implications beside those of clothing or artificial dyeing of their skin.

421

Charles Berlitz reported that John West, a physiologist with the School of Medicine at the University of California at San Diego, researched a very small group of people that lived at an elevation of 20,000 feet, high in the Andes Mountains near Aucanquilcha, Chile.[7] Those people exhibited a distinct blue coloration to their skin. It was determined that the reduced level of oxygen associated with the 'thin' air at such high altitudes resulted in poorly oxygenated blood hemoglobin. That lack of oxygen, a quantity significantly less than the amount found at sea level, imparted a blue color to the skin, an appearance similar to that of an asphyxiation victim.[8]

Tibetan priests living at very high Himalayan altitudes are also known to exhibit this same blue-tint skin coloration. Research shows that the human body can and does eventually adapt to such a drastic reduction in breathable oxygen levels, allowing one to live, thrive, and even perform strenuous labor at such high altitudes. Diet and medication have been shown to assist with the acclamation to those reduced oxygen environments.

In most ancient mythology, the gods were described as inhabitants of the mountains. Author C. W. Ceram also noted that ancient gods were often depicted as standing upon mountains.[9] Yahweh was reported to be a God of the Mountain, the same epithet used for the Canaanite god Baal, the Babylonian god Adad, the Hittite god Teshub, and the Hindu god Indra. Mountains were considered 'sacred' or holy places during ancient times, a place where most gods dwelled.

The Bible states that Yahweh resided on Mount Horeb during the time of Moses. The Persian god Ahura Mazda resided on Mount Hara, while the god Nebo lived on Mount Nebo in the Sinai. Baal had homes on both Mount Saphon and Mount Carmel, mountains that were later also associated with Yahweh. Mount Carmel was considered a 'High Holy Place' since vastly ancient times. Baal's Mount Carmel center was taken over for a brief time by Yahweh, but was later divided into a shared holy place for both religious cults, with side by side alters. Mount Sinai was the even earlier center of the Jebisite god El Elyon, but later also became the mountain that was ultimately associated with Yahweh.

Many of the most ancient megalithic complexes were built at phenomenal heights in the mountain peaks, exemplified by Tiahuanaco and Machu Picchu. The Greek Mount Olympus, along with sites in the Sinai, the Caucasus, and Taurus Mountains were the reported homes of the gods. That situation may have occurred as a result of individual choice. The thin atmosphere, lower oxygen level, cooler temperature, and low atmospheric pressure may have been a matter of personal preference by those 'gods.' Such conditions may have provided a more comfortable environment for beings that came from a base on Mars, which had a thinner atmosphere, lower gravity, and cooler temperatures than Earth. Hence, the legends of blue colored gods in India, the royal 'blue bloods,' and other 'blue' references to the ancient gods may have had a factual basis.

No modern examination of mythological accounts would be complete without mentioning the Earth Chronicles written by Zecharia Sitchin. That series, plus its numerous companion books, develops a theory of extraterrestrial humanlike beings from a world called Nibiru, a planet said to be within our solar system that orbits in an unusual eccentric or 'comet-like' fashion. According to Mr. Sitchin, that planet's royal ruling family colonized Earth around 450,000 BC, creating humanity in their own likeness through genetic manipulation of apeman and their own DNA. Early humans initially functioned as slaves, serving those extraterrestrial colonists. Over time, the visitors mated with earthlings to produce the hybrid species we now know as *Homo sapiens*. Mr. Sitchin's theory asserts that those alien colonists ruled as 'gods' over Earth, building the ancient monolithic monuments, while also civilizing humanity.

That royal ruling 'alien' family fought incessantly for power and control over Earth, using treachery, deceit, and acts of war against their rival family members. Their exploits later became the mythological tales of the gods, found in all the ancient cultures around the world. Those 'gods' were headquartered in the Near East, the area from which Earth's major religions emerged. Those beings possessed supernatural powers, either through genetic differences, or by utilization of advanced devices. They were considered immortal, although the ancient cultures clearly described the deaths of numerous gods, while relegating those beings to life spans of hundreds of thousands of years. According to Mr. Sitchin, one of the first known visitors was Enki, arriving in 432,000 BC. He reportedly was still alive in 2000 BC, making him over 400,000 years old.

As an admirer of Mr. Sitchin's research and narratives, he is held in high esteem, with great respect for his meticulous research and most enjoyable works. He arrives at well-conceived assumptions, through extensive study backed by solid documentation. However, interpretations based on this author's research were unable to substantiate certain portions of his theory, without any implied criticism toward his conclusions. Clearly, the same set of facts can be interpreted in multiple ways, arriving at differing conclusions without contradicting alternate deductions. Such alternate interpretations and speculations expressed in the *Elder Gods* theory merely introduce different deductions arising from many of the same sources, actually expanding upon Mr. Sitchin's *12th Planet* premise in certain areas. This author considers Mr. Sitchin's work to be an accurate portrayal of specific Earth history, from *c.*5000 BC to about 500 AD. The *Elder Gods* theory exposes more archaic eras preceding that period, while adding significant details to his reported time frame, thereby answering some remaining questions or lingering ambiguities.

One such area of divergence exists with Mr. Sitchin's claimed longevity of certain gods, such as the 400,000-plus years old Enki. It is inconceivable for a physical being to live for such extended time periods, regardless of the advanced scientific understanding and technical levels their society might possess. For example, a 400,000 year old being such as Enki would still be subjected to dangers posed by accidental injury and/or natural disasters. A finite limit would exist as to the number of organ transplants, limb replacements, or artificial joints a recipient could receive, before becoming merely a mass of scar tissue. The natural oxidation of organic cells, regardless of the potency of vitamins taken, would still have a debilitating effect on brain functions, which seemingly could not be augmented by a similar transplant procedure. Beside, just imagine the number of times a 400,000 year old man would have to get up during the night to go to the bathroom!

The discovery and understanding of the human telomerase gene provides hope for a greatly extended human life span in the future, but not one entailing ludicrous extremes. A human cell presently can divide about 50 times, its inherent limit at which division (regeneration) stops. The process that copies the long double helix of DNA during each cell division does not copy the last few units of DNA at the chromosome's tip or end, which is known as the telomere. After each division, the chromosomes of that cell become a little shorter until inadequate material is left for that cell to divide further. Eventually, the aging skin and organ cells can not be rejuvenated, as they loose their ability to divide. However, it has been shown experimentally that telomerase, the product produced by the telomerase gene, allows the telomere to lengthen so normal cell division can continue.[10] Since all human cells contain this telomerase gene, it is believed that stimulation of that gene could produce telomerase to lengthen the telomeres, perhaps extending or renewing cell division beyond its current 'natural' limit.[11]

However, this same mechanism is linked with certain drawbacks associated with the cloning process. The first molecular study conducted on Dolly, the initial sheep cloned from a six year old ewe, revealed that its telomeres were considerably shorter than normal for her chronological age.[12] The findings suggest that the cloned offspring not only inherits the donor's genes, but also the equivalent biological age of the donor's cells at the time of cloning.[13] In Dolly's case, at age three, she exhibited the telomere length normally found in a nine-year-old sheep; the equivalent of her actual age, plus her donor's age at time of cloning. If future cloning procedures can not compensate for such 'inherited' cellular aging, the desired rejuvenation associated with this replication procedure will not be achieved.

Such scientific findings provide credibility to the Biblical account of humankind's loss of some longevity after the Great Flood, from a life span of approximately 900 years to one of only about 120 years. If the collection of living creatures brought into the ark was through the process of extracting DNA material only, not through live specimens, the cloning process after the Great Flood would have produced already-aged offspring, depending on the original donor's maturity. The repopulated clones would then pass down their 'aged' status as an inherited trait.

The Epic of Gilgamesh expressly alludes to DNA cloning as the probable mechanism through which life on Earth may have been preserved from certain extinction by that flood. It described a procedure that occurred prior to the arrival of the Great Flood, stating: "...take up into the boat the seed of all living creatures,"[14] without reference to any actual live specimens being involved, only their 'seed.'

Conceivably, the humanlike gods Mr. Sitchin described may have lived about 1,000 years. That would equate roughly with the life spans of the pre-Flood patriarchs contained in Biblical accounts, as well as claims contained in the *Mahabharata* where life spans reached 1,000 years during its Golden Age.[15] To multiple generations of post-flood mortal humans who would have routinely expired during such a lengthy time span, those beings that were capable of a 1,000 year longevity would appear 'immortal.' Subsequent mortal descendants would have been informed of prior exploits long ago by such regional 'gods,' making those gods appear to be immortal.

Most mythology contains some contradictions within its genealogy, accomplishments, and events concerning those gods, as well as discrepancies with the principal characters involved in such narrations. No consensus can be reached as to the actual deeds and actors involved in certain accounts, but the similarities expressed in the various versions would suggest that some historic event did indeed happen. It appears that each new generation of 'gods' would also usurp their predecessors' past deeds, claiming them as their own, further confusing related chronologies while also distorting actual history, but not necessarily the underlying historic event itself.

Both the highest ranking gods and the pharaohs of Egypt took credit for accomplishments of their predecessors; adding their name to prior edifices and claiming those monuments were constructed in their honor. Those rulers could accurately recount archaic deeds and events, claiming them as their own accomplishments, since they had access to the prior historic records of their ancestors. Such claims of past fame also distorted their own mortality, requiring them to have existed prior to their own birth. Therefore, the literal interpretation of any lifeform existing for vast periods of time, as based on those ancient accounts, may simply be erroneous.

As mentioned earlier in this text, the name assigned to a specific god may have been more of a 'title,' signifying a position or duty. Hence, the cumulative accounts of a single named god or a specific epithet likely referred to numerous different beings, not just one person. The god that held a specific post or duty then became known by that title, rather than by their personal name. Longevity attributed to an individual god may have actually reflected numerous holders of such 'official positions' over the years.

The name or title of a god was probably also passed down within each royal family as an inheritance, recycling the name and thus giving the appearance of immortality. Such a practice may also explain some of the inconsistencies in the genealogical accounts of gods, with one text identifying a son of a specific father, while a competing account may reverse their lineage. The gods were clearly mortal, with some critically wounded, while others grew old, although all eventually died, contradicting their 'immortality.' The Egyptian god Ra was depicted as a drooling, old and feeble man when he finally relinquished his reign to his son.

Many authorities acknowledge the likelihood that multiple beings were known by a common name, or usurped prior famous and revered names in an effort to carry on their namesake's mission. It is further understood that several different beings were known to have used such names as 'Thoth' or 'Horus' during different periods of Egyptian history. Many ancient texts infer that there were two gods named Ea. The first was the olden Semitic water god of Akkad, followed by a younger version in much later Babylonia; both different beings, but combined into one god by the numerous scribes of mythology. In *The Greek Myths*, author Robert Graves identified Ea as Anu's brother, likely indicating the older version.[16] But in later Babylonian myths, Ea was described as Anu's son. The continuation of a common name reflecting a specific position would account for the apparent longevity of such legendary beings.

Inference has also been made to the lengthy orbit of Nibiru as contributing to such extended longevity of life, claiming one year on Nibiru is equal to 3,600 Earth years; its required time to complete one orbital revolution. There is no evidence that orbital duration would have an appreciable affect on biological life span. A finite actuarial span would exist for each species, just as on Earth, where the tortoise can live for several hundred years while some insects have a day or two longevity. When humans eventually establish permanent colonies on Mars, which has an orbit about twice as long as Earth, they would not automatically enjoy a 'doubled' life span.

The <u>Earth Chronicles</u> theory also does not explain the inability of the gods to understand the concept and potential of their 'high-tech' weapons and devices. The gods were saddened and amazed at the destructive power resulting from the use of the long forgotten 'deadly seven thunderbolts' (nuclear weapons). Seemingly, only one or two gods of any generation seemed to be able to operate or understand the scientific principals behind many of their own advanced devices. That seems most unlikely for a highly evolved society, unless much of their technology was inherited. At times the gods also appeared to be somewhat dimwitted when dealing with humans. Abraham outmaneuvered Yahweh when he 'bargained' with God over the number of righteous men needed to save Sodom from desolation. Other Biblical accounts and myths relate that additional humans cleverly outwitted the gods. The Mesopotamian gods often appeared ignorant and incorrect, while Egyptian gods were illiterate, except for Thoth, Osiris, and Ptah.

The BOPH gods and their 'cousins,' the humanlike Lunar Pitris or Helpers of the Ancient Ones, are the same beings as Mr. Sitchin's royal lineage of gods, the Anunnaki, including the Igigi. But the <u>Earth Chronicles</u>' *12th Planet* theory does not explain or account for references to alien beings, those not of humanlike form. Such creatures include the 'little gray' humanoids, with their large almond-shaped eyes, that were displayed on rock drawings as being pierced with spears, or the paintings of other alien creatures, such as the one-eyed 'Martian god.'

Still others include the insect-like creatures depicted on rock drawings in Australia, and the beings requiring respirators or space suits to breathe on planet Earth, along with ancient fabled accounts describing amphibious or reptilian creatures. Other accounts told of speechless, short beings, dressed in shimmering suits, which accompanied the civilizing 'white gods' on some of their missions. Additional beings displayed feline characteristics, as represented in certain ancient statues and drawings. The existence of alien worlds and their non-human inhabitants were described in both the *Rig Veda* and the Jewish *Cabala*. The *Elder Gods* theory accounts for such 'alien' beings as the different species that comprised the group known as the Ancient Ones, and perhaps even included some of their loyal 'otherworldly' non-humanlike Helpers.

A final distinction with the <u>Earth Chronicles</u> involves the god's planet of origin. The *12th Planet* concept claims Nibiru as their home world, a planet with a comet-like orbit requiring roughly 3,600 years for one complete revolution. It seems unlikely that such a world could produce humanlike beings. Its eccentric orbit would expose that planet to variable gravitational forces, depending on its proximity to other passing celestial bodies. Its trajectory would also permit constantly changing exposures to various heat sources, likely resulting in both alternating unlivable heat as well as 'lifeless' cold conditions.

Orbital proximity to cosmic radiation sources would subject the planet to intermittent lethal dose levels, sterilizing or killing its indigenous life. Such alternating drastic conditions would produce a constantly changing environment, which would not be conducive for life formation. Any early developing life would seemingly have to constantly adapt or mutate to the ever-changing conditions; but mutation and steady-state evolution could not have worked that quickly.

If life did form by some freak chance, it seemingly would not be compatible with Earth's environment and genetics, or acquire humanlike form. Mr. Sitchin's *12th Planet* concept may still be correct, but would likely refer to a closer and more stable neighbor of Earth. Those celestial candidates would include nearby planets such as Mars or a number of satellites orbiting nearby worlds, such as Jupiter's four moons mentioned in Chapter 2. However, the most likely candidate would be the destroyed Asteroid Belt planet, Maldek. Such likely prospects render any unknown and unacknowledged 'comet-like' planet as being merely a remote possibility for the origin of human life on Earth. Thus, Maldek may indeed be our solar system's tenth planet (aka the *12th Planet*), as referenced from Mr. Sitchin's interpretation of ancient Sumerian texts.

Chapter 36

Since 3000 BC

After the Ancient Ones departed Earth around 3150 BC, the BOPH colonists established themselves as 'gods,' reinforced by their superior knowledge and technical devices. The BOPH gods then took control of Earth, with support from their vast majority of human followers. The Helpers that chose to remain on Earth, which they regarded as their 'home,' had far fewer human followers. That imbalance permitted the BOPH gods' influence and subjugation over early Earth cultures, such as those of Dynastic Egypt, Hindu India, Mesopotamia, North Africa, and China.

The BOPH gods never shared most of their knowledge and advanced devices with humans, or implemented the rapid cultural progress they had previously promised. They realized that their only control over a human population that greatly out numbered them existed with their technical superiority. Such an advantage was never intended to be shared with humans, but merely used to elicit fear and dominance over them. The BOPH gods considered humans to be a lower classification of beings, much below their 'divine' level as 'gods.'

Beside the previously referenced illiterate nature of the BOPH gods and their apparent amazement with the potential of their superior devices, their advanced technology seems to have been loaned or provided to them from extraneous sources. Perhaps such developments originated with their ancient ancestors or the Ancient Ones, rather than being created by their own developmental efforts. That observation seems to indicate a break or disruption within the progress of their culture, such as a major relocation due to a destroyed home world. Their space travel capabilities (or limitations), which required awaiting 'close opposition' with their base on Mars for most contact, a condition that occurs roughly every 26 months, was in stark contrast to the intergalactic craft of the Ancient Ones. A high civilization, one capable of interplanetary space travel, is simply inconsistent with a culture of apparently unenlightened people.

Ancient texts show even the best supporters and friends of humankind, such as Ea and Enki, were still regarded as intimidating beings to the humans of Earth. The Akkadian cuneiform tablets, known as the *Amarna Letters*, depict a Mafia-like 'godfather-reverence' by humans toward even the most benevolent gods. Favors were requested, but stark fear of potential harm was also evident, from the mere act of even addressing such a 'god.' It should be clear that most BOPH gods considered humans to be lower forms of life, to be used as they desired, usually as mere slaves or servants.

But the BOPH gods also realized that they would eventually need the support of Earth's human population, when the Ancient Ones eventually returned from their temporary exile. At that time, Earth would have to finally choose between joining the Cosmic Order and accepting its controlled rate of progress, or remain independent, without benefit of imparted knowledge or the protection provided by the Ancient Ones. Apparently, the BOPH gods devised a plan to handle that eventuality. Perhaps a clue to their strategy can be derived from the *Mahabharata*, which stated the Celestials (the BOPH gods): "...descended from heaven to earth, for the destruction of the enemies of the Gods and the well-being of all the worlds...."[1] That seems to refer to the BOPH gods' plan to demonize the lingering memory of the Ancient Ones within the minds of the human population, with their ultimate intent to permanently eradicate them from memory.

That program was subtle, first changing the Ancient Ones into 'demons,' while usurping all past accomplishments made by the Ancient Ones, claiming such achievements as their own. Henceforth, the bulk of our ancient folklore depicted the lives and deeds of the BOPH gods, rather than accurately crediting such exploits correctly to the Ancient Ones. Thus, the BOPH gods rewrote history, not created it. Although the Ancient Ones never claimed to be gods, usurpation of their feats by the BOPH gods partially accounts for some of the confusion found throughout archaic records that did not accurately identify which 'gods' were being discussed.

Those early narratives of the BOPH beings created their 'position' or classifications as 'gods,' Nefilim, Elohim, or the Anunnaki; as well as their eventual classification as angels or even the divine Supreme Being of certain ancient religions. Such accounts likely also referred to some of the Helpers at other times. A modern version of those same tales, updated to reflect known technology, is contained in Zecharia Sitchin's Earth Chronicles, essentially concentrating on the exploits of the BOPH gods after the Ancient Ones departed our planet. Further references are found within the sacred history and mythical accounts contained in many ancient earthly texts.

The Helpers who remained on Earth also underwent similar degradation, perhaps accounting for the narratives describing 'minor' demons and 'fallen angels.' It was only after 300 AD that certain religions and their human leaders first started to hide the true nature of those humanlike beings, including both the Helpers and the BOPH gods, altering their very existence as dwelling only within a spiritual or supernatural realm. Their deeds were then combined into acts of an invisible Watcher or deity, beings that only the religious leaders could represent or contact. That was done to further control the masses, and promote the later human leaders' own agendas. Since 300 AD, an organized plan was implemented to hide the origins, accomplishments, and nature of the Ancient Ones, as well as the BOPH gods; perhaps in a manner similar to the way that modern world governments apparently now try to hide the truth behind the present UFO phenomenon. That was accomplished with the removal of any written reference made to such otherworldly beings.

The *Mahabharata* noted another aspect of the BOPH gods' plan, stating that Indra, their leader, made a covenant that: "...the Gods would descend from heaven to earth with a portion of themselves."[2] That apparently referred to a partial integration within the human species, through a program of limited breeding. The intent was to produce their own local, regional, and world leaders from their own 'stock,' thus assuring loyalty in promoting the agenda of the BOPH beings.

Even though the first Earth candidate, the proto-Sapiens, ultimately reflected an altered bloodline through interbreeding, either by rape or choice with early Neanderthals, a degree of compatibility apparently remained between Earth species and the 'outer planet' beings. Such an original bloodline 'manufactured' by the Ancient Ones conceivably changed further through later inbreeding between the subsequently 'refined' Cro-Magnon subspecies and a few lingering Neanderthals. Evidence has been found that Neanderthals and Cro-Magnons did mate, at least on a limited scale, based on remains found in both the Sinai and on the Iberian Peninsula.

Even with such ongoing evolutionary changes within the human family since its genetic 'creation' as a hybrid species around 400,000 BC, a genetic compatibility with the DNA material of the original outer planet humanlike beings remained. That basic genetic link preserved the procreation compatibility between humans of Earth and the BOPH gods (and the Helpers of the Ancient Ones). Initially, such inbreeding was utilized only to produce a continuing bloodline to ensure the transfer of rule, from one reign or dynasty to an 'anointed' or chosen subsequent one.

Prior conveyance of power had occurred from one BOPH god to another BOPH god, usually imparting the name or 'position title' with such a transfer. As the population of 'pure' BOPH gods diminished, offspring that resulted from their unions with humans were classified as demigods, something above humans, but below the gods. They then became the primary choice within the line of succession for rule, spawning the term 'Blue Bloods' for kingship royalty. However, as their lineage became diluted further, the tradition of human kingship eventually followed with select, loyal non-related humans becoming the BOPH gods' designated 'puppet rulers' over an ever increasing human population. Such a disparity in population numbers between the two species was always a prime concern of the BOPH gods.

The BOPH beings' previously mentioned preference for high altitude locations, with its corresponding lower atmospheric pressure and oxygen content, provided a more compatible environment for those 'gods.' Josef F. Blumrich, the NASA scientist who analyzed the Biblical *Book of Ezekiel*, concluded that the divine operators of the 'whirlwind' vessel discussed in his book came from a cold climate, one comparable to that of northern Scandinavia, Alaska, or Siberia.[3] The BOPH gods chose not to leave such a preferred environment unless absolutely necessary, leading to a common misconception that the BOPH gods attempted to hide their arrival or presence on Earth. To the contrary, the greater the number of humans who knew of the BOPH gods, the more followers and worshipers they would likely gain. Rather, they stayed in their remote sites by choice, preferring that specific environment to those favored by mortal humans. They also wanted to minimize most casual contact with humans, fearing their true fragility would be discovered, revealing them to be 'false gods.'

With the exception of sexual intimacy, the BOPH gods did not consider humans to be their equal, with certain 'gods' refusing to look upon or deal with humanity. But, by their own acts of sexual intimacy, the BOPH gods may have created their own eventual fate. The biological and genetic compatibility between humans and BOPH gods had been established during remote times, since both their origins were the same, although differentiated and altered through both environmental and genetic manipulations over time. Their original practice of mating with humans only when necessary to produce an offspring to continue their royal bloodline rule was eventually discarded by later generations of BOPH gods. Perhaps those younger BOPH gods 'saw the daughters of men how good they were, and took to themselves wives, and they bore children unto them.' Such promiscuity essentially obliterated any later differences between the BOPH gods and humans. However, a 'pure strain' bloodline might still remain, one that perhaps exists 'behind the scenes,' awaiting Earth's outcome when the Ancient Ones eventually return.

Over the millennia, the dilution of the BOPH gods' bloodline through interbreeding with various levels of demigod/human offspring eventually reached a steady state of blended DNA, resulting in only one genetic strain. Present humans could well be 'second generation' hybrids, as an admix combination of indigenous species and genetically altered extraterrestrial humanlike beings, which later combined with the related but 'manipulated' BOPH gods, those slightly less-altered descendants from the original humanlike outer planet 'seed.'

Obviously, that was not the case with the Ancient Ones, who were truly alien beings that journeyed to our solar system to impart civilization and create harmony. During their temporary exile, their evolving and continuing story may be connected with the modern UFO phenomenon. Their seemingly coy refusal to make 'open' contact with the humans of Earth might be in keeping with their agreement made thousands of years ago for non-intervention in humanity's affairs for some specified period of time. If the hypothesis presented in this writing is correct, Earth may be nearing the end of that agreed upon separation from the Cosmic Order and the Ancient Ones.

The Mayans, known as one of the most meticulous and concise cultures in their record keeping, dated our planet's current period as starting on August 13, 3113 BC, with its predicted end on December 21, 2012 AD. Those dates may reflect the start and planned end of Earth's separation from the Ancient Ones. The increased sightings of UFOs since 1947 may signify the Ancient Ones' early reconnaissance of Earth, in preparation for reestablishment of contact and its subsequent reinstatement within the Cosmic Order. It appears that the final chapters of this saga have yet to be written!

References

Chapter 1

1 David Hatcher Childress, *Lost Cities of Atlantis, Ancient Europe & The Mediterranean*, Adventures Unlimited Press, Stelle, Ill., 1996, p. 64.

2 270 minute taped interview discussing Mr. Childress' book: *Lost Cities of North & Central America*, available from Adventures Unlimited, PO Box 74, Kempton, Ill., Order code DHCR.

3 Jacques Bergier, *Extraterrestrial Visitations from Prehistoric Times to the Present* (hereafter referred to as *Extraterrestrial Visitations*), Henry Regnery Co., Chicago, 1973, pp. 28-29.

4 Peter Kolosimo, *Not of this World*, Bantam Books, New York, 1973, pp. 234-235.

5 Andrew Tomas, *We Are Not The First*, Bantam Books, New York, 1973, pp. 17-18.

Chapter 2

1 Alan and Sally Landsburg, *The Outer Space Connection*, Bantam Books, New York, 1975, pp. 63-64.

2 Zecharia Sitchin, *The 12th Planet*, Avon Books, New York, 1978, p. 253. See also Washington Press release: "Organic Molecules Found in Space," 1-13-2000.

3 Paul Recer, "Experts Confident of Life Beyond Earth," Associated Press article in The Ledger, Lakeland, Florida, 10-15-98.

4 Ibid.

5 Warren E. Leary, "3-D Map Shows Texture of Mars," New York Times article appearing in The Ledger, Lakeland, Florida, 5-28-1999. See also Science News article, "Discovery Sheds Light on Mars' Past," Tampa Tribune, 1999.

6 Andrew Tomas, *We Are Not The First*, op. cit., p. 4.

Chapter 3

1   Patrick Moore, *New Guide to the Moon*, Norton & Co., New York, 1976, p.19.

2   C. W. Ceram, *Gods, Graves, and Scholars*, Bantam Books, New York, 1972, p.164.

3   Warren Smith, *The Secret Forces of the Pyramids*, Zebra Books, New York, 1975, pp. 6-7.

4   Robert K. Moffett, *Secrets of the Pyramids Revealed*, Tempo Books, New York, 1976, p. 15.

5   Graham Hancock and Robert Bauval, *The Message of the Sphinx*, Three Rivers Press, New York, 1996, pp. 41 & 43.

6   I.E.S. Edwards, *The Pyramids of Egypt*, Viking Press, New York, 1972, p. 2. See also Brinsley Le Poer Trench, *Temple of the Stars*, Ballantine Books, New York, 1975, p. 113.

7   David Hatcher Childress, *Lost Cities of Atlantis, Ancient Europe & The Mediterranean*, Adventures Unlimited Press, Stelle, Ill., 1996, p. 351.

8   Robert K. Moffett, *Secrets of the Pyramids Revealed*, op. cit., p. 28.

9   Ibid., pp. 26-29. See also Warren Smith, *The Secret Forces of the Pyramids*, op. cit., p. 15.

10 Herodotus, *History of Herodotus*, trans. by George Rawlinson, ed. by Manuel Komroff, Tudor Pub., New York, 1941, p. 143. See also Warren Smith, *The Secret Forces of the Pyramids*, op. cit., p. 36.

11 Warren Smith, *The Secret Forces of the Pyramids*, op. cit., p. 8.

12 Zecharia Sitchin, *The Stairway to Heaven*, Avon Books, New York, 1983, pp. 262-277, 281-282.

13 Zecharia Sitchin, *The Wars of Gods and Men*, Avon Books, New York, 1985, p. 136.

14 Graham Hancock, *Fingerprints of the Gods*, Crown Publishers, New York, 1995, p. 303.

Chapter 4

1   Graham Hancock and Robert Bauval, *The Message of the Sphinx*, Three Rivers Press, New York, 1996, p.23.
2   Erich von Däniken, *The Eyes of the Sphinx*, Berkley Books, New York, 1996, pp. 124-125.
3   James Bailey, *The God-Kings & The Titans*, St. Martin's Press, New York, 1973, p. 54. See also Graham Hancock, *Fingerprints of the Gods*, Crown Publishers, New York, 1995, p. 115.
4   Ibid.

Chapter 5

1   Robert Lee Hotz, "Universe Is 12 or 13 Billion Years Old," Los Angeles Times article in The Ledger, Lakeland, Fla., 5-26-99.
2   Richard Golob and Eric Brus, *The Almanac of Science and Technology*, Harcourt, Brace, and Jovanovich, Orlando, Fla., 1990, pp. 469 & 472-473. See also James Glanz, "Cosmic Clue May Give Answer to Big Bang," New York Times article in The Ledger, Lakeland, Fla., 11-26-99.
3   Richard Golob and Eric Brus, *The Almanac of Science and Technology*, op. cit., pp. 438, 443. See also Paul A. Driscoll, "Scientists Find First Evidence of Top Quark," Associated Press article in the Tennessean, Nashville, Tenn., 5-1-94; and Curt Suplee, "Elusive Particle is Found," Washington Post, 3-3-95.
4   Richard Golob and Eric Brus, *The Almanac of Science and Technology*, op. cit., pp. 438- 440.
5   Paul A. Driscoll, "Scientists Find First Evidence of Top Quark," op. cit.; and Curt Suplee, "Elusive Particle is Found," op. cit.
6   Richard Golob and Eric Brus, *The Almanac of Science and Technology*, op. cit., pp. 438 & 444. See also Alex Higgins,

"Experiment Yields Evidence Supporting Big Bang Theory," Associated Press, 2000.

7   Richard Golob and Eric Brus, *The Almanac of Science and Technology*, op. cit., p. 473.
8   William Bramley, *The Gods of Eden*, Avon Books, New York, 1993, pp. 105-106.
9   Richard Golob and Eric Brus, *The Almanac of Science and Technology*, op. cit., pp. 438 & 470. See also James Trefil, *The Edge of the Unknown*, Houghton Mifflin, New York, 1996.
10 Richard Golob and Eric Brus, *The Almanac of Science and Technology*, op. cit., p. 34.
11 Paul Recer, "Astronomers Open Way to New Planets," Associated Press, 2001.
12 Walter Sullivan, *We Are Not Alone*, Signet Books, New York, 1966, p. 200.

Chapter 6
1   Cornelius Loew, *Myth, Sacred History, and Philosophy*, Harcourt, Brace & World, New York, 1967, pp. 33, 42, & 69.
2   Ibid., p. 67.
3   Ibid., pp. 68-69.
4   Gualberto Zapata Alonzo, *An Overview of the Mayan World*, Litoarte Printing, Mexico, 1987.
5   H. P. Blavatsky, *The Secret Doctrine*, Theosophical University Press, Pasadena, Calif., 1988, Vol. 1, pp. 429-431.
6   *The Urantia Book*, The Urantia Foundation, Chicago, 1955, p. 198.
7   Ibid., pp. 166, 178, & 198.
8   Ibid., p. 166.
9   *Rig Veda*, trans. by Wendy D. O'Flaherty, Penguin Books, New York, 1981, pp. 37 & 70; in reference to the Asura (aka Sura).
10 *Book of Dzyan*, reproduced in H. P. Blavatsky's *The Secret Doctrine*, op. cit., Stanza VII, verse 1, lines 6, 7, & 8.

11 Erich von Däniken, *Gods from Outer Space*, Bantam Books, New York, 1972, p. 134.
12 *The Urantia Book*, op. cit., p. 144.
13 H. P. Blavatsky, *The Secret Doctrine*, op. cit., commentary on the *Book of Dzyan*, Stanza II.1., p. 53.
14 Ibid., Stanza II.5., p. 60.
15 *Book of Dzyan*, Stanza V, verse 1, lines 1 & 2; as reproduced in H. P. Blavatsky's *The Secret Doctrine*, op. cit., p. 31.
16 *The Urantia Book*, op. cit., p. 164.
17 Ibid., p. 197.
18 Erich von Däniken, *In Search of Ancient Gods*, G. P. Putnam's Sons, New York, 1974, pp. 88-89.
19 Walter Sullivan, *We Are Not Alone*, op. cit., p. 197.
20 Ibid., p. 203.
21 Ibid., p. 202.
22 W. Raymond Drake, *Gods and Spacemen In The Ancient East*, Signet Books, New York, 1973, p. 17.
23 Walter Sullivan, *We Are Not Alone*, op. cit., pp. 203-205.
24 Ibid., p. 206.

Chapter 7

1 Robert S. Boyd, "Saltwater Found in Meteorite," Knight-Ridder Newspapers, article appearing in The Ledger, Lakeland, Fla., 8-27-99. Meteorite found near Monahans, Texas, on 3-22-98, and examined by NASA at the Johnson Space Center by scientific team headed by Michael Zolensky.
2 Walter Sullivan, *We Are Not Alone*, op. cit., p. 121.
3 Brinsley Le Poer Trench, *The Sky People*, Award Books, New York, 1970, pp. 159-160.
4 Ibid.
5 Walter Sullivan, *We Are Not Alone*, op. cit., p. 46.
6 Donald E. Keyhole, *Aliens From Space*, Signet Books, New York, 1974, pp. 136-138.
7 Ibid., p. 138.

8   Patrick Moore, *New Guide to the Moon*, op. cit., p. 199. See also David Hatcher Childress, *Extraterrestrial Archaeology*, Adventures Unlimited Press, Stelle, Ill., 1995.

9   Ibid., p. 197.

Chapter 8

1   Paul Recer, "Experts Confident of Life Beyond Earth," op. cit.

2   Eric Chaisson, *Cosmic Dawn*, Berkley Books, New York, 1984, p.153.

3   Paul Recer, "Scientists Complete First Map of Genes," Associated Press, 1999.

4   Eric Chaisson, *Cosmic Dawn*, op. cit., p. 168.

5   Ibid., p. 169.

6   David Dineley, *Earth's Voyage Through Time*, Knopf Books, New York, 1974, pp. 158-159, & 162.

7   Washington Press release, "Study Finds Existence of Third Branch of Life," 1999.

8   Peter Svensson, "Early Man Shown to be Smarter," Associated Press, May 1999. See also John Noble Wilford, "Fossil Discovery Fuels Missing-Link Debate," New York Times article in The Ledger, Lakeland, Fla., 4-25-99.

9   Encarta 98 Encyclopedia, Microsoft Corp., 1998 ed., Topic: "Homo erectus."

10 Associated Press report, "Wooden Spear Discovery Shows Man Hunted Earlier then Thought," 1998.

11 Herbie Brennan, *Martian Genesis*, Dell Publishing, New York, 1998, p. 25. See also John E. Pfeiffer, *The Emergence of Man*, Harper & Row, New York, 1969, p. 153.

12 John E. Pfeiffer, *The Emergence of Man*, op.cit., p. 156.

13 Ibid., pp. 93-94.

Chapter 9

1   Jacquetta Hawkes, *History of Mankind* (Vol. 1, Pt. 1: *Prehistory*), Mentor Books, New York, 1965, p. 101.

2   John E. Pfeiffer, *The Emergence of Man*, op. cit., p. 153. See also John Maynard Smith, *The Theory of Evolution*, Penguin Books, Baltimore, MD., pp. 299-300.

3   John E. Pfeiffer, *The Emergence of Man*, op. cit., p. 153.

4   Herbie Brennan, *Martian Genesis*, op. cit., p. 25.

5   *The Emergence of Man*, op. cit., p. 155. See also Michael H. Day, *Fossil Man*, Bantam Books, New York, 1971, p.121.

6   News Service article from Paris, France, "Fossil Suggests Nice Neanderthals," 10-13-01.

7   Jacquetta Hawkes, *History of Mankind* (Vol. 1, Pt. 1: *Prehistory*), op. cit., p.102.

8   Michael Pollak, "Neanderthal Isn't Extinct Online," New York Times article in The Ledger, Lakeland, Fla., 5-9-99.

9   Washington Press release, "Neanderthal Bones Date to Human Era," 10-26-99.

10   Barry Hatton, "Skeleton May Help Clarify Genesis of Man," Associated Press report in The Ledger, Lakeland, Fla., 4-17-99.

11   William Howells, *Back of History*, Natural History Library, U.S.A., 1963, pp. 88-89.

Chapter 10

1   Patrick Moore, *New Guide to the Moon*, op. cit., p. 129.

2   Ibid.

3   David Hatcher Childress, *Extraterrestrial Archaeology*, op. cit., p. 33.

4   Patrick Moore, *New Guide to the Moon*, op. cit., pp. 200-201.

5   Ibid., p. 201.

6   David Hatcher Childress, *Extraterrestrial Archaeology*, op. cit., pp. 67, 115-116.

7   Ibid., pp. 40-41.   See also Don Wilson, *Secrets of Our Spaceship Moon*, Dell Books, New York, 1979, pp. 13-14.

8   David Hatcher Childress, *Extraterrestrial Archaeology*, op. cit., p. 100.

9 George Leonard, *Somebody Else Is On The Moon*, Pocket Books, New York, 1976.

10 William Bramley, *The Gods of Eden*, op. cit., p. 59. See also Don Wilson, *Secrets of Our Spaceship Moon*, op. cit., pp. 19-21.

11 Peter Kolosimo, *Not of this World*, op. cit., p. 146.

12 Ibid., pp. 147-148.

13 Patrick Moore, *New Guide to the Moon*, op. cit., p. 169.

14 Ibid.

15 Ibid., p. 201.

16 David Hatcher Childress, *Extraterrestrial Archaeology*, op. cit., p. 105.

17 Don Wilson, *Secrets of Our Spaceship Moon*, op. cit., pp. 239-241.

18 Zecharia Sitchin, *Genesis Revisited*, Avon Books, New York, 1990, p. 280.

19 Numerous sources, including but not limited to: Zecharia Sitchin, *Genesis Revisited*, op. cit., pp. 248-254; David Hatcher Childress, *Extraterrestrial Archaeology*, op. cit., pp. 189-191; and Graham Hancock, *The Mars Mystery*, Three Rivers Press, New York, 1998, pp. 75, 79, & 82; Mark Carlotto, *The Martian Enigmas: A Closer Look*, North Atlantic Books, Berkeley, Calif., 1991, various pages including 53, 74-75, & 78-79; and Richard C. Hoagland, *The Monuments of Mars*, North Atlantic Books, Berkeley, Calif., 1987.

20 Zecharia Sitchin, *Genesis Revisited*, op. cit., p. 253.

21 William Bramley, *The Gods of Eden*, op. cit., p. 60.

22 Zecharia Sitchin, *Genesis Revisited*, op. cit., pp. 254-257. See also David Hatcher Childress, *Extraterrestrial Archaeology*, op. cit., p. 193; and Graham Hancock, *The Mars Mystery*, op. cit., p. 64.

23 David Hatcher Childress, *Extraterrestrial Archaeology*, op. cit., p. 218.

24 Ibid., p. 219.

25 Zecharia Sitchin, *Genesis Revisited*, op. cit., pp. 266-267.
26 Walter Sullivan, *We Are Not Alone*, op. cit., p. 166.
27 Ibid., pp. 165-166. See also Donald E. Keyhole, *Aliens From Space*, op. cit., p. 139.
28 Eric Norman, *Gods and Devils From Outer Space*, Lancer Books, New York, 1973, p. 171.

Chapter 11

1 Walter Sullivan, *We Are Not Alone*, op. cit., p. 121. See also Craig and Eric Umland, *Mysteries of the Ancients: Early Spacemen and the Mayas* (hereafter referred to as *Mysteries of the Ancients*), Walker and Co., New York, 1974, p. 104.
2 Ibid.
3 Frank Edwards, *Strange World*, Bantam Books, New York, 1969, p. 136. Conclusion was based on extensive study by astronomer Frank Halstead, Director of Darling Observatory, University of Minnesota at Duluth.
4 Craig and Eric Umland, *Mysteries of the Ancients*, op. cit., p. 108.
5 Ibid., p. 106.
6 Funk & Wagnalls New Encyclopedia, 1983 ed., Vol. 25, p. 183. See also Craig and Eric Umland, *Mysteries of the Ancients*, op. cit., pp. 106-111.
7 Walter Sullivan, *We Are Not Alone*, op. cit., p. 119.
8 Funk & Wagnalls New Encyclopedia, 1983 ed., Vol. 25, p. 183.
9 Charles Berlitz, *Charles Berlitz's World of the Odd and the Awesome* (hereafter referred to as *World of the Odd and Awesome*), Ballantine Books, New York, 1991, p. 38.
10 Ibid.
11 Ibid.

Chapter 12

1 Zecharia Sitchin, *Genesis Revisited*, op. cit., p. 253.

Chapter 13

1 Jacques Bergier & Editors of INFO, *Extraterrestrial Intervention*, Signet Books, New York, 1975, pp. 3-5.
2 Andrew Tomas, *We Are Not The First*, op. cit., p. 26.
3 Ibid.
4 Kelly L. Segraves, *Sons of God Return*, Pyramid Books, New York, 1975.
5 Andrew Tomas, *We Are Not The First*, op. cit., p. 26.
6 Craig and Eric Umland, *Mysteries of the Ancients*, op. cit., p. 128.
7 David Hatcher Childress, *Lost Cities of Atlantis, Ancient Europe & The Mediterranean*, op. cit., p. 173.
8 Ibid., p. 174.
9 Ibid.
10 Andrew Tomas, *We Are Not The First*, op. cit., p. 26. See also Warren Smith, *Lost Cities of the Ancients-Unearthed!*, Zebra Books, New York, 1976.
11 Jacques Bergier, *Extraterrestrial Visitations*, op. cit., p. 38. See also Andrew Tomas, *We Are Not The First*, op. cit., p. 27.
12 Herbie Brennan, *Martian Genesis*, op. cit., p. 36.
13 Ibid.
14 Jacques Bergier, *Extraterrestrial Visitations*, op. cit., p. 19.
15 R. Cedric Leonard, *Quest for Atlantis*, Manor Books, New York, 1979, p. 151.
16 Jacques Bergier, *Extraterrestrial Visitations*, op. cit., p. 19.
17 R. Cedric Leonard, *Quest for Atlantis*, op. cit., p. 151.
18 Charles Fort, *The Book of the Damned*, Ace Publishing, New York, 1919, p. 130.
19 R. Cedric Leonard, *Quest for Atlantis*, op. cit., p. 151.
20 Charles Fort, *The Book of the Damned*, op. cit., p. 130.
21 Eric Norman, *Gods, Demons and Space Chariots*, Lancer Books, New York, 1970, p. 13.
22 R. Cedric Leonard, *Quest for Atlantis*, op. cit., p. 151.
23 Charles Fort, *The Book of the Damned*, op. cit., p. 129.

24 Erich von Däniken, *The Gold of the Gods*, Bantam Books, New York, 1974, p. 199.

25 Andrew Tomas, *We Are Not The First*, Bantam Books, New York, 1973, p. 29.

26 Ibid.

27 Ibid.

28 Ibid.

29 Charles Fort, *The Book of the Damned*, op. cit., p. 128.

30 Jacques Bergier, *Extraterrestrial Visitations*, op. cit., p. 28.

31 Ibid.

32 Charles Fort, *The Book of the Damned*, op. cit., p. 128.

33 *Scientific American*, June 5, 1852, vol. 7, p. 298.

34 Jacques Bergier, *Extraterrestrial Visitations*, op. cit., p. 28.

35 Charles Fort, *The Book of the Damned*, op. cit., p. 130.

36 R. Cedric Leonard, *Quest for Atlantis*, op. cit., p. 152.

37 Alan and Sally Landsburg, *In Search of Ancient Mysteries*, Bantam Books, N.Y., 1974, p. 20.

38 Herbie Brennan, *Martian Genesis*, op. cit., p. 38.

39 R. Cedric Leonard, *Quest for Atlantis*, op. cit., pp. 151-152.

40 Ibid., p. 151.

41 Andrew Tomas, *We Are Not The First*, op. cit., p. 29.

42 Ibid., see also Charles Fort, *The Book of the Damned*, op. cit., p. 131.

43 Andrew Tomas, *We Are Not The First*, op. cit., p. 29. See also Charles Fort, *The Book of the Damned*, op. cit., pp. 130-131.

44 Craig and Eric Umland, *Mysteries of the Ancients*, op. cit., p. 159.

45 Herbie Brennan, *Martian Genesis*, op. cit., p. 39.

46 Frank Edwards, *Strange World*, Bantam Books, New York, 1969, p. 98. See also Herbie Brennan, *Martian Genesis*, op. cit., p. 39.

47 Jacques Bergier, *Extraterrestrial Visitations*, op. cit., p. 20. See also Frank Edwards, *Strange World*, op. cit., pp. 84-85.

48 R. Cedric Leonard, *Quest for Atlantis*, op. cit., p. 152. See also Jacques Bergier, *Extraterrestrial Visitations*, op. cit., p. 158.

49 Martin Ebon, *Atlantis: The New Evidence*, Signet Books, New York, 1977, p. 108.

50 Herbie Brennan, *Martian Genesis*, op. cit., p. 38.

Chapter 14

1 Peter Kolosimo, *Not of this World*, op. cit., p. 8.

2 Carl Sagan, *Cosmos*, Ballantine Books, New York, 1985, p. 285.

3 Andrew Tomas, *We Are Not The First*, op. cit., p. 24. See also R. Cedric Leonard, *Quest for Atlantis*, op. cit., p. 152.

4 Craig and Eric Umland, *Mysteries of the Ancients*, op. cit., p. 159.

5 Andrew Tomas, *We Are Not The First*, op. cit., p. 24.

6 Herbie Brennan, *Martian Genesis*, op. cit., p. 36.

7 Ibid.

8 John Wallace Spencer, *No Earthly Explanation*, op. cit., p. 83.

9 Funk & Wagnall's New Encyclopedia, 1983 ed., vol. 13, p. 271.

10 Ibid.

11 Ibid.

12 Craig and Eric Umland, *Mysteries of the Ancients*, op. cit., p. 94. Affected area included Oregon, Idaho, Nevada, and Northern California. Additional geological evidence indicates that New Mexico and parts of Arizona also experienced volcanic eruptions and lava cover.

13 Cartography data derived from various sources, including but not limited to: Charles H. Hapgood, *Maps of the Ancient Sea Kings*, Chilton Books, New York, 1966; M.H.J. Th. Van Der Veer and P. Moerman, *Hidden Worlds*, Bantam Books, New York, 1975; David Hatcher Childress, *Lost Cities of Atlantis, Ancient Europe & The Mediterranean*, op. cit.; J. V. Luce,

The End of Atlantis, Bantam Books, New York, 1978; Jacques Bergier, *Extraterrestrial Visitations*, op. cit.; Charles Berlitz, *Atlantis: The Eighth Continent*, Ballantine Books, New York, 1985.

14 Ibid.

15 Ibid.

16 David Hatcher Childress, *Lost Cities of Atlantis, Ancient Europe & The Mediterranean*, op. cit., p. 409.

17 Ibid., p. 396.

18 Cartography data derived from various sources, including but not limited to: Charles H. Hapgood, *Maps of the Ancient Sea Kings*, Chilton Books, New York, 1966; M.H.J. Th. Van Der Veer and P. Moerman, *Hidden Worlds*, Bantam Books, New York, 1975; David Hatcher Childress, *Lost Cities of Atlantis, Ancient Europe & The Mediterranean*, op. cit.; J. V. Luce, *The End of Atlantis*, Bantam Books, New York, 1978; Jacques Bergier, *Extraterrestrial Visitations*, op. cit.; Charles Berlitz, *Atlantis: The Eighth Continent*, Ballantine Books, New York, 1985.

19 Ibid.

20 Erich von Däniken, *Gods from Outer Space*, op. cit., p. 162.

21 Peter Kolosimo, *Not of this World*, op. cit., p. 90.

22 Ibid., p. 91.

23 John Wallace Spencer, *No Earthly Explanation*, Bantam Books, New York, 1975, pp. 82-83.

24 Ibid.

Chapter 15

1 Charles Berlitz, *Atlantis: The Eighth Continent*, op. cit., p. 14. See also Craig and Eric Umland, *Mysteries of the Ancients*, op. cit., p. 159.

2 Robert Charroux, *Masters of the World*, Berkley Medallion Books, New York, 1974, p. 16.

3 David Hatcher Childress, *Lost Cities of Atlantis, Ancient Europe & The Mediterranean*, op. cit., pp. 439-440. See also

Ralph Linton, *The Tree of Culture*, Vintage Books, New York, 1959, p. 224.

4 David Hatcher Childress, *Lost Cities of Atlantis, Ancient Europe & The Mediterranean*, op. cit., pp. 439-440.
5 Ibid.
6 Erich von Däniken, *Chariots of the Gods?*, Bantam Books, New York, 1971, p. 23.
7 Graham Hancock, *Fingerprints of the Gods*, op. cit., p. 221.
8 Zecharia Sitchin, *When Time Began*, Avon Books, New York, 1993, p. 247. See also Charles Berlitz, *Mysteries From Forgotten Worlds*, Dell Publishing, New York, 1972.
9 Graham Hancock, *Fingerprints of the Gods*, op. cit., p. 91.
10 Ignatius Donnelly, *Atlantis: The Antediluvian World*, rev. Egerton Sykes, Grammercy Pub., N.Y., 1949, p. 297. See also Craig & Eric Umland, *Mysteries of the Ancients*, op. cit., p. 159.
11 Ibid., p. 240.
12 Ibid.
13 Merlin Stone, *When God was a Woman*, Barnes & Noble, New York, 1993, p. 88. See also Walter B. Emery, *Archaic Egypt*, Penguin Books, New York, 1961.
14 Kenneth Macgowan and Joseph A. Hester, Jr., *Early Man in the New World*, Natural History Library/Anchor Books, New York, 1962, p. 182.
15 Ibid., pp. 182-183.
16 Ibid., p. 183.
17 Jean Sendy, *Those Gods Who Made Heaven & Earth*, Berkley Medallion Books, New York, 1972, p. 46.
18 James Churchward, *The Lost Continent of Mu*, Paperback Library, New York, 1968, pp. 99-100. See also James Churchward, *The Children of Mu*, Paperback Library, New York, 1968, pp. 180-181.
19 Erich von Däniken, *Chariots of the Gods?*, op. cit., p. 88.
20 Peter Kolosimo, *Not of this World*, op. cit., p. 44.

21 David Hatcher Childress, *Lost Cities of Atlantis, Ancient Europe & The Mediterranean*, op. cit., p. 329.
22 H. P. Blavatsky, *The Secret Doctrine*, op. cit., "Introductory.," pp. xxxii-xxxiii.
23 Ibid., p. xxxii.
24 Ignatius Donnelly, *Atlantis: The Antediluvian World*, op. cit., p. 234.
25 Ibid., pp. 230-239.
26 Ibid.
27 Ibid., p. 237.
28 Ibid., p. 238.
29 Jacques Bergier & Editors of INFO, *Extraterrestrial Intervention*, Signet Books, New York, 1975, pp. 18-19, article by Elton Caton, "The Mima Mounds."
30 Ibid., p. 19.
31 Ibid., pp. 19-20.
32 Jacques Bergier & Editors of INFO, *Extraterrestrial Intervention*, op. cit., p. 32, article by Andrew E. Rothovius, "The Mysterious Cement Cylinders of New Caledonia."
33 Ibid.
34 Ibid.
35 Peter Kolosimo, *Not of this World*, op. cit., p. 90.
36 Ibid., p. 93.
37 Ibid., p. 92.
38 Ibid.
39 Frank Edwards, *Strange World*, op. cit., p. 97. See also Alan and Sally Landsburg, *The Outer Space Connection*, Bantam Books, New York, 1975, pp. 126-127.
40 Ibid.
41 Frank Edwards, *Strange World*, op. cit., p. 97.
42 Graham Hancock, *Fingerprints of the Gods*, op. cit., p. 412.
43 Ibid.
44 William Howells, *Back of History*, Natural History Library, U.S.A., 1963, pp. 88-89.
45 Ibid.

46 Ignatius Donnelly, *Atlantis: The Antediluvian World*, op. cit., p. 27.

Chapter 16

1 Ignatius Donnelly, *Atlantis: The Antediluvian World*, op. cit., pp. 42-43. See also Charles Berlitz, *Atlantis: The Eighth Continent*, op. cit., p. 171.
2 Ibid., (although others have estimated that sea levels have risen as much as 600 feet.)
3 Ibid., pp. 197-199.
4 Ibid.
5 William Howells, *Back of History*, op. cit., pp. 33-34.
6 Ibid.
7 Ibid., p. 129.
8 Ibid., pp. 131-132.
9 Ibid., p. 33.
10 Ibid., pp. 33-34.
11 Jacquetta Hawkes, *History of Mankind* (Vol. 1, Pt. 1: *Prehistory*), op. cit., p. 437. See also *The World's Last Mysteries*, Reader's Digest, New York, 1980, p. 144; Andrew Tomas, *We Are Not The First*, op. cit., p. 23.
12 Andrew Tomas, *We Are Not The First*, op. cit., p. 17.
13 Charles Berlitz, *Atlantis: The Eighth Continent*, op. cit., p. 161. See also *The World's Last Mysteries*, Reader's Digest, op. cit., p. 147, 153.

Chapter 17

1 *Enuma elish*, Akkadian version, Tablet IV, lines 137, 138, 144 & 145; reproduced in *The Ancient Near East*, ed. James B. Pritchard, Princeton University Press, New Jersey, 1958, p. 35.
2 *Rig Veda*, Book 1, Hymn 32: *The Killing of Vrtra*, lines 1, 5, 7 & 11; trans. by Wendy D. O'Flaherty, Penguin Books, New York, 1981, pp. 149-150.
3 *The Urantia Book*, op. cit., pp. 602-604.

4 Ibid., p. 198.

5 Ibid., pp. 611-615, 619-620, & 808.

6 H. P. Blavatsky, *The Secret Doctrine*, op. cit., pp. 160 & 227. See also Peter Kolosimo, *Not of this World*, op. cit., p. 62.

7 Don Wilson, *Secrets of Our Spaceship Moon*, op. cit., p. 247.

8 *The Epic of Gilgamesh*, Akkadian version, Tablet XI, line 24; reproduced in *The Ancient Near East*, ed. James B. Pritchard, p. 66.

9 Ibid., line 27. See also *The Epic of Gilgamesh*, trans. & ed. by N. K. Sandars, Penguin Books, Baltimore, 1964, p. 105.

10 Robert Bauval and Adrian Gilbert, *The Orion Mystery*, Crown Pub., New York, 1994, pp. 121-124.

11 Ibid., p. 193.

12 Ibid. See also Graham Hancock and Robert Bauval, *The Message of the Sphinx*, op. cit., pp. 52-53.

13 Immanuel Velikovsky's interpretation contributed for New York Times article "Man Walks on Moon," referenced in *Velikovsky Reconsidered*, Eds. of Pensee, Warner Books, New York, 1976, p. 266. Article based on thermoluminescence studies conducted at Washington University, St. Louis, Mo., headed by R. Walker. Those studies concluded that disturbances responsible for the anomalies possibly occurred around 8000 BC, but the limited database for extracted material taken from any lunar site creates a wide variation in such inherent dating.

14 *The Kumarbi Myth* sometimes known as *The Story of Alalu, Anu, and Kumarbi*, and also as *The Struggle for Kingship Among the Gods*, referenced in *The Hittites*, O. R. Gurney, Penguin Books, Maryland, 1954, p. 190.

15 Ibid.

16 Ibid.

17 Graham Hancock and Robert Bauval, *The Message of the Sphinx*, op. cit., p.205.

18 Ibid.

19 Zecharia Sitchin, *When Time Began*, op. cit., p. 55.

20 Graham Hancock and Robert Bauval, *The Message of the Sphinx*, op. cit., p.204.

Chapter 18

1 Merlin Stone, *When God was a Woman*, op. cit., p. 80.
2 Ibid.
3 Ibid., p. 81.
4 Ignatius Donnelly, *Atlantis: The Antediluvian World*, op. cit., pp. 162-163.
5 H. P. Blavatsky, *The Secret Doctrine*, op. cit., pp. 653-654.
6 *Enuma elish*, Akkadian version, Tablet VI, line 42; reproduced in *The Ancient Near East*, ed. James B. Pritchard, op. cit., p. 37.
7 Geoffrey Bibby, *Looking for Dilmun*, Penguin Books, New York, 1972, p. 93, then see p.45.
8 Walter B. Emery, *Archaic Egypt*, Penguin Books, New York, 1961. See also Merlin Stone, *When God was a Woman*, op. cit., p. 88.
9 Alan and Sally Landsburg, *The Outer Space Connection*, op. cit., p.100.
10 Merlin Stone, *When God was a Woman*, op. cit., p. 87.
11 *Papyrus of Ani*, Chapter XVII, Sect. 112, from *The Book of the Dead*, trans. by Sir E. A. Wallis Budge, British Museum, London, 1895. See also W. Raymond Drake, *Gods and Spacemen In The Ancient East*, op. cit., p. 136.
12 Gualberto Zapata Alonzo, *An Overview of the Mayan World*, Litoarte Printing, Mexico, 1987: Long Count based on the Goodman-Martinez, Hernandez-Thompson calculation, although the Spinden Correlation (by Dr. J. Herbert Spinden, a noted authority on Mayan culture) arrives at a starting date of 3373 BC; See also Lewis Spence, *The History of Atlantis*, Bell Publishing, New York, 1968, pp. 158-159.
13 *Enuma elish*, Akkadian version, Tablet IV, lines 136-138 & 144-145; reproduced in *The Ancient Near East*, ed. James B. Pritchard, op. cit., p. 35.

14 *Rig Veda*, Book 1, Hymn 32: *The Killing of Vrtra*, line 8; trans. by Wendy D. O'Flaherty, op. cit., p. 150. See also 1.154.1&3, p. 226; 10.82.5, p. 36; 10.121.1, p. 27; & 7.104.21, p. 295.
15 Timothy Wyllie, *Dolphins*Extraterrestrials*Angels*, Bozon Enterprises, 1984.
16 W. Raymond Drake, *Gods and Spacemen In The Ancient East*, op. cit., p. 76. See also Andrew Tomas, *We Are Not The First*, op. cit., p. 116.
17 Ibid.
18 William L. Langer, ed., *Western Civilization*, American Heritage Pub., New York, 1968,   p. 35. See also Cornelius Loew, *Myth, Sacred History, and Philosophy*, op. cit., p. 52.

Chapter 19

1 Alan and Sally Landsburg, *In Search of Ancient Mysteries*, op. cit., p. 22.
2 Charles Berlitz, *Atlantis: The Eighth Continent*, op. cit., p. 155. See also Jacques Bergier, *Extraterrestrial Visitations*, op. cit., p. 158; James Churchward, *The Lost Continent of Mu*, op. cit., p. 189.
3 Jacques Bergier & Editors of INFO, *Extraterrestrial Intervention*, op. cit., p. 12, article by Ronald J. Willis, "The Coso Artifact."
4 Ibid., pp. 13-14.
5 Ibid., pp. 12-17.
6 Ibid., p. 14.
7 Craig and Eric Umland, *Mysteries of the Ancients*, op. cit., p. 159. See also Charles Berlitz, *Atlantis: The Eighth Continent*, op. cit., p. 14.
8 Zecharia Sitchin, *The 12th Planet*, op. cit., p. 324.
9 M.H.J. Th. Van Der Veer and P. Moerman, *Hidden Worlds*, op. cit., pp. 97-98. See also Craig and Eric Umland, *Mysteries of the Ancients*, op. cit., p. 157, and Alan and Sally Landsburg, *In Search of Ancient Mysteries*, op. cit., p. 20.

10 Alan and Sally Landsburg, *In Search of Ancient Mysteries*, op. cit., p. 20. See also Louis Pauwels and Jacques Bergier, *Morning of the Magicians*, Avon Books, New York, 1963.

11 Alan and Sally Landsburg, *In Search of Ancient Mysteries*, op. cit., p. 21. See also Craig and Eric Umland, *Mysteries of the Ancients*, op. cit., p. 158.

12 Frank Edwards, *Strange World*, op. cit., p. 98.

13 Ibid.

14 David Hatcher Childress, *Lost Cities of Atlantis, Ancient Europe & The Mediterranean*, op. cit., p. 266.

15 M.H.J. Th. Van Der Veer and P. Moerman, *Hidden Worlds*, op. cit., p. 100. See also Robert K. Moffett, *Secrets of the Pyramids Revealed*, Tempo Books, New York, 1976, and Charles Berlitz, *Mysteries From Forgotten Worlds*, op. cit., and Jacques Bergier, *Extraterrestrial Visitations*, op. cit., p. 158, stating a height of 18 feet. Descriptions vary somewhat on this column, see following backnote number 16.

16 Ibid., with Jacques Bergier stating a diameter of 18 inches. Note that M.H.J. Th. Van Der Veer and P. Moerman in *Hidden Worlds*, op. cit., p. 102, stated that the Delhi Pillar is often confused with the Dhar Pillar, also in India, a column originally over 45 feet high, estimated to weigh seven tons, but now broken into three pieces.

17 Robert K. Moffett, *Secrets of the Pyramids Revealed*, op. cit., p. 102.

18 Warren Smith, *The Secret Forces of the Pyramids*, Zebra Books, New York, 1975, p. 73.

19 Peter Kolosimo, *Not of this World*, op. cit., p. 239.

20 Erich von Däniken, *The Eyes of the Sphinx*, op. cit., pp. 193, 251-252.

21 Ibid., p. 200. See also Peter Kolosimo, *Not of this World*, op. cit., p. 239 where two statues, one black and the other white, are described as representing 'unusual beings.'

22 Graham Hancock, *Fingerprints of the Gods*, op. cit., p. 333.

23 Ibid.

24 Ibid., pp. 333-334.
25 Paul Recer, "Cave Dwellers Crafted Tough Shoes," Associated Press article, 1998.
26 Andrew Tomas, *We Are Not The First*, op. cit., p. 24.
27 Herbie Brennan, *Martian Genesis*, op. cit., p. 25.
28 Alan and Sally Landsburg, *The Outer Space Connection*, op. cit., p.55.
29 Ibid.
30 Andrew Tomas, *We Are Not The First*, op. cit., p. 48.
31 Ibid.
32 Ibid.
33 Alan and Sally Landsburg, *The Outer Space Connection*, op. cit., p.14.
34 Ibid., p. 52.
35 Ibid.
36 Andrew Tomas, *We Are Not The First*, op. cit., p. 49.
37 Ibid.
38 Alan and Sally Landsburg, *The Outer Space Connection*, op. cit., p.12.
39 Ibid.
40 Peter Kolosimo, *Not of this World*, op. cit., p. 230.
41 Alan and Sally Landsburg, *In Search of Ancient Mysteries*, op. cit., p. 21.
42 Charles Berlitz, *World of the Odd and the Awesome*, op. cit., p. 200.
43 Charles Berlitz, *Atlantis: The Eighth Continent*, op. cit., pp. 134-135. See also Charles Fort, *The Book of the Damned*, op. cit., p. 132.
44 Erich von Däniken, *In Search of Ancient Gods*, op. cit., p.173.
45 Eric Norman, *Gods and Devils From Outer Space*, op. cit., p. 91.
46 Andrew Tomas, *We Are Not The First*, op. cit., p. 54.
47 Alan and Sally Landsburg, *In Search of Ancient Mysteries*, op. cit., p. 21.
48 Ibid.

49 Maurice Chatelain, *Our Ancestors Came From Outer Space*, Dell Publishing, New York, 1978, pp. 110-120. See also David Hatcher Childress, *Lost Cities of Atlantis, Ancient Europe & The Mediterranean*, op. cit., pp. 119-121; Erich von Däniken, *In Search of Ancient Gods*, op. cit., pp. 130-131; Charles Berlitz, *Atlantis: The Eighth Continent*, op. cit., p. 138; and William Corliss, *Ancient Man: A Handbook of Puzzling Artifacts*, The Sourcebook Project, Glen Arm, Md., 1978.

50 Erich von Däniken, *In Search of Ancient Gods*, op. cit., p. 131. See also Charles Berlitz, *Atlantis: The Eighth Continent*, op. cit., p. 138.

51 Erich von Däniken, *The Eyes of the Sphinx*, op. cit., p. 170. See also Alan and Sally Landsburg, *The Outer Space Connection*, op. cit., p.132; and Charles Berlitz, *Atlantis: The Eighth Continent*, op. cit., p. 139.

52 Erich von Däniken, *The Eyes of the Sphinx*, op. cit., p. 170. See also David Hatcher Childress, *Lost Cities of Atlantis, Ancient Europe & The Mediterranean*, op. cit., p. 121; and William Corliss, *Ancient Man: A Handbook of Puzzling Artifacts*, op. cit.

53 Charles Berlitz, *Mysteries From Forgotten Worlds*, op. cit., p. 55.

54 Andrew Tomas, *We Are Not The First*, op. cit., p. 95, quote taken from the *Agastya Samhita*.

55 David Hatcher Childress, *Lost Cities of Atlantis, Ancient Europe & The Mediterranean*, op. cit., p. 19.

56 Erich von Däniken, *The Eyes of the Sphinx*, op. cit., pp. 172-173. See also Charles Berlitz, *Atlantis: The Eighth Continent*, op. cit., p. 140.

57 Erich von Däniken, *The Eyes of the Sphinx*, op. cit., pp. 172-173. See also E. A. Wallis Budge, *Egyptian Magic*, Citadel Press/Carol Publishing, New York, 1991, p. 47.

58 E. A. Wallis Budge, *Egyptian Magic*, op. cit., p. 47.

59 David Hatcher Childress, *Lost Cities of Atlantis, Ancient Europe & The Mediterranean*, op. cit., p. 18.

60 Erich von Däniken, *In Search of Ancient Gods*, op. cit., p. 171.

61 Ibid. See also Charles Berlitz, *Atlantis: The Eighth Continent*, op. cit., p. 143.

62 Erich von Däniken, *In Search of Ancient Gods*, op. cit., p. 172. See also Charles Berlitz, *Atlantis: The Eighth Continent*, op. cit., p. 142.

63 Erich von Däniken, *In Search of Ancient Gods*, op. cit., pp. 178-179.

64 Charles Berlitz, *Atlantis: The Eighth Continent*, op. cit., p. 224; quote taken from the *Samarangana Sutradhara*.

65 W. Raymond Drake, *Gods and Spacemen In The Ancient East*, Signet Books, New York, 1973, p. 28. See also Peter Kolosimo, *Not of this World*, op. cit., p. 9; and Erich von Däniken, *In Search of Ancient Gods*, op. cit., p. 173.

66 W. Raymond Drake, *Gods and Spacemen In The Ancient East*, op. cit., p. 28. See also Peter Kolosimo, *Not of this World*, op. cit., p. 10.

Chapter 20

1 Graham Hancock, *Fingerprints of the Gods*, op. cit., from reference section, p. 554.

2 Erich von Däniken, *The Gold of the Gods*, op. cit., p. 202.

3 Robert Charroux, *Masters of the World*, op. cit., p. 216.

4 W. Raymond Drake, *Gods And Spacemen of the Ancient Past*, Signet Books, New York, 1974, p. 239. See also Irwin Ginsburgh, *First, Man. Then, Adam!*, Pocket Books, New York, 1975, as referenced from L. Ginzberg, *Legends of the Bible*, Jewish Pub. Society of America, Philadelphia, 1972.

5 Ignatius Donnelly, *Atlantis: The Antediluvian World*, op. cit., p. 288.

6 Erich von Däniken, *The Eyes of the Sphinx*, op. cit., p. 165.

7 Herodotus, *History of Herodotus*, op. cit., pp. 133-134.

8   Erich von Däniken, *The Eyes of the Sphinx*, op. cit., pp. 81-83, 86-87, & 94-97. See also Herodotus, *History of Herodotus*, op. cit., pp. 133-134; Peter Kolosimo, *Not of this World*, op. cit., p. 237; and Warren Smith, *The Secret Forces of the Pyramids*, op. cit., pp. 40-41.

9   George C. Andrews, *Extra-Terrestrials Among Us*, Llewellyn Publications, 1995, p. 74. See also W. Raymond Drake, *Gods and Spacemen In The Ancient East*, op. cit., p. 73.

10 H. P. Blavatsky, *The Secret Doctrine*, op. cit., p. 563. See also W. Raymond Drake, *Gods and Spacemen In The Ancient East*, op. cit., pp. 73 & 112.

11 W. Raymond Drake, *Gods and Spacemen In The Ancient East*, op. cit., p. 119.

Chapter 21

1   Rupert Furneaux, *Ancient Mysteries*, Ballantine Books, New York, 1978, pp. 133-135, & 137. See also Zecharia Sitchin, *When Time Began*, op. cit., pp. 32 & 39-42.

2   Rupert Furneaux, *Ancient Mysteries*, op. cit., pp. 138-139.

3   David Hatcher Childress, *Lost Cities of Atlantis, Ancient Europe & The Mediterranean*, op. cit., pp. 30 & 82.

4   R. Cedric Leonard, *Quest for Atlantis*, op. cit., pp. 41-43. See also Maurice Chatelain, *Our Ancestors Came From Outer Space*, op. cit., pp. 219-220; Charles Berlitz, *Mysteries From Forgotten Worlds*, op. cit., pp. 92-94; and Charles Berlitz, *Atlantis: The Eighth Continent*, op. cit., pp. 97-100 & 102-103.

5   Ibid.

6   Edgar Evans Cayce, *Edgar Cayce On Atlantis*, Warner Books, New York, 1968, p. 157; based on a 'life reading' conducted on June 28, 1940.

7   David Hatcher Childress, *Lost Cities of Atlantis, Ancient Europe & The Mediterranean*, op. cit., p. 206.

8   Ibid., p. 207.

9   Ibid., p. 210.

10 Ibid.
11 Ibid., p. 151.
12 Ibid., p. 148.
13 Ibid., p. 150.
14 Graham Hancock and Robert Bauval, *The Message of the Sphinx*, op. cit., p. 52.
15 Graham Hancock, *Fingerprints of the Gods*, op. cit., p. 420.
16 Ibid., p. 415. See also Erich von Däniken, *The Eyes of the Sphinx*, op. cit., p. 253.
17 Graham Hancock, *Fingerprints of the Gods*, op. cit., p. 501.
18 Erich von Däniken, *The Eyes of the Sphinx*, op. cit., p. 24.

Chapter 22

1 Peter Kolosimo, *Not of this World*, op. cit., p. 156. See also *Quest for the Past*, Reader's Digest, Pleasantville, N.Y., 1984.
2 Graham Hancock, *Fingerprints of the Gods*, op. cit., pp. 84-86.
3 Ibid., p. 89.
4 Radio interview with David Hatcher Childress on the *Coast to Coast AM* program with Art Bell on 7-13-2001.
5 Thor Heyerdahl, *Early Man and the Ocean*, Doubleday & Co., New York, 1978, pp. 165, 242-248 & 291.
6 Peter Kolosimo, *Not of this World*, op. cit., p. 143.
7 George C. Andrews, *Extra-Terrestrials Among Us*, op. cit., p. 95.
8 Rupert Furneaux, *Ancient Mysteries*, op. cit., pp. 38-39.
9 Peter Kolosimo, *Not of this World*, op. cit., p. 150.
10 Eklal Kueshana, *The Ultimate Frontier*, The Stelle Group, Chicago, Ill., 1963, p. 68. See also Charles Berlitz, *Mysteries From Forgotten Worlds*, op. cit., p. 124.
11 Eklal Kueshana, *The Ultimate Frontier*, op. cit., p. 69.
12 Ibid.
13 Alan Landsburg, *In Search of Lost Civilizations*, Bantam Books, New York, 1976, p. 193.
14 Eklal Kueshana, *The Ultimate Frontier*, op. cit., p. 69.

15 Ibid.

Chapter 23

1 David Hatcher Childress, *Lost Cities of Atlantis, Ancient Europe & The Mediterranean*, op. cit., p. 149.
2 Ibid., pp. 149-150.
3 Ibid., p. 34.
4 Ibid.
5 *Some Trust in Chariots*, eds. Barry Thiering and Edgar Castle, Popular Library, New York, 1972, p. 68.
6 The Awesome Saw, the weapon of the sun god, is mentioned in the *Enuma elish*, Babylonian version, Tablet III, line 7; reproduced in David Adams Leeming, *The World of Myth*, Oxford University Press, New York, 1990, p. 21. The Olden Copper Lance was referenced by Zecharia Sitchin, *The 12th Planet*, op. cit., p. 71.
7 Graham Hancock, *Fingerprints of the Gods*, op. cit., p. 331.
8 Ibid., pp. 331-332.
9 Erich von Däniken, *The Eyes of the Sphinx*, op. cit., pp. 142, 144-145.
10 Ibid., p. 144.
11 Ibid.
12 Ibid., p. 143.
13 Ibid.
14 Richard F. Dempewolff, ed., *Lost Cities and Forgotten Tribes*, Pocket Books, N.Y., 1974.
15 Ibid.
16 Robert Charroux, *Masters of the World*, op. cit., p. 215.
17 Ibid.
18 Ibid., p. 216.
19 Charles Berlitz, *Mysteries From Forgotten Worlds*, op. cit., pp. 74-76. See also Charles Berlitz, *World of the Odd and the Awesome*, op. cit., pp. 235-236; Warren Smith, *The Secret Forces of the Pyramids*, op. cit., p. 166; and Robert Charroux, *Masters of the World*, op. cit., p. 216.

20 Ibid.
21 Charles Berlitz, *Mysteries From Forgotten Worlds*, op. cit., pp. 74-75.
22 Ibid., p. 74.
23 Ibid., p. 75.
24 Eric Norman, *Gods and Devils From Outer Space*, op. cit., pp. 88-89.
25 George C. Andrews, *Extra-Terrestrials Among Us*, op. cit., pp. 121-123, 164, & 335.
26 Zecharia Sitchin, *The Lost Realms*, Avon Books, New York, 1990, pp. 59-62.
27 Andrew Tomas, *We Are Not The First*, op. cit., p. 99. See also Warren Smith, *The Secret Forces of the Pyramids*, op. cit., pp. 149-150.
28 Ibid.

Chapter 24

1 Andrew Tomas, *We Are Not The First*, op. cit., p. 58.
2 David Hatcher Childress, *Lost Cities of Atlantis, Ancient Europe & The Mediterranean*, op. cit., p. 262.
3 Ibid., p. 263.
4 Ibid., pp. 262-263.
5 Charles Berlitz, *Atlantis: The Eighth Continent*, op. cit., p. 136. See also R. Cedric Leonard, *Quest for Atlantis*, op. cit., pp. 159-160; Erich von Däniken, *The Gold of the Gods*, op. cit., p. 203.
6 Ibid.
7 Charles Berlitz, *Mysteries From Forgotten Worlds*, op. cit., p. 162. See also Andrew Tomas, *We Are Not The First*, op. cit., p. 77; David Hatcher Childress, *Lost Cities of Atlantis, Ancient Europe & The Mediterranean*, op. cit., p. 302.
8 George C. Andrews, *Extra-Terrestrials Among Us*, op. cit., p. 39.

9 Erich von Däniken, *Gods from Outer Space*, op. cit., pp. 67, 69-70. See also Erich von Däniken, *Chariots of the Gods?*, op. cit., p. 78 ff.

10 Craig and Eric Umland, *Mysteries of the Ancients*, op. cit., p. 87. See also Erich von Däniken, *Gods from Outer Space*, op. cit., p. 85.

11 Alan and Sally Landsburg, *The Outer Space Connection*, op. cit., pp. 158-159.

12 Erich von Däniken, *In Search of Ancient Gods*, op. cit., p. 132.

13 Andrew Tomas, *We Are Not The First*, op. cit., p. 20.

14 Donald E. Keyhoe, *Aliens From Space*, Signet Books, New York, 1974, p. 194. See also Peter Kolosimo, *Not of this World*, op. cit., p. 83.

15 Erich von Däniken, *In Search of Ancient Gods*, op. cit., p. 64.

16 Ibid., p. 69. See also Erich von Däniken, *Chariots of the Gods?*, op. cit., p. 78 ff.

17 Erich von Däniken, *Gods from Outer Space*, op. cit., p. 84 ff.

18 Ibid.

19 Charles Berlitz, *World of the Odd and the Awesome*, op. cit., p. 12.

20 Erich von Däniken, *The Gold of the Gods*, op. cit., p. 43.

21 Erich von Däniken, *In Search of Ancient Gods*, op. cit., p. 191.

22 Ibid., pp. 72-73.

Chapter 25

1 William L. Langer, ed., *Western Civilization*, op. cit., p. 31.

2 Charles Berlitz, *Atlantis: The Eighth Continent*, op. cit., p. 15.

3 Ignatius Donnelly, *Atlantis: The Antediluvian World*, op. cit., p. 303.

4 Ibid., p. 274. See also Erich von Däniken, *The Eyes of the Sphinx*, op. cit., pp. 212-213.

5 Ignatius Donnelly, *Atlantis: The Antediluvian World*, op. cit., p. 274.

6   Brinsley Le Poer Trench, *Temple of the Stars*, op. cit., p. 115.
7   Ibid.
8   Charles Berlitz, *Mysteries From Forgotten Worlds*, op. cit., p. 166.
9   Ignatius Donnelly, *Atlantis: The Antediluvian World*, op. cit., p. 303.
10 Herodotus, *History of Herodotus*, op. cit., p. 131. Herodotus was told by Egyptian priests that Egypt's <u>written</u> history dated back 11,340 years before his visit, which is thought to have occurred between 459 and 449 BC. That equated to the start of Egyptian writing between 11,799 and 11,789 BC (i.e. *c.*11,800 BC). See also Ignatius Donnelly, *Atlantis: The Antediluvian World*, op. cit., p. 108; & Peter Kolosimo, *Not of this World*, op. cit., p. 167.
11 H. P. Blavatsky, *The Secret Doctrine*, op. cit., "Introductory.," pp. xlii-xliii.
12 Ibid.
13 James Bailey, *The God-Kings & The Titans*, op. cit., pp. 174-175 & 181.
14 Ibid.
15 Charles Fort, *The Book of the Damned*, op. cit., p. 202.
16 Ibid.
17 Ibid., p. 203.
18 William L. Langer, ed., *Western Civilization*, op. cit., p. 38.
19 Merlin Stone, *When God was a Woman*, op. cit., p. 193.

Chapter 26
1   Robert Charroux, *Masters of the World*, op. cit., p. 29.
2   Ibid., p. 30.
3   H. P. Blavatsky, *The Secret Doctrine*, op. cit., "Introductory.," pp. xxvi.
4   L. Sprague de Camp, *The Ancient Engineers*, Ballantine Books, New York, 1984, p. 145.
5   Ibid., p. 144.

6   Murry Hope, *The Sirius Connection: Unlocking the Secrets of Ancient Egypt* (hereafter referred to as *The Sirius Connection*), Element Books, Rockport, Mass., 1996, p. 204.
7   Ibid.
8   Andrew Tomas, *We Are Not The First*, op. cit., p. 9.
9   Ibid.
10 Pliny, *Natural History*, Vol. II, Chapt. XXXIV. See also Eric Norman, *Gods, Demons and Space Chariots*, op. cit., p. 128.
11 W. Raymond Drake, *Gods And Spacemen of the Ancient Past*, op. cit., p. 194.

Chapter 27
1   E. A. Wallis Budge, *Egyptian Magic*, op. cit., p. 51.
2   Ibid., pp. 51-52. See also Graham Hancock and Robert Bauval, *The Message of the Sphinx*, op. cit., pp. 79 & 109.
3   Graham Hancock and Robert Bauval, *The Message of the Sphinx*, op. cit., p. 109.
4   *The Egyptian Book of the Dead*, (Theban recension), trans. Dr. Raymond O. Faulkner, op. cit., p. 18.
5   Warren Smith, *The Secret Forces of the Pyramids*, op. cit., p. 46.
6   *The Egyptian Book of the Dead*, (Theban recension), trans. Dr. Raymond O. Faulkner, op. cit., p. 160.
7   Sybil Leek, *Reincarnation: The Second Chance*, Bantam Books, New York, 1975, p. 105.
8   Andrew Tomas, *We Are Not The First*, op. cit., p. 51.
9   Paramahansa Yogananda, *Autobiography of a Yogi*, Self-Realization Fellowship, USA, 1981, p. 22 (footnote).
10 Ibid., p. 100 (footnote).
11 Ibid.
12 *Rig Veda*, Book 1, Hymn 32: *The Killing of Vrtra*, line 5; trans. by Wendy D. O'Flaherty, op. cit., pp. 148-149.
13 *Vishnu Purana*, Hymn 32, Vol. II, trans. by H. H. Wilson, Trubner & Co., London, 1865, Chapter XII, p.305. See also R. Cedric Leonard, *Quest for Atlantis*, op. cit., p. 128.

14 R. Cedric Leonard, *Quest for Atlantis*, op. cit., p. 125.
15 *Mahabharata*, Vol. 5., (*The Book of the Effort*), as ref. by Andrew Tomas, *We Are Not The First*, op. cit., p. 117.
16 Ibid.
17 R. Cedric Leonard, *Quest for Atlantis*, op. cit., pp. 134-135. See also Andrew Tomas, *We Are Not The First*, op. cit., p. 110.
18 R. Cedric Leonard, *Quest for Atlantis*, op. cit., p. 134. See also Andrew Tomas, *We Are Not The First*, op. cit., p. 116.
19 Andrew Tomas, *We Are Not The First*, op. cit., p. 109.
20 R. Cedric Leonard, *Quest for Atlantis*, op. cit., p. 125.
21 Ibid., pp. 125-126. See also Andrew Tomas, *We Are Not The First*, op. cit., p. 110.
22 R. Cedric Leonard, *Quest for Atlantis*, op. cit., p. 127.
23 Ibid., p. 134.
24 Ibid., p. 129. See also Andrew Tomas, *We Are Not The First*, op. cit., p. 14.
25 Ibid.
26 Andrew Tomas, *We Are Not The First*, op. cit., p. 116.
27 *I Ching*, ed. Raymond Van Over, (trans. James Legge), Mentor Books, New York, 1971, p. 334.
28 H. P. Blavatsky, *The Secret Doctrine*, op. cit., p. 478.
29 Erich von Däniken, *Gods from Outer Space*, op. cit., pp. 134-135. See also Angelo S. Rappoport, Ph.D., *Ancient Israel Myths & Legends* (Vol. 1, 2, & 3), Bonanza Books, New York, 1987, pp. 24-25; that text refers to seven netherworlds, namely: Adamah, Arka, Ge (aka Gia), Neshia, Zija, Tebel, and Eretz Hatachtonah, a lifeless world of darkness.
30 Erich von Däniken, *Gods from Outer Space*, op. cit., pp. 134-135.
31 Tamar Frankiel, *The Gift of Kabbalah*, Jewish Lights Pub., Woodstock, Vt., 2001, pp. 23-24.
32 Ibid., p. 180.
33 *Book of Enoch* (*2 Enoch* or *The Book of the Secrets of Enoch*), Chapter IV; reproduced in *The Forgotten Books of*

Eden, ed. Rutherford H. Platt, Jr., Bell Pub., New York, 1980, p. 83.

34 George C. Andrews, *Extra-Terrestrials Among Us*, op. cit., p. 54.

35 Ibid., pp. 54-55.

36 Ibid., p. 68.

37 Andrew Tomas, *We Are Not The First*, op. cit., p. 130. See also Robert Charroux, *Masters of the World*, op. cit., p. 113.

38 Andrew Tomas, *We Are Not The First*, op. cit., p. 129.

39 Graham Hancock, *Fingerprints of the Gods*, op. cit., pp. 107-108.

Chapter 28

1 Jean Sendy, *Those Gods Who Made Heaven & Earth*, op. cit., p. 35.

2 Irwin Ginsburgh, *First, Man. Then, Adam!*, op. cit. See also Ellen Gunderson Traylor, *Noah*, Living Books, Wheaton, Ill., 1988.

3 Merlin Stone, *When God was a Woman*, op. cit., pp. 115-121.

4 Ibid.

5 Zecharia Sitchin, *The 12th Planet*, op. cit., p. 328.

6 Cornelius Loew, *Myth, Sacred History, and Philosophy*, op. cit., pp. 25-26.

7 William Bramley, *The Gods of Eden*, op. cit., p. 62.

8 I. P. Cory, *Ancient Fragments*, ed. by E. Richmond Hodges, Reeves & Turner, London, 1876, pp. 12-13. See also Robert Charroux, *Masters of the World*, op. cit., p. 39.

9 Cornelius Loew, *Myth, Sacred History, and Philosophy*, op. cit., p. 124.

10 Brinsley Le Poer Trench, *The Sky People*, op. cit., p. 29.

11 Cornelius Loew, *Myth, Sacred History, and Philosophy*, op. cit., pp. 134 &136.

12 Ibid., p. 107. See also H. P. Blavatsky, *The Secret Doctrine*, op. cit., p. 320.

13 Cornelius Loew, *Myth, Sacred History, and Philosophy*, op. cit., p. 107.

14 Jacques Vallee, *UFO's in Space: Anatomy of a Phenomenon*, Ballantine Books, N.Y., 1974.

15 Cyrus H. Gordon, *The Ancient Near East*, W. W. Norton & Co., New York, 1965, pp. 62 & 134-135.

Chapter 29

1 Max I. Dimont, *Jews, God, and History*, Signet Books, New York, 1962, pp. 28-29.

2 *Lament for the Destruction of Ur*, trans. Thorkild Jacobsen, reproduced by Cornelius Loew, *Myth, Sacred History, and Philosophy*, op. cit., pp. 29-30.

3 Max I. Dimont, *Jews, God, and History*, op. cit., p. 29.

4 Cornelius Loew, *Myth, Sacred History, and Philosophy*, op. cit., pp. 123 & 131.

5 Ibid., p. 145.

6 Jewish History data derived from numerous sources, including but not limited to the *Holy Bible*, King James version, Cambridge University Press, Great Britain, 1994; Max I. Dimont, *Jews, God, and History*, op. cit.; Cornelius Loew, *Myth, Sacred History, and Philosophy*, op. cit.; Merlin Stone, *When God was a Woman*, op. cit.; R. K. Harrison, *Old Testament Times*, Wm. B. Eerdmans Pub., Grand Rapids, Mich., 1970; & H. P. Blavatsky, *The Secret Doctrine*, op. cit.

7 Leonhard Rost, *Judaism Outside the Hebrew Canon*, Abingdon, Tenn., 1976, p. 94.

Chapter 30

1 Elaine Pagels, *The Gnostic Gospels*, Vantage Books, New York, 1981, pp. 38-39, 43-44.

2 *Valentinian Exposition 22.19-23*, from the Nag Hammadi texts; reproduced by Elaine Pagels, *The Gnostic Gospels*, op. cit., p. 37.

3 Elaine Pagels, *The Gnostic Gospels*, op. cit., p. 44.

4 Ibid., p. 70.

5 *Lost Cities and Forgotten Tribes*, ed. Richard F. Dempewolff, Pocket Books, N.Y., 1974.

6 Ibid. See also H. P. Blavatsky, *The Secret Doctrine*, op. cit., p. 350; and E. A. Wallis Budge, *Egyptian Magic*, op. cit., pp. 179-181.

7 George C. Andrews, *Extra-Terrestrials Among Us*, op. cit., p. 63.

8 Ibid.

9 Leonhard Rost, *Judaism Outside the Hebrew Canon*, op. cit., p. 50.

10 Ibid., p. 38.

11 Ibid., p. 45.

12 Immanuel Velikovsky, *Worlds in Collision*, Pocket Books, New York, 1977, p. 299.

13 H. P. Blavatsky, *The Secret Doctrine*, op. cit., p. 492.

14 Ibid., p. 649.

15 Ibid., p. 387.

Chapter 31

1 Robert Charroux, *Masters of the World*, op. cit., p. 29.

2 Biblical compilation derived from various sources including but not limited to Max I. Dimont, *Jews, God, and History*, op. cit.; Cornelius Loew, *Myth, Sacred History, and Philosophy*, op. cit.; Merlin Stone, *When God was a Woman*, op. cit.; R. L. Dione, *Is God Supernatural?*, Bantam Books, N.Y., 1976; & H. P. Blavatsky, *The Secret Doctrine*, op. cit.

3 Leonhard Rost, *Judaism Outside the Hebrew Canon*, op. cit., p. 24.

4 Ibid., p. 23.

5 Voltaire, *Philosophical Dictionary*, excerpts quoted by Noel Langley, *Edgar Cayce on Reincarnation*, Ed. by Hugh Lynn Cayce, Paperback Library, New York, 1968, p. 161.

6 R. L. Dione, *Is God Supernatural?*, op. cit., p. 10.

7   *Hypostasis of the Archons* 89.11-91.1; reproduced by Elaine Pagels, *The Gnostic Gospels*, op. cit., p. 36.

8   *Trimorphic Protennoia* 35.1-24, from the Nag Hammadi texts; reproduced by Elaine Pagels, *The Gnostic Gospels*, op. cit., pp. 65-66.

9   Genealogy of Mary's parents as stated by William Bramley, *The Gods of Eden*, op. cit., pp. 121-123.

10 Ibid., p. 130.

11 David Hatcher Childress, *Lost Cities of Atlantis, Ancient Europe & The Mediterranean*, op. cit., pp. 297 & 298.

12 Various interviews with Dr. Glenn Kimball on the *Coast to Coast AM* radio program.

13 Ibid.

14 *Dead Sea Scrolls* topic derived using various sources including but not limited to Frank Moore Cross, Jr., *The Ancient Library of Qumran*, Anchor Books, New York, 1961; Max I. Dimont, *Jews, God, and History*, op. cit.; Merlin Stone, *When God was a Woman*, op. cit.; & Cyrus H. Gordon, *The Ancient Near East*, op. cit.

Chapter 32

1   H. P. Blavatsky, *The Secret Doctrine*, op. cit., p. 346.

2   Ibid., p. 350.

3   Ibid., p. 346 & 350.

4   Moshe Hallamish, *An Introduction to the Kabbalah*, trans. by Ruth Bar-Ilan & Ora Wiskind-Elper, State University of New York Press, Albany, N.Y., 1999, p. 152.

5   New Testament, John 1:1, trans. Richard Lattimore, *The Four Gospels and the Revelation*, Farrar-Straus-Giroux, New York, 1979, p. 195.

6   E. A. Wallis Budge, *Egyptian Magic*, op. cit., p. 161.

7   Ibid.

8   Samuel Noah Kramer, *Mythology of Sumer and Akkad*, section in *Mythologies of the Ancient World*, ed. Samuel Noah Kramer, Anchor Books, New York, 1961, p. 99 & 115.

9 Jean Sendy, *Those Gods Who Made Heaven & Earth*, op. cit., p. 35.

10 Carl Sagan, *Cosmos*, op. cit., p. 213.

11 H. P. Blavatsky, *The Secret Doctrine*, op. cit., p. 674.

12 Ibid.

13 *The Egyptian Book of the Dead*, Chapter 62, (Theban recension), trans. Dr. Raymond O. Faulkner, op. cit.

14 H. P. Blavatsky, *The Secret Doctrine*, op. cit., p. 293.

15 Erich von Däniken, *Gods from Outer Space*, op. cit., p. 162.

16 Carl Sagan, *Cosmos*, op. cit., p. 213.

17 Robert Graves, *The Greek Myths* (Vol. 1), Penguin Books, Maryland, 1955, p. 27.

18 H. P. Blavatsky, *The Secret Doctrine*, op. cit., p. 366.

19 Various drawings, such as Drawing #86, Erich von Däniken, *In Search of Ancient Gods*, op. cit., p. 79; see also Eric Norman, *Gods, Demons and Space Chariots*, op. cit., p. 19.

20 Peruvian legend contained in *The Earth*, by Jean Elisee Reclus, ref. by Peter Kolosimo, *Not of this World*, op. cit., p. 212.

21 Drawing described by Henri Lote during a French expedition in the Sahara, ref. by Peter Kolosimo, *Not of this World*, op. cit., p. 212.

22 Andrew Tomas, *We Are Not The First*, op. cit., p. 117.

23 Ibid.

24 Ibid., p. 62.

25 Genesis 1:26, *Holy Bible*, Cambridge University Press, Great Britain, 1974.

26 H. P. Blavatsky, *The Secret Doctrine*, op. cit., p. 366.

27 Ibid., p. 92.

28 William L. Langer, ed., *Western Civilization*, op. cit., p. 35.

29 W. Raymond Drake, *Gods and Spacemen In The Ancient East*, op. cit., p. 79. See also Immanuel Velikovsky, *Worlds in Collision*, op. cit., p. 115.

30 Peter Kolosimo, *Not of this World*, op. cit., p. 90.

31 Ibid.

32 Charles Berlitz, *Atlantis: The Eighth Continent*, op. cit., p. 9.

33 Ibid.

34 James Bailey, *The God-Kings & The Titans*, op. cit., p. 80.

35 Peter Kolosimo, *Not of this World*, op. cit., p. 90.

36 Graham Hancock, *Fingerprints of the Gods*, op. cit., p. 483.

37 Ibid., 362 & 381.

38 Ibid., p. 438. See also E. A. Wallis Budge, *Egyptian Magic*, op. cit., p. 185.

39 Lewis Spence, *The History of Atlantis*, op. cit., p. 110.

40 Genesis 2:10-11, 13-14; & Genesis 3:8, *Holy Bible*, op. cit. See also Zecharia Sitchin, *The 12th Planet*, op. cit., p. 286.

41 Ibid., p. 153.

42 Martin Ebon, *Atlantis: The New Evidence*, op. cit., p. 11.

43 Ibid., p. 13.

44 Lewis Spence, *The History of Atlantis*, op. cit., p. 103.

45 Diodorus, *The Library of History*, Vol. III, Ch. 54 & 56, trans. by Oldfather, as included in Appendix A, L. Sprague de Camp, *Lost Continents*, Ballantine Books, New York, 1975, pp. 307-308. See also Ignatius Donnelly, *Atlantis: The Antediluvian World*, op. cit., p. 25.

46 Charles Berlitz, *Atlantis: The Eighth Continent*, op. cit., p. 15. See also L. Sprague de Camp, *Lost Continents*, op. cit., pp. 191, 200, & 310-312.

47 Ignatius Donnelly, *Atlantis: The Antediluvian World*, op. cit., p. 80.

48 Geoffrey Bibby, *Looking for Dilmun*, Penguin Books, New York, 1972, p. 45.

49 Ibid., pp. 90-91, 273.

50 Ibid., pp. 59-60.

Chapter 33

1 Ignatius Donnelly, *Atlantis: The Antediluvian World*, op. cit., p. 49.

2 Peter Kolosimo, *Not of this World*, op. cit., p. 94. See also Warren Smith, *Lost Cities of the Ancients-Unearthed!*, op. cit.

3 Andrew Tomas, *We Are Not The First*, op. cit., p. 67. See also *Eclogue IV--Pollio, The Eclogues and Georgics of Virgil*, trans. by J. W. Mackail Fellow; Longmans, Green, & Co., London, 1905, pp. 14-16.

4 Ibid.

5 W. Raymond Drake, *Gods and Spacemen In The Ancient East*, op. cit., p. 185.

6 Eric Norman, *Gods, Demons and Space Chariots*, op. cit., p. 108. See also Robert Charroux, *Masters of the World*, op. cit., p. 48; & Erich von Däniken, *Chariots of the Gods?*, op. cit., p. 21.

7 Ibid.

8 Various sources used for 'civilizing gods of Mexico,' including but not limited to Harold Osborn, *South American Mythology*, Hamlyn Pub. Group, N.Y., 1968; Charles Berlitz, *Atlantis: The Eighth Continent*, op. cit., p. 151; Alan and Sally Landsburg, *In Search of Ancient Mysteries*, op. cit., pp. 49-50 & 52-53; Zecharia Sitchin, *The Lost Realms*, op. cit., pp. 68, 119-120; R. Cedric Leonard, *Quest for Atlantis*, op. cit., p. 83; & Gordon Whittaker, "The Spaceman in the Tree," a chapter in *Some Trust in Chariots*, eds. Barry Thiering and Edgar Castle, op. cit., pp. 55-57.

9 Robert Charroux, *Masters of the World*, op. cit., p. 47.

10 Alan and Sally Landsburg, *In Search of Ancient Mysteries*, op. cit., p. 47.

11 Ibid., p. 52.

12 Ibid., p. 142. See also Robert Charroux, *Masters of the World*, op. cit.

13 Peter Kolosimo, *Not of this World*, op. cit., p. 89.

14 Ibid.

15 Ibid., p. 57. See also W. Raymond Drake, *Gods and Spacemen In The Ancient East*, op. cit., p. 224-225.

16 Peter Kolosimo, *Not of this World*, op. cit., p. 57.

17 Ibid., p. 32.

18 E. A. Wallis Budge, *Egyptian Magic*, op. cit., pp. 171-172.

19 George Johnson and Don Tanner, *The Bible and the Bermuda Triangle*, Logos Intl., New Jersey, 1976.

20 Ibid.

21 *The Kumarbi Myth* (aka *The Story of Alalu, Anu, and Kumarbi,* and *The Struggle for Kingship Among the Gods*), referenced in *The Hittites*, O. R. Gurney, op. cit., p. 190.

22 Peter Kolosimo, *Not of this World*, op. cit., p. 34.

23 Ibid., p. 35.

24 George C. Andrews, *Extra-Terrestrials Among Us*, op. cit., pp. 285-286.

25 *The Egyptian Book of the Dead*, (Theban recension), trans. Dr. Raymond O. Faulkner, op. cit.

26 H. P. Blavatsky, *The Secret Doctrine*, op. cit., pp. 228-229.

27 Paul Hamlyn, *Egyptian Mythology*, Westbook House, London, 1965, p. 27.

28 Brinsley Le Poer Trench, *Temple of the Stars*, op. cit., p. 51.

29 H. P. Blavatsky, *The Secret Doctrine*, op. cit., p. 167.

30 Peter Kolosimo, *Not of this World*, op. cit., p. 37.

31 Ibid.

32 Ibid., p. 33.

33 Ignatius Donnelly, *Atlantis: The Antediluvian World*, op. cit., p. 156.

34 *Book of Enoch* (*2 Enoch* or *The Book of the Secrets of Enoch*), Chapter I, Verse 6; reproduced in *The Forgotten Books of Eden*, ed. Rutherford H. Platt, Jr., op. cit., p. 82.

35 Josef F. Blumrich, *The Spaceships of Ezekiel*, Bantam Books, New York, 1974, pp. 42 & 78.

36 Ibid., pp. 42 & 133.

37 George C. Andrews, *Extra-Terrestrials Among Us*, op. cit., p. 47.

38 *The Book of the Dead*, Plate XXV, Ch. LXXVIII, Line 14, trans. by Sir E. A. Wallis Budge, op. cit., p. 333. See also W. Raymond Drake, *Gods and Spacemen In The Ancient East*, op. cit., p. 138.

39 Zecharia Sitchin, *The 12th Planet*, op. cit., p. 138.

40 *Book of Enoch* (*2 Enoch* or *The Book of the Secrets of Enoch*), Chapter I, Verse 6; reproduced in *The Forgotten Books of Eden*, ed. Rutherford H. Platt, Jr., op. cit., p. 82.
41 Erich von Däniken, *In Search of Ancient Gods*, op. cit., pp. 68-69 & 72. See also Andrew Tomas, *We Are Not The First*, op. cit., p. 117; & R. Cedric Leonard, *Quest for Atlantis*, op. cit., p. 144.
42 Andrew Tomas, *We Are Not The First*, op. cit., pp. 117-118.
43 From the Sumerian myth known as *Inanna's Journeys to the Underworld*, as reproduced in David Adams Leeming, *The World of Myth*, op. cit., p. 139.
44 Graham Hancock, *Fingerprints of the Gods*, op. cit., p. 397, also photo on p. 486 ff. See also E. A. Wallis Budge, *Egyptian Magic*, op. cit., p. 148.
45 Ibid.

Chapter 34

1 Norris and Ross McWhirter, *Guinness Book of World Records*, Bantam Books, New York, 1974, p. 13.
2 Warren Smith, *The Secret Forces of the Pyramids*, op. cit., p. 143.
3 Various sources, including but not limited to Daniel Cohen, *Monsters, Giants and Little Men from Mars*, Dell Pub., New York, 1977; Eric Norman, *Gods and Devils From Outer Space*, op. cit; Ignatius Donnelly, *Atlantis: The Antediluvian World*, op. cit.; Warren Smith, *The Secret Forces of the Pyramids*, op. cit.; & Peter Kolosimo, *Not of this World*, op. cit.
4 Charles Fort, *The Book of the Damned*, op. cit., pp. 158-159.
5 Ibid., p. 158.
6 M.H.J. Th. Van Der Veer and P. Moerman, *Hidden Worlds*, op. cit., p. 11.
7 Michael H. Day, *Fossil Man*, op. cit., p. 112.

8   M.H.J. Th. Van Der Veer and P. Moerman, *Hidden Worlds*, op. cit., p. 16. See also Peter Kolosimo, *Not of this World*, op. cit., p. 129.

9   Warren Smith, *The Secret Forces of the Pyramids*, op. cit., p. 139.

10 Ibid. See also M.H.J. Th. Van Der Veer and P. Moerman, *Hidden Worlds*, op. cit., p. 16; & Peter Kolosimo, *Not of this World*, op. cit., p. 129.

11 Frank Edwards, *Strange World*, op. cit., 84. See also Peter Kolosimo, *Not of this World*, op. cit., p. 128; & M.H.J. Th. Van Der Veer and P. Moerman, *Hidden Worlds*, op. cit., p. 15.

12 Eric Norman, *Gods and Devils From Outer Space*, op. cit., p. 126. Also reference David Hatcher Childress interview on *Coast to Coast AM* radio program with Art Bell on 7-13-2001.

13 *Coast to Coast AM* radio interview with David Hatcher Childress on 7-13-2001.

14 Warren Smith, *The Secret Forces of the Pyramids*, op. cit., pp. 140-141.

15 Ibid., p. 137.

16 Ibid., p. 136.

17 Ibid., p. 135.

18 Ibid., p. 136. See also Erich von Däniken, *Gods from Outer Space*, op. cit., p. 34.

19 Warren Smith, *The Secret Forces of the Pyramids*, op. cit., p. 136.

20 Zecharia Sitchin, *The 12th Planet*, op. cit., p. 171.

21 Robert Charroux, *Masters of the World*, op. cit., pp. 16 & 227.

22 Ibid., p. 227.

23 Zecharia Sitchin, *The 12th Planet*, op. cit., p. 171.

24 Ibid., p. 172.

25 Ibid.

26 *Book of Enoch* (*2 Enoch* or *The Book of the Secrets of Enoch*), Chapter XVIII, Verse 3; reproduced in *The Forgotten Books of Eden*, ed. Rutherford H. Platt, Jr., op. cit., p. 87.

27 H. P. Blavatsky, *The Secret Doctrine*, op. cit., p. 415.

28 Jacques Vallee, *UFO's in Space: Anatomy of a Phenomenon*, op. cit.

29 Various sources including, but not limited to Daniel Cohen, *Monsters, Giants and Little Men from Mars*, op. cit.; & Warren Smith, *The Secret Forces of the Pyramids*, op. cit.

30 Paul Hamlyn, *Egyptian Mythology*, op. cit., pp. 112-114. See also E. A. Wallis Budge, *Egyptian Magic*, op. cit., pp. 148 & 181.

31 Graham Hancock, *Fingerprints of the Gods*, op. cit., p. 152.

32 Jacques Vallee, *UFO's in Space: Anatomy of a Phenomenon*, op. cit.

33 Warren Smith, *The Secret Forces of the Pyramids*, op. cit., pp. 24-25. See also George C. Andrews, *Extra-Terrestrials Among Us*, op. cit., pp. 43-45.

34 Ibid.

35 Ibid.

36 George C. Andrews, *Extra-Terrestrials Among Us*, op. cit., pp. 44-45.

37 Ibid., p. 45.

38 Robert Charroux, *Masters of the World*, op. cit., p. 239.

39 Ibid., p. 237.

40 Ibid.

41 Ibid., pp. 237-238. See also Eric Norman, *Gods, Demons and Space Chariots*, op. cit., pp. 16-17; Erich von Däniken, *Gods from Outer Space*, op. cit., pp. 87-89.

42 George C. Andrews, *Extra-Terrestrials Among Us*, op. cit., pp. 42.

43 Ibid.

Chapter 35

1 W. Raymond Drake, *Gods and Spacemen In The Ancient East*, op. cit., p. 112.
2 Robert Temple, *The Sirius Mystery*, Destiny Books, Rochester, Vermont, 1987. See also Murry Hope, *The Sirius Connection*, op. cit., pp. 79-89; Peter Kolosimo, *Not of this World*, op. cit., pp. 229-230; & Alan Landsburg, *In Search of Lost Civilizations*, op. cit., pp. 147-150.
3 W. Raymond Drake, *Gods and Spacemen In The Ancient East*, op. cit., p. 113. See also Peter Kolosimo, *Not of this World*, op. cit., p. 171.
4 Peter Kolosimo, *Not of this World*, op. cit., p. 171.
5 William Bramley, *The Gods of Eden*, op. cit., p. 211.
6 Alan Landsburg, *In Search of Lost Civilizations*, op. cit., p. 110.
7 Charles Berlitz, *World of the Odd and the Awesome*, op. cit., p. 151.
8 Ibid.
9 C. W. Ceram, *Gods, Graves, and Scholars*, op. cit., p. 355.
10 Nicholas Wade, "Scientists Extend Human Cells' Life Span," New York Times article in The Ledger, Lakeland, Florida, 1-14-98.
11 Ibid.
12 Rick Weiss, "Study: Dolly Inherits Old Genes," Washington Post article in The Ledger, Lakeland, Florida, 5-27-99.
13 Ibid.
14 *The Epic Of Gilgamesh*, trans. & ed. by N. K. Sandars, op. cit., p. 105.
15 *The Mahabharata*, Book I, trans. & ed. by J.A.B. van Buitenen, University of Chicago Press, Chicago, 1980, footnotes to 58.1.10 & 20, p. 447. See also Mhb. 1.58.10-20, p. 136.
16 Robert Graves, *The Greek Myths* (Vol. 1), op. cit., p. 39.

Chapter 36

1 *The Mahabharata*, Book 1, op. cit., 1.59.1., p. 138.
2 Ibid., Book 1, 1.59.3., p. 138.
3 Josef F. Blumrich, *The Spaceships of Ezekiel*, op. cit., p. 134.

SELECTED BIBLIOGRAPHY

I. Manuscripts, Books, and Texts:

Alonzo, Gualberto Zapata, *An Overview of the Mayan World*, Litoarte Printing, Mexico, 1987.

Andrews, George C., *Extra-Terrestials Among Us*, Llewellyn Pub., St. Paul, Minn., 1995.

Ardrey, Robert, *African Genesis*, Dell Publishing, New York, 1961.

Asimov, Isaac, *Please Explain*, Dell Publishing, New York, 1973.

Bahm, Archie J., *The World's Living Religions*, Dell Publishing, New York, 1964.

Bailey, James, *The God-Kings & The Titans*, St. Martin's Press, New York, 1973.

Bauval, Robert, and Gilbert, Adrian, *The Orion Mystery*, Crown Publishing, New York, 1994.

Bergier, Jacques, *Extraterrestrial Visitations from Prehistoric Times to the Present*, Henry Regnery Co., Chicago, Ill., 1973.

Bergier, Jacques, & Editors of INFO, *Extraterrestrial Intervention*, Signet Books, New York, 1975.

Berlitz, Charles, *The Mystery of Atlantis*, Avon Books, New York, 1969.

-----*Mysteries From Forgotten Worlds*, Dell Publishing, New York, 1972.

-----*Atlantis: The Eighth Continent*, Ballantine Books, New York, 1985.

-----*The Dragon's Triangle*, Fawcett Books, New York, 1989.

-----*Charles Berlitz's World of the Odd and the Awesome*, Ballantine Books, New York, 1991.

Berry, Gerald L., *Religions of the World*, Barnes & Noble, New York, 1956.

Bibby, Geoffrey, *Looking for Dilmun*, Penguin Books, New York, 1972.

Blavatsky, Helena P., *The Secret Doctrine*, Theosophical University Press, Pasadena, Calif., 1988 printing of the original 1888 edition.

Blum, Ralph, *Beyond Earth: Man's Contact with UFO's*, Bantam Books, New York, 1974.

Blumrich, Josef F., *The Spaceships of Ezekiel*, Bantam Books, New York, 1974.

Bramley, William, *The Gods of Eden*, Avon Books, New York, 1993.

Brecher, Kenneth, and Feirtag, Michael, eds., *Astronomy of the Ancients*, The MIT Press, Cambridge, Mass., 1980.

Brennan, Herbie, *Martian Genesis*, Dell Publishing, New York, 1998.

Budge, (Sir) E. A. Wallis, *Egyptian Magic*, Citadel Press/Carol Publishing, New York, 1991.

-----*The Book of the Dead* (inc. *The Papyrus of Ani*), British Museum, London, 1895.

Bulfinch, Thomas, *Mythology of Greece and Rome*, Collier Books, New York, 1962.

Campbell, Joseph, *The Masks of God: Primitive Mythology*, Viking Press, New York, 1959.

Carlotto, Mark, *The Martian Enigmas: A Closer Look*, North Atlantic Books, Berkeley, Calif., 1991.

Cayce, Edgar Evans, *Edgar Cayce On Atlantis*, Warner Books, New York, 1968.

Ceram, C. W., *Gods, Graves, and Scholars*, Bantam Books, New York, 1972.

Chadwick, Nora, *The Celts*, Penguin Books, New York, 1970.

Chaisson, Eric, *Cosmic Dawn*, Berkley Books, New York, 1984.

Charroux, Robert, *Masters of the World*, Berkley Medallion Books, New York, 1974.

Chatelain, Maurice, *Our Ancestors Came From Outer Space*, Dell Publishing, New York, 1978.

Childress, David Hatcher, *Extraterrestrial Archaeology*, Adventures Unlimited Press, Stelle, Ill., 1995.

-----*Lost Cities of Atlantis, Ancient Europe & The Mediterranean*, Adventures Unlimited Press, Stelle, Ill., 1996.

Churchward, James, *The Lost Continent of Mu*, Paperback Library, New York, 1968.

-----*The Children of Mu*, Paperback Library, New York, 1968.

-----*The Sacred Symbols of Mu*, Paperback Library, New York, 1968.

Clark, Adrian V., *Cosmic Mysteries of the Universe*, Parker Publishing, New York, 1968.

Clark, Donald S., *Physical Metallurgy for Engineers*, Van Nostrand Co., Princeton, New Jersey, 1966.

Cohen, Daniel, *Monsters, Giants and Little Men from Mars*, Dell Publishing, New York, 1977.

Corliss, William R., *Mysteries of the Universe*, Thomas Y. Crowell Co., New York, 1967.

-----*Ancient Man: A Handbook of Puzzling Artifacts*, Sourcebook Project, Glen Arm, Md., 1978.

Cory, I. P., *Ancient Fragments*, ed. by E. Richmond Hodges, Reeves & Turner, London, 1876.

Cross, Jr., Frank Moore, *The Ancient Library of Qumran*, Anchor Books, New York, 1961.

Darling, David, *Deep Time*, Delacorte Press, New York, 1989.

Day, Michael H., *Fossil Man*, Bantam Books, New York, 1971.

De Camp, L. Sprague, *Lost Continents*, Ballantine Books, New York, 1975.

-----*The Ancient Engineers*, Ballantine Books, New York, 1984.

Deetz, James, *Invitation to Archaeology*, American Museum Science Books, USA, 1967.

Dempewolff, Richard F., Ed., *Lost Cities and Forgotten Tribes*, Pocket Books, New York, 1974.

Dimont, Max I., *Jews, God, and History*, Signet Books, New York, 1962.

Dineley, David, *Earth's Voyage Through Time*, Knopf Books, New York, 1974.

Dione, Robert L., *God Drives A Flying Saucer*, Bantam Books, New York, 1969.

-----*Is God Supernatural?*, Bantam Books. New York, 1976.

Donnelly, Ignatius, *Atlantis: The Antediluvian World*, revised by Egerton Sykes, Gramercy Publishing, New York, 1949.

Downing, Barry H., *The Bible and Flying Saucers*, Berkley Books, New York, 1989.

Drake, W. Raymond, *Gods and Spacemen In The Ancient East*, Signet Books, New York, 1973.

-----*Gods and Spacemen of the Ancient Past*, Signet Books, New

York, 1974.

Dudley, Donald R., *The Civilization of Rome*, Mentor Books, New York, 1962.

Ebon, Martin, *Atlantis: The New Evidence*, Signet, New York, 1977.

Eclogues and Georgics of Virgil, The; trans. by J. W. Mackail Fellow; Longmans, Green, & Co. London, 1905.

Edwards, Frank, *Strange World*, Bantam Books, New York, 1969.

Edwards, I.E.S., *The Pyramids of Egypt*, Viking Press, New York, 1972.

Egyptian Book of the Dead, The (aka *The Book of Going Forth by Day*), trans. Dr. Raymond O. Faulkner, Chronicle Books, San Francisco, 1998.

Emery, Walter B., *Archaic Egypt*, Penguin Books, New York, 1961.

Encarta 98 Encyclopedia, Microsoft Corp., 1998 ed., Redmond, WA., 1997.

Epic of Gilgamesh, Penguin Books, Maryland, 1964.

Evslin, Bernard, *Gods, Demigods, & Demons: An Encyclopedia of Greek Mythology*, Scholastic Inc, New York, 1975.

Finley, M. I., *The Ancient Greeks*, Penguin Books, New York, 1982.

Fort, Charles, *The Book of the Damned*, Ace Publishing, New York, 1919.

Frankiel, Tamar, *The Gift of Kabbalah*, Jewish Lights Publications, Woodstock, VT., 2001.

Furneaux, Rupert, *Ancient Mysteries*, Ballantine Books, New York, 1978.

Ginsburgh, Irwin, *First, Man. Then, Adam!*, Pocket Books, New York, 1975.

Golob, Richard, and Brus, Eric, Eds., *The Almanac of Science and Technology*, Harcourt, Brace Jovanovich, Florida, 1990.

Gordon, Cyrus H., *The Ancient Near East*, Norton & Co., New York, 1965.

Graves, Robert, *The Greek Myths* (vol. 1), Penguin Books,

Maryland, 1955.

Gribbin, John, *Companion to the Cosmos*, Little, Brown & Co., New York, 1996.

Gurney, O. R., *The Hittites*, Penguin Books, Maryland, 1954.

Hallamish, Moshe, *An Introduction to the Kabbalah*, trans. by Ruth Bar-Ilan & Ora Wiskind-Elper, State University of New York Press, Albany, N.Y., 1999.

Hamilton, Edith, *Mythology*, Mentor Books, New York, 1953.

Hamlyn, Paul, *Egyptian Mythology*, Westbook House, London, 1965.

Hancock, Graham, *Fingerprints of the Gods*, Crown Publishers, New York, 1995.

-----*The Mars Mystery*, Three Rivers Press, New York, 1998.

Hancock, Graham, and Bauval, Robert, *The Message Of The Sphinx*, Three Rivers Press, New York, 1996.

Hapgood, Charles H., *Maps of the Ancient Sea Kings*, Chilton Books, New York, 1966.

Harrison, R. K., *The Archaeology of the Old Testament*, Harper & Row, New York, 1966.

-----*Old Testament Times*, Eerdmans Publishing, Grand Rapids, Mich., 1970.

Hawkes, Jacquetta, *History of Mankind* (Vol. 1, Pt. 1: *Prehistory*), Mentor Books, New York, 1965.

Herodotus, *History of Herodotus*, trans. by George Rawlinson, ed. by Manuel Komroff, Tudor Publishing, New York, 1941.

Heyerdahl, Thor, *Early Man and the Ocean*, Doubleday & Co., New York, 1979.

Hoagland, Richard C., *The Monuments of Mars*, North Atlantic Books, Berkeley, Calif., 1987.

Holy Bible, Cambridge University Press, Great Britain, 1994.

Hope, Murry, *The Sirius Connection: Unlocking the Secrets of Ancient Egypt*, Element Books, Rockport, Mass., 1996.

Howell, F. Clark, *Early Man*, Time-Life Books, New York, 1968.

Howells, Willaim, *Back of History*, Natural History Library, U.S.A., 1963.

I Ching, Van Over, Raymond, Ed., (Trans. James Legge), Mentor

Books, New York, 1971.

Jeffrey, Grant R., *The Signature of God*, Frontier Research Publications, Toronto, 1996.

Johnson, George, and Tanner, Don, *The Bible and the Bermuda Triangle*, Logos Intl., New Jersey, 1976.

Jordon, Michael, *Encyclopedia of Gods: Over 2,500 Deities of the World*, Pub. by Facts On File, Inc., New York, 1993.

Josephus, *Josephus [Complete Works]*, trans. by William Whiston, Kregel Publishing, Grand Rapids, Mich., 1972.

Keyhoe, Donald E., *Aliens From Space*, Signet Books, New York, 1974.

Kitto, H. D. F., *The Greeks*, Penguin Books, Maryland, 1957.

Kolosimo, Peter, *Not of this World*, Bantam Books, New York, 1973.

Kramer, S. N., *History Begins at Sumer*, Doubleday, New York, 1958.

Kramer, Samuel Noah, Ed., *Mythologies of the Ancient World*, Anchor Books, New York, 1961.

Kueshana, Eklal, *The Ultimate Frontier*, The Stelle Group, Chicago, Ill., 1963.

Landsburg, Alan, *In Search of Lost Civilizations*, Bantam Books, New York, 1976.

Landsburg, Alan and Sally, *In Search of Ancient Mysteries*, Bantam Books, New York, 1974.

-----*The Outer Space Connection*, Bantam Books, New York, 1975.

Langer, William L., Ed., *Western Civilization*, American Heritage Publishing, New York, 1968.

Langley, Noel, *Edgar Cayce on Reincarnation*, Paperback Library, New York, 1968.

Leach, Marjorie, *Guide to the Gods*, ABC-CLIO, Inc., Calif., 1992.

Leek, Sybil, *Reincarnation: The Second Chance*, Bantam Books, New York, 1975.

Leeming, David Adams, *The World of Myth*, Oxford University

Press, New York, 1990.

Leonard, George, *Somebody Else Is On The Moon*, Pocket Books, New York, 1976.

Leonard, R. Cedric, *Quest For Atlantis*, Manor Books, New York, 1979.

Linton, Ralph, *The Tree of Culture*, Vintage Books, New York, 1959.

Loew, Cornelius, *Myth, Sacred History, and Philosophy*, Harcourt, Brace & World, N.Y., 1967.

Luce, J. V., *The End of Atlantis*, Bantam Books, New York, 1978.

Macgowan, Kenneth, and Hester Jr., Joseph A., *Early Man in the New World*, Natural History Library/Anchor Books, New York, 1962.

Machinery's Handbook, 18th Ed., Industrial Press, New York, 1968.

Mack, John E., *Abduction*, Macmillan Publishing, New York, 1994.

Mahabharata, trans. & ed. by J.A.B. van Buitenen, University of Chicago Press, Chicago, 1980.

McGaa, Ed, *Native Wisdom*, Four Directions Pub., Minn., 1995.

McWhirter, Norris & Ross, *Guinness Book of World Records*, Bantam Books, New York, 1974.

Mead, G.R.S., *Fragments of a Faith Forgotten*, The Theosophical Pub. Society, London, 1900.

Michell, John, *City of Revelation*, Ballantine Books, New York, 1972.

Mitchell, Edgar D., and Williams, Dwight A., *The Way of the Explorer*, G. P. Putnam's Sons, New York, 1996.

Moffett, Robert K., *Secrets of the Pyramids Revealed*, Tempo Books, New York, 1976.

Montgomery, Ruth, *Threshold to Tomorrow*, Putnam's Sons, New York, 1982.

-----*Aliens Among Us*, Ballantine Books, New York, 1985.

Moore, Patrick, *New Guide to the Moon*, Norton & Co., New York, 1976.

New York Public Library Desk Reference, Simon & Schuster, New York, 1989.

Norman, Eric, *Gods, Demons and Space Chariots*, Lancer Books, New York, 1970.

-----*Gods and Devils From Outer Space*, Lancer Books, New York, 1973.

Osborne, Harold, *South American Mythology*, The Hamlyn Publishing Group, New York, 1968.

Pagels, Elaine, *The Gnostic Gospels*, Vantage Books, New York, 1981.

Pauwels, Louis, and Bergier, Jacques, *Morning of the Magicians*, Avon Books, New York, 1963.

Petrie, Sir W. M. Flinders, *The Pyramids and Temples of Gizeh*, New York, 1883.

Pensee editors, *Velikovsky Reconsidered*, Warner Books, New York, 1976.

Pfeiffer, John E., *The Emergence Of Man*, Harper & Row, New York, 1969.

Phillips, Robert S. Ed., *Funk & Wagnalls New Encyclopedia*, Lippincott & Crowell Pub., U.S.A., 1983.

Piggott, Stuart, *Prehistoric India*, Penguin Books, Maryland, 1952.

Platt, Rutherford H., Jr., Ed., *The Forgotten Books of Eden*, Bell Publishing, New York, 1980.

Popul Vuh, trans. by Dennis Tedlock, Simon and Schuster, New York, 1985.

Pritchard, James B., Ed., *The Ancient Near East*, Princeton University Press, New Jersey, 1958.

Quest for the Past, Reader's Digest Eds., Pleasantville, New York, 1984.

Rappoport, Angelo S., *Ancient Israel Myths & Legends*, Bonanza Books, New York, 1987.

Rapport, Samuel, & Wright, Helen, Eds., *Archaeology*, Washington Square Press, N.Y., 1964.

Ramayana, trans. & ed. by Aubrey Menen, Greenwood Press, Westport, Conn., 1972.

Rig Veda, (partial selection and trans. by Wendy D. O'Flaherty), Penguin Books, N.Y., 1981.

Rost, Leonhard, *Judaism Outside the Hebrew Canon*, Abingdon, Nashville, Tennessee, 1976.

Roux, Georges, *Ancient Iraq*, Penguin Books, New York, 1983.

Sagan, Carl, *Cosmos*, Ballantine Books, New York, 1985.

Scott-Elliot, W., *The Story of Atlantis and the Lost Lemuria*, Theosophical Pub., London, 1968.

Segraves, Kelly L., *Sons of God Return*, Pyramid Books, New York, 1975.

Sendy, Jean, *Those Gods Who Made Heaven & Earth*, Berkley Medallion Books, N. Y., 1972.

Sitchin, Zecharia, *The 12th Planet*, Avon Books, New York, 1978.

-----*The Stairway to Heaven*, Avon Books, New York, 1983.

-----*The Wars of Gods and Men*, Avon Books, New York, 1985.

-----*The Lost Realms*, Avon Books, New York, 1990.

-----*When Time Began*, Avon Books, New York, 1993.

-----*Genesis Revisited*, Avon Books, New York, 1990.

-----*Divine Encounters*, Avon Books, New York, 1996.

Smith, John Maynard, *The Theory of Evolution*, Penguin Books, Maryland, 1958.

Smith, Warren, *The Secret Forces of the Pyramids*, Zebra Books, New York, 1975.

-----*Lost Cities of the Ancients-Unearthed!*, Zebra Books/Kensington Publishing, N.Y., 1976.

Spence, Lewis, *The History of Atlantis*, Bell Publishing, New York, 1968.

Spencer, John Wallace, *No Earthly Explanation*, Bantam Books, New York, 1975.

-----*Limbo of the Lost*, Bantam Books, New York, 1973.

Stone, Merlin, *When God was a Woman*, Barnes & Noble, New York, 1993.

Sullivan, Walter, *We Are Not Alone*, Signet Books, New York, 1966.

Temple, Robert, *The Sirius Mystery*, Destiny Books, Rochester, Vermont, 1987.

The Four Gospels and the Revelation, trans. by Lattimore, Richard, Farrar-Straus-Giroux, New York, 1979.

The World's Last Mysteries, Reader's Digest, New York, 1980.

Thiering, Barry, and Castle, Edgar, Eds., *Some Trust in Chariots*, Popular Library, New York, 1972.

Tomas, Andrew, *We Are Not The First*, Bantam Books, New York, 1973.

Traylor, Ellen Gunderson, *Noah*, Living Books, Wheaton, Ill., 1988.

Trefil, James, *The Edge of the Unknown*, Houghton Mifflin, New York, 1996.

Trench, Brinsley Le Poer, *The Sky People*, Award Books, New York, 1970.

-----*Temple of the Stars*, Ballantine Books, New York, 1974.

Umland, Craig and Eric, *Mystery of the Ancients: Early Spacemen and the Mayas*, Walker and Co., New York, 1974.

Urantia Book, The Urantia Foundation, Chicago, 1955.

Vallee, Jacques, *UFO's in Space: Anatomy of a Phenomenon*, Ballantine Books, N.Y., 1974.

Van Der Veer, M.H.J. Th., and Moerman, P., *Hidden Worlds*, Bantam Books, New York, 1975.

Van Doren, Charles, *A History of Knowledge*, Ballantine Books, New York, 1992.

Velikovsky, Immanuel, *Worlds in Collision*, Pocket Books, New York, 1977.

-----*Earth In Upheaval*, Pocket Books, New York, 1977.

-----*Oedipus and Akhnaton*, Pocket Books, New York, 1980.

Vishnu Purana, Vol. II, trans. by H. H. Wilson, Trubner & Co., London, 1865.

Von Däniken, Erich, *Chariots of the Gods?*, Bantam Books, New York, 1971.

-----*Gods From Outer Space*, Bantam Books, New York, 1972.

-----*In Search of Ancient Gods*, Putnam's Sons, New York, 1973.

-----*The Gold of the Gods*, Bantam Books, New York, 1974.

-----*The Eyes of the Sphinx*, Berkley Books, New York, 1996.

Waters, Frank, *Book of the Hopi*, Ballantine Books, New York, 1969.
Wigoder, Geoffrey, Ed., *The Encyclopedia of Judaism*, The Jerusalem Publishing House, Ltd., Jerusalem, Israel, 1989.
Wilson, Don, *Secrets of our Spaceship Moon*, Dell Books, New York, 1979.
Wyllie, Timothy, *Dolphins * Extraterrestrials * Angels*, Bozon Enterprises, 1984.

Yogananda, Paramahansa, *Autobiography of a Yogi*, Self-Realization Fellowship, USA, 1981.

II. Articles and Reports

Associated Press Report, Ancient Site Found, 1998.
-----Wooden Spear Discovery Shows Man Hunted Earlier Than Thought, 1998.

Boyd, Robert S., New Planets Thrill Astronomers, Knight-Ridder Newspapers, 1996.
-----Europa May Have Life-Supporting Ocean, Knight-Ridder Newspapers, 1998.
-----Saltwater Found in Meteorite, Knight-Ridder Newspapers, 1999.
Broad, William J., Think You're From Mars?, New York Times, 1999.

Callahan, Rick, Comet May Be Made Of Early Material, Associated Press, 1999.
Cooke, Robert, Scientists Discover New Evidence that Universe Began With Big Bang, Newsday, 1995.
Crenson, Matt, Cosmologists Bringing Universe Into Focus With Math, Associated Press, 1996.

Davis, Bob, A Universal Mystery Is Said to be Solved, Wall

Street Journal, 1991.

Driscoll, Paul A., Scientists Find First Evidence of Top Quark, Associated Press, 1994.

Egan, Timothy, Study of Prehistoric Human Inconclusive, New York Times, 1999.

Fordahl, Matthew, Team Finds Evidence of Early Oxygen-Producing Organisms, Associated Press, 1999.

Gannett News Report, Neanderthal Bones Date to Human Era, 1999.

Glanz, James, Cosmic Clue May Give Answer To Big Bang, New York Times, 1999.

Hatton, Barry, Skeleton May Help Clarify Genesis Of Man, Associated Press, 1999.

Higgins, Alex, Experiment Yields Evidence Supporting Big Bang Theory, Associated Press, 2000.

Hotz, Robert Lee, Universe is 12 or 13 Billion Years Old, Los Angeles Times, 1999.

Joshi, Vijay, Egyptian Writings May Be Oldest, Associated Press, 1998.

Leary, Warren E., 3-D Map Shows Texture of Mars, New York Times, 1999.

Ledger Wire Service from New York Times and the Associated Press, Scientists ID Half of Misssing Universe Matter, 1997.

Levy, David H., What Rocks Say, Parade Magazine, Parade Publications, New York, 1999.

Maugh II, Thomas H., Ancient Site Yields Unexpected Discoveries, Los Angeles Times, 1998.

News Service article, Fossil Suggests Nice Neanderthals, Paris, France, 2001.

Pollak, Michael, Neanderthal Isn't Extinct Online, New York Times, 1999.

Recer, Paul, Satellite Finds Possible Presence of Dark Matter, Associated Press, 1993.
-----Evidence of Huge Asteroid Uncovered, Associated Press, 1997.
-----Cave Dwellers Crafted Tough Shoes, Associated Press, 1998.
-----NASA Defends Theory of Life on Mars, Associated Press, 1998.
-----Experts Confident of Life Beyond Earth, Associated Press, 1998.
-----Fossil Find Suggests Arctic Once as Balmy as Florida, Associated Press, 1998.
-----Ancient Fossil May Be Primate Ground-Dweller, Associated Press, 1999.
-----Scientists Complete First Map of Genes, Associated Press, 1999.
-----Astronomers Open Way to New Planets, Associated Press, 2001.

Schiffmann, William, Scientists Point To Other Solar System, Associated Press, 1999.
Schmid, Randolph E., DNA Testing, Associated Press, 1998.
-----Oldest Fossil Life Sign Found, Associated Press, 1999.
Siegel, Lee, Discovery Backs Big Bang Theory, Associated Press, 1992.
Siegfried, Tom, Universe May Hold Clue to Dinosaurs' Fate, Dallas Morning News, 1998.
-----Conferees Agree to Disagree About God, Dallas Morning News, 1999.
Suplee, Curt, Elusive Particle Is Found, Washington Post, 1995.
Svensson, Peter, Early Man Shown to be Smarter, Associated Press, 1999.

Tampa Tribune *Science News* article, Discovery Sheds Light on Mars' Past, 1999.

Wade, Nicholas, Scientists Extend Human Cells' Life Span, New York Times, 1998.

-----Pioneer, Company Join to Map Human DNA Within Three Years, New York Times, 1998.

Warren, Jere and Baker, David, The Missing Link, Knight-Ridder, 1995.

Washington Press release, Study Finds Evidence of Third Branch of Life, 1999.

-----Neanderthal Bones Date to Human Era, 1999.

-----Organic Molecules Found In Space, 2000.

Weiss, Rick, Study: Dolly Inherits Old Genes, Washington Post, 1999.

Wilford, John Noble, Day Apes Straighten Up To Stand On Own 2 Legs, New York Times, 1995.

-----Fossil Discovery Fuels Missing-Link Debate, New York Times, 1999.

-----Human Family Gets Larger, New York Times, 2001.

Witze, Alexandra, Jets From Black Hole May Answer Puzzle, Dallas Morning News, 1997.

Index

Abraham 343, 344, 347-350, 367-368, 429
Abydos 166, 221, 230, 240, 250, 252, 254
Adapa 366, 388
Ahura Mazda 354, 362, 390, 402, 422
Akapana 258
Akkad (Akkadian) 13, 184, 193, 292, 296, 302, 328, 337, 342-343, 347-348, 366-367, 370, 383, 388, 393-394, 428, 434
al-Mamun, (Caliph) Abdullah 24, 212
al-Maqrizi, Ahmed 212
al-Masudi 292-293
Alalu 188-189, 192-193, 196, 198, 245, 338, 439
Alexander the Great 143, 297, 311, 319, 324, 357, 404
Alexandria, Egypt 144-145, 296-297, 299-300, 332, 355, 367, 373
Amarna 364, 388, 414, 434
Amenhotep 364-365, 370
Amenti 390
Amshaspends 56
Anatolia 175, 244, 359
Ancient Ones (Elder gods) 54 & Following Pages
Andean, Andes Mountains 143, 161, 209, 241, 244, 255, 264, 267, 286
Angels 56, 127, 199, 202, 332, 344, 363, 367, 376, 388, 398, 403, 405, 413, 435
Antarctica 118, 143, 145-146
Anu 187-188, 318, 367, 399, 428
Anunnaki 56, 127, 337, 367, 429,

435
Apeman 78, 80, 137, 139, 389, 410, 423
Apep 399
Arctic 142, 145
Aryans 320
Ashur (deity) 296
Ashurbanipal 216, 292, 296, 309, 388, 394
Assyria, Assyrian 292, 296, 343, 347, 352, 394
Atlantis 145, 157, 166, 232, 238, 328, 391-393, 420-421
Attis 359
Atum 364, 383
Australia 92, 117, 145, 217, 290, 382, 405, 420, 429
Australopithecus 78-80
Autotrophs 73
Avesta 216, 297, 324, 362
Aymara 158
Azazel 333-334
Aztecs 392, 397, 401, 415

Baal (deity) 247, 342-343, 351, 363, 368, 398, 422
Babylonia 13, 166, 182, 192, 279, 292, 347, 353, 364, 367, 370, 394, 401, 405, 422, 428
Bahrain 190, 194-195, 394
Bauval, Robert 185
Benben 188
Bergier, Jacques 5, 130
Berlitz, Charles 117, 177, 217, 236, 278, 287, 323, 422
Berosus 13, 192-193, 293, 309, 321, 394, 396
Bibby, Geoffrey 394
Bible 22, 127, 171, 202, 236,

Fontechévade man 87
Fort, Charles 161, 294
Frankiel, Dr. Tamar 330
Furneaux, Rupert 236

Garden of Eden (see Eden)
Gilgamesh 13, 184, 296, 394, 426
Giza 14, 22-24, 26, 29, 31-32, 165-166, 185, 247, 249-250, 252-254, 258, 276, 292-293, 316
Gnostic, Gnosticism 202, 310, 318, 322, 329, 357, 360-362, 368, 374
Gobi 109, 140, 157-158, 160-161, 166
God 9 & Following Pages
Gomorrah 344, 348
Gondwanaland 76
Goyon, Prof. Georges 29
Gozo 166, 239, 242
Graves, Robert 428
Gravettian 284
Great Flood 13, 157, 165-167, 169-173, 181, 184-185, 214, 234, 236, 239-240, 247, 250-251, 257, 262, 292-293, 296, 322, 331, 339, 348, 365-366, 375, 389, 393-394, 420, 426
Greece 9, 224, 242, 244, 275, 281, 377, 386-387, 391, 393, 395, 416
Grigori 332, 413-414
Grimaldi 283-284
Gudea 404
Günz 118-119, 122, 147-149
Gupta 303
Hadrons 37
Hagar Qim 240-241

Hancock, Graham 226, 250-251, 260, 405
Hapgood, Prof. Charles H. 144, 146
Harran 343, 347-349
Harrison, Dr. R. K. 351
Hathor 219, 229
Hawass, Dr. Zahi 253
Hebrews 331, 333, 337-338, 342-343, 347-351, 353, 363, 365, 370, 372, 383, 393, 413
Heliopolis 188, 307, 310, 315-316, 364
Hermes (see Thoth)
Herodotus 12, 26, 233, 293, 307-308, 313, 421
Hesiod 306, 403
Heterotrophs 72
Heyerdahl, Thor 271
Himalayas 170, 303, 325, 377
Hindu 8, 22, 50, 56, 166, 182, 202, 231-232, 308, 320, 322-323, 327, 383, 386, 391, 399-402, 404, 408, 412, 414, 422
Hinduism 376
Hittites 245, 351, 416
Hoagland, Richard C. 105, 221
Hopi Indians 389, 420
Horus 195, 395, 399, 428
Howells, Prof. William 174
Hoyle, Sir Fred 61, 227
Hurrians 189, 351
Hutin, Serge 163, 273
Hyksôs 349, 351

Ice Age 66, 74-77, 79, 82, 118-119, 122, 142, 147-148, 151, 153, 159, 170, 290
Idfu (see Edfu)

Index

Ragette, Friedrich 275
Rama 308, 322, 395
Ramayana 308, 322-323
Rawlinson, Sir Henry 394
Red Sea 143
Reis, Piri (Admiral) 143-144
Rephaim 414
Rig Veda 51, 54, 58, 182, 199,
    320-321, 324, 326, 384, 386,
    401, 430
Rishi 309, 320
Riss 118, 151
Rosenberg, Dr. Gunther 23, 26
Rost, Dr. Leonhard 363-364
Rta (Order) 51
Ruzo, Dr. Daniel 130

Sacsahuaman 238, 241, 244, 265
Sagan, Dr. Carl 266-267, 418
Sahara Desert 165, 289, 419
Sais 307
Sanchuniathon 305-306, 334, 341,
    370
Sanskrit (texts) 34, 51, 55, 58,
    183, 218-219, 221, 234, 294,
    309, 320-33, 325-327, 384, 401,
    406
Saqqara 33, 166, 212, 215, 221,
    240, 254, 316
Sargon 352
Schliemann, Heinrich 243, 263,
    381-382
Schoch, Dr. Robert 239, 251
Schröter, Johann 68
Sendy, Jean 14
Senzar 294, 325-326
Serpent People 231, 329
Serpent Symbol 230-231, 361
Seth (Set) (deity) 399

Seti I, Seti Temple 221, 230,
    250, 393
Shemsu-Hor 159, 195-196, 315
Siberia 77, 115, 159, 171, 222,
    409, 437
Sibylline Books 298-300
Siderites 62
Siderolites 62
Sin (deity) 343, 348, 367
Sinai 342, 351, 377, 423, 436
Sirius 57, 419-420
Sitchin, Zecharia 14, 27, 106,
    124, 188, 412-413, 423-424,
    426, 429-431, 435
Smith, Warren 212, 318, 409,
    411
Smithsonian Institution 5-6, 90
Smyth, Prof. Charles Piazzi 14
Sodom 344, 348, 429
Solutrean 160, 285
Sphinx 27-28, 234, 248-249,
    251-253
Steinheim man 86
Stonehenge 225, 233, 236, 243
Strabo 233, 293, 312, 392
Stromatolites 73
Sumer, Sumerian 8, 13, 195-
    198, 203-204, 217, 291-292,
    296, 302, 342-343, 347-348,
    365-367, 370, 386, 393-395,
    431
Surid (king) 292
Swanscombe man 83, 85-86
Syncellus, Georgios 310

Tartessos 236, 287, 293, 392
Ta-Neteru 390
Tassili Mountains 279, 405
Taylor, John 14, 25

M. Don Schorn

About the Author:

M. Don Schorn started his professional career in 1968 with a thermoplastics molding company. As a graduate mechanical engineer, he combined his interests in plastics and cars working for several manufacturers supplying component parts to the automotive industry. Mr. Schorn continued his postgraduate education with a curriculum in Plastics Technology and individual course study in various technical and managerial programs. His extensive manufacturing and design experience led to the development of a number of new processing techniques and numerous patentable innovations.

Utilizing his extensive plastics and manufacturing background, Mr. Schorn later joined a Detroit manufacturers' representative firm as a product development specialist. Working with various OEM automotive divisions, he assisted in finalizing product specifications and part designs, ISO quality criterion and certifications, along with direct marketing and sales efforts. After a successful professional career spanning more than 27 years, he retired early at the beginning of 1995 to pursue a second career in writing.

Since then, M. Don Schorn has studied cosmology, paleoanthropology, geology, and archaeology, along with extensive analysis of ancient records and sacred texts. Those studies provided both comprehension and factual data necessary to complete five manuscripts as of this date. Four of those books are non-fiction works, including the trilogy collectively known as the *Journals of the Ancient Ones*, which introduces the *Elder Gods* theory that reveals Earth's primordial development and the emergence of humankind. The author's other non-fiction work, *Reincarnation...Stepping Stones of Life*, is an enlightening examination of the reincarnation concept and its implementation as a way-of-life. Mr. Schorn's first fictional work is his *Emerging Dawn* novel, which details a near-future global search for ancient artifacts that are connected with the Mayan *End-Time* prophecy anticipated to occur on December 21, 2012.

Other Books Published
by
Ozark Mountain Publishing, Inc.

Conversations with Nostradamus, Volume I, II, III.........by Dolores Cannon
Jesus and the Essenes.....................................by Dolores Cannon
They Walked with Jesus...................................by Dolores Cannon
Between Death and Life.................................. by Dolores Cannon
A Soul Remembers Hiroshima.........................by Dolores Cannon
Keepers of the Garden....................................by Dolores Cannon
The Legend of Starcrash..................................by Dolores Cannon
The Custodians..by Dolores Cannon
The Convoluted Universe - Book One, Book Two..........by Dolores Cannon
I Have Lived Before.....................................by Sture Lönnerstrand
The Forgotten Woman......................................by Arun & Sunanda Gandhi
Luck Doesn't Happen by Chance............................by Claire Doyle Beland
Mankind - Child of the Stars....................by Max H. Flindt & Otto Binder
The Gnostic Papers...by John V. Panella
Past Life Memories As A Confederate Soldier..................by James H. Kent
Holiday in Heaven.......................................by Aron Abrahamsen
Is Jehovah An E.T.?...by Dorothy Leon
The Ultimate Dictionary of Dream Language....................by Briceida Ryan
The Essenes - Children of the Light.........by Stuart Wilson & Joanna Prentis
Rebirth of the Oracle............................by Justine Alessi & M. E. McMillan
Reincarnation: The View from Eternityby O.T. Bonnett, M.D. & Greg Satre
The Divinity Factor..by Donald L. Hicks
What I Learned After Medical School ....by O.T. Bonnett, M.D.
Why Healing Happens..................................by O.T. Bonnett, M.D.
A Journey Into Being................................by Christine Ramos, RN
Discover The Universe Within You...................by Mary Letorney
Worlds Beyond Death................................by Rev. Grant H. Pealer
Let's Get Natural With Herbs............................by Debra Rayburn
The Enchanted Garden...by Jodi Felice
My Teachers Wear Fur Coats...................by Susan Mack & Natalia Krawetz
For more information about any of the above titles, soon to be released
titles, or other items in our catalog, write or visit our website:

OZARK
MOUNTAIN
PUBLISHING

PO Box 754
Huntsville, AR 72740
www.ozarkmt.com
1-800-935-0045/479-738-2348 Wholesale Inquiries Welcome